Readers love the
Little Goddess Series
by AMY LANE

Vulnerable

"What can I say about Amy's writing that I haven't already said? Not much. She's fantastic, I love everything she writes."

—Love Bytes

"I strongly recommend you read this book, as I would hope it would please you as much as it did me. It will give you hours of enjoyment…"

—The Novel Approach

Wounded, Vol. 1

"There is much darkness in this book, but there are rays of light as well. I look forward to furthering this series."

—Prism Book Alliance

Wounded, Vol. 2

"It's another great read, so full of emotion and drama, magic and mystique."

—Jeannie Zelos Book Reviews

By AMY LANE

LITTLE GODDESS
Vulnerable
Wounded, Vol. 1
Wounded, Vol 2
Bound, Vol. 1
Bound, Vol. 2

Published by DSP PUBLICATIONS
www.dsppublications.com

Bound

Volume Two

AMY LANE

DSP PUBLICATIONS

Published by
DSP Publications

5032 Capital Circle SW, Suite 2, PMB# 279, Tallahassee, FL 32305-7886 USA
www.dsppublications.com

Bound, Vol. 2
© 2015 Amy Lane.

Cover Art
© 2015 Anne Cain.
annecain.art@gmail.com
Cover content is for illustrative purposes only and any person depicted on the cover is a model.

ISBN: 978-1-63476-459-9
Digital ISBN: 978-1-63476-460-5
Library of Congress Control Number: 2015910609
Second Edition December 2015
First Edition published as *Bound: The Third Book of the Little Goddess Series* by iUniverse, 2007.

Printed in the United States of America
∞
This paper meets the requirements of
ANSI/NISO Z39.48-1992 (Permanence of Paper).

CORY
Therapy

"GIVE ME...." Green's hands were tight in my hair, demanding, and I found myself ravenous for him when I should have been done, sated, replete.

"Anything," I whispered against his cock, letting it slip through my lips and slap me gently on the cheek before taking him into my mouth again.

He groaned. His hands were rough—Green was never rough—and his urgency, his lack of finesse, made me want him in the back of my throat, made me want him everywhere. I took him there, to the back of my throat, and his next sound was even more raw, more urgent. Suddenly his hands were under my arms, and that carefully shielded sidhe strength was at work as he hauled me up effortlessly until I was straddling him, my knees on the rough stone of the bench, the center of my body poised over his glistening phallus. Moving with the violence of speed and want, he reached under my skirt and ripped my cotton panties off crotch first, then shoved me willingly down on top of him.

I wasn't ready. I was swollen, and the friction of him rubbing on my tender, used sex was such an exquisite pain, such a rough pleasure, that I screamed, "Yes!" so he wouldn't stop.

"Give me...," he demanded again, and I was helpless to deny him.

"Anything...," I told him, meeting his mouth and letting him possess me with lips and teeth and tongue. He moved me up and thrust himself into me again and again, and I collapsed against him, barely able to sustain consciousness, much less hold my weight up. Still he pounded as I gasped helplessly into his shoulder, begging him, pleading with him to bring me, to make me come.

One rough hand reached in front of me to touch my little bundle of nerves, and another grasped my bottom—a clever, clever finger sliding into the cleft, finding the other place, the one nobody talks about—and probed, invaded, and now I did scream, because it was terrible, unbearable, gorgeous, and I needed to come.

"Give me…," he shouted, and his eyes were burning, and he was demanding a response from my body that we usually avoided—because it was unpredictable, because I did great and terrible things when I was this frantic—but my orgasm was coming, my power was coming, and I was moaning uncontrollably and powerless to stop it.

"Anything…," I moaned again. "Oh God, Green, please…."

"Everything…," he corrected, and I closed my eyes and thought seat cushions, because my knees were raw. Then I shoved myself down over his member, over his busy invading fingers, until I felt him against my cervix and deep inside of me. The pain and the pleasure were too beautiful, and stars exploded behind my eyes and my throat was rough with shouting, and I came and came and came. So did he, both of us shivering, jerking, trembling with the force of what we'd brought into our bodies.

"Everything," I whispered against his neck when it had all subsided.

He cupped the back of my head in his big hand and stroked my hair. We didn't move for a long time after that, and when I finally moved it was to look up to his rough chuckle.

"Seat cushions?" he asked.

"My knees hurt," I said mildly, peering at the thick cotton cushions that were now under my knees—in fact, they stretched full length down the bottom and back of the granite bench.

Green was instantly contrite. "I'm sorry… I should have…."

"Don't you dare be sorry for that!" I ordered. "Don't think about being sorry, don't imagine being sorry, don't pretend not to be sorry when you are…." I trailed off, too tired and too replete to even stay angry over this. "Just don't," I finished. "Just hold me…." Abruptly I was falling asleep on his chest, and he was still inside me.

"Nice colors, luv," he said, a smile in his voice as he let me fall asleep.

I cracked my eyes open. They were olive green, scarlet, and twilight purple. I had just enough left in me to shake my shoulders. "Come colors," I said crudely.

Green shifted, that amazing strength able to pull his pants up with one hand while the other lifted me against him. I sighed when he was no longer inside me, because that feeling never seems to last long enough. "What colors?" he asked when we were situated again—although it felt like I'd never moved my head from his chest.

"The colors I see behind my eyes when we explode," I said thickly. A part of me reflected that it had been one hell of a day.

"At least we know you're starting to control it...," he mused. I could tell he was thinking something important, and I was suddenly tired of important.

"And we gave Adrian a hell of a show."

"Not just Adrian, I think...." So softly I barely heard him, and I was too tired to ask. "I think I have to give you to Bracken now, luv."

"Mmmm...." It was the last noise I remembered making before being slid into one of Bracken's T-shirts and into bed. When Bracken moved next to me, I burrowed into him and slept until the alarm went off the next morning.

Green's homecoming was over. It was time to get back to real life.

"I THINK you should go see Hallow," Bracken insisted as we walked out to the track.

"No." I'd been walking stiffly all day. What can I say? In a life of rather spectacular sexual activity, the previous thirty-six hours had been something pretty special.

"You're in pain!" he said.

"I'm uncomfortable!" I returned. "Women have been living with it for years."

"Well, you shouldn't have to."

I turned to him and grinned. "Give it a rest, O Mighty Warrior Sex God," I told him. "You did your part here too. Now let me run, and some of this will work itself out." I hoped so—I was going for a mile and a half today, and I didn't know if I knew Davy well enough to explain why it was going to be a bit tougher than usual.

"Why won't you just go to Hallow?" he asked, damn his persistence.

"It's not our day anyway," I evaded, unwilling to explain human embarrassment one more time when I wasn't sure why I still had it.

"No," he said shortly, "it's Renny's."

We were both silent then, because Max had met us at Renny's door this morning, hastily dressed in boxers and nothing else, and looking sheepish and uncomfortable.

"Oh... jeez...," I said painfully. "Max... this was so not a good idea...."

"It's the one thing we don't need words for," he answered, evading my eyes.

I'd patted his cheek and wished him well, and now I wished more than ever that Renny had come with us to school—because out of everybody who talked to Hallow, she needed it most.

"Nicky's taking her time slot today," I told Bracken now. And Nicky needed the time too. Before we'd even had a chance to knock on his door, he'd been on his way out—only stopping to give Eric a long, lingering kiss in the doorway. Eric had looked me in the eyes with thinly disguised apprehension, but I'd winked and smiled, and he'd been relieved. Actually, I was relieved as well. I felt a lot better about Nicky and Eric than I'd felt about his freefall into free love. Maybe because I knew him—I knew what he'd wanted for himself before Green and I had come along and screwed up his life, and random copulation had never been in his plans. "C'mon—Davy's waiting."

"This human worries me," Bracken said suddenly, so suddenly that I stopped my trot out to the track and he almost plowed into me.

"I'm sorry?" I asked, genuinely puzzled.

Brack wouldn't meet my eyes. "She's vulnerable, she's alone—and you want to protect her, and it's only natural. But it's not your place, and...." He shook his head. "You will blame yourself if something happens to her," he said at last.

I swallowed, because he was right, and tried a reassuring smile. "She's on twenty-four-hour sprite watch, Bracken. Even I know that's all we can do, right?"

He nodded, and I reached up to kiss him. Then we both continued out to the track, but his words niggled at me, especially after Davy joined me on the track and we started our warm-up round, her sprites chirping in unnoticed colors above her head. Davy was chatty and blithe and positive—but she wasn't stupid. Kyle obviously loved her, and I didn't think he wanted to mess with her mind any more than necessary, and now, after the other night, she was left with some serious questions.

"So... Cory... I've got to ask...," she started after a few paces, "are you and Bracken... I mean is Kyle.... Are you guys into anything... I don't know... illegal?"

In spite of the seriousness of the question, I had to laugh. "No," I said simply. "In fact, I think Green's businesses are run more aboveboard than most." He had to be above reproach in all the obvious places so no one would look hard enough to figure out that "Green, Inc." was actually the same guy running the show since the gold rush. "Why do you ask?"

Davy shook her head. "It's just… I hope you won't take this the wrong way, but I got this feeling that Kyle knew who you were before we walked in the other night… and that he was really ready to not like you."

I nodded, still out of breath enough to be glad she was doing most of the talking. "You'd be right."

"Why wouldn't he like you?"

I risked a smile at her. She liked me. After Chloe's antipathy, Renny's nervous breakdown, and the mess I'd almost made of my entire love life last night, it was good to have someone on my side.

"Let's just say that Kyle's last boss and Green had some… serious differences of opinion," I understated, "and Kyle had some good reasons to think I was not a nice person. But he didn't know the whole story, either."

Davy thought about that for a few beats of our shoes on the rubber track. We were running in the rain, which I found exhilarating, but she was wearing a rain poncho. I wondered how she could breathe with that thing on. "That's really vague," she said at last.

"It is," I replied honestly. "But…." I sighed—as much as I could, anyway. "Davy, there's just some stuff that Kyle has to tell you. I'd love to. I… I'm not good at dodging questions or any of that shit. But Kyle's your…." I fought not to say "beloved," because she would think it was just a quaint word—but to us, it meant so much more. "Kyle's your boyfriend, and he's known you longer, and most of these secrets are his to tell and not mine, okay?"

"Okay," she said unhappily. "I just don't know. I mean… when I'm with the two of you, it doesn't seem like there's any secrets at all. You're just… real, you know? It's only later when it seems like you have something to hide."

"We are real," I said, and it felt like one of the most honest statements I had ever made. "Davy—if you believe nothing else, believe that we're real." Her boyfriend was a vampire. I was a sorceress. The irony was, we were as real as it got.

"So, where's Renny today?" she asked, making a concerted effort to lighten the moment.

"Boyfriend troubles," I replied, and changed the topic to Renny and Officer Max, which, as much prevarication as it involved, actually seemed to be a safer topic. But the conversation bothered me. I hated lying—even halfway, like I was with Davy—and Bracken was so right. The more I knew her, the more I felt responsible for her. At this point, my anger at Kyle was escalating past reason. His silence wasn't letting me do my job! It seemed perfectly clear to me, but somehow Bracken and Green had it all turned around.

That night, as we were all sitting in the living room studying, Green asked me casually how my meetings with Hallow were going.

"Fine!" I said brightly. "Nothing to report, really."

Bracken looked at me darkly. "Actually," he said, with an evil glance my way, "yesterday was our day, and we missed it."

"Like I said," I returned blandly, "nothing to report."

"Bracken?" Green asked, and I had the feeling he knew anyway, because, dammit, Hallow wasn't a legal therapist and Green wasn't a twenty-first-century human male, and although Hallow wasn't about to go blabbing everything we said to Green, he was going to keep him apprised as to how his people were doing.

"She's absolutely correct," Bracken replied, looking up from the notebook on his lap. He was doing homework—whose I wasn't sure. "There's nothing to report because she doesn't tell him anything."

"That's not true!" I protested. It felt like I'd been doing nothing but spilling my guts for the last two weeks!

"The hell it isn't. You think I don't see how frustrated Hallow is when you leave? And whatever you say to *me* is so cryptic I need a damned 'Earth to Cory' decoder ring to figure it out."

I shot Bracken an evil look of my own. "Oh, really? Do you have it with you? Can you figure out what I'm thinking right now?"

"Define the cosine vector, *due'ane*," he replied mildly, sneaking a glance at the muted television to watch the Kings waste another play-off opportunity. "We're still on number three."

I took a deep breath and concentrated on my knitting. I was sitting on the floor, leaning on the couch between Green's knees as he worked on the laptop, and Bracken was sitting on the other end of the couch, his legs extended toward me. Every now and then I reached out and stroked Green's calf or the curve of Bracken's instep, and then returned my busy hands to the needles and cable hook. Green's sweater had two different cables on it. I was so proud of the crawling things that worked their way up the silk/cashmere that it was all I could do not to jump up and make both men fawn all over my accomplishment like spaniels, but somehow I didn't think they'd think it was as cool as I did.

"Cory...," Nicky said from the couch across from us. He was leaning against Eric with his feet up on the arm of the couch, and Eric was reading a book on business law. Just the fact that the book wasn't putting him to sleep impressed the hell out of me.

"I know you know the answer," I said grumpily. "Give me a second here."

"The cosine vector is 200 miles per hour," Nicky said calmly. "If you didn't know it five minutes ago, you're not going to know it now. What I was going to say was, talking to Hallow will help."

"Oh, Jesus, not you too...," I whined. I recognized it as a whine, but dammit, they were ganging up on me. "Renny, anything to add here?"

Renny was in cat form, curled up against my thigh. She purred, rubbed her head against my knee, and looked at me patiently from glowing brown eyes. I squeezed my eyes shut and groaned. Yes. Apparently Renny agreed with the men.

"Just because I don't like dumping my shit all over someone else's yard, that doesn't mean my shit is any more interesting or special than anybody else's shit," I said succinctly. "Bracken, what's the next goddamned problem?"

"You are, beloved," Green interrupted evenly. "And your *shit* is special because it is *your shit* and you are important to us, and we don't want you to make a stupid mistake because you can't see your pretty yard for all the *shit* in your eyes."

Suddenly I felt tears start, and I couldn't seem to wish them back. I stood up abruptly. "I'm going to go knit with the vampires," I said grandly and stalked out of the room so they could worry about me without me personally being there to suffer through it.

There were no vampires in their common room. It was pissing down rain outside, which they hated as much as the living. When I put out a gentle mental "*halloo...*" to Marcus, I got a rather confused image of red light and bare limbs and a bed so big it made mine look like a crib, and I cut off that line of thought immediately. As quietly as possible, I slunk back into my room.

Green was waiting there for me, laptop engaged, fingers tapping implacably. When he saw me in the doorway, he looked up and smiled. "I like what you've done with the place, luv," he said, nodding at the magically redecorated walls. I had forgotten he hadn't seen my room since that odd and revealing afternoon with Bracken.

"Thanks," I said and flopped into the overstuffed chair next to his. Apparently this conversation was as inevitable as moonrise. I might as well be comfortable.

"It actually gives me an idea of how to make our people invulnerable to Hollow Man, if you want to know the truth—but I need to make a trip back to Marin to make sure it will work."

"Good," I said numbly. Any news on that front that didn't involve us shouting at each other was good. "What would we have to do?"

"Mmm…." He tapped furiously for a moment, hit Send, and finished his reply to me. "I'd sooner wait and see if it worked before I propose it to you, luv. It's not necessarily something high on your wish list, and we've got enough on your plate."

"Okay," I agreed, waiting. Tired of waiting. "What do you want me to say, Green?" I asked. My knitting bag was still looped around my elbow, and I found myself looking at my unusually still hands.

Green looked at me until I looked back, and his emerald eyes were intense and sober. I shifted uncomfortably for a moment. Then he started to speak, and my entire world went as quiet as my hands. "I want you to say that you're beautiful and magnificent, and that you deserve every good thing you've ever gotten. I want you to say that you don't need to earn our love—and that you'll honor the love we give you by not thinking ill of yourself for stupid human preconceptions that you've disproved a thousand times over. I want you to say that you forgive yourself for making mistakes, for being one of the Goddess's children, and for not knowing every answer to every situation. I want you to say to yourself, if not to me and Bracken, that you are worthy." He stopped. I hadn't been looking at him for a few sentences. Instead, I was staring at my still hands, and they were wet with tears, and I couldn't say anything at all.

"And if you can't say that, *ou'e'eir*," he continued, his own voice taut, "I want you to get rid of whatever is getting in your way. And if that means dumping your *shit* on someone else's lawn, that's what it means."

Oh jeez. My shoulders shook for a moment, and I still couldn't meet his eyes. I nodded my head mutely, because that seemed to be the only answer I could give. Green got up and kissed my forehead. "I've got an appointment, beloved," he said. "I'll send Bracken in a couple of minutes, give you time to pull yourself together, okay?"

I nodded. Bracken came in fifteen minutes later, and I was still weeping soundlessly. He pulled my yarn bag out of my arms and slid my jeans down my hips, then pulled me into bed and let me cry myself to sleep against him. And the whole time, I had no words, no words to give any of them, not one lousy curse or protest or syllable of agreement or disagreement, just tears. It was the damnedest thing.

Nobody mentioned it the next day, and I was hoping everybody would just let it drop, but as Bracken and I neared Hallow's door and I saw Nicky, Mario, LaMark, Renny, *and* Officer Max sitting on the floor of the hallway, I realized that their silence on the matter was just more time to plot.

"Oh, for fuck's sake...," I huffed when I spotted everybody.

"Cory...," Nicky said, his hands out like he was soothing a dangerous animal.

"Cory *what*?" I demanded. "I wasn't planning on skipping out. It's a shrink appointment—what the hell is the honor guard for?"

"We're here to watch over Bracken," Max said evenly. Ever since he'd fallen for Renny instead of me, he had been the one person completely unafraid of my moods. Right now I despised him for it.

"Bracken and I were going to see Hallow together," I answered with, I thought, excessive reason.

"Not today," Bracken corrected. "We need to do that—but not today." He bent down so he could say it softly, and I turned around to glare at him. He looked implacably back, and I turned around to glare at the whole goddamned lot of them. They were calm, reasonable, and unassailable.

"There was no reason for a fucking ambush," I hissed. "What's it going to take to get you people off my back?"

"I don't know...," Renny said pleasantly. "How about Hallow walks you to the door and says 'Well, Cory, it's been a good session. I look forward to next week.'"

I frowned at her. "Does he ever actually do that?"

Everybody but Max nodded at me, and I blinked, feeling bad. I guess I was usually so busy escaping at maximum velocity I had missed out on that part.

"Fine!" I snapped, pulling out of my surprise and jerking my hand from Bracken's. He had been holding it gently, like you would an egg, since I'd seen everybody lying in wait like velociraptors. "In half an hour, that'll happen, and you all can get the hell off my back." And with that I opened Hallow's door, hitting it with my shoulder and flinging it back into the wall with so much force that Hallow choked on the sandwich he was eating and even I jumped in surprise. That didn't keep me from slamming the door in everybody's face, though. Screw them all.

"Lady Cory…," Hallow gasped. "Are you actually early?"

Jesus, I was. I would get them for this, I swear to the Goddess I would. "Look," I said ungraciously, not caring, "I've got an appointment to go running with a human in mortal peril in forty-five minutes. What's it going to take to get you to escort me to the door in a half an hour saying we've made progress or some sort of crap like that, and that you actually look forward to seeing me next week?"

Hallow blinked and forced back a smile. "I beg your pardon?"

"You heard me! Which part of my soul do I have to bare, which ventricle of my heart do I have to eat, what in the blue fuck do I have to say to get you to walk me to that door in twenty-nine minutes and say 'Well, Cory, this has been very productive and I look forward to seeing you next week?'"

"Is that a requirement of the session?" he asked, sounding confused.

"There are four of my ex-friends and two lovers who are going to be *very* sorry out there, waiting to hear those words from your mouth, so I need to know what I have to do to make it happen." The anger that had borne me up was far from fading, my voice was rising to a shrill shriek, and just ask me if I gave a flying fuck.

Comprehension dawned on Hallow's face. "Oh," he said. "I take it Green and Bracken are getting impatient."

"Impatient? They're getting overbearing! I mention one lousy idea about how to get Hollow Man off our back, and suddenly they think I have a death wish. Do they think I'm stupid? Do they think I'd risk Bracken's life? How about Nicky's life? What about Green's heart? Too goddamned much rests on my breathing in and out to just throw my life away—what do they think I'm going to do?"

"I don't know… what do they think you're going to do?" He was still confused, and I was still pissed off.

"All I said is that if I blooded this asshole like any other vampire, he'd be bound to me, and then we could kill him, and they think I have a self-esteem problem."

"Well, do you?" Hallow risked a nervous glance behind him at the clock and seemed reassured that only three minutes had passed.

"Would I know it if I had one?" I shot back. "And Renny—damn. The woman is cat more often than she's human, and she thinks *I'm* the one with a problem? And Max! Max was so screwed up he actually thought he wanted me for like eight months. Two weeks of fucking Renny like a lemming, and he's totally besotted and *I'm* the one who needs therapy? Nicky spends two weeks in a traveling orgy and *I'm* the one who needs some goddamned therapy? And what about Bracken? Asshole can't even admit there's a goddamned ghost in the goddamned garden, because then he'd have to admit that he's still angry with that ghost and that would just fucking kill us all, then wouldn't it—and *I'm the one who needs some goddamned therapy!*" My voice damned near shattered the windows, and suddenly I was out of words and embarrassed by my anger in front of this relative stranger, and all of my impetus rushed out of me as the blood rushed to my face. I sat down abruptly.

"I beg your pardon, Master Hallow," I said quietly, the sudden silence so loud my swallow seemed to echo in it. "How are you today?"

He breathed out on a bemused laugh. "Well, I for one feel very relieved. Was all that catharsis good for you?"

Oh, Jesus—how loud had I been? "No," I said, embarrassed. "You don't think they heard, do you?"

"Not at all. They might have heard your voice raised, but I don't think they could make out the words," he said kindly.

"Magic shielding?" I asked inanely.

"No, hellifically old building." He nodded.

"Ah." I could actually hear the clock tick. "Do you mind if I knit?" I asked politely.

"Knock yourself out," he invited.

I pulled out my bag and situated myself in the deafening silence, then looked at Hallow expectantly. "So... any questions I can answer today, Professor Hallow?" I asked, feeling like I was eating my heart just to prompt the whole process that I had dreaded for weeks.

"A few," he said firmly, as though he was ready to get down to business. "Would it matter?"

"Well, I thought questions were the point," I said, confused.

"I meant, would it matter if everybody heard what you said about them?" he prompted, and I flushed.

"Yes," I said, shamed. "They rely on me. They *follow* me. Even…"
I choked, because this truth was still painful. "Even Bracken. You don't…
go off… on people who follow you."

Hallow nodded. His look of perpetual worry deepened, and I felt
my stomach clench. This was totally going to suck. "You didn't say ex-
lovers," he said, and it was such a non sequitur that now *I* was the one
who was confused.

"I'm sorry?"

"You said 'ex-friends'—and as mad as you were, I knew you
weren't serious. You didn't say 'ex-lovers.' Why not? It wouldn't have
mattered—you were just 'going off,' as you said. You were going off in
a totally safe place, with a totally safe person, and as upset as you were,
you still didn't say 'ex-lovers.' Can you tell me why?"

I shrugged. "My love is a matter of life and death—to both of
them." I shrugged again, my flush intensifying. "You don't say shit like
that when it's that important. Not even when you're mad. Not even when
it's safe."

"Not even in your own head?" he prompted gently, and I was
instantly horrified.

"Goddess, no!" I gasped, the pain of even the thought too awful to
contemplate. "No. Not even to think about." I wanted to make him even
take the idea back, as childish as I knew that to be.

He nodded again, and I was starting to dread the slow, thoughtful
incline of that noble head. "You're awfully controlled for someone so
young, Lady Cory." He didn't miss my wince with the honorific, but he
didn't say anything about it, either. "You didn't even lose control when
you lost control. Can you remember the last time you completely lost
your cool about something?"

Crap. It took me a minute to discipline my mouth and be sure my
voice wouldn't betray me. "Of course I do," I said casually, working
the cable needle deftly, knitting, knitting from the needle, knitting some
more. "You couldn't have missed it. I was covered in Adrian's blood,
I almost killed Bracken and Arturo, and a hundred vampires died." I
swallowed, proud of how good I was getting at saying that without
completely losing it. "I don't want to let that happen ever again."

"Which part?" he asked, an emotion in his voice that I couldn't
define. I looked sharply at him, and he went on. "The part where you lost
your lover, or the part where you killed the people responsible?"

Fucking hell. I looked him in the eyes and shook my head. "You know, Master Hallow, this whole therapy thing is sooooooo going to suck large," I said, so much feeling dripping from my voice that I was surprised it didn't melt the floor.

Hallow cocked his head sympathetically. "You owe me fifteen more minutes, my lady," he said gently, and I thought with a shocking jolt of venom that I could really hate this guy.

Fifteen minutes later, nothing had changed my mind. I felt like I had been put through the wringer, and my anger at my people hadn't dimmed one itty-bitty little teeny tiny bit. Hallow walked me to the door as promised and put his gentle hand on my stiff shoulder. Then he spoke in a voice meant to carry. "It was good talking to you, Lady Cory." He gave a little bow as he said it, which made my mortification complete. "I look forward to talking to you next week."

I smiled at him pleasantly and said, sotto voce, "If you think I'm ripping my soul open like that for you next week, you're high."

"If you don't," he said softly, "I'm going to insist to Green that you take a full hour at least twice a week." Then, louder, "So—next Tuesday, then?"

"If I don't eat your liver first," I smiled, and he smiled blandly back before gesturing Bracken inside his office. I glared at everyone left, and they all had the grace to look ashamed.

"I'm going running," I snapped. "If anyone tries to follow me, I'll fry them to the last grizzled pubic hair."

"Cory, it's not safe—" Nicky started, and I cut him off with a glare.

"Fuck you, Nicky, and the posse you're riding on." And with that I shouldered my backpack and took off, not even bothering to look behind me, because I was serious and I was pretty sure they were more afraid of me than they were of Bracken.

By the time Davy joined me on the track, I'd run half a mile on sheer pissed-offness. I'd run it too fast in the driving rain, and I was winded, sore, drenched, and irritated—but I was still angry, so when Davy came up beside me I didn't slacken my speed.

"Wow, Cory, you're going pretty fast," she said, surprised, and I just nodded, knowing that talking was beyond me right now. "Any particular reason?"

"I want my husband to live," I puffed out, and Davy, being a smart young woman, nodded and said nothing else for the rest of the run. It turned out to be pretty short, because in two more laps I had to slow down against my will, and we walked in silence for half a mile before my breathing slowed and she asked me if I wanted to talk about it. I shook my head.

"I just got blackmailed into therapy," I said sourly. "Ask me if I want to talk about anything else today."

Davy barked out a laugh. "That's harsh. What did he use as blackmail?"

I sighed, and it came out as a shudder. "My running time," I said, still blowing a little. It was pounding down frigid cloud-piss, but between my temper and the run, I was overheated. Frustrated, I pulled off my sweatshirt and my white T-shirt, leaving me in my black sports bra, walking faceup in the cleansing rain. Davy stopped suddenly, her yellow rain poncho making a whisking sound.

"Wow!" she breathed. "Cory, that is one hell of a tattoo on your back. Does it mean anything?"

I stopped, right there on the rubberized track. "Yes," I said through a suddenly rough throat. "It means a lot… but it's sort of hard to explain."

"Give it a try," she asked, lost in the weaving of leaves and blood that was written on my back.

"They're symbols," I said gruffly, "for people I love. It… it was sort of our way of binding ourselves to each other, so that… the world would know we belonged to each other."

"Which one is Bracken?" she asked.

"He's the sword with the red cap on it. And the blood." I shrugged. "It's sort of an ancestral thing for him."

"Who's the hawk?"

I shrugged again. "Nicky." She'd met him.

"But you two… you're like brother and sister…," she said, puzzled.

"Yeah. We should be, but… but our world is complicated."

Davy laughed. "It's the same world I live in."

"It is," I answered, and a wave of discomfort and worry suddenly crashed into me and broke. "You just don't know it. Look… Davy…." And at that moment, we both took a breath that we didn't finish.

"Holy crap, what is that stench…?" She choked, and as quick as that, we were wearing the shield I'd practiced two days before, and the fight with Hollow Man was on.

"Davy, we've got to get to Bracken and the others," I said breathlessly, calling silently for Green. "That smell is a bad thing, and we don't want to be here when it pounces."

I'd left my backpack in the locker room today, and I fleetingly mourned it as I grabbed Davy's hand and pulled her at a dead run toward the gate at the far side of the field from us. She was reluctant to go, and my shoulder twisted backward as I jerked her body forward and she finally took the hint and joined me. *A hundred meters*, I thought with fractured logic. We were both runners—we could make a hundred meters in a fairly brief amount of time.

And then something hit the shield with a ring like a marshmallow church bell, sending Davy and me flying in my cushioned bubble of power, bouncing us off the ground like kids in one of those big inflatable playpens. And the smell.... *Why couldn't my shields ward off the smell?* I thought dismally, but there was no time, no goddamned time to figure it out.

"What in the hell...." Davy pulled herself to her feet, and I grabbed her hand and dragged her back into our full-out run.

"Shut up and keep running," I panted. "And if I go down, go get Bracken."

"What's after...?" And we were hit again. It was moving too fast to see, and it didn't shatter my shield, but the invisible wall did get weak on the bottom, and we both went down face first. My nose exploded in white pain, and between that and the stench, my stomach cramped— but it wasn't just me out here, it was Davy and me, and I needed to get her to safety. Both of us came up wiping blood from our knees, hands, and mouths, but I was the one who bounded to my feet again and went lurching for the end of the field.

"Shit!" I spat, reinforcing my goddamned shield and taking up that dead run one more time. I'd done something serious to my face when we went down, and not only could I not clear the stars from my vision, but my first breath had me choking on blood. *Twenty-five meters*, I thought, gasping from my mouth. We had twenty-five fucking meters and my mad was on.

"Beloved," Green's voice was alarmed in my head. *"Where is everybody?"*

"Funny story." Even my mental voice was winded. *"I'll tell you about it sometime. Could you send them this way?"* With that, I felt the whoosh of a body that was too unwieldy to move with the Goddess's speed, and I turned toward it, my anger and my power smacking together with my furious backhanded gesture, and without warning a

familiar, bulky-sized human materialized, hurtling away from us and landing against the bleacher wall with a nasty melon-hitting-concrete sound.

"Oh, fuck," I muttered, sickened even as I turned and grabbed Davy's hand and once again resumed our sprint. I was going to have to barf sometime soon. The stench of Hollow Man hadn't diminished, and I had to believe he had more to throw at us than poor Chuck Granger, whose blood and gray matter were currently being puddled onto the track by the pissing rain. What a fucking waste.

There was one more whooshing attack of air and malice before we hit the gate and the split in the stadium, but I backhanded it just like I'd backhanded Granger, and Green was in my head to give me some added power. I heard it crash and screech behind us in a mess that must have surely bent and twisted some of the bleachers, but I kept Davy's hand and kept running blindly through the split, past the stadium, and up toward the campus until I met an unmovable force of muscle, angst, and panic that wrapped its arms around me and murmured affectionate things like "dumbshit" and "fuckwit" into my hair until the shaking stopped.

"Jesus, Bracken, where'd you come from?" Davy asked between spitting blood, and I remembered myself and my duty and my nose gushing blood and pulled away from Brack's furious, warm arms.

"Green called me," he said, and I nodded.

"I called him." Hugging Bracken had made even the scrapes on my hands and knees run blood, and suddenly I could taste it down my throat, clear and coppery. Not now, I begged, and tried to keep my composure even as I popped a cold sweat. I'd dropped my sweatshirt and T-shirt on the track in the initial run, and when I looked down for something to wipe myself on, all I saw was my Lycra sports bra and running shorts, plastered to my body in the dripping rain.

Bracken swore and reached under his sweatshirt to rip his T-shirt from his body and hand it to me, careful not to touch my skin again.

"Where're the boys?" I asked into the wadded T-shirt, my voice clogged and nasal. I nodded at Max and Renny as they came sprinting toward us.

"Jeez, that's a big cat!" Davy breathed, and I shook my head. Max was holding various parts of Renny's clothing and looking pissed off—I was pretty sure he'd scooped those up behind her after she changed.

"You have no idea," I mumbled, suddenly nauseous and cold and feeling foolish about being mad enough to leave behind all these people running to my rescue. "Nicky and everybody?" I prompted Bracken.

"Checking out the area." He was making helpless gestures like he wanted to touch me. "We were halfway here when they said the noise stopped. I assumed that since I was still...." His usually stoic face threatened to crumple, and his voice got thick. "That if you were okay, that meant he had stopped the attack and left."

"I'm sorry," I said softly, meaning it.

"You should be," he snapped, and he looked so miserable that I reached out and touched his face, heedless of the recently slowed blood that went running down my face all over again.

"I was mad, Bracken. I'm sorry. I didn't expect an attack today. I just needed some space, that's all." My voice was getting thick and slurred as my nose swelled. Wonderful.

Suddenly, three big birds touched down about ten feet from us, and after checking to make sure that Davy was wrapped up with scratching a reluctant Renny behind the ears, they turned and approached us.

"There're two dead men in the bleachers," Nicky said quietly, for my ears only. "And I think we should get the hell out of here before anyone sees them and you two bleeding like an auto wreck."

"In a second," I said, picturing again what Chuck Granger had looked like with his skull cracked open. I closed my eyes tightly, fighting nausea with everything I was worth.

"Give it up and barf, baby," Bracken ordered gruffly. "Then we can get the hell out of here."

Good advice. I fell to my hands and knees, and my shoulder sang in pain. That was good, because the extra pain made it easier to let go. I closed my eyes, because I hadn't eaten lunch and I knew the rain would be washing away my own blood and stomach acid that I didn't want to see, and heaved. Above me I could sense Bracken's restive movements—he wanted to touch me, to stroke my hair from my face, to comfort, and he couldn't. I finished and spat and used an offered corner of the bloodied T-shirt to wipe my mouth. Davy came and fussed at me, but I shook her off and took Nicky's proffered hand so he could help me to my knees. Max came and helped, giving me Renny's green hoodie to put on over my sports bra. It looked familiar, and I cast the big tawny cat rubbing up against Davy an exasperated look as I realized it was mine. Renny-the-cat licked her whiskers and yawned, and I stuck my tongue out at her as I started to ease the sweatshirt on and tried to pull my thoughts together. *Other things to worry about*, I thought grumpily, *but damn, it sure would be great if the stuff in my closet stayed mine.* My shoulder protested loudly when I finally moved it—I must have done something big to it when I was dragging Davy along behind me. Fucking fabulous.

"What about…," Max asked, looking at my friend meaningfully, and I sighed and rubbed my bloody hand across my bloody face and through my sopping hair.

"Davy…," I started. She looked at me, her eyes shrewd and expectant even as she hugged Renny to her. "Davy—you need to go to Kyle's apartment and thtay… *stay* there. And you can't be alone."

"But Kyle's there," she said, sounding puzzled.

"Not weally," I replied slowly, shaking my head against her questions. "Not until thunthet… *sunset*, anyway. I'm going to send…." I looked over my shoulder at Max, and he nodded. "Max and Renny and Mario with you."

"No," Mario said unexpectedly, and I looked at him in surprise. "I'm your honor guard, Cory, like it or not. I'm not leaving you and homeboy here for the rest of the day."

"But… I…. Max and Wenny can't be awone…," I said helplessly. All at once, this leadership thing seemed too large for me. I ruthlessly squashed that thought, but not before Green caught it. "*Take it easy, beloved,*" he said gently, and the smell of mustard flowers made me strong. "Okay—who *is* going with them?" I asked. "Howwow Man ith out there, and Kyle's going to be vewy pissed when he wakes up. I don't tink two of us are going to be enuff." My fucking nose hurt like the ass of the fucking lowest butt-reaming demon in the fucking pit of fucking hell. Talking was getting painful and unintelligible, and I was starting to shiver and I wanted out of the goddamned rain almost as much as I wanted Green, but this had to be dealt with.

"I'll go," Nicky said unexpectedly, and I shot him a supremely grateful look and kissed his knuckles in thanks. Then I remembered our physics exam.

"*Green?*" I asked helplessly and was relieved when I didn't have to voice the weak-assed question.

"*I'll have Hallow take care of it,*" he said, and I nodded.

"Don't wowwy about physics," I said quietly to Mario and LaMark. "Gween will deal."

"Oddly enough, the last thing on my mind," LaMark muttered, and my blood spattered with my laugh.

"Oh, jeez...," I swore. "Is dere anyding we can do to top this goddabbed bweeding?"

Between Bracken's proximity and my broken nose (it must have been broken—with the hurt and the breathing and the goddamned blood there wasn't another option) it turned out that there really *wasn't* anything we could do about the bleeding. By the time we pulled up to Green's hill, I had soaked through what was left of Bracken's T-shirt as well as one of the sweatshirts Nicky had left in the SUV, and since those were the only extra clothes in the car, I was freezing my ass off as well. Somewhere between where we'd met by the stadium and the parking lot, my shoulder had good and well frozen up with agony, so the entire trip up the hill was one long misery of pain, blood, and cold.

Max had called right when we hit the freeway and told us that Davy had taken them to a little apartment near the school and that they were all drying off in the living room, pleasantly telling her that there was no need to wake Kyle up and hoping she wouldn't press the issue. Nicky got on the phone and asked how long I'd had sprites watching her, because they had made themselves busy at Kyle's house and the place was spotless. I had him ask them what they could do about Davy's insistence on asking questions, and he said he'd do what he could. He also told me that she had a split lip, and that it had scabbed over by the time they got to the apartment. Lucky Davy.

Green was waiting for us as we pulled up, his yellow hair dark with rain and his lovely face clouded with worry. I had a sudden, horrible feeling in the pit of my stomach—I had done this to him, I thought miserably. I was the reason he was standing in the rain, pacing and afraid. Wonderful.

He greeted me with grim, flashing eyes and a general pat down to check my injuries. I yelped as he touched my arm, and he practically had to fight my hand away from my nose, soaked-through T-shirt and all.

"I'b thorry," I garbled, trying not to cringe away from his touch in guilt and shoving that pathetic wad of bandage back up against my face. "I'm bweeding like a thucking thtuck boose."

Mario sputtered as he got out of the car. "Are you sure that's not a stucking mucked foose?" he asked, putting a gentle hand on my shoulder and shooting Green a wary look.

"With Cory's mouth, I think she meant a mucking fucked stoose." LaMark shot back, aligning himself next to me and giving my "gentle" beloved one of those superbright smiles that usually melts knees.

"I think," Green said deliberately, "that she is bleeding like a fucking stuck moose. And I also think that you two need to get out of the rain."

"We tried," Mario said philosophically. Then they deserted me like the cucking fowards they were, leaving me face-to-face with one very unhappy beloved while the other one parked the car.

It was hard to look sheepish when I couldn't wrinkle my nose or show my mouth, and after a minute I found I was squinting uncomfortably against the rain as it fell. "Uhb… bewoved…," I said hesitantly, and he swore savagely and hauled me against him, mindful of the shoulder but with the suppressed violence of a pulled bowstring.

"It would serve you right if I let you bleed," he said, and his voice was as close to sounding petulant as a two-millennium-old being possibly could.

"I d'ow," I said. All of my misery must have oozed through the rag in front of my face, because he heaved a giant sigh and kissed my temple reluctantly, but the sweet weirdness that was his healing felt just as wonderful when the tingle of knit tissues and realigned bones faded. Then he ushered me to the shower, and half an hour later I was no longer bleeding, my nose and shoulder no longer hurt, and I was warm and dry on his couch. But that awful feeling in my stomach was still there. It wasn't helped by the fact that both he and Bracken had insisted I eat as soon as I got out of the shower, and the stew that Grace left simmering on the stove sat like a rock.

"So, beloved," he said after a moment, "you've told me about the attack, and about the two dead 'meat puppets' as you called them. You told me that you knew one of them from high school and that he probably gave the Hollow Man part of your name."

I nodded. I thought the name part might be crucial—knowing that much about me was probably what had given Hollow Man the power to sneak up on me. The more I'd thought about it in the car, the more I thought I should have known he was there before Davy did—certainly before he steered Chuck Granger into my shield.

"What you have yet to tell me is what you were doing out on the track alone." His voice was even, but I'd known him long enough—and I knew him well enough—to know that he was still boiling mad.

"It's...." My voice trailed off as Bracken glared at me from across the couch. His look was part misery, part anger, and part dread. He didn't want to tell this story to Green any more than I did.

"You said it was sort of a funny story, really."

I nodded, pursing my lips.

"I'm not laughing yet."

Ouch. "You sort of had to be there," I said numbly.

"Bracken?" Green looked at where he sat on the overstuffed chair, far away from me, and Bracken's miserable expression was more than I could stand.

"It's not his fault," I cut in, embarrassed. "It's mine. He was with Hallow, and I went hauling off for the track."

"Why?" Green asked pointedly. "And if he was with Hallow, why didn't anybody else go with you?"

"Please, beloved... it's sort of between me and...." I trailed off because the look on his face said his patience was thinning and that the "between them and me" thing wasn't going to fly. "I told them to go piss up a rope, okay?" I blurted. "I finished my... my *thing* with Hallow and told them to fuck off and that if they followed me, I'd fry them all. They... they just did what I said, that's all."

Green looked at Bracken, and he returned the look with so much self-directed anger that I couldn't stand it.

"Don't let him do that, Green," I begged, feeling tears threaten for the first time since we'd gotten home. "I waited until he was in Hallow's office so he wouldn't make a big thing about it. I was angry, and I went haring off into the wild blue, and bad shit happened...." My mouth quirked upward in spite of the heaviness of my heart. "I know you know the feeling."

Green shook his head in disgust and flopped down on the couch next to me. "Yes, luv, I know the feeling," he conceded, taking my hand in his and rubbing his thumb over my knuckles.

"Bracken?" I begged, holding my free hand out to him. He looked away from me, and a string in my heart popped. "Please, Bracken, please?" I begged, and he closed his eyes. Even before he heaved himself out of the chair and plopped next to me, I knew I'd won.

"Well, Corinne Carol-Anne," Green said into my hair even as I brought Bracken's knuckles to my lips, "I do hope you at least got something out of your session with Hallow today."

"I don't want to talk about it."

"I know you don't," he said, and even Bracken laughed. "Can you at least tell me why it's so hard to talk to someone else?"

I was going to say no. But I'd just put my life in danger, and by proxy, Bracken's, as well as Davy's and the lives of everybody else who had run to my rescue, and maybe my own sense of privacy needed to be invaded. "Can you tell me why it's so important that I do?" I asked, surprising even myself. "Why can't I just talk to you and Bracken and people here? You're all... smart and wise and shit. Why can't it just be you?"

"Because you can't even say what you're really thinking to us," Bracken spoke up unexpectedly. "You... cloud it with language and with this thing you do where you're trying not to sound 'smart and wise and shit'—and I'm not sure if you're worried that you'll sound like something you're not or more worried that the world will see that you're something you are, but you don't talk to us."

I blinked, and so did Green.

"And look who is all 'smart and wise and shit,'" Green said. I leaned back into him, and he put his arm around my shoulder. Bracken leaned back into me, and I stroked his hair.

"See?" I said brightly. "I don't need anyone but you."

"Yes, you do," Bracken said soberly. My fingers stilled in his hair. "Because Green will let you get away with that. And so will I. Because we love you, and we don't want to watch you hurt. But Hallow won't. Hallow won't let you get away with lying to yourself or lying to him. And that's why you need to talk to someone not us."

There were so many things I could have said to that. I could have said, "Fine, Bracken, you go have a conversation with Adrian, I'll talk to Hallow." I could have told Green, "You tell me about the other things in your life that hurt more than Adrian's death, and I'll go talk to Hallow." Hell, if nothing else, I could have begged and pleaded and wept, and I don't think they could have denied me. But....

"I'm not good enough for either of you," I said softly. "If this is all you ask of me, then I can't say no."

"If this is what it takes for you not to believe that," Green replied, "then this is what we're asking of you."

"Okay," I said, sinking into the comfort sandwich that the two of them made. "Okay."

GREEN
Exploring Options

GREEN MANAGED to spell her to sleep before Kyle got there. He didn't feel particularly bad about it, either, because when she was strong and happy her will was too strong for him to influence like that. But when she was stressed or recharging her batteries after something like today's attack, all it took was comfort and relaxation, and then the suggestion of sleep would have her soft and warm and breathing quietly in his arms like a child. The aptness of the analogy was not lost on him, either.

"Do you want me to take her?" Bracken asked as soon as he felt her hands slacken in his hair and fall to her sides.

"Not really, but it would probably be best. Davy's boyfriend is going to be storming in here about ten minutes after sunset, and it would be good to have the both of you quietly locked away, I think."

"She'll hate the thought of hiding," Bracken stated, sitting straight and swinging around to pick Cory up.

"Well, she won't be hiding, will she? She'll be sleeping, sexing, or studying, right?"

Bracken nodded, raised an eyebrow, and said, "I'm all for option B."

Green laughed and shifted her off of his lap. "You're all talk, mate. You were so relieved to have someone take up the slack it almost had you walking funny."

And now it was Bracken's turn to laugh as he hoisted their beloved in his arms. "Yeah, yeah—and you were pretty happy to do just that. But seriously, how are you going to deal with Kyle? He's going to be pissed."

And Green's expression hardened. "Well, now, he's not the only one to have something to be pissed about, is he?"

Bracken sobered. "No. He's not." His voice turned inward, and Green took his cue.

"I promised her I wouldn't let you do that. Today wasn't your fault, Bracken."

"I should have...."

"Should have what? Known? Stopped her? We love her because she's strong willed. You think we're going to be able to tell her what to do all the time because we wish it?" Cory'd had this argument with Bracken the past winter, he knew, but some things needed to be said twice. "Then she wouldn't be who we love, right?"

Bracken nodded. "Right." He shook his head as though pushing the lesson in. "Right," he repeated and set off for their room.

A few minutes later, Nicky called to tell them that Kyle was on his way—and that he wasn't driving. In the ten minutes that followed, Green managed to surround himself with Arturo, Mario, Eric, Joe, Steph, Ray, Leah, Willow, Sweet, Twilight, Cockleburr, Grace, Marcus, Phillip, and Chet. Cory had offered Kyle a place with their people; vampires were communal creatures—they depended upon each other for society, sex, and blood. Green wanted Davy's beloved to have an inkling as to what Cory's offer truly entailed.

Sweet opened the door to Kyle's frenzied pounding and greeted the furious vampire with a serene smile and a gesture into the front room. Green looked up calmly from his station on the stuffed chair and invited Kyle to sit down on the couch. Kyle, thrown off his guard by the courtesy and the warmth of the greetings, accepted the place on the couch with little grace and grunted a churlish negative to Leah's offered throat.

"You people need to stop offering me food," he snarled, frowning at Green. He was still wet from flying through the rain, and his hunting face with the deepened grooves and elongated jaw was barely receding. "That little werekitten sitting with Davy right now could have lost her gullet."

"Since her boyfriend is a cop and probably packing the silver bullets we gave him for Christmas, I seriously doubt that," Green said smoothly.

Kyle blinked. "A what?"

"A human policeman on our local force." Green found that his smile was all teeth. "He's been... exceedingly useful... in recent months."

"You people...." Kyle shook his head and tried valiantly to remember his former anger. "My girlfriend is *bleeding*. Her lip is split because of...."

"Because of an enemy we had nothing to do with," Green interrupted.

"Her lip is split open!"

"That's too bad. My beloved had a broken nose and a dislocated shoulder from the same incident. I'd say you got off easy on the worry department, didn't you, mate?" And Green's voice hardened and his eyes grew flinty, and now every bit of his frustration with this vampire and with Cory's situation with his human began to roll off his bow-tight body in waves.

Kyle swallowed in surprise—a truly convulsive movement in a vampire. "Dislocated shoulder?" he asked blankly.

"From hauling Davy behind her, I believe," Green snapped. "Something she wouldn't have had to do if Davy had known what kind of danger she faces just being attached to you!"

"I can take care of my beloved!" Kyle snapped, but there was desperation in his voice. He didn't believe it, and neither did anyone else in the room.

"What are you afraid of?" Grace asked suddenly in exasperation. "If she's worth your love, she's certainly not going to turn you away because of what you are. You could at least tell her the truth."

"Yes," Green added unequivocally. "And you could at the very least protect her by finding a kiss to keep you well. If not us, then at least Andres!"

"Oh yeah—a kiss is a wonderful idea," Kyle snapped out sarcastically, "because I want to see the woman I love passed around from vampire to vampire like a flask of whiskey at a campout."

There was a sudden shocked silence among Green's people, which Leah broke with her trademark humor. "Oh, are we doing that sort of thing now? Because Officer Max is totally hot. I've wanted him since he started coming by last summer!"

Eric looked at her consideringly. "You think? I don't see it."

"Oh, yes," Willow nodded, pale gray-green face dreamy with hunger. "I'd have him. Of course, Renny would chew my spine off while I slept," she added, her eyes twinkling.

"Yeah, Green," Sweet said impishly, "if we're passing around lovers, I'll take either one of them—Cory or Bracken!"

"I get Cory first!" This from Marcus. "Phillip and I have had a thing for her since Adrian brought her home."

"Mmmm… more you than me, roomie," Phillip disagreed. "For me, it would be too much like kissing my sister."

"Not that that's a bad thing for the fey," Arturo said, flashing the silver caps he'd put on his teeth just for style. "But since I haven't kissed her either way, I wouldn't know."

"A thing that makes us all much more comfortable with each other," Grace added crisply.

Kyle was human enough—and shamed enough—to flush. "Okay," he said gruffly. "I get it. I was wrong about that." He didn't say anything more, and the chatter around Green died down.

"I think," Green mused, eyeing his people with meaning, "that young Kyle and I need to go walking in the rain for a bit."

Green liked taking newcomers to the Goddess grove. He liked their surprise, he liked their appreciation, and he liked reliving the memory of making it and his first wonder at what he had helped to shape. Kyle looked around at the trees in their erotic poses and swallowed again. The rain was dripping from the branches, singing on the moss on the ground, whispering to them of silent bodies, hushing skin, and promises in the dark.

"Who are they?" he asked, voice rough. "They must be... there's something very personal about this. Like the wood had no other choice than to twist itself into their shapes."

"It *was* personal," Green replied simply. There was more rainy silence as Kyle digested this. Green allowed a certain amount of ambient light, and the two of them were standing at the bole of the oak tree Nicky had perched in a few nights before, staring into the low-lit grove, and the leaves of all the trees were dark and shiny from the wet.

"I'm glad," Kyle admitted. "It's beautiful when it's personal."

"Mmmm," Green agreed. Then, delicately, "Crispin would have made you share her, wouldn't he."

Kyle bit his lip, and Green, looking at him sideways, could see that his fangs had extended just a little in agitation. "Yes," the young vampire said softly.

"Mmmm. We're not Crispin. If you don't choose us, you need to go to Andres." He was brusque now, trying to give Kyle space and, more importantly, trying not to overlay his own strong personality on the vampire's connection with the hill. It was important that he looked to Cory more than Green.

"I've made a reservation at that hotel...," Kyle said hesitantly. "I'm going to see Andres this weekend."

Green nodded. "You need to leave tonight. Cory killed two humans controlled by the Hollow Man today. There are going to be questions and policemen, and Davy can give more of us away with her ignorance than she would with her knowledge."

Kyle shook away his shock. "Yeah—okay. I spelled her to sleep as soon as she told me the story. We'll be packed and on the road before she wakes up."

"Good. Come back with your decision made. You put my beloved in danger with Davy's ignorance, and that isn't going to happen again."

Green had a mild autocratic streak (Cory would have used a different adverb), and its timbre in his voice put Kyle's back up. "And what are you going to do if I don't?" he snapped.

"Oh, that's easy. My people will hold you down while Cory bloods you, that's what we'll do." He turned to the young man with his eyes flat and his lovely, sensual mouth pursed and grim. "Don't test us on this, Kyle. For everybody's safety, you need to resolve this situation now."

Kyle nodded and managed a weak grin. "That's... really sort of merciful and terrifying at once, do you know that?"

"Well, so is my beloved," Green replied, letting his own fond grin sneak out. "Terrifying, I mean. I'm the merciful one. You won't deal with me again."

"Why am I now?" Open curiosity.

Green let out a breath and decided to be brutally honest with the young vampire. They did, after all, have a few things in common. "Because I can be an arrogant bastard sometimes, if you want Cory's answer to it. But mostly because she came home today covered in blood and freezing cold and soaked in guilt. And you and I both know it wasn't her fault. Sometimes we do for our beloved what we can't do for ourselves." He looked at Kyle meaningfully—and finally, finally he made eye contact.

"I hear you," he conceded. "I'll tell Davy, at the very least. I promise."

"See that you do." Green gestured toward the trapdoor to the inside. "And now I think it's time that you sent my people home and got on the road. Agreed?"

"Absolutely."

Cory emerged from her room about an hour later, yawning, with Bracken at her back holding a physics text and what Cory called her "backup" knitting bag. Study time.

"Why didn't anybody wake me?" she asked through her yawn. "I'm expecting Kyle any minute."

"He's actually come and gone," said Green casually, waiting.

Her eyes snapped open, and she spoke with careful emphasis. "Where, exactly, is he going?"

"To the hotel in the city." He looked up from his computer and saw that Bracken was edging away skittishly, as though from a rabid dog.

Her eyes narrowed. "Dammit, Green...."

"Corinne Carol-Anne," he said abruptly, stilling her with her full name, which he knew she missed the sound of since they had decided to use it sparingly. "Two days ago, I was asleep and Bracken knocked on the door—do you remember that?"

She blinked, surprised. "Y... yes...."

"What did you say to him when he was there?"

She shrugged. "I don't know... to take Max to school to keep an eye on Nicky, since Renny wasn't going...."

"Mmm-hmmm... why didn't you wake me up?"

She shrugged. "You were sleeping, Green. It was just standard stuff—I thought I'd spare you. You were so tired...."

He waited. She was stubborn, but by no means stupid.

Comprehension dawned. "But Green, this wasn't the same thing at all. I'm supposed to be the queen of the vampires. What I did the other day was minor shit. This was big deal queenship stuff...."

"And you are still learning to be queen," he said gently. "Nobody expected you to suddenly take over the reins overnight, luv. Let me do for you when I can. Please?" he added when she would have protested. "I will be gone enough, and it will be hard enough to just desert you and go—let me do these things for you when I can." He heard the note of pleading in his own voice and tried not to cringe.

Abruptly she closed the distance to the couch, threw her arms around him, and buried her face in his neck. "No problem," she said. "No problem at all."

Bracken sat down in the overstuffed chair and opened the physics text, but she stayed buried in Green's arms for many more minutes before they got to studying. Later that night, Cory stretched, yawned, and moved herself off to bed, turning at the doorway expectantly. Bracken looked at Green, and Green smiled and nodded. "Of course, beloved," he said gently. "Go get ready, and I'll be there in a moment."

She nodded in a sleepy, contented way that said their time together would be more snuggling than sex, and then wandered off to his bedroom.

Bracken picked up the physics book and had turned toward the hallway when Green caught his attention.

"The sylphs' mating cycle is coming round again," he said softly, not wanting Cory to hear.

"I figured." Bracken frowned. "I didn't think you needed to be there for all of them."

"I don't—maybe one out of four, if they're as tight together as I think they are. But…." Green took a breath. He hadn't let *anyone* in on his plan to protect his people, but Bracken was crucial to what needed to be done, and to keeping Cory balanced enough to do what needed to be done. "I want to try something with this cycle. This is going to be a trial run, but when the real thing comes around, I'm going to need you and Nicky to know what's coming."

"Have you told Cory yet?" Bracken was obviously nonplussed. Of the two of them, Green was the one she talked to most easily.

"No. She's having such a hard time finding balance with all of us…. What I'm thinking about doing will involve the four of us, and unless it works with the sylphs, I don't want her to know the specifics…." Oh, Goddess, was he actually blushing? Eighteen hundred years old, and he couldn't discuss how to cast a spell in sex without blushing? God, Goddess, and other, what was the use of living so long!

A slow grin had bloomed on Bracken's unrepentantly beautiful cheeks. "We're going to try to do that thing again—the one we did when you healed Twilight and we blew each other's minds."

"Among other things getting blown, yes," Green said dryly, pulling his composure back around him like a cobweb cloak. "But this is only a test run. I was just thinking that…."

Now Bracken looked positively eager, and Green had to laugh. He was sure to his bones that Bracken would be happy to bed Cory and Cory alone until his dying day. But he'd also been raised a sidhe, with all of the freedom that entailed—a little adventure wouldn't bother him at all. "You were thinking that if it was powerful when we were all apart, it would be absolutely nuclear if we were all in the same bed." His voice was practically throbbing with excitement.

"I think it could be protection against what the Hollow Man does against our blood, yes," Green affirmed. He outlined it, discussing the sexual logistics and the magic, and Bracken followed, his grin growing wider by the moment.

"That would be soooooo awesome," he said when Green was done, using some of Cory's own language. Then, as though remembering who they were talking about, he added, "She'll never agree to it."

"She might, when she sees how this one works." Goddess, he hoped so, he thought wretchedly. The only way to go through with this plan was to go through with it consensually. If she wouldn't agree—and wholeheartedly, without being dragged into it kicking and screaming— then it couldn't be done.

Bracken nodded, and Green could see he was hopeful. "Well, the least we can do is try," he said, and Green nodded in agreement. Bracken moved off to his bedroom again, because Cory was either getting impatient for Green or fast asleep. He turned at the doorway. "Green— that other thing aside—when the mating cycle kicks in, even if you're only going to be gone for one or two nights.... Leader, you have to tell her you're going before you leave. She's not ready for you to be gone yet, not so soon."

"I hear you," Green agreed.

"You'd better," Bracken laughed, but not happily. "Otherwise we'll both be hearing it from her."

"And she needs you to put her back together," Green said bleakly.

"It's what we do." And with that bit of philosophy, he was off to bed.

CORY
The Physics of Breakthroughs

FOR MOST of the next three days, I worked at Grace's store, studied like mad, and enjoyed Green's company while he was home. He had another trip coming up soon, but he wouldn't commit to when—something to do with the mating cycle of the sylphs, but he wouldn't say anything more.

But Sunday, Green was down in Old Town Sacramento, having dinner with Eric and Hallow someplace obscenely expensive that I'd be uncomfortable in anyway—and since I'd made it my unofficial policy to see Hallow only during those times when I was required to tear open my intestines and show him what was wounded where, it was better that I stay at home. As I had been brushing Green's hair (I loved doing that—it was like playing with raw silk), Bracken had stuck his head in the room and asked if I wanted to go with him to the Camp Far West property, where he was going to help the Avians with some big caveman house-fixing ritual. They also needed a little bit of everyday magic, and I could help as well. After only the slightest hesitation, I said yes.

I actually liked traveling the back roads of the lower foothills this time of year. It had been raining pretty steadily for the last month, and now, mid-February, the small farm patches in Ophir were green with long grasses that would be Weedwacker fodder come fire season but were the closest thing many folks had to a lawn. I liked the smell of the usually dry earth, now wet and happy, and the peeping wildflowers in their too short season. Around the middle of March, the whole drive would be crazy with lupines and poppies and those purple-flowered things that turned into spiral sticker-burrs in the summer but were really pretty now. In the summer, the place would be brown and lonely feeling, in spite of the closeness of the properties and the oak trees that huddled the area together—but now, in the rain, it felt vast and social. It's too bad that springtime in the foothills is usually only the week between when the rains stop and when the thermometer climbs to the nineties as a prelude to settling into its nice comfortable niche around 102.

But the Avian property wasn't in Ophir—it was out by Sheraton. If we skipped over the freeway to Luther, we could cross Highway 49 and travel the back roads to Highway 193. From there it was a right turn on McCourtney, which wound peculiarly among big farmsteads before it started doing some really stomach-turning things. First it snaked through a wildlife preservation place that nobody knew about, where Green had just bought some mine-shaft-riddled property for the cave trolls. Beyond that was a levee, with the man-made lake on one side and a pit of rocks on the other, which had always terrified me because there wasn't even a faint guard rail on either side and the bridge was one way. Between the kinky-snake things the road did around the wildlife preserve and the rip-your-guts-open-on-the-rocks thing, the second half of the trip was not nearly as pleasant as the first.

Bracken knew this and made an effort to fill the moments between motion-nausea by the wildlife preserve and stark terror by the levee with easy conversation. Except conversation with Bracken was never as easy as it should be.

"How in the name of the three-headed one did you pass that test?" he asked for the umpteenth time.

"I told you." I was glaring straight ahead on this part of the road. If I wasn't careful, I'd get (surprise!) sick. "I just explained how I'd solve the problem as a moron who can't do math."

He pulled his lead foot up a tad as we came out of the turn, but the centrifugal force still pushed me to the side of the car. "Give me an example, Cory. For sweet Goddess's sake, I've been trying to talk you through this for a month—give me a clue so I know how to help you for the rest of the semester."

My stomach rebelled, and I tried desperately to hold on to the lunch he'd forced me to eat before we left the hill. It wasn't going to happen, but I tried anyway by concentrating on physics. "You want a clue? Fine. There's a goddamned car traveling on a goddamned curve. The car's initial vector is its weight times its speed going fucking forward. The idiot behind the…" (*oomph*) "…fucking wheel took the goddamned curve at sixty fucking miles an hour, which is a vector going thirty or so miles to the…" (*bleagh*) "…right and another vector going thirty or so miles forward, so that if the goddamned wheels break loose and we go speeding off the damned hill we will have so much momentum taking us good and forward that we will jump off the twenty-foot drop and so much momentum taking us to the side that we can slam into the trees before we have the gravity vector slamming us down off of that drop and into the ground when we die." I took a breath. It didn't help. "Pull over asshole, I have to hurl."

He held my hair back as I lost my dinner on the nonexistent shoulder, but when I was done and ready to get back in the car, I could sense his suppressed laughter. I couldn't blame him, really.

"I don't think I used to do this quite so much," I mumbled after I'd rinsed and spat from a bottle of water we kept in the SUV.

"Define 'quite so much.'" He put both hands under my arms and lifted me up like a rag doll, then kept his arm around my shoulders.

I scrubbed my face with my hand. "I mean, before last summer, the last time I'd gotten sick to my stomach was probably when I fell off my friend's horse in the sixth grade and broke my wrist. I meet you, and I can't seem to keep anything down."

"As flattering as that is to my ego, I could point out that you met Adrian and Green first," he said, stowing me securely in the car and closing the door.

"Yes, but I only seem to throw up around you," I pointed out sourly as he got in and started the engine.

Bracken turned to me and grinned so brightly that the dimples I hardly ever got to see popped in and I started to feel marginally better. "Maybe it's the price I pay for bringing out the best in you as well."

I laughed in spite of myself. "Shut up and drive the fucking car," I said, but my foul mood was ebbing and so was my nausea. I thought the humor might be enough for me to cope with the terror of the one-lane bridge.

"Car's not getting any action tonight, baby. Green's SUV is in the city—and unlike Green, that monster doesn't share."

I laughed a little more. "I'm serious, Bracken. I mean, I've always gotten carsick, but it wasn't always a guaranteed upchuck. Lots of people get queasy when they get hurt—but it's getting to the point where if I'm not throwing up, you guys know I'm fine."

Bracken nodded. "Yeah, I know. Green and I were talking about it the other night."

"You guys talk about me?" The idea was foreign, but it shouldn't have been. As much as I tried not to discuss either of them in front of the other one, sometimes it was just a by-product of shared acquaintanceship—it should have occurred to me that they would discuss *me* when I wasn't there. I just didn't think I was that interesting.

Another nod, this one exaggerated. "Yes, Cory. We discuss the care and feeding of Corinne Carol-Anne, so that one of us might not step where the other one just shit. Is that okay with you?"

I shrugged. "I guess I didn't think I was that high maintenance." Before he could say anything about *that,* I hurried up with, "So what about Cory-the-vomit-comet? What did you two come up with?"

He was *dying* to say something about "high maintenance," I could tell, but he restrained himself. "It's sort of like an exhaust valve for your power. Your magic is fueled by emotions. When you get hurt—physically or emotionally—or when your sense of perspective gets confused, you purge your human fuel. You fill up on magic, you dump your humanity—it's sort of a counterpoint."

"That would be almost poetic, considering the subject matter," I said thoughtfully. "I just wish I could sweat blood, or something less disgusting."

Bracken laughed, and I realized that we had actually finished the kinky-snake part of the road and were at the one-lane bridge. He could be a handy guy to have around sometimes. "Yeah, but this way all I have to do is hold your head. The other way, it would be an all-over sponge bath, and that could be inconvenient at times."

And we were over the bridge and to the property. Forget everything bad I'd ever thought about Bracken's ability to make conversation—when it counted, he was freaking brilliant. And since I wasn't sweating blood, the sponge bath didn't sound like a bad idea either.

It wasn't until later that I realized the most important thing about that conversation. Without prompting, without bitterness, without anger or pain, Bracken had used Adrian's name. At the time, I thought it was what Hallow would have called a breakthrough. It wasn't until later that I learned what a real breakthrough was all about.

When we got to the house, I was impressed by how much everybody—Avians, vamps, weres, and sidhe—had accomplished. It had started out as a one-story ranch-style house with four bedrooms. Thanks in part to some brilliant architecture by Green, a little magic, and a lot of hard work, it had become two stories, three if you counted the basement darkling under construction—with fifteen bedrooms and six baths, not including the darkling. It wasn't fancy—nothing that would draw the attention of *Better Homes and Gardens*—but the middle rooms in the top story had clear fiberglass ceilings and ladders to the roof, with clear fiberglass posts that (with a little glamour thrown in) were difficult to see, but easy for man-sized birds to perch on. It was, in fact, an aerie—and the thirty or so displaced Avians who had put in their lot with Green and me after their old leader was overthrown would be very comfortable here.

They were glad to see me and Bracken—if they didn't get periodic visits from the sidhe themselves, or me, Green's glamour tended to fade—but mostly the bird shape-shifters were just happy for company. The Avians had needed some pride and some space—but that wasn't the only reason to set them up so far from Foresthill. Green didn't want what had happened to Nicky to happen to all of the other Avians. The atmosphere at the hill was so sexually charged that he was afraid more accidental bondings would happen unless there was some distance. But that didn't mean that most of them hadn't come to like us. Besides, they all knew LaMark and Mario, who were living at the hill now, and if we didn't bring them, we usually brought gossip.

Tonight, the gossip was grim. Nicky, who had come up earlier on his motorcycle (just ask me what the thought of a motorcycle on that road did to me), was surfing the net on the house PC, and when we walked in, he looked at us accusingly. "You guys are late. I almost called Green."

I grimaced. "Sorry, Nick. We had to take an upchuck detour."

It was his turn to wince. "Eww." Then, seriously, "Have you *seen* the press those two bodies are getting? They're going to open the track tomorrow, but I'll be surprised if you and Davy don't get questioned blue."

I sighed, and Bracken gripped my arm before moving to where the other Avians were working. They were laying drywall in the darkling tonight—the cave trolls had lined it with granite to help keep the foundation sound, but not even vampires wanted to live in a giant granite box.

"We have to go tomorrow," I said. "If I don't go running, Davy will want to know why, and if Kyle hasn't told her anything, I need to run damage control." Then, reluctantly because I didn't want to know, "Have they released the name of the other body?"

Nicky shook his head, looking studiously at the screen. He was lying.

"Give it up, Nick." I tried to sound sharp, but it was a nice gesture on his part. "I just want to know, okay?"

"Yeah. I know. His name was Shane Ruskaff."

"Jesus," I breathed out.

"He went to your high school."

"Yeah. He and Chuck used to hang out together... get high, get laid...." Make fun of punk-goth chicks like me and honors students like Renny, and beat the hell out of runaways like Mitch and Ray who had been too poor and too dispossessed to turn to any outside authority for help. And wait down by the lake at night for the vampires to come and roll their minds, so they could be free and then pretend they didn't remember.

"It wasn't your fault," he said. I'd heard it all weekend from Green and Bracken. Bracken, of course, blamed himself. Although unwilling to say anything, and certainly not willing to rub it in when Bracken felt so awful about the whole thing anyway, I think Green blamed him just a little bit too.

"Yeah," I said brusquely. "Can I climb to the aerie now? Last time I couldn't, and I had to redo the glamour from down here. I think that's why it died so early—I'm not that good with glamour yet."

"Cory, I mean it," Nicky said seriously. I didn't want to have this conversation with him. I'd been having it for three days—there was nothing he could add to it, and telling him that would just make him feel like crap.

"I know you do. Thanks. The aerie?" I smiled brightly and looked expectant, and Nicky glowered at me.

"You've been driving them crazy, haven't you?" He wasn't moving toward the aerie. He was, in fact, standing nose-to-nose with me, so close and so intense that I could see the black specks in his golden eyes. I didn't want to look him in the eyes, but he was only a little taller than I was, so my next choice was his button-up shirt with the cityscape on it. Nicky loved trendy.

"I always drive them crazy." I analyzed his shirt, staring at the single place where orange became yellow. I double-checked my face, and found my smile was intact. "C'mon—I think Bracken's going to be working in hyperspeed, and I may have some time to do my homework when this is finished."

"Dammit, Cory, you were defending yourself. You were defending *her*. You could have been killed—"

"So yes," I snapped, wanting this over with. "Yes, you're right, I had the right to smack them out of the sky like really big psychotic bugs running on magical steroids. I get it. I've heard it. They weren't nice people. I know that too. And hey, the fact that I knew them and loathed them in high school was strictly incidental—and it's not like I haven't committed mass murder before." I swallowed, because my voice had gotten loud and I was aware that several of the men (there were very few female Avians in the world in general) were looking at me sympathetically.

"Well," he snapped back, clearly out of patience with me too, "have you just gone and thought about the fact that maybe, considering what we know about how the guys addicted to Hollow Man end up anyway, that the way they ended up was a fucking mercy!"

I caught my breath, because in spite of all the cajoling Green and Bracken had done this weekend, that subject had not come up. "No," I grated, "I hadn't thought about that." And I didn't want to. I squeezed my eyes shut tightly, adjusted my expression, and tried again. "The aerie, Nicky? Please?"

He grabbed my hand and practically hauled me to the middle of the house and up the ladder to the roof, then stood there watching me do my job with crossed arms and a twisted expression. Buffing up the glamour was no problem—in fact, it was fun—and afterward I sat on one of the fiberglass benches and stared into the star-laden sky. Sacramento was many miles and a few foothills to the south, and Woodland was barely a smudge off to the east somewhere, so the stars out here under the rolling bare hills that made this country were all our own.

"Pretty sky…," I said, feeling relaxed for a moment. "Sometimes I'm jealous of the guys out here, with all this sky to fly under."

"Do you want me to move out here?" Nicky asked tightly, and I looked at him in surprise.

"No!" I said, feeling a little panic. No. "I like you at the hill. You're… you're…." How could I finish that sentence? "No," I said at last, forlornly. "Look, Nicky, I know I yelled at you guys the other day, but… but…."

"This isn't about that," he said softly, coming up behind me. It wasn't raining, but it was cold, and I felt his hands cup my shoulders tentatively, then move more firmly to wrap around my body and keep me warm. He had a smell, I realized with surprise. How was it that we'd had sex, not once but twice, and I hadn't noticed his smell? It wasn't mustard flowers like Green, or sun-on-stone, like Bracken—it was subtler, less overbearing. It was dusty and animal, like a dog or a cat that had been outside all day. Dusty feathers? Something. Something comforting. The comfort that was his smell made me suddenly frantic to keep him nearby.

"Then why would you want to move out?" I had been all ready to defend myself with the whole "how are you holding up" thing, but Nicky leaving the hill had me nearly in tears.

"I don't," he said and, Goddess help me, I leaned into him. In all our time together, I had never wanted to lead Nicky on, ever—but dammit, I didn't care that he had other lovers, I needed him as a friend. "I've been trying to think about how to… how to make this whole thing easier on you. I thought that…."

"Then don't even talk about it," I snapped, looking out into the smoke-colored hill shadows and the silver grasses of moonlit horse country. "It's not…." My voice rose, and I tried to find a word to describe how it would feel to know that Nicky wasn't down the hall, ready to talk to or study with or to step in and help in unexpected ways. "It wouldn't make it easier on me. It's not convenient," I finished weakly, and he laughed a little in my ear.

"Convenient?" he goaded.

"Just don't move," I begged at last. "Green and I like having you at the hill."

"Sure, Lady Cory," he said gently. I had the feeling that he was laughing at me, but I didn't care. Nicky was staying. "As you wish."

"I wish you to be happy," I said softly, feeling wretched. "I want you to be happy, and I want you nearby. Is that awful? Am I being horrible and possessive? I don't care who else you love, Nicky. I… I've just come to depend on you, that's all."

"What makes me happy is being there for you," he said seriously, and I nodded, accepting his embrace as gratefully as I'd accepted anything from Nicky since he'd brought me coffee during an all-night study session in San Francisco.

I kissed his hands, linked in front of my chest. "I'm grateful for you, Nicky," I said under the clear cold sky.

"You're welcome," he said, and I nodded. Far away, near the flat black of the lake, a hawk that wasn't a hawk wheeled under the moon and went diving for some poor sleepy fish who wasn't expecting nonbirds that flew in the night.

"Is Tim really going to eat that fish?" I asked, thinking *ick* thoughts.

"No," Nicky laughed, "he just likes catching the damn things." We laughed a little together, but we didn't move for a long time. I was grateful, I thought breathlessly under the moon, still scenting sun-warmed dust and feathers from his body. Nicky would be there for me. As unfair as it was of me to ask him, he'd be there. Thank you, Goddess, for Nicky Kestrel.

That night, after we'd made the trip home (easier this time—nothing to throw up!) and I'd stayed up to make sure Nicky made it safely, and after Bracken and I had made love, I perched my chin on Bracken's chest and looked at him, worrying at the precious curve of his ear with my finger.

"What?" he asked softly.

"There will be police tomorrow."

"Yes. You can take care of them, right?"

I'd done it before inadvertently, and I still knew how to talk to people with power in my voice and make them believe that what I was saying was actual fact. "I can try."

"That's not what you were thinking about," he chided gently, pulling his hand through my hair and taking out the band, which was hanging by a little clump at the back of my head. "You were thinking about Nicky."

"Among other things." My head was once again becoming crowded with things I didn't feel like sharing. Maybe, a little voice nagged, they were right. Maybe I needed to dump my shit in someone else's yard just so I could have some room in my head for something nice, something peaceful—something *besides* shit.

"But Nicky first. Yes."

"Yes what?" I knew Bracken didn't read my mind—at least not as often or as easily, like Green. But it was getting to be spooky how well he could read me. I just didn't know if he was saying yes to what I was really thinking.

"Yes, you can and you should make love to Nicky on other nights besides date night." His mouth clenched a little as he said it, but not too much, and I wrinkled my forehead at him. Oh, yeah, he did know what I was really thinking.

"It would… complicate things," I fretted. His hand smoothed down my back, touching the tattoo that Davy had noticed on Thursday. I could practically hear his own tattoo—similar in the weaving of Green's lime leaves and my oak leaves and Adrian's roses, but wound from his wrist to his elbow—cooing to mine in simpatico.

"What complicates things is that you worry. Nicky knows that Green and I come first. You worry that giving him more than this little tiny part of yourself will lead him on. But all it does is give you more to worry about and more for him to be hurt about."

"You don't even like Nicky."

"I didn't like that he thought he had a right to you," he corrected, and I looked at his face in surprise. I hadn't thought Bracken read Nicky that way, but he had, and he'd been right. "He doesn't think like that anymore. He's trying to find a way to have a path to you. You need to clear the path, beloved. You are stuck with each other, for better or worse, and it would be better for us all if it was a peaceful thing."

I sighed. He pulled me up so I was sprawled almost completely on his body and then rubbed my cheek with his own—an oddly tender gesture that had the tension melting from my spine and the lines on my face easing just with the kindness of his love. "I'll think about it," I promised.

"You think too much," he groused. "It would have been better for us all tonight if you'd stopped thinking and come back from the aerie all sweaty and mussed."

"He was asking if he should leave the hill," I said, and I heard my hurt reflected back at Bracken in my voice.

"Give him a reason to stay," he said softly, and I nodded, thinking about it until he threatened to go get Green and have him will me to sleep. Of course Bracken could do that on his own, but Green had more finesse. When I woke up in the morning, I could smell dust and feathers under Bracken's stone-and-sun smell, and my conclusion was still the same. I had marked my back for Nicky; maybe it was time I let him into my heart.

The police were there at the track that day. Young, bland-faced officers who reminded me only a little of Max before he'd started being a person and stopped being a cop. In fact, I was almost glad that Renny and

Max had fought once again about the same thing, and that Renny was too blue for her fickle felinity to see her through another day at school. On the one hand, it was one more thing on my worry list—I didn't think she was going to make it through school at this rate, and I didn't know what else she wanted to do with her life at the hill. On the other hand, she was worse at the dodge-and-evade thing than I was, and Nicky and Bracken had their hands full.

We got there just as Davy arrived, and I put a careful hand on her arm at the questions. She cast me an unfriendly look but followed my lead and evaded the police with wide eyes and "No, I didn't see either of those guys enter the track"—"I didn't see anyone who looked strong enough to do that to them." Both statements were, of course, true. However, as innocent as Davy and I appeared, the cops had it in for Bracken.

"You look pretty big, sir. I imagine you could throw a guy a few feet," the oldest of the cops said. Wow—that was subtle.

I stepped in quickly. "He wasn't even here, officer," I said tersely. I probably should have been all smiling and obsequious and crap, but Davy was looking murder at me and the cops were looking at Bracken like he was a total psychopath, and it was time to get out on the track and talk. Panic, urgency, fear for Davy, the warmth that was Bracken vibrating like heat off a rock next to me, and that new, subtle dusty-musky thing that was Nicky when he was thinking of me—I let it build in my chest as I spoke.

"He wasn't here. You don't need to know his name. He's not nearly as freakin' big as he looks right now. In fact, we're all pretty fucking nondescript. Say bye-bye now."

"Bye-bye," the two men echoed blankly, and I steeled myself for Bracken's ironic look before he took my pack and dragged Nicky up the stairs.

If I hadn't been able to guess from Davy's seething anger, her first words to me after we'd stretched in silence and started trotting down the slick brown track made it painfully obvious that Kyle hadn't talked to Davy about anything important.

"What are you, a Jedi master?" she hissed after we were out of earshot of the blank-eyed officers and the incriminating yellow tape.

"Do I look like Carrie Fisher?" Ah, if only.

"No, but you just totally… you had that guy agreeing to whatever you said…." Her voice trailed off. It was impossible. What was impossible always seemed to make people doubt what their senses told them was true.

"Did you have a good weekend?" I asked, hoping against hope that she was just being dense and Kyle hadn't wussied out.

"Yeah—I loved that hotel you got us into," she said, and for a moment she had some real enthusiasm. "And that boss guy, Andres, was really dishy." The anger melted away—probably helped along by her unwillingness to deal with "that's impossible!" She chatted about her trip for the next mile, and I asked appropriate questions (and made appropriate comments—Yes, Andres was dishy; really, wasn't it interesting that they had a suite with no windows in the core of the hotel) while the whole time I was thinking that Green and Bracken really were going to have to hold Kyle down so I could compel him to take care of his own goddamned business.

"Is Kyle going to take Andres up on his offer?" I said finally, at the same time thinking *please please please please… anything.* This bizarre suspended state of emotional constipation was starting to piss me off.

"I don't know…." We had been planning for two miles today, with a quarter-mile cool down—but now, with another quarter mile to go, Davy was slowing down. I looked at her in surprise, and when she cast a furtive glance at Bracken, who was sitting in the stands, getting wet and watching us with tranquil eyes, I figured she wanted more time to talk. I slowed down with her, secretly grateful because my body was bitching at me big time about the extra quarter mile, and she nodded. "I think he's ready to sign on with your boss." She gnawed her lower lip.

Frickin' hallelujah. "Is that bad?"

"Nobody's said anything about that attack," she said at last, her eyes darting to the blank-eyed cops, who had still not recovered from the double whammy I'd thrown at them. "I woke up on the way to San Francisco, and Kyle said it was because we needed to avoid police questions. When I asked him why the police would want to know, and if he knew what had attacked us…." She shook her head. "He said you and your boss would take care of it. He told me he'd explain everything in San Francisco. But instead we spent this really great time in San Francisco in this fabulous room with no windows, and when we were coming home early this morning, I realized we hadn't talked about it at all. I brought it up and he looked at me—jeez—Cory, he looked at me like he might never see me again and told me that he'd tell me tonight.

I don't—his eyes. It was like… it was like he was saying good-bye and begging me not to go, and… and at the same time, that attack thing was really weird. And…." She looked up, and I didn't have to even see what she saw to know what she was talking about.

Now we both looked. The destruction had been cleared, leaving only the two policemen loitering there in the rain, but the tape remained.

Davy cleared her throat. "And what did you do?" she asked at last. "Besides your Jedi thing today, I mean. Because suddenly we were running, and there was that stench, and you were making these fly-swatting motions. I heard sounds, I felt stuff, but I couldn't see anything. But everybody's talking about these two guys getting killed, and we were here, and…."

And suddenly I couldn't lie to her one more time. "Yes," I said abruptly, swinging around to face her. I wiped my face clear of drizzle and tried like hell to look her in the eyes. I couldn't do it. I was telling the truth, and I still couldn't do it. "They tried to kill us, Davy. I can't tell you how, but I can tell you that. I was acting out of self-defense." My breath caught. It was the truth, and it hurt, and just saying that brought up a vision of the dumbass kid I had gone to school with, leaking his brains out onto the rubberized track. I swallowed because, dammit, if I didn't toughen up, who would protect Nicky and Bracken? Who would protect her? I made an effort to haul breath through the bed of nails that my lungs had become. "Yes, Davy. I'm responsible for that yellow tape. But until your boyfriend steps up and deals, I can't tell you how. And I can't go to the police about it. They wouldn't believe it, and they'd arrest me—and too many people need me for that to happen."

"But what did you *do*?" she asked, her voice harsh. Her eyes were wide and bright, and her lower lip, pink-blue in the cold, was trembling. Goddess fuck it all. This was why I didn't get human friends, I thought wretchedly—because her misery was my fault, and I couldn't even make it go away.

"Kyle will tell you tonight," I promised rashly. "He will tell you. Just the fact that he let you remember that conversation means that he's planning to tell you." For both our sakes, I hoped that was true.

"Let me remember…." Her voice rose indignantly, and I held up my hand.

"He loves you, Davy. All you have to do for answers is love him enough to not tell him good-bye. I think you do. I've staked a lot on

it. But until you talk to him, this is where it's going to have to stay."
Her perky brown ponytail was plastered to her neck under her hood, her
eyes were red with tears of frustration, and she looked miserable and
confused—a wet kitten in a yellow rain poncho—and I found myself
looking past her shoulder so I wouldn't start to cry too. I was staring past
the gray to the green of the football field when I saw Green.

Confident, beautiful—he was striding across the field, his pretty,
pretty yellow hair swinging in a perfect horse-tailed braid down to
below his fine and tight behind. And now I did cry, because there was
only one reason for him to be here dressed in a crème-colored suit and
a long white trench coat. I don't remember what I said to Davy then,
and I was suddenly no longer tired as I hurtled across the field and into
his arms.

He caught me, picked me up, and kissed me soundly—and I was
so sick of worrying about the human world and what it thought and how
to blend into it that I didn't care. I wanted him to kiss me, I wanted his
hands on my bottom, I wanted to hold his face, and I didn't give a fuck
about what the world saw, because, dammit all, he was leaving us again.

"I won't be so long…," he mumbled between kisses. "I swear,
luv—a week at most. I promise it won't be long."

I didn't answer, because I didn't want him to make promises it
would hurt him to keep. I just kept kissing him until his hands moved
behind him and detached my legs, and suddenly I was being handed
to Bracken. I turned into Bracken's chest with a whimper, and he and
Green shook hands or some sort of manly shit like that, and then there
was that big, long-fingered, tender hand stroking my hair. He leaned in to
whisper, "I'll be home soon, beloved." Then he gave Nicky a firm good-
bye kiss and was gone.

I peered out of the shelter of Bracken's arms as that yellow braid
disappeared beyond the bleachers, and I saw Nicky. Nicky had spent
two weeks losing himself in other people's flesh, trying to kill the pain
of being bonded to the both of us. He had just embarked on a very sweet
love affair with a very nice man in order to build a place in his heart that
was his alone. He had just offered to move away from the home he loved
to make things easier on me.

He looked as lonely as I'd ever seen anyone look in my life.

I said his name and opened an arm, still in the circle that was
Bracken, and he made a forlorn little noise and launched himself at me.

We stood there, the three of us, shivering in the drizzle and trying to pull ourselves together now that Green was gone again.

Eventually Brack and Nicky needed to go get our packs. I was surprised that when they moved away, Davy was still there, sitting on a sideline bench and staring at me with eyes so lost she made the wet-kitten analogy look like a pacing jungle cat.

"I don't understand," she said through a hoarse throat.

"It's...."

"Don't say it's Kyle's job to explain it to me," she snapped, angry. "You and Bracken—you love each other as much as anyone I've ever seen in my life. But... what I just saw... what kind of woman are you?"

I wanted to say I was a lost one, but she'd think the wrong thing. I wanted to say I was powerful, but she'd picture me in black leather with a whip or something—and that was so beyond funny I didn't even want to start. I was suddenly more than aware of the difference between human and not quite human, and I wanted—desperately, I wanted her to see me as just like her.

～ "In... in my world... in our world... we don't have 'boyfriends' or 'fiancés' or even 'husbands'...," I said, watching with distant eyes as two of the men in my life grabbed their stuff.

"But you and Bracken...."

"Hush," I ordered, without heat. They had turned and were looking at me now, and I knew that with their hyperhearing, they could hear every word. "You asked and here I am, giving you hard truth." I looked down at the toe of my sneaker and made myself stop digging a muddy hole in the turf of the field. "The hard truth is that my world and Kyle's world are very much the same. We don't have those people, the way you think about them. We have lovers, and they can be anybody—friends, brothers, warm bodies in the night—and we have beloveds, and we love them beyond death. We love them so much that death has no meaning, and life has no meaning without them. And there's not a number or a type or a box for these people. They are who they are."

My voice fell evenly, almost songlike from my throat. This story was passion and pain and still a churn and a roil in my heart, but what fell from my lips was poetry. I could no longer deny, even to myself, that the men in my heart were poetry. "Adrian was my beloved, and Green was his beloved, and then Green was my beloved, and for the briefest, happiest time of my life, we were... we were something so sublime that there's not even a word for it. But Adrian died, quickly, violently, and… Green and I lost our beloved, and Bracken lost his brother, and… and the grief.…"

I looked at her now, and she was listening, no judgment, no anything. She was simply mesmerized by my song. So I looked across the track and met Bracken's eyes, and I kept singing.

"The grief was the howl of the earth when it's ripped asunder. It was, and still is, the scream of a wind as it uproots trees, houses, people's dreams. It's a shriek in our hearts like an unholy music box, and when we least expect it, the box is opened by a careless hand and we are all razed to our knees, our hands over our ears, wailing in counterpoint." Suddenly the churn and the roil in my heart took over my chest and my throat and tightened my tongue and my face. "And Bracken and I held each other in our grief, and we found that when we touched, that wail became a melody—heartrending, but not harsh. And he is my beloved too."

"And Nicky?"

"Nicky's my lover. By necessity—don't ask me to explain. We must be this thing to each other, or he dies. And so must he and Green. The four of us… we're so tangled in love, so bound by emotion, by bonds of fate and pain and life and death—not even we can see where love for one of us ends and the other begins." I took my eyes from the toe of my mud-covered white running shoe, from the shiny red-brown track, from the gold of Bracken's sympathetic eyes as he neared us, shouldering our packs as he shouldered my sorrow and confusion and defensiveness. Now I truly looked at Davy, and I saw myself as I must have been last year, when it was just me and my vampire against the world. I was smaller then.

"We live in a vast world, Davy. Bigger than you can conceive, more complicated than you ever thought possible. And Kyle has made you a part of it, and that's for him to explain. It's scary. There are deaths and pain and brutality that I don't ever want you to imagine, much less know." I turned to Bracken and was going to take his hand, but he wrapped his arm around my shoulder, giving me just enough room to turn to her as she sat on the wet metal bench in the rain. "But there's sweetness here too, Davis Stacia—remember that when you talk with Kyle. So much of it hurts, but there is sweetness, and beauty, and love."

"Will I think it's worth it?" she asked, but the heat from Bracken's arm was seeping through my wet T-shirt, and suddenly Davy and Kyle were their own concerns and not mine.

"Absofuckinglutely," I called over my shoulder. I leaned my head against Bracken as we walked. Halfway down the track, Nicky caught up with us and took my free hand, his skin warm against mine, the scent of dust and animal faint under the wet. The last I saw of her was the sprites I had assigned to watch over her, hovering about six feet above her head, blinking merry blue and red and purple and green twinkles in the gray.

BRACKEN
Twisted Routes

DAVY DIDN'T show up to run with Cory for the next three days. Watching her steel her expression for the disappointment when her friend didn't show was as painful as pretending with her that it didn't matter if she did.

The sprites checked in periodically, telling us that Davy was okay, which was, I think, the only reason my beloved didn't track her down just to make sure, and Cory ran with Renny and her iPod instead.

Renny and Max were "taking a break" (Max's words, tortured and wounded as they were), which meant, I thought, that neither of them could think of a way to resolve their original problem—should Max become a part of our world, or shouldn't he. Cory remained hopeful on the matter—saying shrewdly that Max was already a part of our world, he just didn't realize it yet—and I was content to rely on her judgment.

So for three days, Nicky and I sat, thankful for the heavy gray clouds that, for this week, were not spewing water, and watched the women run the track. Renny, as feline in human form as when she wore fur, did not prattle as much as Davy, but every now and then one of them would gasp a quick comment and the other one would smile or nod, and then their footfalls would resume regularity, comfortable in their companionship.

Today, Nicky looked up from his textbook long enough to comment, "It's hard to watch her hope."

"Yes," I said quietly. "I don't even know what she's hoping for, and it's hard."

Nicky turned to me, a rust-colored eyebrow arched. "You don't know?"

I shook my head. Nicky and I had reached... *détente,* I guess was the word. I knew Cory hadn't taken him into her bed without the "date night" restriction yet, but she'd been free about taking his hand, kissing his cheek, or wrapping her arm around his waist and accepting his arm around her shoulder. Nicky seemed grateful and even content with these attentions, and in his turn, he was careful to give me precedence in all matters concerning Cory, which was all I think I ever wanted in the first place.

"She's hoping that a part of her is still human," Nicky said, his eyes back on the two women on the track. Even as a human, Renny's legs seemed to blur independently of her body. It suddenly occurred to me that Renny was probably not comfortable running as a girl—she was out there for Cory. Considering her jealousy of Davy, I was touched on Cory's behalf.

I sighed. "Dominic, I love her with all of my soul," I said softly, "but I saw her, all those nights ago when Adrian wanted me to see the love of his undeath. She didn't even know what she was then, and I knew she was too good to be human."

"Yeah, Bracken, I know," he acknowledged. "But when I met her, human was all I was hoping for. It's a hard dream to let go of."

I didn't know, so I couldn't argue. One more thing to bring up to Hallow—who, after pulling thoughts from her like teeth from a tyrannosaur for a month, was taking to her new attitude of grudging expansiveness with an almost ghoulish enthusiasm. For her part, Cory had left their last session looking like her stomach hurt, and had run as though Hollow Man were after her all over again.

She wasn't running like that today, however. She was tired today— we all were. Renny had decided to come back to school, so in addition to staying up late and helping Renny with her own studies, first exams had arrived for all of our other classes. We had all stayed up to write papers, prep notes, and finish our reading. It didn't bother me so much— after around our fortieth year, my species as a whole doesn't need much sleep. I often got up when Cory was sleeping and visited the common room. Even Nicky and Renny, with their quick metabolisms and shape-shifter energy, weren't too affected by the three days without. But Cory's footfalls were sluggish today, and her arms pumped clumsily and out of sync, and I realized that I'd become accustomed to her strength and her energy. She had been right—she had taken up running to build her strength, and it was working, but not today.

Nicky noticed it too. "Think she's up to going out to Camp Far West tonight?"

"No," I said decisively. "But we still need to go." The vampires were coming up to paint and lay flooring for the entire house. Someone needed to be there, someone of rank, to keep things running smoothly. Nicky and I qualified, mostly because we were sleeping with the two most powerful people in the hill, but also because we had helped organize the thing and knew what everybody was planning. We'd ordered the supplies and read the directions as well.

"So…," he asked, looking at me dubiously.

"We let her fall asleep and sneak out of the hill." I kept my voice tranquil, but I was not nearly so sanguine about the plan. With the mood she'd been in since Green left, "sanguine" was probably a good word choice—that was a lot of my blood she'd be willing to spill if she realized I'd gone out unprotected on my own. But she was tired, and I was not, and I'd be damned if I hauled her up that road to get sick again and then let her sleep cold and miserable in the car, which would be the only place to sit out of the way while we were working.

Nicky thought this over very carefully. "It's a good thing you're the one sleeping with her regularly," he said after a moment. "I don't know if I'd want to be you when she wakes up."

"If you're lucky, you'll get some backlash action," I said as I gathered backpacks, and he brightened. Eric had left this morning, looking sadder than I'd seen him since he'd left the hill the first time. I had given him a hard time about how, in the old days, he wouldn't have let business interfere with his personal life, and he'd given me a twisted smile. "In the old days, I didn't have a business," he returned with a hug, and I felt for him. I couldn't imagine any business pressing enough to make me leave the hill I loved, or the woman I loved more. But leave he did, although he promised to return soon. I didn't know the details, but I knew that he and Nicky had come to some sort of understanding that did not include Nicky sleeping with the rest of the hill in the meantime. Nicky seemed to have found his balance, and I was happy for him.

I gazed wistfully out at Cory as she and Renny finished their run, Cory guzzling water from the bottle she'd left by the track. Now if only….

When we got home, she crashed within an hour, dozing off as she was knitting on the couch. The sitting room was semifull—a few of the sidhe along with Sweet and Ellen Beth were in there watching a movie, and Renny was curled into a lonely ball at Cory's feet. I eased away from the couch and signaled to Nicky, who in his turn nodded and stood up as well. Arturo intercepted us at the doorway, shaking his head in disgust.

"Where do you think you're going without her?" he asked. Grace stood by him, her arms crossed and her eyebrows raised. They had been talking quietly in the kitchen, hands clasped, half smiles on their faces, as we had made our stealthy way toward the door.

"The Avian property," I hushed, looking over to where she was sitting. She had turned so that her cheek was on the arm of the couch, and a part of me wanted to go pick her up and move her because that was just going to tweak her neck. "I thought you'd be going, Grace."

"Mnn." She shook her head no. "Too much to do keeping their food fed." She smiled playfully, and I realized how much we'd missed her, relaxed and happy at her home, since Chloe had arrived. Humans.... Goddess, could they complicate things. "There are perks to being den mama," she added, and Arturo looked at her sideways.

"I should hope so." He turned back to us. "You realize she's going to be pissed enough to crack the sky. And Grace and I are going to have to pick up the pieces."

"Yeah, Arturo," I said, dodging inside the kitchen to grab an apple, "but she loves you guys—you'll be fine. If she catches the two of us, she'll cut off our balls and serve them to Marcus and Phillip for lunch, so can we go? And, hey—could you give us a ten-minute head start and then pick her up and take her to her room? She'll never sleep like that."

"Any other duties you'd like me to take over?" he asked sourly, but Grace elbowed him sharply in the ribs, so he gestured for the door, and we practically ran Chloe over on the way out.

The apple was not enough, so we stopped by the Starbucks in Lincoln on our way and practically bought out their entire pastry section, then drove off into the night. Near the turn from 65 to McCourtney, there was an enormous grain silo that was lit up pinkly against the dark. After that, there was nothing but houselights, headlights, and starlight for miles, and this night, the moon was down. I drove quickly—if Cory wasn't there to get queasy, I enjoyed driving fast—and Nicky and I discussed the frustrating topic of Hollow Man.

We had sent Ellis and Leah to the address Ellen Beth had given us, but it was an apartment and already rented out to someone else. Not even the stench of our adversary remained. When we had turned the hill out to search for Sezan and Crispin the previous summer, we had at least known our enemy was in Folsom—and probably not in one of the newer neighborhoods, either. But Hollow Man had attacked us in Auburn, in

Sacramento; he'd even left a trail of sylph dust in Marin County—and he'd originated in Houston, of all places. We didn't have enough people, or enough leads, to guess where he was. About all we could do was protect ourselves from him and hope the next time he attacked we'd take him out.

"And that doesn't even count the people he controls," Nicky said with disgust. "I have no idea how he made those guys fly. Twilight said he had power like Cory's—sidhe magic, but bigger—but I can't imagine Cory throwing people around like missiles."

"I don't think he was throwing them around," I mused. "His big thing is infection. I think he just 'infected' those guys with power—sort of the same way you infect a culture with greed, or a mob with anger." Next to "how is Cory," this had been a hot topic at the hill, and we all had our theories.

"I'm sorry… I didn't quite hear you." Nicky shook his head, and I reached out and turned down the radio. We had just hit the place in the road where the curves started, and without the moon, it felt like our headlights were cutting a tunnel through the foliage. The radio made things less lonely.

"I think he… infects them. With himself, with his blood. It makes sense—that detestable asshole and his buddy, they would have been totally vulnerable to Hollow Man. They would have been begging for his bite, for sex, for whatever. We're so used to the idea that the Goddess's changes clean out our blood for the weres and vamps that we forget that humans live in fear of blood diseases." I had been thinking about this carefully—especially with Cory's suggestion that she blood this enemy—and the idea scared me more now than it had when she brought it up.

Nicky was shaking his head again, almost like a dog hearing a whistle, but he was concentrating on what I was saying. "That's the best theory I've heard so far…." He grimaced. "Speaking of hear, do you hear—watch out!"

I squinted at the road but saw nothing. Then the car struck an unmovable object, and it was all I could do to keep it on the road. I cut the next blind corner on the wrong side, praying there was nobody coming toward me, and swore. "It's him, isn't it?" I asked, and Nicky held his hands over his ears and whimpered in answer. Fuck. I couldn't see him—he could be fucking *anywhere*. I looked to Nicky for help, but he could barely function over the sound, and the keening he was making was grating on my nerves. I concentrated on the road and hit the accelerator, and swore again when the road veered right and he hit us on the left, trying to force the car off the steep verge.

This part of the road came with a cell phone blackout, and we needed help. Without even asking permission, I grabbed Nicky's hand as it clutched his ear, drove like a madman, and thought of our beloved with every ounce of intensity I could spare.

CORY
Distorted Destinations

CHLOE'S INDIGNANT squawk pulled me out of the nicest dream. I was in bed, sleeping, surrounded by all of them—Bracken, Green, even Nicky—and we were all soft and sweet with each other, and the sex was there, but the touching, the balance—it was like one of those chords in choir that gives you goose bumps of perfection.

Chloe's shriek was so discordant it made me mad enough to smack her.

Renny thought so too, because she did one of those cat-splang things that makes you think of cartoon cats with their claws in the ceiling. By the time she settled down into a crouching ball of hiss in the corner of the couch, I'd looked blearily around the living room and realized that Bracken and Nicky were both gone.

"I'll fry them!" I shouted and saw that the elves in the sitting room were looking at me sideways, half-amused and half-alarmed. I grabbed my knitting bag, which had my wallet and car keys in it, and charged the door—barefoot, bedheaded, and wearing sweats, a T-shirt, and an old Mr. Rogers cardigan I'd smuggled out of Green's closet.

I was nearing the door when I ran into Arturo with enough force to send me backward into Grace, who'd moved in hyperspeed to catch me.

"Not tonight, little Goddess," he said calmly, with so much parental authority in his voice that the temper I'd been about to spill off my tongue rearranged itself. Unfortunately, what came out sounded a lot like whining. "Arturo—they're out there in the dark without me. I was supposed to go with them...."

"And *Nicky* and *Bracken,*" he emphasized, "both agreed that you were too tired and that you should stay home and get some rest. And if Grace and I hadn't agreed with them, we would have woken you up," he said firmly.

I was glaring at him, I realized, like a child glares at a parent, but I couldn't seem to help myself. Uncle Arturo, I'd called him, and usually that was a good thing—when it went my way. "Aren't I supposed to be some sort of authority here?" I snapped, and I realized how arrogant that sounded when I saw his lips quirk upward.

"Yes, *mija,* and if you shake your rattle and stomp your little foot hard enough, we will all rush to do your bidding," he said mildly, and after sustaining my glare for another five seconds, I found I was giggling with him.

"If you try to change my diaper, I'll cook you," I muttered, and he ruffled my hair in response.

"Now see, Mom, *this* is what I don't understand," Chloe snapped, breaking the moment. Grace sighed behind me, and I wasn't imagining the tightening of her arms around my shoulders before she released me and straightened toward her daughter. "You tell me she's some sort of 'mighty leader,' and then you go and treat her like a child. Who *is* she to you?"

"She's twenty, Chloe," Grace snapped over my shoulder. "Even Alexander the fucking Great had people to remind him to rest." And with another silent hug, she moved away. "I've got things to do—was there something you wanted?" Grace moved toward the hallway, leaving Chloe to glare at me as though the whole thing were my fault.

"You know, Chloe," I said in disgust, "you might try to not be a flaming bitch to the woman who birthed you, okay?"

"Like you know so much about mothers," Chloe sneered. "Look to your own relationship with your mother before you start lecturing me about mine, okay?"

"What do you know about my mother?" I asked, a sneaking suspicion forming in my mind. I hadn't heard from Mom since she'd crashed into Grace's store, but that didn't mean she hadn't been calling. Something in my voice must have gotten Renny's back up, because she came up by my side and growled softly.

"Keep that… *thing*… away from me," Chloe said uneasily. I didn't think she was over watching Renny just appear naked in front of her.

"That 'thing' is my best friend," I snapped, suddenly as out of patience as Grace. "Why can't you just deal with us like people?"

"Because you 'people' think you're so damned special! You're just the same as the rest of us—just ask her boyfriend."

"What about Max?"

"He's no better than any other man—I saw him tonight at Denny's with a blonde with big boobs—wha' the…."

The rest of Chloe's venom was lost as Renny let out a snarl and literally ran over her on the way to the door. Muck a ducking fuck.

"Damn," I muttered as I started toward the door. Quicker than blinking, Renny turned girl, opened the door, then turned cat and left. "I don't know where she thinks she's going—I'm going to have to drive."

"Grace will drive," Arturo spat, stepping over Chloe's prone and sputtering body, "mostly because Bracken took your car." And with that, he blurred down the hall to go get Grace from the darkling. I realized he was right. Nicky drove the Ninja, and Bracken drove my SUV—which he had taken when they slunk out of the common room like the cowards they both were. There were other vehicles down there—the garage was huge, there were at least twenty—but none that I had the keys to. I was *so* going to grab Renny by the scruff of her neck and haul her back into the house when Grace blurred in and opened the door to the one automobile I least wanted to get in.

"Oh, you've got to be shitting me," I groaned as I opened the door and let Renny into the flamboyantly purple hearse that Green had bought specifically for the vampires. It looked young and funky, and it was set up so that in a pinch, between three and five vampires could lay out, flip a switch, and be protected from the sun for the rest of the day. The previous summer we'd had to stuff Adrian in the trunk of Arturo's Cadillac to keep him safe from the brutal June sun—I remembered wishing we'd had this car at the time, but I sure didn't want to drive in it now.

"It's what we've got, sweetie," Grace muttered as she turned over the engine. Practically before it caught, she threw the hearse into gear and backed out of the garage, spewing gravel everywhere as she threw the car forward and tore off down the driveway. I made sure my seatbelt was fastened and looked sourly at Renny, who was still in cat form, then held on tight as we made the hardest of rights and disappeared down Foresthill Road.

By the time we squealed across the I-80 overpass and into Denny's parking lot, I was praying Max was there—because between Grace's frustrated anger and Renny's vicious jealousy, this whole situation was going to need more than my ham-handed humanity to chill everybody out. Grace hadn't spoken a word during the twenty-minute flight over what should have been forty minutes of road, and Renny had kept up a feral, nonstop growling. It was funny how, even when I was sure we were all going to die on that damn road, it never occurred to me that

Max had found an alternative to Renny even on their so-called "break." Sometimes we read people better just because we're *not* close to them. There would be an explanation, of this I was sure.

My faith wasn't shaken even when we narrowly missed plowing into Max's Mustang and slammed to a halt on the blacktop behind Denny's. It was one of Green's places, so it was impeccably kept up, but it was still a Denny's, and after eating at Grace's table for nearly three months straight, the smells behind the restaurant did nothing to make me long for dinner. Grace jumped out of the car before the engine died, and Renny was right behind her. I got out on my side a little more sedately. It pained me to admit it, but after three nights of little sleep and no sex, I really was as tired as Bracken had thought. It did not excuse my two scheming dumbass lovers, but it was true.

Grace stood stewing by the car, and Renny went pounding up to a pained-looking Max and his very surprised blonde companion—who had, like Max, a pair of nearly crossed blue eyes. They didn't look so charming on her, but they were definitely similar.

Renny stood on her hind legs, planted her forelegs on the woman's stiff shoulders, and growled, her whiskers coming up and her mouth opening slightly to reveal that enormous pink tongue as she smelled her prospective victim. I assumed she was searching for the smell of sex with Max, which Renny would know well by now. What she smelled instead, I was sure, was the feminine version of her lover, which explained her puzzled snarl and her immediate retreat to prowl ruminatively around Max's black-and-silver Mustang.

"Your sister, I presume," I said blandly, and Max nodded with a sigh.

"I saw Chloe when she stopped for gas. I knew something like this was going to happen." He muttered something that sounded like "vindictive bitch" under his breath and then covered his eyes. "Sorry, Grace," he apologized, and he sounded sincere.

"Don't be sorry." Grace shook her head and sighed, the anger seeming to seep out of her at hearing the thought voiced by someone else. "It's true." She slumped against the hearse.

I turned with a sheepish smile toward Max's sister, who was still staring wide-eyed at the giant cat that had, as far as she knew, just threatened to eat her throat out while her brother stood by and watched. It was a nice night, I thought inanely. Chilly, as it should be in late February, but with a promise—a smell of magnolias and honeysuckle and early roses on the air. A certainty of spring.

"Hi," I said greenly into that mix of old Denny's and new Mother Nature. "I'm Cory. It's nice to meet Max's family."

"What in the hell is that animal doing out without a leash?" she sputtered, finally sure Renny wasn't going to shed any of her blood.

"We usually keep her on one," I said, straight-faced, "but tonight he's hanging out with you."

Max coughed to smother a laugh and said, "Michelle, meet Cory. Cory, Michelle. Cory's a member of my girlfriend's family." He said it smoothly, without even a hitch, and I raised my eyebrows at his careful duplicity. He was as good at this as I was. "In fact, she's one of the heads of the family."

"Max overstates things." I was running out of things to say, because Michelle was looking at me like I was sprouting mold spores.

"You're responsible for this?" she asked incredulously. Max held up his hands, absolving himself of any responsibility for her actions. "My brother was a nice boy. You and your freak show have totally turned him into some sort of hippie-loving heathen, and I want to know what you're going to do about it!"

"I'm at a loss…," I said, looking to Max. For his part, he held out one hand and gestured to his sister, as though he knew the only cure for her was to let her rant herself out.

"He doesn't believe in God anymore, do you know that?" she asked, stomping her foot. She was wearing a denim skirt and a plain brown shirt, too large, with three buttons at the collar. She might have had big boobs, like Chloe had said—but if she did, they were covered by the demure/butt-ugly clothes.

"I know for a fact that's not true," I answered calmly. I did know—Bracken had told me about their conversation.

"He talks about this 'Goddess' of yours like she's a real thing. He told Daddy that he couldn't go to our church anymore because he said that any church that taught 'intolerance as dogma' was not somewhere he wanted to be. Daddy's been preaching at that church for all of Max's life!" Michelle was obviously distraught, and I could read from Max's expression that this was a part of his life he hadn't wanted us to know. Suddenly Renny was there, rubbing against Max's legs in sympathy. He looked at her sadly, then dropped his hand to rub her tenderly between the ears.

"I take it your church is against gay rights?" I said quietly to Max, and he nodded, quirking his mouth up in a depressing parody of Green's usual expression.

"Against gun control, gay rights, abortion, sex education, science fiction, and money for the arts... et cetera, et cetera...."

"Et cetera," I finished. I turned to Michelle sympathetically but determined that she not hurt my friend anymore. "Sweetheart, your brother is a good man. He is compassionate, and brave, and honorable in ways that you will never know. We know this about him—we treasure this about him. Can't you accept this...." Oh shit. A sudden feeling of dread washed over me, almost sending me to my knees. "Accept this about him the way we...." Oh, Jesus. It flooded me, and I struggled to stay upright.

"Cory...." Max was by my side, and Renny was suddenly a naked girl in the chill evening, holding my elbow. I could see them as clear as the purple sky above me—Bracken squinting at the road, Nicky clutching his ears—and I could feel their panic. Oh, shit. I knew that road, those twists. There was a cell-phone blackout there, and they were under attack, and they were scared and they were....

Longing. Longing to go back to the living room where they could see me one last time. Fuck it all if that was the last time they would see me.

"*Bracken!*" I didn't know if I screamed it out loud, but Green was suddenly in my head. Max and Renny were talking to me, so I choked out, "Brack and Nicky... attacked." And then my skin turned cold and I went back to the place in my head where I could see them, feel their panic, let them know I was there.

"*Vampires,*" Green said in my head, his panic as breathless as mine. "*Call them.*"

Of course. The vampires were near them. They were just a couple of hills and a lake away. I screamed to Marcus and Grace and could barely hear Max's sister saying, "Oh my God!" as Grace launched herself into the air and disappeared into the night. Then I was in the thick of it—in Marcus's head, in Grace's head—seeing a giant slice of sky between my feet and the ground and a brutal, chill, and humid wind whipping my hair around my face, and I heard, for the first time, the brain-chatter of my brethren as they called to each other through the night.

It was too loud, the wind and the blur of the wide and treed green under me, the starlight and the brain-chatter, and I almost shrieked and yanked myself out of their minds—but Bracken swore and something smacked the SUV sideways, and I could feel the wheel jerking skin from his palms as he wrestled the damn thing on the road. I had just enough of myself left to start reciting vectors as I pulled together for him and started ordering vampires.

"Tell Bracken to stay on the road until the levy." I didn't know how to separate Green from the vampires in my head, but he knew who I was talking to because Green said, *"Done,"* and Bracken's emotions grew a little less frantic, a little more sure.

And then I made a picture in Grace's and Marcus's heads, as clear and simple as I could, and waited for their replies. I could taste Marcus's coffee in my throat when he spoke, and Grace's diet soda, and it was the first time I'd been able to do either thing with just their thoughts in my head, but I didn't care. I felt a terrible, breathless pause, and suddenly I was back in my own body, breathing like I'd been underwater for a minute. I could feel my real heart beating in my real throat and the bruises of Max's fingers as they dug into my arm, and I could hear the bizarre monologue of stupid questions from his dumbass sister, but I knew that a minute ago I hadn't been there in my own body. Even now I was more aware of Green inside my head holding my mental hand than I was of my own flesh. The wind blowing through Grace and Marcus as they called the other whipping black shapes through the sky; then the lake beneath Marcus's feet, and the levy with the iron bridge only a stone's throw before him; then, after a pause, the phalanx of vampires building as they flocked to Grace and Marcus—all, all were more real to me than the laboring of my own heart and the bursting of frozen lungs.

The vampires formed two circles, one inside the other—the vampires I'd blooded on the outside, led by Marcus and Phillip, facing out; the ones I didn't know as intimately on the inside, led by Grace, facing inward. They hovered there, flying people dressed in jeans and slacks and gauzy dresses, as varied as people in a government courthouse, against the black reflection of the stars drowned in the water and the silver of the rising moon on the sweep of horse country. Their urgency had brought out their hunting faces—the pointed teeth, the elongated jaws, the stretched tendons in their necks and the pulsing at their temples—and in their human clothes, they looked alien and feral and frightening.

For a moment they were still, seeming to listen, but when their nostrils flared and the howl of revulsion passed among them, I knew they'd been waiting for the stench of emptiness, of foul selfishness, that took the Hollow Man beyond death and beyond even a vampire's redemption.

A hundred heartbeats after the stench descended, we could hear the whine of the SUV's engine. It sounded off, as though it was overheating or running badly. Fifty more heartbeats and it burst from the cover of the foliage, the horrid dark blur of the Hollow Man battering at the side of the car as it came. The front windshield was spiderwebbed with cracks, the grill dented inward, the hood crumpled—and even through the shattered glass, Marcus could see that both airbags were deployed. They were smeared with red.

"*Easy, beloved,*" Green prayed inside my head. "*Nicky's moving, and Bracken's still on the road.*"

Not for long. Not if he listened to Green. Not if he trusted us. I knew he trusted us. Please Goddess, please God, please Goddess, please God don't let us let him down.

The engine whined faster, and the only sane part of me started whispering vectors again. *Seventy miles per hour equals how many feet per second on the x-axis times the cosine of gravity on the y-axis and how many feet did he have before the car hit the goddamned lake and let the vampires be close enough please let them be close enough open ranks open ranks open ranks,* "Open your Goddamned ranks!"

And the SUV launched itself off the levy, whining in acceleration, missing the slope of wicked rocks and heading straight toward the vampires. And the vampires opened ranks to receive it—and then closed the ring again as soon as the vehicle stopped moving horizontally and started its fearful trajectory downward.

I waged a silent battle with myself while Marcus, Grace, and Green shouted *"Now! Do it now!"* And even to save Nicky and Bracken, I was afraid, but the car was plunging toward the water, and drowning was one thing that could kill them both and Green promised me it would work and….

Power flooded through the vampires in the outer ring—from their hands, their eyes, their mouths—a glow of sunshine power that should have killed them, but because we'd shared blood, shared power, and because Green was inside me sheathing my power with his, it didn't. It formed a giant bubble like the one I'd used to protect Davy and me, but this one was a boil of light surrounding the outer ring of vampires and keeping everybody inside safe.

The car crashed into the floor of the bubble of power with a scream of tortured metal and pulverized glass. Through Grace I could hear the thump of Bracken's big body as the momentum snapped his seatbelt and threw him through the windshield to lie bleeding on the layer of light suspended over the water. My body bucked, dying for oxygen, as I fought to sustain the shield's strength, then calmed as the shudders from the collision subsided. Nicky morphed as soon as the windshield disintegrated—all but the most serious of the wounds inflicted during the terrible journey would heal with his change. He flew frantically around the car's crippled space until one of the vampires let go of the power so he could rip the door off and let Nicky free.

The stench disappeared as soon as the shield went up, and there was an agonized shriek that rent the air and made Nicky positively insane with the pain of the sound. I realized that there were power bursts flashing from the vampires, from their mouths, their hands, and their eyes, as they targeted the Hollow Man. He flew ineffectually around the glowing ball that was the whole stinking lot of us working together protecting our own. His shriek intensified, and again, and Phillip caught him in his boiling glare and pinned him against the sky. Through Phillip's eyes I could see his body start to smoke, start to shake—but then Grace called my name, and the shield remained but the power to kill disappeared as I called my attention to Bracken. He was spurting crimson lifeblood through holes and gashes made by metal and glass, many too deep for a redcap to heal, even one who was a full-blown sidhe.

I screamed Green's name in my head. He'd been inside me the whole time, giving me power and focus and allowing the vampires to conduct but not to destruct. And he was a healer, a sweet, sweet god of healing, and he was inside of me and I was inside of Grace as she laid her hands on Bracken's face. Bracken's mouth bubbled blood, his chest heaved, and he was bleeding through rips of tattered flesh on his arms, across his stomach, and his beautiful face. He was also losing air through a hole in his chest that showed the bloody pink of struggling lung—and I screamed mentally, physically, every way.

I was tired, I was taxed to everything I had—but this was Bracken and I needed Bracken to live, and Green needed me to live, and Grace screamed my words through a throat that shredded with the force,

"Please, oh Bracken please…" and we flooded her with healing power. His flesh began to reknit itself, the hole in his chest covering with blood, with bones, with muscle, with skin. The blood stopped bubbling from his lips, falling from his skin, from his limbs, from a cut in his face that sliced through his eye and his cheek showing shiny bone. Cut by cut by gash by rip in a queasy slide of body, bone, and spirit, we made my Bracken whole.

He sat up, still on the floor of my bubble, and I heard Marcus groan inside my head, a sound echoed by the other vampires. They were agonized, in pain, because Green had pulled the focus of his power from protecting the vampires to healing my beloved, and they could stand so much of me, only so much, and I was hurting them. I was exhausted, the blood pounding in my head, but I wasn't in my head to feel it, and Bracken's pain was mine—on my cheek, on my chest, on my flesh—and I couldn't, couldn't think, couldn't mesh with Green, couldn't sustain us, and the Hollow Man had fled, broken and hurt, and we were safe for the moment, oh Goddess we were safe, and….

My power cut off like a shorted fuse, and abruptly I was myself, inhaling and screaming on the exhale again and again until my throat was raw, my body sore, battered, exhausted from channeling the power and from the healing that had passed through. I was a weapon, not a healer, and I had felt Bracken's wounds even as they'd healed. Eventually not even my weak screams could continue. Max and Renny held me up, although my body had gone limp and dead as I'd left myself and become Marcus and Phillip and Grace and most of the kiss of vampires. Now I took my own weight for a moment, but just as they let go of me, I puddled to the ground like poured pudding, coughing weakly from aching lungs.

"He's okay," I whimpered. "Oh, Goddess, they're okay."

Max and Renny pulled me up, alarmed when my legs couldn't hold me, and Max swung me up into his arms. Two months ago he had wanted me, and when he'd laid his body next to my fevered one to feed me life force, he'd helped to make me strong. Tonight, I felt nothing—no flicker, no buzz, no hum of life coming from him. He was merely big, and warm, and human.

"Max will make it better," Renny said, a thread of panic in her voice. "Let Max hold you—he'll make it better."

"But she's not… feeding…," Max said, puzzled.

"I need to get back to the hill," I said, as strongly as I knew how.

"Why isn't Max making it better?" Renny sounded plaintive and scared, and I had to laugh.

"Renny, you dork, why do you *think* he can't feed me anymore?" I laughed weakly. "Jeez... no wonder you two are making us crazy."

And suddenly, loud and intrusive, Max's sister got her say. "Good grief, will someone please put some clothes on her!"

Max and Renny locked eyes over my body for a painful, intimate moment. And for just a moment, Renny—who had a house cat's way of saying "fuck you" and "talk to the fuzzy butt" with a flip of her wild, flyaway hair, and who looked as comfortable without clothes as I felt in sweats—was suddenly as naked as I'd ever seen another human being in my life.

"I've got an extra T-shirt and some sweats in the trunk," Max said thickly.

"I remember," she whispered and reached around my back to take the keys shyly from his pocket.

While Renny dressed herself, Max situated me in the passenger seat of the car so that Renny eventually had to crawl into the back from the driver's seat. Michelle sat herself behind Max, and now that we were in close quarters, her nonstop bitching was starting to permeate the haze of fear and exhaustion that I'd been swimming in since I came to.

"What do you mean she flew away? People don't fly. What happened to that woman, Max—and how did she know you? Where is that big cat? Where did that naked girl come from? Max, how can you just put a naked girl in your car? Daddy will be so disappointed to know that you keep company with whores and drug addicts. Aren't you a policeman, shouldn't you know better? Who are these girls—how can you just put them in your car—what about the car they came in?"

"Grace will get the car when she gets back," I said, partly in an effort to make her shut up.

"And what was that *light* coming out of you?" she asked, leaning forward as Max started the motor so she was so close to my face as I leaned sideways that I practically jumped backward before my muscles gave a whimper and I decided against it. "Are you a Satanist? How could you conjure that weird light—what was that screaming? It sounded like someone was dying and setting you on fire as you went? Max, how could you associate with people who practice witchcraft? What in the hell happened back there?"

Max turned to me with long-suffering eyes. "Cory, you couldn't… you know… put the whammy on her or something, could you?"

"Max, that'll be my first order of business as soon as I can stand up on my own." I was totally sincere.

Renny leaned forward, blocking Max's sister out completely, and asked me quietly what happened.

"He almost got them." I coughed, the pain of the possibility making me weaker. "Hollow Man was slamming into the car, and the SUV didn't have much left, and Bracken was already bleeding. We had him jump the rail at the Far West levy, and the vampires channeled me and put a shield around it… and Bracken…." My voice broke. "He was all torn, and bleeding… so much blood…." I was shaking all over, and I saw the parts of his body exposed that shouldn't have been, and the picture behind my eyes was obscene, like a dog slaughtered on the road, because neither the God nor the Goddess had ever intended her creatures to have their viscera see the light of the moon. I was suddenly as nauseous as I'd ever been and not sure I had the strength to even throw up. Bracken wasn't here, I thought wretchedly. I couldn't be sick if Bracken wasn't here to pick me up afterward.

Renny took my hands, rubbing on them with her shape-shifter heat and blowing on them to warm them up. "They're okay, right? C'mon, Cory, tell it all, you need to see them whole. I heard you say it when you came to, you need to say it now."

"Nicky turned bird as soon as the car was still," I said, and I felt stronger just knowing. Nicky was okay.

"Good," she said, "good. Now tell me about Bracken."

"Green…. Green was in my head, and I was in Grace's head, and she laid hands on Bracken and… he healed." Strength. Bracken was alive, and Green was alive, and Nicky was alive, and I was strong.

I felt Renny's tears on my hands, and she laid her cheek against them, catlike, stroking me with her cheek. "You see," she whispered, "they're okay. They're not going to leave us. We'll be okay."

I nodded, and her words calmed me. "We'll be okay," I agreed, my nausea fading. "They're okay. They won't leave us."

There was silence then, a sweet, blessed silence, when even Max's sister recognized that something larger than her own small world had happened. I closed my eyes and drifted for a moment, so lost in exhaustion and aftermath that I almost didn't hear Renny say softly, "I didn't know what you were up against, Max." She freed her hands from mine and reached diagonally to stroke his cheek. He didn't take his eyes from the road, but he bit his lip and captured her hand and gave it a squeeze. "You take whatever time you need. I'll wait."

"I didn't know what kind of fear you were living with, beloved," he replied, just loud enough for Renny to hear. "I've seen it up close and personal, and I still didn't know until I watched Cory just... die and explode... out of sheer fucking panic. Life's too short and there's too much bad shit that can happen to put it off just because I'm afraid."

"It's a big decision." The hope in Renny's voice was painful to hear.

"It's the right one," he said, and they were quiet then, the silence in the car heavy with the things they wanted to say privately to one another, and I wanted to be home so I could be alone with my fear and my joy and so they could be alone with each other.

When we got home, Max was actually going to heave me up the stairs from the garage, but Arturo, bless his heart, met us and saved Max the trouble.

"You're not that heavy," Max told me as he shuffled me into Arturo's arms.

"Bullshit," I mumbled. "I outweigh Renny by twenty pounds."

Michelle snorted behind him. "Drug addiction will do that to you."

Arturo turned outraged eyes to her. "Max?" he asked, the veiled threat almost visible in the dark of the garage.

"Oh please, would you?" Max begged, and Arturo obliged by bending forward and catching Michelle's slightly crossed eyes with his own impossible gaze of copper lightning until he had her complete attention.

"You are among decent people, woman. You will only say decent things." He turned away from her in disgust, and the look he shot Max was weighted with sympathy. Michelle's mouth fell open slightly and her head bobbed once, and a blessed peace fell.

Arturo's touch didn't feed me either—he was too in love with Grace for that—but he was still Uncle Arturo to me, and he made me feel safe like Max didn't, so I snuggled into his embrace for a moment, just a moment, of comfort.

"They're okay, Arturo," I said.

"I know, little Goddess," he murmured back. "And the vampires are okay too. They're carpooling home, the lot of them."

"Carpool…?"

"Too tired to fly." He laughed quietly, but I couldn't join him.

"I was so scared," I whispered. "I didn't want to hurt them. If Green hadn't been there, in my head, keeping them safe…."

"He was, Corinne Carol-Anne." My eyes were closed, so I didn't see the corridors of home blurring past, but I felt his avuncular kiss on the top of my head. "He was there, and you did what you had to… and now our hill feels safer, just because you're home."

"I'm tired," I confessed, feeling weak, and then I felt guilty for saying it because Arturo was suddenly glaring into my face, all concern. "It's no big deal," I protested, "I just need a nap…."

"You just need one of the men," he snapped. "You must be more than tired to even admit it." He grunted, thinking, and then wheeled out of the sitting room, doing a complete 180 and pounding up the granite stairs to the trapdoor of the Goddess grove, calling behind him for Renny to bring me a blanket.

We came up the trapdoor and into the garden, which was palely glowing in the moonlight. "Will he come, you think?" he asked, sadness in his voice. Adrian had been like a wayward son to Arturo.

"He always comes when I need him." I was certain—I didn't know how I could be, when he didn't come every night, but he was, always was, there in the grove when I needed him.

"Good." Renny came up with the quilt Grace had made me and one of those fuzzy fleece blankets that are always soft, and suddenly I was swathed in covers and stashed on the stone bench memorial, the one with Adrian's face engraved on the side, grateful for the seat cushions I'd conjured after that rough and urgent night with Green.

"I need to leave you alone, Corinne Carol-Anne," Arturo sighed when I was situated. "We have sidhe who need reassurances, and four mortals in the hill…."

"And Green's gone and I'm out of commission. Yeah, go. Thank you for everything." I snuggled deep into the covers, feeling my eyes close, feeling Adrian's presence and breathing the fragrance of the roses, ripe and plentiful in all of the recent rainfall. I barely felt Arturo's kiss on my cheek and Renny's halting good-bye. I dozed, listening to the sounds of birds and wind and early spring crickets, until I felt a chill on my forehead and a breeze where there was none. I opened my eyes and he was there, translucent in the night, spangled blue eyes perpetually sad and, tonight, concerned for me.

"You're weak!" His voice was almost solid with anxiety. "Why are you weak and nobody's here to make you strong?"

I told him haltingly, letting him hear my panic over Bracken, over Nicky, my fear of hurting my people, the awe and terror of holding the power of a nova sun. When I finished, I was crying softly, trying not to hiccup, and longing, longing with all my heart for him to be real. He had never been warm, but he had been solid, real, flesh around my body, strength to feed me, love. *Oh, Goddess, Adrian... why? We all miss you so much, hurt for you so much, why is it that all we have left is the memory of a dream in the garden?*

"Shhh...," he whispered as my tears got out of control. "Hush." His hands made a chill breeze as he brushed my face with them, and I leaned into that because I had nothing else.

When I was calm again, I found I had drifted off, and I came to in a panic, afraid he had left. "Still here, luv," he confirmed, a little laugh in his transparent voice, "but I was wondering... how weak are you?"

"Not ready to join you yet, beloved," I reassured, because there had been a time not so long ago when I had been a stalled breath away from being his companion here in the garden.

"Good to hear." He grimaced, and I felt frustration rolling off of him in breezy waves. "Luv, Bracken's going to have to come up here to get you, right?"

I hadn't thought of that, but, "Yeah—I guess." And I wanted him here, oh Goddess I wanted him here.

"Is it all right if I... if I spend a bit of time getting Fuckhead to talk to me, you think?"

A ghost shouldn't have that much yearning. "Of course, beloved," I told him, dammit, drifting off again. "You make him talk to you—of course."

And then my eyes drifted closed again, and Adrian was a presence, a fragrance, a longing in my dreams.

BRACKEN
Unforeseen Ends

"YOU DRIVE like my grandmother, has anyone told you that?" I complained from the back of Phillip's Lexus. Marcus was driving, because of all the vampires, Grace and Phillip had suffered the most from wielding Cory's power.

"No, and since your grandmother was a tree in Wales who got chopped down around 1800, I know for a fact it's not true." Marcus smiled as he said it, in that perpetually goodwilled way that Cory had told me was the hallmark of the good high school teacher.

"Well, has anyone told you that you drive like *your* grandmother?" I snapped, a little relieved that the Goddess overlooked figures of speech, because right now the cramping and nausea that came with a lie were the last things I wanted.

"Yes, Bracken. You. You've told me that I drive like my grandmother. Right now." And even Marcus's perennial patience was waning. I didn't blame him, not really.

Cory's power had snapped off like a blown fuse, and the SUV and I had both plunged unceremoniously into the lake. It wasn't spring yet, after a long snow season, and the water was not warm. I could have swum to shore, but that hadn't stopped Marcus from going in after me. While vampires weren't susceptible to cold and heat, they still registered discomfort, and driving home in wet clothes was probably making him chafe like mad. Add to that the pain and the high they were all feeling from wielding Cory's power, and Marcus was probably the sweetest tempered of the lot of them.

"Seriously—can we go just a little faster?" I begged, not caring that I was pissing him off.

"So help me, Bracken, I will pull this car over and make you walk ho——"

"She's weak!" I yelled, feeling helpless and hating it. "She's weak, and we're not there."

Marcus laughed a little. "Well, I hope to heaven she's weak. No one should be able to wield that much power and not feel a little bit woozy, you think?"

"Look, brother, I'm sorry it hurt you....," I started reasonably.

"Don't be," Marcus returned, surprising me. "If it hadn't been you and Nicky, she never would have tried it." He sounded dreamy, and the high of the power was suddenly thick in the car, like sweet smoke.

"It was good?" Nicky asked, curious.

"It was fabulous," Phillip said from a raw throat. He'd been pretty much walleyed since we'd put him in the car, and it startled me to hear him speak. "It was like... like holding a solar flare when you haven't seen the sun in twenty years...."

"Well, I'm sorry you didn't get a chance to finish him off," I finished, subsiding. They were doing their best. It became my mantra for the rest of the trip.

"That's okay, brother," Phillip whispered, and I could see in the dark of the car that he was smiling like a shark dreaming of red water. "She'll wield that through us again. I know she will. Oh... Goddess... I know it will happen." He shivered, and now the car smelled like incense and sex, and I could only pray a cop didn't pull us over because he'd get the totally wrong impression.

"She's okay, isn't she?" Nicky asked beside me, and he sounded young and uncertain so I found myself nodding.

"Yeah. Yeah, Nicky, she's okay—it's just... we weren't there. She woke up and we weren't there, we just left her at the hill...."

"She wasn't at the hill," Marcus corrected, and then he did one of those blank-faced things that I'd learned long since was a blooded vampire talking to his kiss mate. "Grace says they were at the parking lot at Denny's, sorting out Renny's love life...." Grace was in another car. As soon as Cory's power had faded, every vampire and Avian with keys in their pockets had flown off for the aerie, where everyone was parked. They'd been back in minutes to pick us up, but we hadn't loaded into the cars with any sort of order.

"Why would she leave the hill?" Nicky burst out. "The whole reason we left her there was so she'd be safe and strong—what in the seven hells was she thinking?"

Marcus laughed a little and shook his head in the rearview mirror. "I bet she was thinking just like the two of you—that her presence was needed to make things right. In any case, she just saved your asses, so I wouldn't get on her back about it right now, you think?"

"She's weak," Nicky repeated, looking at me with distress. "We can both feel it. She needs us."

"We'll be there," I said and pulled Nicky into my arms, where we shivered together for the rest of the interminable journey.

Nicky and I practically ran out of the Lexus while it was still moving and pounded up the outside steps into the living room, where a room full of tense elves looked at us in relief. My mother was suddenly hovering around me, her feet three feet off the ground, her invisible wings buzzing fast enough in anxiety to let her hover. She fluttered around me, brushing my face and back and chest with a thousand maternal touches. I finally managed to grab her hands, calm her down, and give her to my father, who gathered her into his rock-quarry embrace and whispered reassurances to her. "I'm fine," I told them quietly. "I really am fine." I looked around the gathered crowd and didn't see the one face I wanted desperately to see.

"She's in the grove," Arturo said in response to my unasked question, and I had just enough energy to blur up the adamantine granite stairs, so I was moving with some serious velocity when I hit the trapdoor—only to have it freeze on me, sending me hurtling back down the stairs almost into a bewildered Nicky, who had the presence of mind to change form as I blew by him. As Nicky shrieked in alarm, I landed, winded, on my back in the hall, staring up the stairs and wondering what in the blue fuck had just happened.

"Uhm," I said, staring up at the ceiling. With some deliberation, I picked myself up and walked back up the stairs. I grabbed the granite handle, put my shoulder against the door that was never locked, and pushed—then harder—then frantically as I realized it wasn't going to give.

"Cory?" I called. "Cory, are you all right?"

"She's fine, fuckhead!" said a voice on the other side of the door. I froze.

In a surprised ruffle of feathers, Nicky was standing right next to me. "Was that who I think it was?" he asked. I had to open and close my mouth a couple of times to dredge up an answer.

"No one," I said, my mouth dry and my gut clenching. "It was nobody." *Oh, Goddess… not now. Do we really have to do this now?*

"No one? Fuck you, mate. I was your brother, your lover, your *friend* for your whole goddamned life, and now I'm no one?" If I didn't know that it couldn't exist, I would have said the owner of that voice was hurt—and enjoying getting a little back. I swallowed against the anger and betrayal that thought brought on and tried appealing to reason.

"Cory—Cory, could you let me in?" I begged and was relieved to hear her strained and muffled voice from somewhere above me.

"I'd love to, Bracken," she said weakly, "but it's not my call."

I hit the door with my shoulder again, and pain shivered down to my neck and elbow because, dammit, the door was made of sturdy oak with a granite overlay. "Fuck it all, open the door!"

"I'm not holding it closed, Brack…." She sounded distressed, and I hit the door again, feeling my flesh give and my shoulder creak.

"Then who is!" Damn, that last charge would have shattered me if I were human, and I felt a sense of urgency grip me. She was up there and she was *weak*, and he… it… something wasn't letting me in.

"I am!"

"You don't exist!" I shouted childishly, but I couldn't help it, and I charged the door again.

"Bracken, you're hurting yourself!" She was crying.

I started frantically pounding the door even as the other voice said, "He's hurting us all! Damned stubborn rock pile of a brain—I don't exist, do I?"

"You didn't love us enough to stay!" I shouted and lost all track of the pain in my shoulder and the pain in my chest, and I charged the door until my bones shattered and reknit and blood started pouring down from the round of my shoulder where my flesh split. But still I hit that damned door again and again and again, calling to Cory and to the Goddess and to everyone but the owner of that voice—that Goddess-blighted, smug and sorrowful voice on the other side of the door—until the skin of my arm and shoulder ran warm with blood for the second time that night, and my neck and collarbone snapped in protest, and I was forced to my knees in pain and despair for a moment to let it heal. She needed me. She needed me and I wasn't there, and he wasn't either, not really, not the way she needed us, and how dare he keep me from her when he couldn't be there the way I could? How dare he be there when he'd left us, left me, and I'd had to live with that hole in my heart for months and pretend it didn't exist so I could love her with a heart that felt whole? "Please…,"

I begged again, feeling my pride seep out of me with my sweat. "Please don't lock me out."

"You started it, jackass!" And that pricked my temper and melted my resistance because fuck it all, it wasn't true.

"The hell I did!" I shouted, pounding the door futilely with my fist until it too ran dark and crimson, not caring that half the hill, Chloe and Max and my parents included, were gathered at the foot of the staircase listening to me talking to someone who shouldn't exist. "You *died*, asshole—do you remember that? You left *me*! My whole damn life I was terrified of leaving you behind, and then you go and leave me? How dare you! How dare you come back here and listen to her and comfort her when the one thing that kept me whole this last year is that at least we didn't make her choose...." I was sobbing. The kind of sobs that men, even sidhe, don't like to admit they have, when their chests heave and their tears flow and their noses run. "You left me, Adrian." My momentum faded, and abruptly I was the little boy in the garden begging to fly, except this time Adrian simply kissed my cheek and disappeared into the dark without me.

"How could you leave me?" I finished, wiping my face with my bloody hand. There was a terrible pause, and then the trapdoor creaked open. After a heavy moment, I heaved myself to my feet and went through the door.

He was waiting for me, shaking his translucent head, with bloody see-through tears coursing down his pale cheeks. "You really messed yourself up, mate," he said kindly, gesturing to my bloody shoulder.

"I repeat," I said, trying for dignity, "you started it."

Adrian was about to reply when Cory made a sound and struggled over to me on unsteady legs. She reached out to touch my shoulder just as her knees buckled, and I had to catch her before she went down.

"You're hurt!" she said, breaking, her hands fluttering around my shoulder. I was still buzzing with Green's power, and the cuts and cracked flesh were starting to heal already, as they had been during my frenzied pounding at the door, but she turned a face streaming with tears to me.

"You're weak!" I returned, trying to distract her, but she bit her lip and shook her head and put her hands on my chest, pressing what was left of my wet sweatshirt against my still tender skin and feeling, I realized, for the giant wound that had healed under Grace's hands a little more than an hour before. She held her palms up to me, sticky with watered blood that I was no longer shedding, and a sob caught at her throat.

"You were hurt," she repeated in a whisper, then leaned her cheek against my chest, smearing my blood across her cheek, her chin, and her hair. She shivered there in my arms, and I met Adrian's sympathetic gaze. He was growing less substantial even as I looked at him. I wondered at that, and at what strength of will he must have to stay here for us, to feel our need for his company and to manifest here, where he could feel us love him. How many nights had he come here, knowing I missed him, only to have me deny his existence?

"I left you," he said quietly after a long moment of me reading his misery in his transparent eyes, "because you could survive it. You're strong, Bracken. I was only ever as strong as the people I loved. You're stronger for them—it makes a difference."

"I miss you," I said nakedly, having nothing else. "I miss playing chess and beating the hell out of each other. I miss a thousand things we did that had nothing to do with making love and everything to do with being with my brother." I stopped and thought, what the hell—I was already baring my soul. "I miss knowing if we could have shared her, loved her together. I think it would have worked." I shifted her in my arms as she whimpered a little, and felt her hand come up to touch my cheek.

"Of course it would have worked, mate," Adrian said gently, dropping an almost invisible kiss on the top of her head, so close to me I could feel the chill of where his flesh should be. "We're bound together, the lot of us. You don't abandon the people you love because they love the people you love."

Cory snarked, her breath feathering against my throat. I laughed against my will, and even Adrian smiled. "I thought ghosts were supposed to be wise," I said.

"I'm very wise." He flashed an extended fang with the insouciance I remembered, then passed a disintegrating hand in front of his face with a pained expression. "I'm just not that coherent." He moved his transparent gaze to meet mine, and the light moment was gone. "I died twice, and my love is still enough to keep me here, Bracken Brine. You may be pissed at me, but please, my brother, honor that."

I closed my eyes and swallowed, and managed to dredge up an unlikely smile of brotherhood. "I've always honored you, Adrian. You never knew how much."

I don't know what he would have said next, because at that exact moment, a dying sprite appeared right over us, to drop exhausted into Cory's lap even as I held her. She caught the tiny body, like the child of a hummingbird and star shine, as it fell, and her shocked grief was heard in her indrawn breath. She leaned forward, cupping the sprite as it told her something in a tiny voice like the buzzing of wings—and then, even as its light dimmed, she let out an anguished cry.

"No. No no no no no no no.... Oh, Bracken...," she wailed, burrowing into me for a comfort she could never find even as she cupped the still, dark body carefully in her hand. "It's one of Davy's sprites. He got her, Bracken. Davy's dead."

And I looked to Adrian—my brother, my lover, my friend—for help dealing with this one crisis that I didn't know if I could share, and Adrian gave me a look of profound sorrow even as he disappeared.

I held her. I held her until I felt her shivering with the cold, with reaction, with shock, and then I took her downstairs, where we were surrounded by our people, who didn't know what had happened. I caught Arturo's eye, and he cleared the bottom of the stairs, pausing only when Cory looked up from my chest and said, "Nicky?"

Nicky stopped and came toward her, and she held her hands out to his face, his shoulders, his chest, all sheathed in tattered clothing with a few healing wounds. She gave him the same fluttering motions she'd given me. "You're okay?" she asked, holding his face in her hands. He closed his eyes and wobbled a little, and I knew he was feeling the same pull I was, holding her in my arms. She was pulling strength from us in giant gulps of skin-on-skin.

"I'm fine," he assured her, taking her hands in his and kissing them with enough tenderness to make me swallow. "You?"

"Davy's dead," she whispered. My mother drew near, and I nodded at her to take the tiny body from Cory's hand. "I failed her. But you're okay... you're okay. You and Bracken are okay...." She trailed off and leaned her head against my chest again, pulling her hands in toward her chest while Nicky and I exchanged a helpless glance.

"Goddess...," he muttered. "Take her to bed, Bracken. Feed her. Green will be here soon."

It was a good plan and I followed it—undressing her, kissing her human skin with its red-brown freckles, watching her close her eyes as though each kiss were too exquisite to bear. We showered, washing the blood off my body, the blood I'd smeared on her hair just to hold her, and when we were dry, I kissed her, trying to still the sobbing breaths she hadn't stopped taking. Her touch on my flesh felt like frantic, felt like panic, felt like grief, and even as I moved inside her, the holy dark crashing over the two of us and taking us under then over in an explosion of stars and pleasure-pain, I knew she was checking me, making sure my body was whole, making sure I wouldn't leave her. Her every touch was a blessed silken cord, binding me to her side like Adrian's soul was bound to Green's hill.

When we were done, we lay silently, face-to-face, and her eyes shimmered in the dark. I reached out and touched her wet cheek, singing the lyrics of "Don't Cry" softly.

"Pretty words," she said, capturing my palm against her cheek and planting a kiss in the center. "Go to sleep, beloved."

"You're not okay yet," I yawned through half-closed eyes.

"You can't fix that tonight, Bracken Brine," she said. "Sleep." And it was almost like she'd put power in her voice, because that was the last thing I remembered.

CORY
Finishing Techniques

LONG AFTER Bracken fell asleep, I lay watching his face in the dark. Sometimes I saw him whole and unblemished as he was here under my hands, each puff of breath a burst of invisible white in the purple space of our room; sometimes he was mangled and dying under my hands, on the floor of the shield I'd tortured our people to create. The T-shirt and jean jacket he'd taken off to make love to me had been shredded and were still damp and bloody. I prayed somebody or something would clear them before we woke in the morning.

Sometimes I didn't see him at all. Instead I saw Davy, alone and distraught, sitting on a football bench in the gray, so confused she couldn't even move to get out of the rain.

Apparently Green defied radar to fly home in the Cadillac, because after about an hour he slid in behind me. I didn't even hesitate to turn toward him. We came together in the shadows, and I welcomed him inside of me—praying, praying that he would help ease the confusion, the pain, the panic, and the grief. But when it was over and he held himself above me, shrinking from my body as we trembled in aftermath, he looked into my eyes, his clean, alien profile ghosting in the faint light, and knew that he hadn't.

"I can't heal you when you blame yourself, luv," he whispered. His eyes, so green they were even emerald in the dark, glistened faintly. I was hurting him. I didn't want to hurt him.

"I know… I'm sorry… I'm so sorry…." And the tears were coming again, and I put a mental boot heel on my emotions and ground them back into my gut. "I'm sorry, Green," I said, hoping I sounded mature and in control. "I'll deal with it. I promise I will."

He smoothed my hair back from my face unhappily and sighed. "You don't have to be brave with me," he said, and I nodded.

"She was mine, Green," I said. "She wasn't yours to protect, she was mine, and I don't want to burden you with this."

"Luv…." He would have pressed it. I half wanted him to press it, but at the same time, I knew that if he did, I would yell at him—I would say awful, human, venomous things to him that I didn't mean—and I couldn't do that to Green, not to my Green whom I loved more than life. I couldn't burden him with my anger, with my blame. This wasn't a grief we shared, not like Adrian. This was my failure, my stupidity, and I wouldn't place it in his hands.

"Go to sleep, beloved," I ordered gently. He smelled like sylphs and sex, and I was pretty sure he had taxed himself to the extreme to help me while he was busy working sylph magic and then taking a three-hour drive in one and a half to come to me. "Go to sleep. I'll be better in the morning, I promise."

"If you're not," he said, rolling over to my other side and wrapping his arms securely around me, "I'll call Hallow."

"No you won't," I said with certainty. He wouldn't call Hallow—not when he could help me himself.

Only a little later, Nicky crawled in behind Green, and I pretended to be asleep as he passed his hands over my face and kissed me over Green's shoulder, then settled down to sleep.

I couldn't sleep. My brain was a giant puppy chasing its own tail; it was a worm Ouroboros devouring its problems and regenerating what should have been eaten. It was an endless cycle of all of the ways I had royally fucked up and could not redeem myself.

Green. Bracken. Nicky. Vampires. Davy. Green (I was trying please Green am I doing okay why aren't you home so I know if I'm doing okay Green don't let me let you down…). Bracken (obscene hole in his chest, his power pulling blood that poured through the shield into the water, battering the trapdoor and baring his broken heart for all of us to hear…). Nicky (loving me enough to leave if I wanted him to but I didn't want him to I loved him I loved him but not like I loved Green and Bracken and was that fair but I wanted him here dammit please don't take him away). Vampires (do it, Cory, do it, flood us with sunshine but what if you die? Do it, order us lead us we'll do it please do it kill us if you have to but lead us we need you we need you we need you…). Davy (don't want to…). Davy (don't want to…). Davy (don't want to don't want to think about Davy don't want to remember her desolate, forlorn, bereft, doubting her beloved doubting me doubting herself Davy did you know the sprites were watching would you have mourned them when they died for you Davy did you know your boyfriend was a vampire that I am more than human that the world was full of magic or did you die alone did you die confused did you die in terror did you die in the dark not seeing the sprites I had at least sent to keep you company...).

Green   Bracken   Nicky   Vampires   Davy GreenBrackenNickyVampiresDavy   bracken   nickyvampiresdavy   and around and around and around and aroundandaroundandaround and oh Goddess make it stop make it stop make my mind stop make it stop what did I do what can I do what can anybody do to keep their lovers safe to keep their people safe to keep their friends safe from the bad guys from their ignorance even from themselves....

Ad nauseam. At four in the morning, I sat up in bed and wiggled out from all those lovely, loving male bodies to take a shower. I thought briefly about walking into the kitchen and getting something to eat, but the vampires were out there, and I'd almost killed the vampires trying to defend my lovers, and I didn't want to deal with them right now.

I turned on the little light next to the bed and pulled out my knitting. It was wonderful—so peaceful, so ordered. There was something hypnotic about the stitches, something lovely and peaceful and perfect. It was a light worsted-weight yarn, which meant I was working on a gazillion stitches for Green, my beautiful sidhe lover, and I needed to work on it, needed to hurry up and finish it, give him my token, my sweat and my tears and my soul, and it was lovely, so lovely, to make a stitch and another and know each stitch was perfect and there was no bad answer and no bad decision to making the next stitch.

Eventually the men woke up. They looked at me—I didn't see them, but I could hear their eyes violating my silence—and then they looked at each other, and then they nodded to Green. Bracken went into the shower and Nicky left the room for his, and Green crouched at my feet. "How long have you been up?" he asked hesitantly.

"Not long," I said pleasantly. I looked up from my perfect ordered stitches and smiled a little. My eyes were blurring, his lovely clean face losing its lines and muddling into a pale, shining halo, and I should have taken the opportunity to stretch my neck and my hands—but my knitting was so pleasant and calm, and it called me, and the potential for disaster in Green's sad emerald eyes was endless.

"Have you eaten?" he asked.

I worked my cable needle and shook my head. "MmmmNnn," I murmured the negative, not really hearing him. "I'll get something later." (*Stitch stitch cable three backstitch stitch stitch purl two stitch....*) Green left the room, Bracken came out of the shower, something about going to eat that I didn't hear but said no to anyway, and still my hands moved. My neck ached, my shoulders were cramping, my hands were cramping, but the next stitch called and the next and the next.

I looked up at one point and there was a plate with breakfast on it. Shortly after that, Renny padded in and nibbled at my sausage with delicate carnivore teeth, and I was so grateful for her in this form that I relaxed my hand and petted her, my muscles spasming into her fur. Then I set the knitting on my lap for a minute and petted her some more, allowing her purr to resonate on my legs and through my feet, and it felt wonderful. She licked my face with her sandpaper tongue and curled up around my feet again, and my knitting called.

I looked up to see her eating a plate of pasta, stopping every so often to lick the sauce off her whiskers, and wondered who had brought that in. When I looked up again, she was gone and so was the food. My head pounded, and my eyes felt like they'd been sandpapered, and I turned back toward my knitting—and the next thing I knew, someone was forcibly pulling it out of my hands.

I sprang to my feet and tried to fight back, but my shoulder picked that moment to seize, and then my calves did that charley-horse thing— and in a massive scrunch-twang of agony, my body arched back in one big tight bowstring of a cramp. I let out a whimper through a dry throat and fell awkwardly back to the chair, wondering how long it had been since I'd taken a drink of water or even spoken or swallowed. Then I rounded on whoever had taken my yarn and needles from my hands.

"Dammit, Green, I said in a minute!" I snarled, fighting upright through the cramping, reaching for my work, and the hand that blocked my grab was not gentle as it closed in on mine. A sense of rough peace seeped through my fingers, of sweet, sweet healing, and I realized that I hadn't stretched in too long a time. How long had I sat here, hunched over my knitting, as my muscles screamed in pain unheard?

"You need to eat, Corinne Carol-Anne," he snapped, and my full name falling from his lips whipped me into myself for a moment.

"I'm fine," I said with an attempt at a smile. It hurt. My whole face hurt—my forehead, my cheeks, my neck. I wobbled on my feet because

my muscles were seizing and tried to keep my balance and focus my
eyes. "Really, beloved. I just need to clear my head. I'll be out in a few
minutes."

Green swallowed hard and nodded. His eyes looked odd, and I
realized they were red rimmed, as though he was exhausted or grieving
or worried. His hair was pulled back in a rough queue and looked as
though he'd been dragging fingers through it, and I wondered what else
had happened to make him look so ragged. "Grace wants to know if
you're weaving in your ends or just tying them in knots," he said out of
the blue.

"Tying them into knots…." Then I caught myself. "When did you
talk to Grace?"

"Just now, before I came in," he said slowly, as though that would
mean something.

I scrubbed my face with my hands, trying to orient myself. "What
time is it?" I asked blearily.

"Twelve a.m." I blinked again, hard, trying to clear my vision. He
looked angry—bitterly, furiously angry—and I started to worry.

"Impossible." I tried to laugh this off too. "I wasn't here very lon—
" I broke off, because he had grabbed my shoulder with one hand and
my chin with the other and was forcing me to focus on his face. I blinked
hard, because I could barely do it.

"Twenty hours, Corinne Carol-Anne," he rasped. "Twenty hours
you've sat there in that chair and tried to kill yourself over sticks and
string, and I want to know why."

"I'm fine!" I protested. Jeez, talk about being overprotective! "I
was just…."

"Tying things into knots," he snapped.

"I'm fine," I said again. My body screamed in the pain of enforced
position, and I squinted at him, the light from the little lamp suddenly
too dim. For a brief flashing moment, I wondered if the Goddess was
punishing me for something as I reached creakily for the ceiling,
desperately trying to chill my body out.

"Fuck it all, Cory, if you say that one more goddamned time, I'm
going to ship you off to Hallow's with your knitting as a gag," Green was
saying. His eyes were crackling, literal emerald sparks that looked like
rabid fireflies. "You… you can't even see yourself right now—you're

unhinged. You were catatonic for nearly an entire day, and now you're telling me you're fine?"

I didn't hear the second half of what he was saying. I was still stuck on that first part.

"You can't send me away, Green." Where did that voice wobble come from? "I'll do better, I promise!" He couldn't send me away. "It's just... I'm sorry I'm not strong enough when you're gone." I nodded, trying to get him to agree with me, but he was just looking at me with those red-rimmed eyes and an unbearable sadness, and he was going to do it, he was going to send me away, he was going to leave me again.... "You can't leave me again!" More wobble—even some wailing in that one—and I tried, oh I tried to get my voice, my face, my body under control. "You can't make me go, beloved," I begged. "I know I screwed up... I almost let Bracken die, I'm sorry, I'm so sorry.... Please don't go... please don't make me go. I'm lost without you, Green. I know I said I'd be okay, but I'm so lost, and I feel like a kid left home alone, and I said it would be okay but now I'm scared.... I'll try to do better, beloved, but you can't g... you can't g-g-g-g...." Oh, God, I was going to lose it. I couldn't lose it, Green depended on me. The whole hill depended on me. How could I be an almighty leader one moment and a mewling baby the next? I would control it, I would I would I would....

"You can't gooooooooooo...." I had never tried to hold sobs like this back, and they hurt, they ripped, they destroyed on their way out. Green's arms came around me and he picked me up to him, in that way I bitched about but really treasured, and it was a good thing, too, because I felt too weak to stand once I started crying. Relief, blessed, blessed healing, seeped into my back and my shoulders and my head and my ears, and my body let me know in no uncertain terms that the day had been one long misery that I'd never acknowledged.

Green moved to sit on the bed and leaned back, moving his hand through my hair and whispering tired, quiet reassurances until I could breathe again. We sat there for the longest time when I was done, playing games with restless fingers.

"Oh, Goddess," I said at last. "Can you forgive me?"

"Can you forgive me?" he asked, his hands moving my hair out of my face as he looked seriously at me.

I blinked. "For what?"

"I left you, Cory. You said it again and again and again…. I left you here, and you felt overwhelmed and like you had to lead the hill alone."

He looked so sad. "There's nothing to forgive," I said to our twined hands.

"Don't lie to me," he growled, the anger taking us both by surprise. I looked up again and thought he looked more than sad—he looked exhausted and worried, and I realized *I* had done that. I had made his eyes red-rimmed with tears and tiredness and frustration.

"I'm sorry," I said miserably, reaching up to touch his face. "I'm sorry I'm not as strong as I thought." I had been so sure I could do this— so sure I could make him proud of me. "I'm sorry I need you and that I fuck everything up when you're not here. I'm sorry. I shouldn't be mad, Green. We talked about this in December, and I knew it was coming and I should have been okay. I shouldn't be mad at you, and my head knows that it's stupid, but I think about you walking away one more time and I just want to… to beat the shit out of you, and that's not mature or grown up or even rational… but I can't keep them all safe by myself, and I need you. I'm sorry… I'm so sorry…."

"Sh…," he soothed. "It's not your fault." He smiled just a little, and the crinkle at his eyes made him look young and whole and well, and I rubbed my cheek against his chest like a cat. "It's okay. You know…." A laugh came out, but it wasn't the laugh I loved from Green, with an open mouth and an open heart. It was a closed laugh, with pain and bitterness, and it hurt me. "When I walk away from you, I want to kick the hell out of the whole world. But that's us, luv… that's because we don't like being apart. It makes us… or me, at least, want to blame something for the hurt. And… and there will be no more trips for now, but… but we're going to have to live with them in the future, okay?"

I whimpered. *Jeez, I'm a total pussy.* He needed me to tell him it was okay, but I whined at him instead. I tried again. "O… ooo… ok…."

His laugh this time was real, and it warmed me to my toes. "Don't hurt yourself, Corinne Carol-Anne." He laughed, and I laughed too, a free laugh this time, but the laughter faded and we squeezed each other at the end of it.

"We'll have to work on it," he said after a moment, "but what you must accept now, right this moment, is that you haven't let anybody down." I made a negative sound in my throat, but he shook his head at me. "In fact," he insisted, "you did just fine. You keep talking about screwing up—beloved, you kept them all safe."

"But Bracken...." Oh, that hurt to think about.

"Is safe and whole because of you." He rubbed my back absently and I relaxed into that touch, feeling again the healing in the tortured muscles at my neck and shoulders. "The Hollow Man almost got him—and Nicky—but you saved them. There's nothing to apologize for."

"Nicky was talking about moving out!" I said indignantly, and Green laughed.

"As though we'd let him do that," he agreed.

"We need him." I nodded, wanting the reassurance that Nicky wouldn't leave me too.

"Damned straight."

"I could have killed the vampires." I was angry at myself all over again for this.

"Impossible," Grace said from surprisingly close, and I looked up, startled. She had just slammed the door open and was coming in with a tray of food, and when I looked beyond her to the doorway, I saw Bracken and Nicky and Arturo, and half the vampires and the other half of the hill. Had they all been there listening as I had an emotional supernova? I almost whimpered with mortification.

"We didn't know...." I hid my face in Green's chest.

Grace bent down so I had to look at her. "We did know, Cory," she said gently, her freckled cheeks wrinkling with a kind smile. She set the tray down on the end table and patted at Green so he'd make room. "Those of us who'd tasted your blood, we knew. We knew you couldn't hurt us—not with Green inside you."

"I did hurt you." I felt them again, at the end, grimacing with the pain of my power before I'd been forced to withdraw.

"And then you stopped." Her hand, cold and compassionate, touched my sweaty face. "We're okay, Cory. And I've got to tell you, the unblooded vampires are going to be hammering down your door from here on out, because they are mighty impressed. And it doesn't hurt that Phillip can't stop talking about it like it was taking blood while having sex hovering seventy feet in the air." Grace snorted. Then she stood, long, lanky, and capable, and I had a sudden wish that her daughter could see her like this. "I've brought you food—both of you." She glared at Green, and I touched his face again. So worried. He looked so worried. "You're going to eat every last damned bite, and you're going to let Bracken and Nicky in before they gnaw at the carpet in frustration, and…." She looked at me with a mother's look, a look of frustrated love. "And you, my dear, are going to cut yourself a fucking break, okay?"

I nodded. So much easier to say than do.

"Good." She nodded decisively, then gestured for Bracken and Nicky to come in.

Bracken reached me first and bent a hesitant kiss to my lips, then stepped back and peered tentatively into my eyes. He looked like hell—pond-shadow eyes red-rimmed like Green's, handsome, grim mouth flat and narrow with tension. And a terrible hesitation to him, as though afraid of what he'd find in my eyes when I looked at him.

"What?" I said, unsure of what he wanted.

"Do you know me?" he asked. I was confused and looked it. "You didn't know me this afternoon." He took one of my hands as I cuddled into Green. "You didn't know any of us. You didn't look up, you didn't talk, you didn't answer. You just sat there and stared at your hands."

"I'm sorry," I said again. I took his hand, then reached for Nicky, and he squeezed between the end table and the bed, where Bracken wouldn't fit, and took my other hand. "I'm sorry, both of you. I was just…." My voice sharpened. "You assholes *left* me when I was sleeping, and then you almost died!" I looked at Bracken, accusing. "And you hurt yourself, trying to get to Adrian…." I was going to supernova again, and I was too tired, I didn't have the reserves left to flare. "And how am I supposed to protect you if you don't stay with me?" I had left Davy alone and sad, and she was dead.

"And how are we supposed to take care of you if you don't take care of yourself?" Bracken asked, frustrated. "How could you not know me?"

"I knew you," I promised, stretching up from my position in Green's arms to stroke his short hair because I was feeling bad all over again. "How could I not know you? I just… put off dealing with you, that's all."

"Well, deal with us now." Bracken pouted, nudging Green, who scooted again so Bracken could flop over on the bed. Nicky leaped across us, startling everybody, and landed, light as the bird he'd channeled, on our other side.

"What do you want me to say? Besides I'm hungry, that is...." I looked hopefully at Bracken, who handed me the sandwich Grace had left and then gave Green his.

Bracken let us eat for a moment in silence, and then typically Bracken pointed to the elephant at the room and figuratively screamed, *look, it's a big gray thing!*

"Davy," he stated, and I almost choked on my sandwich.

"My problem," I garbled, and then Green smacked me in the back of the head. On purpose. I swallowed in surprise and glared at him. "You hit me!"

"Let's try that again," he replied evenly—as though Green, the most patient man I'd ever known, hadn't just tagged me in the back of the head like a mother would smack a wayward adolescent reaching for a cookie.

"My *fault*," I said again, and he shook his head and moved his hand back, making me duck.

"You get one more chance, and then I'm calling Hallow up at dark thirty in the fucking night and dragging him up here."

"I thought you were going to send me down...."

He closed his eyes in pain. "You, beloved, Corinne Carol-Anne— you of all people should know that was an empty threat. The Goddess herself would have to pry you from my cold dead hands to get you off my hill. Now, let's try this again. She's not your fault. Her death is not your fault. She was Kyle's to take care of, and he left himself vulnerable, and it's still not his fault either."

"You didn't see her, Green," I said after a really long pause while the sandwich lost the -wich part but I still kept eating the sand. "She was so lost. We completely blew apart her world, and destroyed her faith in everything, and... then he got her anyway."

Bracken was lying on his stomach, so he could watch me eat I guess, and he nudged my leg and frowned up at me. "Your little human would have been okay," he said after a moment. "Why did you like her?"

"Uhm...." (*chew chew chew, think about the question, chew some more*) "She didn't ask questions. She just... I don't know... accepted me and liked me, that was all."

"I could point out, luv, that this is exactly why we like you." Green's pale attenuated fingers pushed the hair out of my eyes, and I found myself smiling at him with silly eyes and a loose mouth. He liked me. All the ways I felt I had screwed up, and he still loved me, still wanted me here. Out of nowhere, the roiling of the sacred dark crashed into my loins like a tide, then receded, leaving a cleansed slate of sleep sand in its wake. I took a deep breath and tried to pull my thoughts back to Davy, back to pain, but whereas the night before I had begged both Green and Bracken to make love to me to block those things out, right now I simply wanted Green because he was all that was not pain. He made me happy, and I wanted him. I breathed in again and felt my whole tight angry body simply melt against Green's chest, his arms, his thighs, and for the first time since his return, I let him comfort me. I let him be my strength, my backbone, my grief, and my healing.

"Mmmmm....," I mumbled, suddenly sleepy and pleasantly aroused at once. "I could point out that that's why I like you guys too." I didn't want to move. The hand holding the rest of my sandwich rested limply in my lap, and a foggy part of me wanted to finish it and then make wild furious passionate love to any one of the three men on my bed, but most of me was simply content to hum with desire and put that other thing off until later. Gently, Bracken took the sandwich from my hand, and Green moved me so that Brack could shuck my jeans from my hips. A quick flip and a little maneuvering, and my bra went with my jeans. Then I was set between Bracken and Green, and their hands were mesmerizing, quietly relaxing on my body, and they were both touching me, and if I'd stopped to think about it, I would have realized that Green had powered me into sleep. But that was okay, because apparently I was too dumb to give my brain a rest on its own, and besides, they were taking care of me. They were feeding me power and strength and love, and that's what we did for each other, and sometimes you're on the receiving end, and that was something I had to get used to.

So I fell asleep pleasantly horny, and woke up unpleasantly hungry. I tried to slither out of the puppy pile unnoticed again, but Bracken woke up immediately and put a heavy hand on my arm as I was halfway to the bottom of the bed.

"I'm starving," I confessed, hoping he'd be thrilled that I was eating and stay away from the emotional stuff for a while.

"I'll get it," he rumbled. We both wriggled, sans dignity, to the bottom of the bed and stood up, looking anxiously to Green and Nicky, who were on the outside edge, to make sure they hadn't woken up.

"But...." I could get my own food, right?

"The vampires were still buzzing about you when we came to bed," he said, arching his eyebrows at me. "Quite frankly, I don't think you're up to being Lady Cory tonight."

I sat down abruptly on the bottom edge of the bed. The sprites liked to do my sheets in watercolor abstracts, and this set was different shades of rose on an aged green—it was one of my favorites, and I stroked it restlessly before looking up. "Yeah," I said after a moment, "you're probably right." I couldn't look at him—it hurt to admit.

"Back in a minute." And I barely heard the door close behind him.

With a small sigh, I stood and stretched my fingertips toward the ten-foot ceiling and moved to the chairs where my knitting was. I didn't want to work on it—no, after my marathon of self-denial, I could probably wait a day before I worked on it again—but I did want to see it. The fibers were wool, cotton, silk, and cashmere—the blend itself was magical—but touching it with my hands was like touching love, and I had done the yarn proud. I had nearly finished the front in one day, and it was some of my best knitting ever. The stitches were flawlessly even, the cables perfectly executed.

I seriously considered ripping the whole thing out.

Bracken had said he could feel my love in his sweater. Would Green be more sensitive? Would he be able to feel the pain I'd denied as I worked on it? Would the butter-soft fibers score his chest and make him remember that I was weak and worried and difficult? Would his fine green-pale skin chafe under my personal flaws as a human's wouldn't under the perfect knitting?

I was a silk strand away from pulling the needles out and yanking on the yarn when Bracken came back in and said, repressed panic and all, "Cory? You're not...."

I dropped the knitting abruptly on the maple end table. "No," I said through a dry throat. "I'm not knitting again." I pulled my knees up to my chest, squashing my body sideways into the overstuffed brocade. Bracken set the tray on the table and handed me a sandwich, then sat down beside me on the floor and rested his head against my hip.

"Then what are you thinking?" he asked gently.

I looked at Nicky, who was on the edge of the bed, and at Green, right behind him. Both men were lying on their stomachs, their heads pillowed on their outstretched arms, their faces turned toward me. The shadows illuminated the lines of their muscles down their upper arms, the droop of their lashes on their cheeks, the hollows of their underarms as they met slim-muscled torsos—Green's was smooth and bare, Nicky's had a patch of cinnamon-colored hair. Green was propped up a little on his side, and his sand-colored nipple was almost more visible in the dark than it was in the light. Nicky's chin was gruff with stubble, and Green's hair in the darkness was the brightness of a lemon cookie. Their features were slack and sweet in sleep, and my heart was suddenly tied up into a little tiny knot.

"I'm thinking…." I swallowed and cleared my throat. "I'm thinking what I'm always thinking—that love makes us strong and vulnerable all at the same time."

"Mmmm." His hand came up to my knee, and he leaned a little more, using his arm as support.

"I'm also…." This was always hard to put into words. "I'm also thinking that I can't imagine what it must be like to be Green, and to open my heart up again and again for such a long time, only to have it broken by the inevitable."

"It's frightening, isn't it?"

I shuddered and wiped my fingers on my T-shirt so I could stroke his silky dark hair. I had known it was a birthright when he'd first cut it, trying to prove something to me. I hadn't known that to the European fey, at least, it signified immortality. When he'd cut it again, after he'd been bound to my lifespan, I had cried for two days.

"It's terrifying," I whispered, trying to put a finger on the feeling that had gripped me for the last few months, the thing that had driven me to keep our people safe, to risk myself for Bracken and Green in ways that frightened them. I searched hard for an analogy, went back to high school, to poor, beleaguered Vicki Morrison, who'd found herself pregnant at fifteen. Until she and the baby had been taken into foster care, I'd been the only one to talk to her. "It's like… like I held my friend's baby once," I said into the quiet. "And it was all good, you know?" An understatement—it had been breathtaking, like holding thunder. "The kid was cute, waving her tiny little fist with the fat perfect fingers, and those unfocused eyes were all crossed and everything… and suddenly it hit me that I drop shit all the time, right? I drop my purse, I drop my backpack, my wallet, whatever. But this… this perfect little creature… she owed her whole existence on the gamble that I wouldn't drop *her*." I shuddered again, and my fingers tightened in his hair and I grabbed his shoulder instead. "You didn't know me, Brack." I couldn't even look at him when I confessed this. "I was such a bitch in high school, so afraid that friendship—any friendship—would just suck me down into loserdom. I was such a bitch to Adrian when we first met. And now you and Green and Nicky love me, and...."

"And you're afraid you're going to drop the baby," Bracken, his hand stroking my knee.

"I had to give her back to my friend, like, right then." I remembered that, because it had hurt to give her back. It had been terrifying, but sweet. I shook my head. "I can't give you guys back. I *refuse* to give you back, Bracken." I closed my eyes, seeing them, all of them, breathing in the quietude, sleeping in the shadows, their hearts beating for me. "But holding on to you all scares me to the hairs on the tops of my toes, every goddamned day."

"If you think it's any different for us, beloved, you're sadly mistaken," Bracken told me.

"Which baby did you ever drop?" I asked, and it heartened me to hear that puff of breath that signified laughter.

I guess he had no answer to that, because he changed the subject and reached for my knitting instead. "You did a good job while you were completely psychotic. What are all these little ends sticking out, though? There weren't any of those in my sweater." His fingers flexed in the delicious cream-colored yarn.

"That's because I wove them in," I said dryly. "You're supposed to do it as you finish off the yarn—I don't."

"So that's what Grace meant—are you weaving in your ends or tying knots." I nodded affirmative, and he stroked the fabric again. "Why don't you do them as you go?"

I shrugged, took the knitting from him, and tucked it safely in my bag. "I don't know. I just like to... touch the finished product, say good-bye to it. I can do that if I take an hour when I'm done and weave in all the ends."

Bracken made a noncommittal sound in the darkness, and I felt myself nodding off. So I was not ready, I was exposed and unprepared, when he suddenly said, "Davy. You need to weave in your ends with her."

Abruptly I was awake, and without warning, I was in tears. I wasn't fighting them—they came freely—and I was somewhat surprised to find that they didn't hurt when I didn't fight them. I'm so stupid sometimes—how many times did I have to cry to learn this lesson? Still…. "That wasn't fair, Brack," I complained thickly, wiping my face with my hands, and still they kept coming. He sat up and wrapped his arm around my back, and I leaned my cheek against his hair. "I wasn't ready." My breath caught on a sob, and he waited patiently, but I breathed it out and thought I was done.

"We're never ready, beloved," he whispered, stroking my hair, "but she's gone. You know it. We'll find out how, and if Kyle survives, we'll help him. But you need to grieve."

"Remember that night at the Chevron station?" Not one of our best moments. "That old man died, and you told me 'It's more mete that others grieve.' Remember? You phrased it so old-fashioned, it stuck in my head. I just keep thinking…." Oh Goddess, I was hiccuping with the effort to hold it together and to keep my sorrow civilized. His arm tightened around my back, and he took my tear-puddled hand in his and kissed it. "I just keep thinking that she's not mine to grieve for. She's got friends and family and people who have known her for years, and I just ran around the track with her—she didn't even know who I was…."

"Shhh… sh… sh…." He rose to his knees and gathered me in close, whispering things in my hair. "If you grieve because you'll miss her, then she's yours to grieve for," he told me. "But if it's only guilt… well, then, deal with the guilt."

"I'll miss her—I'll miss her—I'll—" And then it was gone, that barrier in my chest, that tough I've-got-everything-under-control-and-every-emotion-in-a-box blockade was gone, and I wept freely and quietly for my friend. When I was done, and Bracken was mopping my face with my T-shirt, I said, "She never got to hear me sing." Because it was a talent I was particularly proud of, but too shy to share. "Would it be okay if I sang for her?"

Bracken nodded and kissed my forehead. "I think it would be perfect," he said, and his throat sounded rough. I'd put them through a lot this last day, I thought dismally.

"Would you sing with me? Would Green?" Bracken nodded, and we both looked toward Green, his eyes closed, his chest moving in and out in the silence of sleep—or so we thought.

"I'd love to sing with you, beloved," he said, opening his lovely green eyes, "if only you'd shut up and come to bed so I can hold you too."

Of course I did. Green and Bracken held me tight until I slept soundly through the rising of the sun and beyond.

GREEN
Alien Forms of Worship

NO ONE saw them enter the church. According to the press, a week and a half ago, Davis Stacia Kelly, daughter of a prominent businessman, had been murdered after leaving dinner with her family in Stanford Ranch. During supper she'd told them she was moving in with her boyfriend, whom they had never met. (Oh, yes, Kyle was high on the suspect list—or would have been, if anyone could remember what he looked like or where he lived.) Her father was well known, her mother was on a lot of community boards, and the evening attendance at the Episcopalian service on K Street was both healthy and well publicized.

For the three vampires, two werecreatures, two sidhe, and little sorceress, it was like being top ten on America's Most Wanted and strolling into a police station for a drink of water. It was possible they might escape unnoticed, but only because a church with a thousand cameras was the last place anyone would expect the supernatural.

Cory had no idea how risky it would be.

"Are you going to tell her?" Bracken asked Green nervously as they watched everybody else load into the Suburban.

"Nope," he replied, smiling at Cory as she scowled at the folds of her black dress and hauled the thing in after her, trying to keep it out from under Renny's cat feet and Nicky's dress shoes.

"There's going to be cameras everywhere, Green…." And Green turned the full force of his gaze on Cory's *due'alle.*

"You promised," he said. His voice didn't rise, but his position was unspeakably clear. "So did I. Neither time nor place did then adhere, yet you would unmake both?"

"They make themselves." Bracken sighed. "Do you ever mangle *Hamlet? Twelfth Night? Romeo and Juliet?*"

"Frequently." Green gathered his camel dress coat around his crème-colored suit and straightened Cory's scarf at his neck as he moved to the front of the vehicle. "If it be not now, it will be to come, and if it be not to come, it will be now."

"We're going to get cau-aught," Bracken sang to himself as they got into the Suburban, but Green could tell that it was just because it made him feel better to worry.

Everyone was dressed for the funeral except Renny, who had insisted on coming in cat form. Given who would be waiting in the back of the church, Green thought that bringing a werecreature might be the prudent thing to do.

The trip down to Sacramento was actually a pretty lively affair—as though the vampires who hadn't known Davy were making things easier on Cory, Renny, Bracken, and Nicky, who had—and it was hard to be depressed as they cleared Foresthill and took the freeway entrance east. The foothills had blossomed green under the rain, and the wildflowers had finally emerged. Since the fate of their child was the reason for the split between the Goddess and her mate, Easter wasn't really celebrated among the Goddess's get, but its counterpart, Oestre, the spring equinox, was coming soon, and Northern California's traditional two weeks of spring were there. The air coming in through the side windows was a complicated braid of cool and warm, flowers and damp concrete.

Green watched intermittently in the rearview mirror as Cory smiled and bantered with the vampires and tested the air coming in through the vented window, her expression both dreamy and sad. She caught Green's eyes and answered his questioning brow with "I didn't give up anything for Lent."

"Sure you did," he said in an undertone for her only. "You gave up me. I came home early, that's all."

"Do you think anybody will notice us?" she asked seriously, the first time she had acknowledged the risk they were running.

"We're getting there late—I hope not." He waited to see if she would catch the evasion, but she was looking out the window again.

"Do you think we practiced enough?"

"Yes," he answered unequivocally. "You'll make the angels weep, dearest."

"I didn't know the angels listened in on us," she bantered back.

"For you, I'm sure they'll eavesdrop."

She grinned at him, and he felt better and better about this mad exposure to the media. Anything to help her heal.

Contrary to myth, vampires don't actually spontaneously combust upon entering a church or touching holy water. Given the nature of their recovery from death, they had no choice but to believe in the Goddess, and believing in her counterpart as well was not a hardship—most vampires simply chose to worship at the feet of the Goddess instead. It seemed only fair, since God had been the one to deny them sunlight.

So there was no spectacular conflagration when the six of them entered the back of the church. It was a classically imposing structure, squarely built in tan stucco with plain arches at the sides and an exquisite spire and delicate bell at its front. It was placed in a neighborhood of tastefully expensive homes with manicured flowerbeds and neat sidewalks, just before K Street did something really flaky and turned into a street with another name near a couple of roundabouts that would have had Bracken inventing new swearwords in Elvish if he'd been driving. Parking was hellific, but the press had already done most of its opening shots, so few cameras were whirring as they parked the car in front of one of the houses nearly two blocks from the church and then hiked to the entrance in the spring drizzle.

They left Renny curled up in a shadow on the side of the building, then walked through the stone-tiled foyer to the inside, using their preternatural quiet so as not to disturb the ritual of mourning inside.

The interior had an almost Spartan grandeur—whitewashed stucco walls, small stained-glass arches set in high up, burgundy carpet, and dark wood pews. Its simplicity spoke of an earnest faith that Green admired—but he was reasonably sure the admiration would be one way, should those attending the funeral get a really good look at him or Bracken. But the front of the church was crowded and the back empty, and he thought that maybe, if they parked themselves in the back and left the moment they were done, no one would remember anything but Cory's heartbreaking voice.

The pastor walked up to greet them, an imposing man in his fifties with dignified-looking gray hair, pale gray eyes, and a definite sense of his own importance.

"All friends of the deceased are welcome...," he began. Then he took a second look at Green and Bracken, then a third, and his face narrowed and hardened. "But friends of Satan are friends of nobody."

Cory looked at him in shock, and then looked Green in the eyes with surprise and sadness. Green hadn't told her that he and Bracken wouldn't be able to wear their glamour—an ancient treaty between the God's people and the Goddess's forbade any sort of disguise in a place of worship. Her lips parted, and Green worked hard at a shrug and a smile. She took his hand in hers, and he felt her lips whisper across the pale skin of his knuckles. Then she turned toward the minister like a warrior doing battle. She tightened her expression, her freckles scrunching up around her nose. "A minister, of all people, should know that dichotomies don't exist," she said mutinously. "Just because we're not God's creatures doesn't mean we're the other's."

They had stopped three pews before the crowd began, and she kept her voice controlled enough that no one looked back, but her words brought an arching of grayed eyebrows and a tilting of a heavy, long-boned head. "Who are you?" he asked, keeping his voice civilized.

"We're friends of the deceased," Cory replied with dignity. "And we'd like to honor her in song."

"You—all of you—knew Miss Kelly?" he asked, and Green was wondering if the man heard thunder as he realigned his world with their presence.

"My beloved knew her," Green answered, before Cory could do battle again. "Some of us are here for her, but most of us are here for Davy. If you please, all we ask is a song." He nodded toward the front of the church, where a group of girls who looked like high school friends were engaged in a weepy version of "Blessed Be the Tie That Binds." "We can sing just as well from the back of the church as from the altar. Nothing will be defiled, and an innocent child will be honored. Don't tell me that God is forbidding things like that now as well."

The pastor flushed and nodded toward the pew against the back wall with a sole, familiar-looking occupant. "Something tells me you'll be quite comfortable there," he said stiffly, and Cory sighed.

"Try not to think you're better than God," she snapped. "Not even he hates us, you know." The man tossed her a startled look before regaining his measured dignification down the aisle of the church.

Kyle didn't glance at them as they sat down, but Cory looked at him with narrowed eyes and a firm purpose during the rest of the service, and Green knew she was either mentally rehearsing the song or mentally rehearsing what she was going to do to Kyle to make him want to live. She was most definitely not paying attention to the rest of the service, and for that Green was only grateful—he could hardly bear to watch her compare herself to other humans and wonder if she was better or worse as it was, and watching human reactions to grief would only confuse her. Most humans were not honest when they grieved.

Several people got up and spoke, telling anecdotes of Davy's childhood, of her days in school—the words "good" and "sweet" and "will be really missed" coming up so often that Green had a brief, extremely irreverent, and nearly unkind thought that creative writing should be mandatory in American human education—before the minister nodded grudgingly to the back of the church.

The three of them stood, Cory in the center of Green and Bracken, and paused, all taking their time from Green. Then, with his nod, they launched into a song that quite frankly reminded Green of Adrian. When Cory suggested it, she'd said that it was the song she'd never been able to sing for him. "I didn't know Davy well enough to have a song for her," she'd added with an embarrassed shrug.

"What song would you sing for me?" Bracken had asked curiously.

"'Lifetimes' by Sheryl Crow," she'd replied promptly, then looked at Green sideways. "You're not going to ask?"

"Do you want to tell me?"

"You have too many songs to name one." It was said with soft eyes, and he'd smiled gently. Something in his eyes must have troubled her, though, because she'd frowned a little. "A lot of living gets you a lot of songs!" she'd defended and then turned away before they could continue.

Now she had a little line drawn between her eyebrows as she concentrated and stood, shoulders back, carrying the lyrics with a subtle melody that was meant to depend on dreamy instrumentals. He and Bracken sang the instrumentals for her, unselfconsciously and clearly, so subtle as to blend behind her, their voices only emerging when the song called for backup vocals.

Cory's voice lifted in melody, and suddenly, although his voice never faltered, Green was seeing Adrian behind his shuttered gaze, as he'd first seen him—filthy matted hair, the fury of ten years of hell burning in his spangled eyes.

The song progressed, and he was seeing Cory on that first night—plump, barely aware of herself as a power or even as a woman, stoically cleansing the scene of a tragedy. She'd had no idea, none at all, of the joy and pain that would follow, and her bravery had impressed the hell out of him, just as it impressed him now.

The lyrics rose in a supplication for healing, and abruptly he was there again in the church, singing softly without even a flicker in his voice and wondering if there had ever been any way to save Cory from the gradual alienation from her own species. And if there had been, would he have risked it? He listened to her now as they sang together, her throaty alto stretching surprisingly as the song climaxed, risking a look at the startled, moved group of mourners who had caught their breath to hear beauty as it spelled their hearts in plain notes. He remembered the feel of her power, pulsing through the resisting bodies of nearly sixty vampires as they had fought to save Bracken and Nicky, and he could still feel beneath his fingers the satin of her flesh as they moved in the night.

As the song crested in its melancholy climax, a wave of sadness crashed over him, foaming about his mouth and nose until he could hardly breathe. When he had fought his way clear, it receded, leaving in its wake a feeling of... transparency, of insubstantiality, that was so comforting that Green almost stopped singing from fear. No. His body was offering to fade, to become transparent, to drift into nothingness until the hot breeze of a foothill summer blew through his precious temperate garden and carried even his memory away. It happened to the fey, even to the sidhe, when the weight of living became more than they could bear, but it couldn't happen to him. *She needs me,* he thought in panic, and the feeling passed, leaving his singing uninterrupted, the moment as though it had never been. But he would remember it, use it as a goad. Melancholy must never be allowed to take over, because once he had faded, he could never return. And his people needed him. *Cory* needed him—hadn't the last few days proved that? Being needed was all he'd ever lived for.

The song wound down, their voices twining, releasing, until only Bracken's voice remained, trailing off in the final haunting vocal, and they were left in the stunned silence of the grieving assembly. There was no protocol for responding to song in church, Green knew, no relieving applause, no way of acknowledging that the people who had moved you, struck a chord in the emotions that still vibrated in your throat, had done you good. So it was in that awed quiet, they bowed slightly and moved out of the pew at Green's signal, followed by their people and, as they all hesitated and looked at him expectantly, followed by Davy's beloved as well.

Green's people kept stoic faces as they caught sight of Kyle's mask of bloody tears and hoped that the assembly would still be too caught up in the web of song and sadness to react. How could he show up here, among humans, and let them see that tell? It was more madness than Green and Bracken and their telltale ears and facial features—these could be explained away as deformity or foreign visitors, but blood is blood, and every human who actually looked would recognize that the scarlet streaks down Kyle's face were the same vital element that his lover had lost all over the concrete outside her father's house in Granite Bay.

Phillip and Marcus flanked him immediately, with Grace taking position at his front, and together the lot of them made a somewhat dignified—albeit mysterious—exit from the church. Cory glanced behind them once as they left, her gaze weaving in and out of her people behind her, and Green heard a barely suppressed snicker.

"What?" Bracken whispered as they cleared the great wooden doors.

"The minister," she said. "He looks like he swallowed his tongue."

"Good," Bracken said darkly. "Pompous prick…."

As they walked down the concrete steps to the sidewalk below, Kyle said distinctly, "Let me go."

Cory replied, low and clear, "We have business, Kyle. Wait until we find some shadows…."

"We passed an alley about a block from the car," Nicky supplied, looking around nervously. The moon was just coming off full, so it was brighter than the pinkish lights that lined the street and shadows were harder than usual to find.

Cory nodded. "You hear that? Just wait."

They walked quietly past the two remaining news vans waiting for shots of the emerging crowd, past the white stucco houses, almost ridiculously tiny after the vastness of Green's home. Many of them one or two bedroom, but with sweet, manicured flower gardens—monetary wealth with scant family size was Green's estimation.

The promised alley was the sunken driveway to a detached garage on one of the larger properties, but there were thick seedless mulberry trees in both the lower yard and the upper yard, and the closest streetlight was four houses away—the darkness was both complete and eerie. The vampires looked more at ease than since the moment they had walked into the church.

Cory had turned to face the bereaved vampire when Kyle apparently lost all sanity and blurred past his escort to seize her arm, snarling, "I said let—"

It was as far as he got before Bracken and Green grabbed an arm apiece and shoved him against the concrete wall of the sunken driveway. Bracken was growling, his eyes throwing off amber sparks, and Green felt the unmistakable surge of the redcap's power before Cory touched his shoulder and murmured—not in his ear, but loud enough for him to hear—and he charged down, breathing in deep, shuddering gasps.

"No," Cory said evenly, sparing a glance for Bracken before turning her attention back to their objective.

"No, what?" Kyle spat. His eyes were spitting red sparks in the spring darkness, whirling with the vampire's change. He was struggling silently with Green and Bracken, and between the tendons popping out at his neck and temples, his emerging hunting face, and the blood of his tears crawling across his cheeks and chin like demented spiders, his face was a truly terrifying mask in the dark. Cory was unafraid.

"No, we won't let you go." She swallowed, and Green saw her spine stiffen and her "leader face" fall firmly where it belonged. "And no, we won't let you stand in the middle of the street and fry like an ant when the sun comes out. No. You no longer have a choice in the matter." She walked toward him as she said this, until she was face-to-face with an angry vampire. Her complete faith that Bracken and Green wouldn't let him hurt her was evident in her posture, her voice, the way she didn't even have to look at them, and the way she stood toe-to-toe, looking up into the face of an enraged killer, and told him that she hadn't given up.

"Who's going to stop me?" Kyle growled, his throat thickened with the change, his words fouled by lips that wouldn't fit over his long and pointed teeth.

"I won't have to stop you," she said softly, reaching her hands up to his crimson cheek. She stroked her thumb over the bloody tears tracking down his face while he strained away from her touch. Then she cocked an eye at Green, who nodded. "I just have to make you want to live." She popped the thumb in her mouth, closed her eyes, and sucked in her breath—her face transfiguring, glowing with Adrian's violet light, her features shown for the loveliness they truly were. "Coffee... damp earth… dew… the smell of fish and…." Her nose wrinkled, a very young, human expression that contrasted with the mystery of what she did with her vampires. "Fish and worms… and a voice… older… loved…."

She opened her eyes and looked into his softening face, waiting until his eyes stopped whirling red with anger and for his teeth to start diminishing. "Fishing with your grandfather when you were young," she told him. "That's what you miss most about your human life. That's why you loved Davy—she made you feel like the world was hopeful again, like each rising held something to look forward to."

"How did you…." But before he could finish the question, she popped that same thumb into his mouth and nicked it on a not-quite-receded fang, waiting breathlessly until Kyle swallowed in surprise before moving her hand down to his shoulder. Now it was Kyle's turn to close his eyes and suck in his breath, and then his body sagged so abruptly that Green and Bracken let him go, lowering him gently to his knees.

"Oh, God…." Kyle's voice thrummed with agony, and then it rose, the pain so exquisite not one of them watching could hear him without tears. "Oh, God…. Sunshine… sunshine…. You bitch… it's a lie… there will never be sunshine for me again…. Oh, Davy…." And now he sobbed, wept, cleansed himself the way he had needed to but hadn't, because he hadn't had a Green, or a Bracken, or a Nicky to hold him.

Cory held him. Cory lowered herself to her knees and wrapped her arms around him, whispering soft things against his ear until his sobbing subsided. When he was down to gentle hiccups—a human gift from the Goddess, those—she leaned her forehead against his, and now Green and Bracken could hear her, because her words held purpose and control.

"Okay," she said. "And now you're going to feed, because you haven't and you're almost crazy with it. And then—hear me out—" Because Renny had stepped forward and he'd made an animal whimper of hunger in his throat, but Cory wouldn't turn him loose on her friend unless she knew she had command. "Now listen." He turned his bloody, grief-wrought face toward her, and she ran a hand over his cheek and leaned into him, so close that, looking down at them, Green could only see the tiniest sliver of air to define the two of them. "You're going to feed, and then you're going to fly with your kiss mates." She closed her eyes, and Grace and Phillip and Marcus opened their eyes wider, looking at Kyle with whirling crimson anticipation.

"You're going to fly with them, and share flesh and blood—and by the end of the night, you won't think of hurting yourself, because it would hurt them, and you will love them as much as I do, right?" She nodded slowly and waited until Kyle nodded with her, their communication so intimate that Kyle lowered his head, barely brushing her lips with his. Cory let him, for just a moment, before she slipped gracefully back and called for Renny. There was sadness then, and Kyle reached out to caress Cory's cheek, but Cory caught his hand in hers and moved so that Renny could plant her paws on Kyle's shoulder, and he lowered his head and carefully extended his fangs only. They punctured a fur-covered carotid, and Renny began to purr, writhing her body sinuously and rubbing against Kyle's chest until he groaned and released her, leaving her so clenched for fulfillment that she mrewled pitifully and wound herself around Green's legs. Green dropped a hand to her ruff and sent a little bit of will into her, watching bemusedly as she shuddered and growled and then plopped dazedly at his feet. Kyle stroked her head absently and wiped his mouth with the sleeve of his black leather jacket.

He looked immediately to Cory for guidance, and she gestured to Marcus and Phillip, who nudged Green and Bracken out of the way to take their new brother by the arms and heave him to his feet. Then Grace stepped forward and extended her fangs. They were of a height, so she didn't need to bend—she simply leaned forward and sniffed at his neck, her eyes dilating slightly, her unnecessary breath coming in pants. She traced a delicate line down his throat with her tongue, and he groaned and shuddered. Then she traced the same line with her fang, and he moaned with such wanting, such terrible skin hunger that Green's heart went out to him—he'd been without his kiss for far, far too long. As the crimson welled up along his neck, Grace lapped at it, then Marcus, then Phillip, their tongues doing gentle things along his skin. Kyle's moan became more demanding, more pleading, until the three of them wrapped their arms around him and around each other. Grace emitted a hiss of satisfaction, clamping her fully extended feeding fangs into his throat with full and eager lips. All of them shuddered, groaned, and came in time with him, and the only thing keeping them on their feet was each other. A raw, completed, hungering sound burst from Kyle's throat, and the huddle of vampires burst open just enough for them to bend at the knees and as a whole launch into the air, Kyle's animal cries of grief, of relief, of release wailing through the night, his brethren's answering calls never far behind.

Cory sat down abruptly in the middle of the driveway, her full black skirt pooling around her. Green squatted down beside her, taking inventory. Her gold button-up sweater was dark in places from Kyle's wept blood, and she herself had tear tracks, glistening in the faint glow from the streetlight.

"Well, that sucked," she muttered, her voice choked.

"You were magnificent," he said truly, and she shrugged and wiped her cheek with the sleeve of her black peacoat.

"Nicky?" she asked, looking away from Green's admiration in embarrassment. "Nicky, honey, could you keep an eye out for them for a bit? You've got your cell phone in your pocket, right?"

"Yeah...."

"Good." She looked in the sky, where a human might be confused by the perspective of the tall old trees into thinking fluttering shapes were simply large bats flickering in the distance. "Make sure they come home—if they haven't started by, say, three a.m., give us a call. I think he'll be all right, but I don't want the others in danger because he still has a death wish. Okay?"

"No problem, Lady Cory," he said without any irony, and she made a face. Nicky stepped forward and went to kiss her cheek, but she turned and took his lips, seeking the intimacy she'd missed purposefully when Kyle had tried. Their lips tangled for a moment, and she leaned in, making the kiss real and passionate and true before pulling back.

"Be safe, right, Nick?"

"Absolutely," he said, giving her a parting kiss on the brow. Then he had changed, in that quick, graceful way that the Avians did better than any other were, and was gone.

Cory sighed and held her hand to Green so he could pull her up, but he bent to one knee and scooped her into his arms.

"Green... I'm fine. It's all good—I can walk...."

He kissed her hair. "I know—but, for a minute, could you pretend that you need me?"

She whimpered a little in her throat and leaned against his chest, her hand spreading beneath her cheek and flexing a little, like she was making sure he was real. "No pretending necessary."

And they gathered together and went to find the car.

They arrived at the hill around nine, changed, and mooched about the front room until Bracken put in *Rent* and they watched it. Cory brought her knitting, but she was working on something smaller and brightly colored and made it a point to glance up at the movie and make comments while she paused her work, so Green and Bracken exchanged glances and agreed to let it be.

"For you?" Green asked.

"Mm-nn." She shook her head. "Matching hats for Gavin and Graeme." She smiled slightly. "Since I'm a superhero and all."

Oh damn—another harsh subject. He sighed. "Beloved... about Chloe...."

Cory's hands stilled, and she looked up at Green from her spot in the middle of the couch. "Yeah, I know. She's not fitting in. We're going to have to... I don't know... banish her? Shun her? Brain-wipe her? Something."

Green nodded, glad she understood. "I was hoping to bring it up to Grace in a few days, after Kyle is comfortable. Chloe, every time she's here, she's destructive. She's angry. She says and does things that hurt Grace—that hurt you. I just can't allow her to stay."

"But the boys?" Cory said anxiously. "We can let them remember, right?" She bit her lip and looked at him pleadingly. "I would... you know. Grace would really miss those kids, if she wasn't allowed to keep in touch."

Meaning Cory had fallen hopelessly in love with the two children, and she wanted to know they were safe and that she could make them hers as she hadn't been able to with Davy. Green smiled and took the hand lying quietly in the wool, bringing it to his lips and grazing it in a very tender, private way. "I am helpless to deny you anything, beloved."

She rolled her eyes and said "Bullshit!" But he could tell she was pleased. Then her smile faded and she grimaced. "I'll tell her," she said softly, tugging at her hand.

"We'll tell her," he corrected, raising an eyebrow and keeping her hand where it belonged for just a moment longer. "It's a decision that's best for the hill, not one that just affects the vampires."

Cory nodded. "Deal." Then a sudden thought. "Hey—you guys never told me what happened to Max's obnoxious sister."

Bracken looked up from her other side—he had been playing chess with Twilight, who was sitting in the stuffed chair to his diagonal. The chess set was a special-edition *Simpsons* set—Bracken had gotten it from Adrian's room. Different chess sets had been Bracken's running

Christmas gift to Adrian from the time he was a child, Green remembered, and he was happy to see this one out. Tonight Bracken was losing, to his immense irritation.

Bracken was unaware of Green's scrutiny, and replied to Cory, "We had Marcus mind-wipe her." He shook his head in disgust. "It was pretty sad—Marc rolled her mind, and suddenly she went from the poster child of judgmental harpies to a jiggling ho-bag. Max said he was so embarrassed he almost told Marc to do her and let her remember it, but Grace made him take her home."

Cory laughed a little, then laughed a lot. "Poor Max," she giggled. "He's such a good guy—no wonder he had such a hard time with us."

Green released her hand and said thoughtfully, "The thing is, Corinne Carol-Anne, that Max is just the better side of human. I know you worry about getting along with your own people, but it's not that you don't—it's that you're very careful about who you do like. You pick people who are accepting, who are honorable. Chloe and Michelle aren't. Max is, and Davy was. It's that simple."

Cory's silence was ominous—then she squinted up at Green impishly. "I'm going to show you how well-adjusted I'm feeling today by not answering that," she said after a moment.

"You're going to school tomorrow?" he returned playfully. It was Monday, and they hadn't gone that morning.

"Uh-huh," she answered affirmatively, looking slyly from her knitting.

"You're going to see Hallow?" he asked, keeping his voice playful.

"Uh-huh," she answered back, her eyes dancing gently, although she kept her head tilted down.

"Then I'll let you slide," he responded grandly.

She reached behind Bracken and yanked out an unused but squashed throw pillow that she chucked at Green. He fielded the pillow and stuck out his tongue, she returned the gesture, and they let the matter lie. But when he had gone back to his laptop, he caught her gazing at him thoughtfully, traces of her playful smile still on her face. She winked at him when he caught her. Finally, he thought, she was starting to understand herself and her place in the many worlds she inhabited. And she felt good about it.

At ten o'clock, just before they were about to retire (the three of them in Cory's bedroom—Green had put off his other "appointments" until after Davy's funeral, and Cory had been too grateful to protest or even to mention it, in fear that he'd have to see someone else after all), the vampires returned. Cory caught their brain-chatter midyawn, so caught up in what they were doing when they returned that she almost choked on her own tongue.

When her focus returned to the room she was in, she started talking, stopped, flushed, and tried again. "Uhm... they're... they're.... Marcus and Phillip are taking him to that room with the ginormous bed," she said after a moment, then looked up and caught Arturo's eye. He was reading a book of Walt Whitman's poetry in a corner of the room. "Uhm, Arturo, I think Grace wants you." She swallowed and blushed again. "Now," she added, nodding. Arturo got up with some alacrity and practically blurred to the back bedroom. Only a few minutes later, Nicky walked through the front door, shaking moisture from his hair as he did so.

"It started raining again," he complained by way of greeting.

"I'm glad you're back, Nicky," Cory replied mildly.

She pushed herself up off the couch using Bracken's shoulder. He sighed and conceded his queen, shaking his head at Twilight and saying, "I used to think I was good at this."

"You play like someone has been letting you win," Twilight said guilelessly, and Green hid a smile at Bracken's startled look as he too moved off the couch.

Cory greeted Nicky with a hug, and he moved toward the kitchen with its big raw-wood table and started hunting for something to eat. He was still bitching about the weather. "You people keep telling me that summers here are hot, but I swear it's never going to stop pissing down water, frozen or no."

Cory laughed and then moved him out of the way to reach into the refrigerator and pull out one chocolate cream and one banana cream pie. "You'll think that, and then one week it will go from sixty-five to ninety-five in three days' time and you won't know what to do with yourself." She put the pies on the table and then set down silverware, and was turning to get plates when Nicky just dove into the middle of the banana cream pie with a fork.

"Ge' i' qui'," he garbled with his mouth full. He swallowed. "Don't mess with plates, I'm taking no prisoners."

Green and Bracken had already grabbed forks and were diving in, so Cory sat on her knees on the chair by Nicky and joined them. They wolfed pie in companionable silence, and when they had slowed down a little, both pies almost completely demolished, Green licked the whipped cream off the corner of his mouth and said, "So, does anyone want to hear about my plan to protect us?"

"I do," Bracken said smugly, and Cory looked at him from narrowed eyes. Then Green started talking, and her eyes got very, very wide indeed.

Somewhere in the middle of his description of how Green and the sylphan leaders had healed their entire enclave of sylphs of everything from scrapes to bad haircuts the night Bracken and Nicky had been attacked, her jaw dropped open. When he suggested using the same means to *protect* everybody in the hill, her eyes glazed over a little.

"I'm not a porn star," she said stiffly, and Bracken almost spit pie crumbs.

"Of course not," he said, wiping his mouth with the back of his hand. "They usually have bigger boobs."

"Ass. Hole," she replied succinctly, socking him in the arm, and Bracken grinned back without shame.

"That will probably be Green's pleasure," he said back, enjoying the way her mouth opened and closed before she could come up with a retort.

"Oh, fu…." She trailed off on the insult and/or instruction. They could all see her realize—that was the idea. She wrinkled her nose and shook her head. "How do you know I can even control it?" she asked accusingly. "We've never tried to… harness it like this."

Green grinned, a blinding expression that had worked on all genders since he'd been of Goddess's age. "Two words," he said. "Seat. Cushions."

She flushed so thoroughly, with so much arousal, that the great, shiny, blue-tiled kitchen, which had been companionable and pleasant before, was suddenly charged powerfully with want. Everybody was abruptly aware of the fact that Cory shared a bed with all three men, and that the possibility of them all being in that bed together and naked made their breath catch.

"That was a fluke," she mumbled, not meeting any eyes at all.

"That was control," he corrected throatily. She stood up, and so did he, like a mountain lion following the motions of a jackrabbit. He pinned her with his gaze, and she looked up at him—flushed, warm, panting slightly, the tip of her tongue coming out to lick her lips before she gnawed on her lower lip in an attempt to keep the many fertile imaginings in her mind from running all over her face. "And you have control now, don't you?" He nodded, waiting for her to catch the motion herself. She did, mesmerized by his eyes, lost like a light-struck deer. "You control the sex, and you control the magic, and you control us, and we can use that control—but only if you're game."

She swallowed hard, still nodding. Her mouth moved, her wide, full mouth, and she licked her lips again. The whole room was still caught in her panting breaths and in the heartbeats that all three of the preternatural males could hear, feel, smell throbbing beneath her skin.

"But what about her?" Nicky asked after a moment, swallowing a couple of times before he got it out. His eyes were locked on the two of them. "I mean...." He laughed a little and took a swig of milk from the glass next to him, rubbing his lips together. "Everything she's ever done has affected things, not her. Will she be able to protect herself?"

Green smiled, because he'd thought of that. "Cory, come here for a moment, will you?" Her breath caught, but she did, her body coming just a heartbeat from touching his all along the front, and he lowered his lips to her ear, his hair falling between her and her other lovers as he whispered against the whorls of her skin. "Turn around and face them, beloved."

She did, breaking off eye contact at the last possible moment, and looked shyly out at Bracken and Nicky from under the curly fall of her rust-colored hair. Green's pale hand moved hotly across her hip, pulling down the waistband of her jeans and pushing up the hem of her oversized man's T-shirt until a patch of skin tantalizingly close to her bikini line was showing, drawing Bracken's and Nicky's gaze like a bright toy. He bent and whispered in her ear again, asking her for the words she'd written in that fit of whimsy the night he'd come home from his longest trip. Her flush intensified, and she whispered—even though she knew Nicky and Bracken could hear, she whispered—and the throaty sound of "Cory loves Green" made the temperature in the kitchen kick up another few notches. There were spots of high color in Bracken's bright-pale face, and Nicky was blotchy scarlet with the blood flooding under his skin.

Bracken sucked in a breath so tightly past his lips and teeth that the whooshing sound seemed to vibrate, and Nicky made a strangled "ungh" sound near his throat and tongue. "That's amazing," Bracken said on his exhaled breath, at about the time Nicky said, "God, that's hot."

She looked down, surprised, and the little moue of embarrassment was accompanied by a feeble struggle to cover her skin with her hands, but Green's hands were there to expose it. There, upside down and written across her hip beneath the gently rounded bone, was her name, a crooked little heart, and Green's name, shimmering in dazzling gold.

"But how….," she asked as her struggling stopped and she became content to let them look at her with hot, dilated eyes and desire.

"You know how it happened," he chided. "Touch, blood, and song—it's how all strong magic happens." She groaned a little, and he moved his lips against her neck, enjoying this moment, this locked moment of wanting between the four of them, very, very much.

"Green," she said with as much attitude as she could muster, "that wasn't blood."

Bracken whispered, "Cory, you're killing me," and Nicky said "ungh" again.

"Even better," Green said smugly, knowing that if he didn't have her around the waist, her knees would buckle, because she was melting against him—against his thighs, against his erection, a puddle of want coating his skin. "It's made of the same animal essence, but it's given freely, given in pleasure, and the song written in touch with it will bind the wearer so tightly to her lovers that she'll be safe from—"

"From unbeing?" She came out of the spell of desire just enough to sound curious and sharp about this. Then he kissed her neck again and she whimpered.

"From about anything," he said and then looked up with smoldering eyes at Bracken and Nicky. "You need to think of her names," he told them. "All of them—good, bad, silly…. If he tries to get her with blood, she needs to be so tightly bound with all the ways we know her that her body wouldn't even think of unmaking itself, right?"

They nodded, eyes still locked on that glowing strip of bare skin. The two of them, so different, so alienated in January, actually swallowed in tandem.

"When?" Bracken asked coherently.

"Nine days," Green said. "The equinox is coming—Oestre. It's a powerful day for us on its own—life, rebirth, redemption, resurrection. It will give us a boost." For fun, he ran his hands down to her hips, letting her shirt fall, then continuing down the front of her thighs before wrapping his fingers around the inside of her legs, palms against her skin.

The two other men shuddered.

"What do we do?" Nicky asked, sounding like he was trying to keep it together.

"Resume our lives until then?" Green answered, lips trailing along Cory's throat. "You go back to school and we keep as safe as we can. We've defeated him a couple of times now—he's wary. Some vigilance on our parts should serve us we...." He swallowed the last part of the word, he knew, but her skin... he had no stomach for planning and strategy when she was warm and confident in his arms.

"I mean what do we do *now*?" Nicky asked pitifully, but Green wasn't feeling particularly merciful tonight.

"Tonight we go to bed alone and beat off," Bracken said harshly, but then he stood up and moved to where his beloved was practically lying vertically against Green, and bent to kiss her so hard and so passionately that she actually moaned and shuddered, almost brought to climax by the taste of his tongue in her mouth. Then he was gone, quickly enough that Green's hair fluttered with his passing. Nicky came to her too, touching lips gently, rubbing the side of his nose against her cheek, teasing her until Green couldn't stand it anymore and brought his hand to cup their lover's head and pull him in for a kiss that would arouse as much as it teased. When she whimpered again, pleading, Nicky pulled away and Green swung her up into his arms and blurred to his bedroom. Nine days from now, they would be together, skin to skin, and it would be mind-blowing, amazing, and shattering. Tonight she was writhing with passion, with feeling, with life, with want for all three of them. Tonight she was his.

CORY
The Winder and the Swift

I SAT in Hallow's office, looking at that generic brown-framed government clock accusing me of wasting its little clicks, and sighed. Two minutes down, twenty-eight to go. I adjusted my knitting, wiggled into the horrible orange Naugahyde chair that I was sitting in sideways, and resolved to beg for mercy.

"Hey," I said on a deep breath, making him jump. He was just settling down to lunch and grading a stack of essays on the difference between male and female neuron responses and how they affected sexuality, and for a moment I felt the weight of being such a shitty and reluctant client descend on me full force. He actually had a *job* to do on this campus, and then he had me to look forward to. On that note, I tried again.

"I'm sorry." I looked at him and shook my head. "Look—can we do this next week? Today I'll just sit here and let you enjoy your lunch, okay? I mean… I know why everybody is worried about me, right? I am young. For the things…." A vision of Bracken lying on that power bubble, and the knowledge that only Green and I could save him, slid in front of my eyes. I blocked it out. "For the things I've had to do, the responsibilities I've taken on, I'm young and inexperienced, and I wasn't exactly… brimming with self-confidence when I became a part of this in the first place. I acknowledge that. I realize that I've been trying to be all 'human' on campus and 'supernatural woman' off campus, and that's dumb. You can't put yourself in boxes any more than you can put other people in boxes. I tried to put Green and Bracken and Nicky in boxes, and that was dumb too. Green was my 'gentle lover' and Bracken was 'the guy I fought with' and Nicky was 'the friend' and we'd just ignore the once-a-month sex—but Bracken is gentle and I fight with Green and I want Nicky to be a bigger part of my life, and you just can't define things like that. Friends are friends whether they're human or werecat or Martian, and lovers are lovers, and you can't minimize them or write them off of a whole emotional range just because it makes it easier for your poor simple overloaded human brain to deal with. You can't wrap up your friends and emotions in cubbyholes, because there aren't enough cubbyholes, and you want more and more and more and more—and soon you're just like the Hollow Man, coming apart at the seams, unmaking everything you touch just because you want everything whole and perfect and to be a part of it in the worst way. So I understand all that. I understand that I'm going to need to talk to you, and that you'll help me feel better about my screwups, and that I can't talk about my screwups to Green and Bracken—because they are, bless them both, stupid in love with me and don't see them until I'm catatonic, and then it hurts them so much to help me that I feel bad all over again—so you're going to be very necessary in the future, and I thank you for it. But not today. Today I'm tired, and I'm sad, and I'm scared and terrified and excited all at once, and I just want to sit and let it wash all over me until I'm clean and ready for what I need to do next, okay? So can we not play the whole 'emotional dentist' thing? Today I'll just be a kid knitting in your office, and you'll get to eat your lunch in peace."

Hallow sat quietly through my request, and I could swear he was trying not to laugh. Finally, after a few attempts to speak, he just shook his head, breathed out through his nose, and said, "Absolutely, Lady Cory. You're under no obligation to work anything out with me today."

I nodded happily and gave him a pleased smile, then turned back to Green's sweater. We did our things for a few blissful moments of silence until Hallow spoke, and I was the one who jumped this time.

"Is that it? Is that 'The Sweater'?"

Of course Bracken had told him about it. He'd gone first today and was waiting outside with our honor guard. "Yeah," I sighed. "I hope he likes it. I mean...." This was embarrassing to voice. "I hope all the weirdness" (pain) "that I was going through doesn't make it... hurt or anything when he wears it."

"Here." Hallow stood up and moved so he could run his hands over the fabric I'd worked on during that awful day. Eventually he shook his head and gave the fabric one last stroke. "Mmm... no," he said. "Love, sadness, melancholy, confusion... a desire to keep him safe... but nothing he wouldn't want to touch from you." He returned to his desk, while I shook my head and went to go with my first instinct and frog the whole thing. "Stop!" he commanded, and I raised my eyebrows at him.

"Sadness, melancholy, confusion?" I asked. "Do you think that's not going to hurt him to touch?"

"How many times does he have to tell you he loves all of you before you believe it?" he asked bluntly, and I swore and sighed and put my needles back in place and started knitting again.

"Fine," I muttered. "Like he hasn't had a sad enough time of it in two lousy millennia of living."

"We live with it or we die, Cory," Hallow said evenly. "Give him credit for knowing which side of the fence he wants to be on."

I swallowed and worked my cable needle. "It's awful," I said after a moment. "Knowing that I'm the one keeping him here. It's scary and awful. I'm so fragile, and he's so badly needed, and I can't hardly bear the idea that his existence is pinned on the hope that I will live."

Hallow sighed, and I looked at him in surprise. His sky blue eyes were glistening, and his beautiful alien features were lined with pain. "You're very astute," he said after a moment. "And you were right to keep that particular observation to yourself. And now to me."

I nodded again and felt a few tears slip down my cheek before I dashed them away with the sleeve of my bright green Sac State sweatshirt. Silence descended again, but this time when Hallow broke it, I was glad of the interruption.

"So are you going to make a sweater for Nicky?" he asked, and I shrugged, because I'd been fretting over this triviality for a month.

"I would," I said hesitantly, "but the elves wear such classic stuff it's easy to spend a month or two on it. Nicky's so trendy, you know? I'd hate to work on something forever only to have Nicky look at it and think, 'Mmm… not really me, but I'll wear it to make her happy.' I think I'll make him a throw or something."

"That is a dilemma," Hallow said wisely. "But sweaters are so much more personal than blankets. He might be hurt if you go that way. How about a vest? Not quite so much work, and you can make something trendy before it goes out of style."

I brightened. "That is an excellent idea," I said happily, and now the quiet lasted for the next fifteen minutes while I knit and let my mind focus on a brightly colored wool vest with cables, a V-neck, and nifty sleeve finishing. He'd love it.

When our time was over, I stood up and stretched and Hallow walked me to the door, opening it for me with a rather sly "Thank you so much for your time today, my lady—I think we really had a productive session."

Everybody in the hallway heard him, and I smiled gratefully. Only the two of us would ever have to know that I had begged for mercy and weaseled out of any therapy today.

As we trotted out of the C-shaped English building, I went left toward physics and Bracken, Nicky, and Renny went right, toward the gym.

I stopped in confusion. "Oh. I hadn't thought...."

"You met her because it was something you wanted to do for yourself, right?" Bracken said implacably.

"Well, yeah... but I didn't even bring my clothes or my shoes...."

"I did," he said without blinking. "I brought Renny's too." Renny grimaced at him, and I could tell that she hadn't known this.

"Oh." We'd been so broken the week before, I hadn't thought about it. Apparently everybody else had. I tried to think of a rational reason why I shouldn't run today, and nothing came to mind. "Okay." And off we went.

Later, as I was trotting around the track, my iPod playing Green Day's "Jesus of Suburbia" for this lap, it occurred to me—obvious, I know—that Hallow was an elf, and elves couldn't lie. This meant he'd been telling the truth about our "really productive session," as he'd called it—and now, thinking back on what I'd said, I found myself flushing self-consciously and suppressing a giggle. Renny looked at me from her quiet padding at my side, and I shrugged, not wanting to put it into words.

That evening, Grace and I were working in the back of the store at the class table, untangling twisted hanks of yarn and winding it into balls so they wouldn't be tangled when the customers bought them— or rather, Grace was winding them, because I often got impatient when setting the hanks up on the swift and the resulting tangle was a yarn lover's nightmare. My job was looking through our stock to see what needed to be wound, and relabeling the wound yarn with all the pertinent info. Grace's job was to put the yarn on the umbrellalike swift that kept it taut for winding, feed it to the ball winder, then wind the ball. It was sort of a fun thing to do, actually—an interim thing, a setting up of the working materials before they were used, and it was soothing to watch the swift whir around and the ball of yarn spin and grow. We had worked companionably for a little while—both of us had plenty on our minds, I was sure—when we heard a customer ask Renny, who was at the register, where Chloe was this evening.

"I don't know," Renny said in her quiet, polite way.

"Well, I have to tell you that I'm sort of relieved," the woman said confidentially. "Sometimes she's just so angry. I love this place. It needs to be happy here."

Renny and I met guilty eyes across the store, and I carefully avoided looking at Grace as I dumped what looked to be the last load of miswound skeins on the table in front of her.

"She's right," Grace said quietly, "she's right. Chloe... I.... When she was a little girl, she'd never let a grudge go. I thought... I thought it would be something that would mellow as she got older, but it hasn't...." She took a deep, cleansing breath and tried again. Grace was often loud in her joy and self-contained in her grief. I had seen her be both. Tonight she was being self-contained, keeping her pain in her chest, and I knew from experience that keeping it in hurt more—but she needed to talk before she needed to cry, and maybe she didn't even need to cry with me.

"It's what brought her here, you know," Grace went on, setting a hank of truly amazing hand-dyed merino lace-weight on the wooden umbrella swift and threading it through the winder. Slowly she began winding, keeping her movements in careful check because the Goddess's speed didn't always work with plain God's physics. "Her damned bulldog tenaciousness just wouldn't let her let this go... but it's what's killing her here. She's too inflexible for us. She's not happy, I'm not happy...." Grace gave a controlled sniff. "She's going to have to go, isn't she?"

And for the first time, I felt the true and personal weight of leadership descend on my chest. Green and I had made a decision, and now it was going to affect our friend, and she was going to abide by it because that was who we were. It wasn't life or death, it wasn't supernatural power, it was the life of a friend, and I had to live with it and it really sucked.

"Yeah," I said after a laden moment. "Yeah. She's going to have to go." Grace nodded, keeping her back to me as she kept up that controlled movement with the winder and the swift.

"But Green and I were hoping we could let the boys keep their memory... maybe come visit once a year, if that's okay." Grace let a breath out with a big shudder, and I thought it would be safe to add the rest. "And... and if you can have them in the hill eight nights from now...."

"For the protection spell?"

"Oh, jeez... does everybody know about that?"

And now a sound came out that sounded like a snork of laughter through painful tears. "Yes, Cory, we all know about that. I can't believe you're surprised."

"Only at how fast the news travels," I said. "We just thought this up last night."

Grace turned toward me, her face conspicuously devoid of bloody tears. "Well, I'm pleased that you thought of me and the boys," she said evenly, begging me not to make this a big deal. "And I'll do my best to get them there. And the night after that, Phillip and Marcus and I will take care of Chloe—wipe her memory, have the people up in Redding do the same with her husband—and we'll send them all on their way."

She sounded so matter-of-fact, but I knew this was hurting her. "We'll do it—Green will, I mean," I said, and she nodded. Tentatively I stepped forward and held out my arms, tilting my head to let her know that if she didn't feel like letting go on me, walking away was an option. She smiled just a little and caught me up in a ferocious hug, and I hugged her back just as ferociously. "I'm so sorry," I whispered. "I'm sorry we couldn't be more for your family."

"Oh, sweetie...." She sniffled against my shoulder. "Don't you know by now that *this* is my family?"

"Good," I said. "Good." And we hugged and hugged and held, until the service bell rang again and duty called and I didn't think she could do this anymore without crying and the copious cleanup that would require. We separated and she gave me a motherly peck on the cheek, and then she turned back to her work. I went to move some more inventory from the back of the store to the front to give her some space, and our night pattered on. As I wove my way between the shelves of yarn and the bolts of cloth and books I heard a familiar voice in my head.

"Well done, beloved."

"Thanks, Green," I thought back. *"You know I only learn from the best."*

Right before closing time, we sent Bracken out for food while Renny and I counted the drawers in the back, and Renny brought up my appalling lack of privacy again.

"So... what is it?" she asked, looking at me sideways from cat-curious eyes.

"What's what?" Even when I was working at the Chevron, money counting had taken me a while, and some poor college student had cashed in her coin jar to buy a skein of Lorna's Laces to make her girlfriend a pair of socks. I'd contemplated learning how to make socks, but Bracken and Green were size eighteens at least—and even that wouldn't have stopped me, but unless it's deep snow, they abhor shoes. I'd make them for Nicky, but he tended to lose things in trans, and I didn't know how unglued I'd come if I spent two weeks on a pair of wool socks only to have them disappear into the ether.

Renny came to a pause in her counting and waited for me to do the same. "What's the big 'ritual' that you guys are doing on the equinox?" She spoke sotto voce, but everybody's hearing was so acute I was wondering why the two nymphs working up front didn't run into the back to hear the answer.

I shrugged, trying to be neutral. "You know… usual gang bang…. No big."

I expected Renny to snark or to make some bad, blunt pun—but she just looked at me, troubled, until I was forced to look back at her. Max had moved his stuff into her room, and Green had given him a special place to keep his guns and other assorted cop paraphernalia since he was going to keep his job as long as possible—even I had to keep my gun as far from the fey in the hill as I could. (It was in a safe made of old oak, behind my shoe rack where Bracken couldn't touch it.)

Renny looked good. Her tawny hair had been brushed smooth and braided, and she was wearing my collared gold-yarn sweater, which the sprites had cleaned since the funeral. (It was one of Renny's favorites, but if I outright gave it to her, or knit one for her, she'd move on to other items in my closet.) She had even put on a pound or two, so her piquant little face looked softer, and in general she no longer looked like one of those lost faerie children climbing out of the brush and getting ready to disappear on the wind like a bubble.

"What?" I asked, wondering at this seriousness.

"That's not really how you think of it, is it?" Suddenly I felt like the weight of her happiness depended on my answer.

I thought carefully. "Only when I'm not with one of them. When I'm with them, it feels like…." I remembered that moment in the kitchen—with Green's touch behind me and Bracken's in the front, with Nicky's taste in my mouth and the smooth muscles of taut arms wrapping me in sex and cocooning me in want—and nothing seemed wrong, nothing at all, as long as the lot of us were fused together and sated. I jerked my attention back to Renny and tried to still my breathing. "It feels like perfect," I said at last, feeling inadequate.

Renny grinned at me, and I realized she'd been cat so much in her short life that her canines were getting round and pointy. "Excellent," she said, and I had to laugh. "No, really!" she protested. "Because that's the night I wanted to bite Max, and I was sort of hoping it would be like...." She smiled dreamily and just a touch sadly. "I was so out of it when you guys made the Goddess grove, you know? But I remember that night. I don't remember who I was with, because unless it was Green all that mattered was that it wasn't Mitch, but I remember that it was awesome. I'd like Max to know what that feels like, you know? It's not an everyday thing."

I laughed again, and it was the sweetest, lightest sound that I think I'd made in a hundred years. "You're right," I agreed, feeling comfortable in my own skin for the first time since the night before. "It's definitely not an everyday thing." At least not yet.

"You're nervous," she stated wisely.

"Of course I'm nervous!" I said, going back to counting money. "Wouldn't you be?"

"Well, yeah—but I'm not you. You do things that terrify me frequently." She smiled slightly and went back to counting her drawer. "I mean, you took physics!"

"Yeah, well, that terrifies me too," I said. I was the sudden recipient of another one of Renny's smiles, and I was dazzled. Bracken and Green talk about what my smiles do to them, and I wondered if either one had seen this expression on Renny's face before, because if I'd been a man it would have made me weak in every knee but the "wee" one.

"I'm glad to hear it," she said happily. "I sure do like you more, knowing that you're not always as assured as you seem."

I was way too stunned to reply, and I watched Renny guilelessly count her drawer for another couple of heartbeats before I had the wherewithal to go back to my own business.

And suddenly I was grateful, more than grateful, that the Goddess had given me Renny, my catlike friend who would comfort me as a giant housecat or as a girlfriend and who knew me and who cared. She was more human than Chloe or Michelle or even than Davy, who had needed to think about her humanity. Renny never thought about what made her human or what made her not—she just responded to good or bad, and she thought I was good, and wasn't that all we need in a friend?

"Renny," I said, eyeing her teeny-tiny feet, "if I made you a pair of socks, would you remember to take them off before you turned cat?"

She thought about it, glanced at me, and nodded. "I'd make it a priority," she said, and I thought I'd take a look at Grace's sock yarn before we left.

But in spite of Renny's assurance that it was okay to be nervous, and in spite of the men's best efforts to keep me on an even keel and not to tax out my poor, warped emotional operating systems, the next days crawled by like slugs on quaaludes. Every time one of them touched me—if Nicky bumped my hand as he walked down the hall, if Bracken spooned me in sleep, if Green rubbed my calf as I sat on the couch and studied—my heart would beat faster and the well between my thighs would gush and my nipples would tingle, and my body would go on instant high sexual alert. By unspoken consent we had all agreed to no sex after Green had taken me to bed that night (good night!), and the four of us were so high-strung and horny that the whole hill felt like it was hovering on the edge of a thunderous sex storm that would make the running of the grunion look like a game of fish pattycake.

The tension was at its worst on Tuesday night. The Kings were winning against Golden State in the background, and I sat edgily and tried to study with my back against the arm of the couch. Quiet as a sidhe's ghost, Bracken walked up behind me and put a hand on my shoulder, and I shrieked loud enough to wake a vampire in the daytime. Green was with an appointment—"no sex" between the four of us couldn't possibly stop those—and tonight he was with Ellen Beth, who, it looked like, might just decide to live. However, Nicky, LaMark, Mario, Arturo, Grace, Renny, and Max were all relaxing in the front room with me, and they all about smacked the ceiling with their feet—knocking over board games and half-filled soda cans and sending a book flying into the air to hit the low-hung ceiling fan and get shot against the back wall of the kitchen.

We all watched the book rebound in a splatter of paper and fall on the blue-tiled floor face-first, its pages rumpling beneath it in abandon. I tried to apologize but was giggling too hard to get it out.

"I'm... I'm so... sorr... so... oh, fuck it...." I buried my face against my knees and howled with laughter, and everybody's obvious disgust as they cleaned up the mess made me laugh even harder. Finally the last giggle bubbled out, and I risked a look up. The room had emptied and it was only Bracken and me. He was sitting on the end of the couch looking at me sympathetically, his hand hovering above my shin like he was getting ready to rub my leg but was afraid to.

I looked at him, not even sure what expression was on my face, and he nodded reassuringly, like he was soothing a wild animal. "Is it okay if I touch you?"

"Please do." I tried to smile, also reassuringly—but again, I wasn't sure what came out.

His hand came down and rubbed my shins through my jeans, then my calves, and I sighed a little and melted into the couch.

"That's nice," I murmured.

"You've done this before," he said, not referring to his hands passing heat through my jeans.

"It's scarier this time," I said, not talking about that either.

"What makes it scarier?" His face seemed to catch the shadows— what few there were in Green's warm, well-lit sitting room—and there, his eyes and mouth were darker and grimmer than I knew them to be. But he still didn't look as scary as the feeling of what the four of us would do.

I didn't even need to think about this one. "Part of it is the premeditation. It's killing me. Green, Adrian, and me? It was all spontaneous, at least to me. I mean, they could have been planning positions like generals planning attack strategies—but to me, it was all a surprise. This... this just seems so cold-blooded, that's all."

"Sort of like... I don't know... date night?" he asked meaningfully, and I cringed.

"Ouch," I said, humbled.

"You did that for me," he said frankly. "Don't feel bad, but we don't need it anymore. You'll find your balance with Nicky—and honestly, I think this will help. But as for the rest of it, don't sweat it. It's just touch." He continued the rubbing, moving down to my bare feet and managing to rub sensuously without tickling. "That's all sex is, you know, pleasurable touch."

"Touch squared," I said, trying not to be uncomfortable and squeamish, and... and human. "When you touch me... when we touch...

it's like…." I remembered that day after we'd registered for school. "It's like freefall, Bracken—from the tallest, rockiest cliff on the planet. When I touch Green, it's like riding a whale from the depths of the ocean to the top of a jump and crashing into the surf."

"What about Nicky?" he asked curiously. I searched for an analogy and found one right outside the door.

"It's like walking outside and smelling spring—not quite so spectacular, but lovely, you know?" He nodded, pleased with the comparison, and I went on. "But the thing is… any one of these things is huge and exciting. Cliff diving onto a whale on the first day of spring is going to be a little overwhelming."

His shoulders shook with laughter, and then I had to laugh, pressing the back of my hand against my mouth so it wouldn't get hysterical. When we were done, his hands had moved to the backs of my knees. "Yeah," he agreed when the laughter had passed, "but remember that when the whale has jumped and spring arrives and you've fallen off that cliff—we'll all be there to catch you."

"Yeah," I nodded, feeling a little better.

"Can I hold you without freaking you out?" His hands stilled on my knees, and I wondered if we all had really been so high-strung that we'd forgotten the simple act of just laying our bodies parallel and breathing in tandem.

"God, Bracken, I wish you would." He stretched full-length on the couch and I lay on top of him, savoring his warmth and the hardness of his chest under my cheek and the scent of sun-heated rock that was all Brack.

"So," he said overcasually, "what's your Adrian analogy?"

I had to think for a bit, to remember—maybe because I just hadn't been that good with analogies before Adrian had died, or maybe because he'd been gone for almost a year and analogies were the first things to go—but I came up with one. "It was like sitting outside on a perfect summer night, and staring up at a billion bright stars, and his touch was like a breeze just north of cool, and climax was like reaching up to the stars and clutching one, blazing bright and cold."

He thought about it, a slow smile spread over his usually grim, alien features. "Yeah."

"Yeah?"

"Absolutely." There was a pause then. "Are you still scared?"

"I'm never scared when one of you is with me. Even Nicky."

"I'd think especially Nicky," he said, and I made a "hm?" noise, so he continued. "Lots of people are afraid of cliff diving, of whales, of swimming in the ocean. Not a lot of people are afraid of evening in the spring."

"I'm going to make him a vest," I said, hoping Bracken would understand what this meant and why it was important.

"I think that's very wise," he replied, so I guess he did.

"It was Hallow's idea."

"And listening to him is very wise too."

Lying on my beloved was lovely—so restful, so perfect, that I sailed off to sleep, listening to his heartbeat, not afraid of anything, least of all being touched by the men who loved me.

School was difficult the day of the ritual, and damned if I could remember what, if anything, I learned. I don't think I was alone, though.

We'd weighed the risk of the Avians being exposed to Hollow Man versus the likelihood of them accidentally bonding. Most supernatural creatures didn't even know about Avians, and they were unlikely to be on Hollow Man's radar, so we decided it would be best if the Avians all bunked at the aerie on ritual night.

Given all that, LaMark and Mario watched in some amusement as Bracken walked into a metal light pole while he was watching me trip over the bike racks next to it. Renny kept leaving a book or a jacket or a water bottle in each class, and she was actually tired after our run because she kept scampering to her previous locations to get her stuff— and Nicky apparently spaced out during their Elizabethan Lit class and, according to Renny, the professor had to wave a hand in front of his eyes and jump up and down to ask him a simple question about Henry VI. (Nicky grumpily explained that he was an old English guy who had died early after living a very wimpy life that somehow provided fodder for three plays—I figured I'd ask Green about him later.)

It was still light when we came home, but I practically ran out of the SUV as it pulled up because we'd caught every possible red light on our way out of Sacramento and then had caught the worst of the traffic between Roseville and Auburn. We were late for banquet, and one of my day's mishaps was to step into the world's largest puddle—the one everybody avoided because it was really a pothole by the bike racks in the center of the quad—and I was covered in mud. Bracken had taken the twisty part between Auburn and Green's hill so quickly that I felt bruised from fighting the centrifugal force trying to fling the SUV off the road.

I was breathless and flustered as I buzzed through the almost full sitting room on my way to the hall, waving a hello to everybody there and pausing only long enough to ruffle Graeme's and Gavin's hair and tell them how glad I was to see them. Steph and Joe were their keepers tonight, and Joe was entertaining the boys with different dog sounds while they waited for Grandma to wake up. He could bark as well in human form as he could when he was a big Labrador retriever—the boys were riveted.

I told the kids to do *exactly* what they were told, and made sure Steph and Joe knew that the boys needed to be spelled to sleep as soon as they'd eaten and been put in one of the guest bedrooms with a secure door. Then I scurried away down the hall to my room, where I tore off my clothes in record time and hopped in the shower.

The shower was the best part of my day. It's impossible to be pounded by hot water without letting some of the tension seep out your feet, and Bracken (or our little sprite and brownie housekeepers) had been very conscientious about putting some really soothing smells in our soap—chamomile, aloe, ocean breeze, whatever. It was less sweet and more real than the stuff you buy in stores, and tonight it did its job and chilled me right out.

Suddenly time was not an issue, and I spent long enough in the water that it was probably dark when I got out.

My mind wandered during my marathon shower, and I let it. I was dressing in front of the bathroom vanity, staring dreamily at my own reflection, having just about gotten to where I'd completely forgotten about what was going to happen after banquet, when Bracken walked in. I smiled at him, feeling relaxed about it. He was Bracken and I loved him, and my body was quiet with the shower, and it gave him a big happy hello as I saw him in the mirror.

"Hey," he said. He took the comb from my fingers and started grooming me like a big gorilla, twirling little ringlets around his fingers, making the whole thing a mess of curls around my face.

"Hey," I said back and let him do his thing. He bent and kissed the nape of my neck, and I shivered and dropped my head to give him better access. He continued, kissing down the backs of my shoulders, then down the curve of my spine. I was wearing a black dress with a mandarin collar and an open back (the better to show off my tattoo), and nearly every kiss hit bare, sensitized skin. I made "mmmmnnn" noises, and he straightened a little and unhooked the collar. The front of the dress fell forward. I wasn't wearing a bra, and he put his hands on my naked breasts from behind me, pinching my nipples ever so gently as he did so, and I tried futilely to keep my clothes on my body. I ended up trapping my dress against his hands with my own hands, and as he moved his palms in circles I made a strangled sound in the back of my throat.

"You know…," he whispered in the hollow of my ear, "I saw this comedian once…."

"If he wasn't telling a dirty joke, I don't see where this is going…."

"Give me a chance…." He nipped my earlobe, and I gave up the dress struggle. Then I was just facing the naked top half of my little ol' body and his giant beautiful self in the mirror. I looked at him—it was easier—and tried to capture my dress as he unzipped it the rest of the way and slithered it down my hips. "So anyway, this guy was talking about the death penalty and how we needed to make it more humane…."

"This is so romantic," I said, but I couldn't summon any sarcasm because he'd pulled me back against him, and I was wearing pantyhose and nothing else now against the roughness of his jeans. Even through his jeans, he was as hard as a rock, and suddenly banquet seemed like a burden I couldn't bear.

"Hush…. What he said was that instead of making someone wait and wait and wait, just knowing they're going to die—because that would be awful—we should just pop our heads into their cells one night and take care of business… bang… the end. That the anticipation was the most awful part…." As he was talking, his hands slid from my breasts down to my now flat stomach, then under my pantyhose as he started the top rolling down past the V at the juncture of my thighs that I refused to see in the mirror, and then they were down my thighs, and he stepped on them and hauled me up by main strength until they popped off my feet. I let him. I reveled in his hands on my waist—then they slithered down again to palm my inner thighs, and my brain was torn between going completely bye-bye and trying to figure out what he was telling me. He turned me in his arms and kissed me gently, teasingly, pulling back from me when I wanted more, kissing the corners of my lips, my chin, using his long fingers to tease my spine, my hip, the cleft of my bottom, and I was almost in tears because I wanted him so badly that the world seemed to stop breathing just so my skin could beg for his touch.

He picked me up, wrapping my legs around his waist, and my tender, aroused sex was abraded by his jeans. He carried me into the bedroom, and I tried to make some sort of protest—we had things to do, and then we had things we *must* do, and it wasn't going to be like this, not just the two of us, not spontaneous, not wonderful…. With another part of my brain, I heard my door open and close quickly, and before I could look up and see who had come in, Bracken laid me on the bed and kissed the hollow of my throat. Now my eyes crossed under kissed lids with the effort to not lose myself.

"Cory…," he said slyly.

"Mmmmnnnnnnmmmmmmmm?" I wanted to be lost.

My beloved smiled, pulling back just enough for me to see his lazy grin.

"Bang," he said, and Green and Nicky joined us on the bed.

ARTURO
Yarn Over

ARTURO NEVER let Grace know how hard it was to get Chloe to leave the boys there that night.

Chloe skewed up the driveway in her pale, colossally sized Toyota Tacoma just as Arturo was finishing his walk of the land. He had been making preparations for the banquet all day and had put off his walk until the very end—for one thing, he wanted to be fresh and strong for the ceremony that night. When he'd been a god, they'd had many such ceremonies, and he'd reveled in them. The only thing that gave a god more energy than his subjects fucking each other blind was the slew of joyous births that followed, and he'd always been enthusiastically in favor of both events. There had been other gods who'd taken more joy in spilled blood than in touch, blood, and song, but blood magic without the touch and the song was dark magic, frightening and uncontrollable, and Arturo had always tried to be a merciful god.

He'd be the first to admit, though, that in the merciful god department, he didn't hold a candle to Green.

For instance, he would have killed Chloe weeks ago for torturing his beloved the way Chloe had been torturing Grace. But then Grace would never have forgiven him, so it was probably a very good thing that Arturo wasn't in charge. That's what he'd told himself when Green had changed the power flow in the hill, and nothing had happened since to change his mind. Cory's ups and downs didn't bother him—she was young, and just as it had been hard for him to adjust to being a subordinate to Green, it would be difficult for her to adjust to being a goddess. Arturo had no doubts whatsoever that Cory would someday achieve immortality, but unlike Green, he was not looking forward to the day. He'd seen it happen before, to humans he'd loved, and he knew that the Goddess had a way of balancing the universe. Not one of the humans who'd become immortal wouldn't have traded their immortality for the thing they'd sacrificed to get it. Not one. The problem was, the immortality was usually a sort of consolation prize, given for something *truly* valuable, and Arturo didn't want to see Cory go through that sort of pain. But he did want to serve under her for longer than a mortal lifetime, so he wasn't planning on telling any of them about his doubts.

And speaking of sacrifices....

Chloe squealed to a halt, spewing gravel, and threw herself out of the truck with force. If he'd told her then that she looked exactly like her mother, she might have lunged for his throat, but it was true nonetheless—and even Arturo knew she had a right to be pissed, even if she couldn't put her finger on why.

He'd had to compel her over the phone, using all of the formidable power in his control, to get her to leave the boys for the night and then turn around and go back to the hotel she'd been staying at. Grace had been paying Chloe an absurd amount for working in the store in order to keep her nearby until the situation was settled. Chloe was in possession of dangerous knowledge, and unless her attitude toward her mother changed in a hurry, that was knowledge they were going to have to strip her of—because she couldn't be allowed to walk around knowing not only who lived at Green's hill, but how to get there as well. They had been lucky so far that she hadn't brought anyone who didn't belong there, but given her simmering anger, Arturo didn't know how long that situation would last.

So tonight, she'd been spelled to come and drop the boys off, and she didn't know why, and she didn't know why she couldn't resist the compulsion. That would have made Arturo angry too, but he still didn't sympathize with her. She'd hurt Grace, and that flushed all his sympathy down the crapper without queries, questions, or comments.

So now, as she stalked out of the car, Arturo approached Gavin and Graeme with a smile. He'd noticed that Graeme, the younger, was adventurous and precocious and oddly protective of his older brother, who did not share these traits. Graeme reminded him a lot of Grace, and Gavin was too sweet a child not to adore on his own. He did not spare even a glance for Chloe, not even when he thanked her perfunctorily for bringing the boys.

"Why do they need to be here, Arturo?" Her voice was waspish, and now he eyed her with distaste.

"You've put them in danger by tracking your mother down. We're doing something tonight that will keep them safe."

"Does my mother know I'm not invited?" She gave him a look that was pure Sixth Grade Queen Bee, and he had a moment's remorse. She could have been so much like Grace, if only she had chosen the right parts of her character instead of the angry parts.

"Yes," Arturo answered levelly, making sure she understood the full implications. Her lips parted and her eyes widened, and for a moment, just a moment, he could see the hurt child that she had been.

"You're lying," she denied.

"I can't lie," he said, surprised. "It would make me ill." He thought for a moment. "The vampires, they can lie... and so can the weres, but to my knowledge they try not to. Nobody wants an unfair advantage here."

Her eyes had narrowed, and she was suddenly pure bitch again. "I don't know what in the hell you're talking about."

"You don't want to know." He bent down to the boys and winked conspiratorially. "Hey—your grandmother wants you to go upstairs and wreck your dinner with whatever's in the refrigerator. I think Joe and Steph are up there, if you want to go see...." It was apparently what they wanted to hear, because Graeme gave him a hug, Gavin jumped up and down, and they both raced up the stairs for the hamburgers and spice-fried potatoes he knew Grace had specially asked Joe and Steph to make for the boys. The fact was, the only one who thought the group of lovers would make it to banquet that night was Cory.

"Why wouldn't my mother want to protect me too?" Chloe asked, and now a little bit of sympathy actually slipped through.

"You don't want our protection, Chloe," he responded at his gentlest. "You don't want your mother's love. You want her to suffer for dying...."

"Leaving...."

"*Dying.*" He sighed and ran his hands through his black-as-black hair. "Your mother's story is legend, Chloe. She sat out on her porch for an entire summer and *longed*, simply *yearned* to live long enough to watch you grow up. Adrian flew by and heard that yearning from three hundred feet up, and landed and talked to your mother. His mother had sold him into slavery when he was a child. Your mother, with her fierce love, her yearning to see you grow into a woman, she enchanted him. And she almost didn't make it after her transition—that part we don't talk about. She almost died of a broken heart until she took on the whole hill as her children, and we let her. We *loved her* for it. And now here you are, talking of pain and anger, and you're taking the love she had for you and your sister—the love that has made the lives of our entire hill wonderful—and you're spitting it back in her face. What you don't understand is that this time, you may break her heart, but you won't break her—because if you don't want her love, we'll take it. We'll *revere* that love. It is you who will yearn and yearn and yearn and not realize that you're the one who killed what you wanted most."

Chloe took in a sharp breath and looked longingly after her children as though she wished she could go snatch them from the doorway and take them far, far away. "This isn't my fault," she whispered.

"Tell your mother," Arturo bit out. "You've broken her heart, and I've had to pick up the pieces."

"You're too young for her," she was searching for reasons to be angry, and this one was too absurd for words.

"I'm actually much older," he understated. Then, more seriously, "Your mother's illness was not your fault, and neither was her death. What you are doing with your chance to know her now? That is entirely on you, little girl. You may either grow up, or grow old without her, but make your mind up quickly."

"Why? What can you people do to me?" But she was gnawing on her nail—a habit she had picked up from her mother, actually—and he knew she was not as insouciant as she appeared.

He told her the truth. It was all he could do, but he still regretted it later. "We can make you forget," he said simply, and watched her face whiten with shock. "Now go away," he ordered. Cory and the others were due home soon, and he didn't want them to worry about this situation. The hill was wound tightly enough as it was.

For a moment, the child Grace had loved stared nakedly out at him—and for a moment, he was tempted to love her as Grace did. She looked hurt and confused and desperate, and he'd seen that look on Cory's face too many times to just write Chloe off as a lost cause. But where Cory would have filled with resolve or remorse or compassion, when Chloe's expression changed, it did not change to understanding.

Her eyes narrowed and her lip curled, and Arturo realized he'd made a mistake somehow in his dealings with her, but he couldn't figure out where.

"You go ahead and make me forget, you bastard," she hissed. "But I'll be damned if you'll be able to forget about me." And with that, she jumped into the truck and peeled out of the driveway. Five minutes later, Bracken skidded into the driveway, and Arturo breathed a sigh of relief. They had just missed each other, and he could only be grateful.

The boys had eaten by the time Arturo got up there. After Cory's breathless greeting, he took them to a small guest room that he'd outfitted specially with a new Xbox and as many games as he could find, and sat down to play with them. For about half an hour he competed fiercely, listened to the boys cheer, and encouraged them to try again when they failed. Graeme was the better player, but Arturo noted he let his brother win sometimes. He thought for a moment of Adrian and Bracken and felt his heart sproing hard, like a tightly wound steel string breaking with resonance, and it was with great regret that he took the controls from Gavin and, while Graeme was setting up the next game, thought drowsy thoughts until the sandy brown eyelashes fluttered to his freckled cheeks and he flopped gently backward onto the bed next to him. Arturo finished the game (it was some game where wildly animated cars zoomed around a racetrack—he enjoyed it very much) and then moved Gavin up on the bed, listening to Graeme's indignant monologue on how *he* would *never* fall asleep when they were company, and how *he* wanted to see the vampires again more than anything.

"Well," Arturo said, feeling more than a little bit bad about this very necessary deception, "he may miss the vampires at banquet, but tomorrow there will be pastries downstairs, and I bet he'll see more sidhe and were-animals in one place than he's ever dreamed of."

Graeme took in an excited breath. "Will we? I like the were-animals... and the sidhe, too, of course, Arturo." He added that last dutifully—but Arturo knew that, to the little boy, sidhe were just odd-looking people. Still, he'd made the effort, and Arturo was touched.

"I'll tell you what, boy," he said gently. "Tomorrow when you wake up, I promise to take you with me when I walk the hill. I'll carry you and your brother on my shoulders and we can run like giants, and then you will enjoy the sidhe as much as the werecreatures, yes?"

"Is that a promise, Arturo?" Graeme asked wistfully. "Because Mom keeps promising to take us home. Dad's mad at her for staying so long, but she keeps staying here and staying here, and I like you and everything, but...." He bit his lip, an adult sadness creeping over his long-boned little-boy's face. Graeme had rusty brown hair and milk-chocolate eyes, and of the two of them, he was the most like Grace.

Arturo was determined to give him something wonderful to remember, because he had the feeling that Chloe would fester with bitterness, bad memory or no memory. Some people were just destined to nurse their own splinters until they infected the soul.

"That is a promise, little man," he said formally. "I *will* take you with me when I walk the hill—I'm not lying. Do you know what happens when we lie?"

Graeme shook his head gravely.

"We totally puke our guts out all over our shoes." Arturo suppressed a smile as he borrowed Cory's vernacular. An awed smile broke out over Graeme's features, and Arturo felt better for what he was about to do.

"Really?" the little boy asked, and Arturo nodded, accepting the spontaneous hug from him with another sproing in his heart.

"Really, truly," he said, and while Graeme's face was hidden over his shoulder, Arturo spelled him to sleep. The little head got heavy all of a sudden, and the breathing came evenly through the soft pink lips. Arturo leaned forward, taking Graeme's weight in the hand nearest the bed, and settled him down next to his brother. Then he eyed the two of them, side by side, breathing evenly, little pieces of his Grace, lodged in his heart just as surely. He begrudged every moment their mother spent with them that Grace would not.

By the time he emerged from the guest room, Grace was awake, frantically bustling around the kitchen, and the banquet was underway. Unless you had been born and raised sidhe, this particular banquet was no place for children. As Arturo came down the stairs, he found himself smiling at the various stages of dress and lack thereof among the diners. They would eat formally—Green had never favored the massive orgies that had been indulged in by Titania and Oberon, two rulers Arturo had never served under but had reason to particularly dislike—but there was no doubt in anybody's mind as to what would happen after they had eaten.

He smiled down the table at a shyly seductive Renny, dressed in emerald baby-doll satin. She blushed at Arturo's wink and then smiled coyly at a very nervous Max, who was wearing black jeans and a black silk shirt. Max smiled back at her, and he looked as besotted as Mitch ever had. Arturo was suddenly very, very glad he hadn't kicked the young cop out the past summer when he'd thought Max was in love with Cory. There was a core of decency to the man that Arturo had to respect, even if he'd found Max's sister too annoying to even be allowed to remember her night in the hill.

Arturo sat at the head of the table. Tonight he was the ranking leader—but everyone knew what Cory and her lovers were doing as they ate, and nobody cared who was leading the banquet, so Arturo felt free to sit back and watch the flirting, the seduction, the play of aggression and retreat that built up the static at a banquet until when the participants touched, the charge it released sent ripples of electricity through everyone else in the room.

At last Grace walked down the stairs wearing a cream-colored pantsuit with a flounced bottom and a tie that went right under her full, soft breasts, and Arturo got a hard-on that would have shattered solid rock.

Goddess, how he wanted that woman.

She was still bustling, ordering sprites and nymphs in serving and cleanup, although in breathless twos and threes and even (in the case of the vampires) in fives at the least, the banquet room had started clearing out. Cory had still been in the shower when Arturo left the boys' room, but Bracken had been about to open the door to her bedroom. He'd flashed a nervous, excited, sex-saturated smile as Arturo had passed, and Arturo had winked at him in turn, having every faith that the three men would manage just fine. And now he had no more thought for Bracken or Nicky or even Green and Cory, short of what their activities could give him now, if only his damned stubborn woman would leave things be for just this once.

He could wait no longer—the thundercloud feeling of anticipation was growing laden and heavy. He walked up behind Grace, giving a significant look to Bracken's mother, Blissa, who giggled at him and scurried away to be with Crocken, then grabbed Grace's hips and pulled her against him without subtlety or finesse.

"Woman, you are making me crazy!" he growled in her ear. He was rewarded with a sideways look from brown eyes, and a glance away. She hadn't fed—her skin stayed pale and cool—and the possibilities of that made his growl rougher.

"There's more to do…," she protested, and he kissed her neck, next to the dark red curls she'd sculpted against her head. He wanted to run his fingers through them and make them wild and hazy around her face, but first he had to get her into her room.

"It will be done when you rise tomorrow night…," he whispered into that hollow of her neck where the flesh was just so.

"You want me to just leave it?" She tried for asperity, but what came out was a breathless plea to let it be okay, this once, to serve herself before her family.

"Oh yes… by all means leave it," he rasped, the edge of impatience making the suggestion an order. He calmed himself down and tried another tack. "Or you could clean it up all by your lonesome while I watch you with hungry eyes… but in the meantime, Cory and her lovers are in her bed, and do you know what they're doing?"

"Unnhh?" Grace moaned. Arturo turned her toward the stairway, then whispered, in exact detail, how Cory was pleasuring and being pleasured by the three men who loved her most.

Grace beat him up the stairs and into her room, but not by much, and then he took charge. He loved her body—he would have loved it more if it had been warm, but her heart was so warm that he could live with the coldness of the skin. Her stomach was soft and baggy and carried the marks of two children on it—*Chloe, that snot, was ten and a half pounds… we had to break her collarbone to get her out of there*—and her breasts were softly stretched mouthfuls. Her skin, when she'd been alive, had been tinted with honey, and in death there was the memory of that warm gold in her freckles, in the brownness of her areolas, in the tan on the tops of her thighs and the backs of her hands that lingered after more than twenty years. Dusty sunshine, diet soda, sugar cookies, and cool lake water—all the things that Cory could taste when she tasted Grace's blood were there in the place between her thighs that wept when he kissed it, and kiss it he did. She closed her eyes when he tasted her, because she loved him and was afraid of what she'd see in his eyes if she opened them, and then he made her open them when he surged inside her into that cool, moist, tight place that gripped him and pulled at him until he wanted to pour his warmth into it and make it beat with the sound of his own heart. She groaned quietly, because she tried not to make much noise when their bodies were meshed and pounding, and he delighted in making her scream.

And he knew what she wanted now. She had fasted just for him, because he'd asked her to. Her eyes were flared in passion, and even as she moaned she was scenting his skin and the sweet, sweet elven ichor that ran underneath. She wanted... she wanted.... She clenched around him, begging with her body, and he heaved above her, his smile taunting.

"Say it," he demanded, his voice rough with sex.

"Please...." Grace was breathless, and her lip curled in a half smile that left her fangs extended. He grinned, wickedly feral, back at her.

"Say it...."

"*Goddess*.... Oh please...."

"What do you want?"

"I want to *feed*...." And with that she lunged upward, locking her teeth into his artery, clamping her lips down and drawing, needing him like mortals needed breath, and he screamed with the power of it....

And Cory came, the power washing through the walls of the hill, through their skin, into their loins, making them safe, making them whole. Making them climax like a strike of lightning, like thunder through their hearts, making them shudder and scream in each other's arms as the shivers of orgasm washed over them again and again and again, endlessly, until they lay, washrag limp and spent, Arturo's blood and sweat and come coating Grace like the life that she'd wanted badly enough to die for.

Arturo had to catch his breath, and when it was caught, he saw his beloved lying motionless. She usually breathed, because she was still a young enough vampire to have muscle memory that insisted she do just that, but now she simply lay more quiet than death—unblinking, unbreathing, unbeating—until Arturo kissed the skin at the crook of her arm just to make her gasp.

"Sorry...." She was full of his blood now, the sweetest of wines to a vampire, and she blushed with it. "I'm sorry, beloved...."

He drew in his breath, and she bit her lip—no fangs extended, just white teeth, sucked clean of his blood. "You never say that...."

"I should." She turned to face him, fine brown eyes clear and her face as soft as her body. "I should have called you beloved last summer, when we first... the night the Goddess grove was made," she said earnestly.

"Good night." He grinned, and she rolled her eyes.

"Exceptional," she said dryly. "Which would make tonight...."

Arturo shuddered delicately, like a cat, with too many emotions to count. "Spectacular," he breathed. "Terrifying. To bind people with loyalty, like they did this winter... that was something. But to bind them with *safety*...."

Grace nodded, a convulsive swallow working her throat. "It's the one promise a parent can't make to a child," she agreed, taking a self-conscious swipe at the blood trickling from her lips, then licking her fingers. "We can promise them good schools and love and time to play and allowance, but safety... the binding of flesh and blood against evil...." She shook her head. "It's haunting that we can't promise that."

"Yes." And he hadn't been able to filter the sadness out of his voice. She looked at him sharply, just looked, and he felt his misgivings unpacking themselves from his heart. "Their power, what they can do... it doesn't come without a price, Grace... and Green's pinned his hopes on her immortality...." His voice broke a little, and he was *shocked* because he'd thought he had contained these worries so well.

"Shhh...." She stroked the side of his face. "Sh...." She didn't try to reassure him beyond that, but when his breathing quieted, she smiled softly at him, tilting her face to the side as she lay on her back. "They will have children," she said, the hope in her voice painful to hear.

"Yes." He smiled brilliantly—silver caps, white teeth, hope.

"I want to raise their children. And if Cory becomes immortal, she can still keep having them, right?"

"Yes." He laughed a little with the sound of her glee.

"I will tend her children, one after another, into immortality, and you will be by my side," Grace proclaimed, as poetic as she ever became. She didn't even ask the question of the last part, and Arturo's smile became lazy and self-satisfied. At last, the woman believed she was his.

"Then we'll make it okay," she confirmed simply. "Whatever the sacrifice, we can have hope."

Arturo nodded. "And sex," he growled. The hill, the air, the walls, the earth... all of it cried out that the promise of flesh and power was still vibrating with impending fulfillment.

"Goddess, I hope so," Grace prayed. She moved to kiss him, to lick from his chin downward, to taste him, and the night spun on.

A breath away from dawn, she nudged him from a light sleep, and he groaned. "Beloved, it's almost time," she whispered.

"No," he said and wrapped his arms around her body, which felt warm now after all they'd done.

"Arturo...." She was getting stern. "You know what could happen if you're here at dawn." It had happened to Adrian and Cory—it had changed Cory's life forever.

"Mark me, woman," he growled against her neck. "Mark me, and mark me, and mark me, and maybe someday I'll trade my immortality for your life."

"Arturo!" she gasped and tried to wriggle to face him, but he wouldn't let her, and although both of them were supernaturally strong, he was older and stronger.

"Lie still," he said, surprised now to find his throat clogged with tears. He was three thousand years old, and he wept, on average, once every two hundred years. He had thought Adrian's death had wrung him dry. "Lie still, and I'll lie next to you, and we'll pretend we're like human lovers and that dawn is a time for hope."

"Oh...." No words. His beloved was caught without words, and that alone was worth having the mark of her soul with its sacrifices and pain and regret.

He leaned over, and she turned her head. He kissed her—long, lingering, playing with her fangs as they emerged, cutting his tongue on them, knowing the cuts would heal in a moment. They were kissing when dawn came, and she made a stunned, protesting sound. Then her flesh went still, and her soul, more beautiful and shining than the sun shearing through the canyon below the house, melted through him, and he could smell her and taste her and hear her rough voice in his blood and his veins and his pores and his heart....

He keened with loss when she was gone, and her body was deadweight in his arms. He kissed her cooling cheek and laid her down in the bed, arranging her so she would rise comfortably without mussed hair or a pillow dent in her cheek. Then he climbed out of bed and got dressed to walk the land. He went to wake the boys, and although Gavin mumbled and rolled over, Graeme forced himself to wake up. He perched on Arturo's shoulders and respected the request for silence, and the two of them rushed across the earth of the hill, the unlikely red dirt that sprouted soft green grass and amazing flowers in every color. Arturo would occasionally nudge him and give a quiet point when he saw the other sidhe greeting the dawn with quiet meditation and bare feet.

He saw Green and Bracken in the distance as he went walking, their gaits so companionable there could be no question but that they had shared something important the night before, but he didn't approach them. He would have told Graeme (had the boy asked) that he was too wrapped in his own thoughts. He told himself that he was still absorbing the alien texture of Grace's mark on his soul, the warmth of her that he did not get from her body. However, Green, had Arturo known it, had seen him wipe tears from his cheeks that he hadn't realized he shed; Graeme couldn't see his face from his perch in the clouds.

CORY
K4tog

I WAS naked and they were not, and our first few moments were a
breathless flurry of hands on jean buttons and wiggling out of socks and
tossing underwear onto the light fixtures until everywhere I turned was
smooth, warm skin over wiry or bulky or sleek muscles—until I felt
engulfed by them, swallowed by men, frantic with the need to feel their
skin all over mine.

I lost track of who had his mouth on my breast, on the softness
of my stomach, the sweetness between my thighs, but it went on and
on until my skin became electric like a field of buzz so the kiss on my
shoulder, my neck, my stomach was as exquisite as the tongue on my
nerve bundle, bursting with yes. I knew who was kissing me, and when
I tasted me squared on Bracken's lips after quivering to the point of
screaming as he delved into my center and tasted the firing of orgasmic
neurons, I groaned and whimpered, even with his tongue in my mouth.
I wanted to taste them too, but there was not enough of me, only one
mouth of me, only too much of my skin to be stroked, to be nipped, to be
pleasured and laved.

Bracken kissed me and kissed me until I was drowning in us. Then
I was rolled, turned, so that I was straddling his lap, and his body was
so deep inside of mine that I could feel him against my cervix—stopped
by the physical, pushing, trying to reach even farther. I howled into his
shoulder with the pleasure—the aching, wonderful pain of being invaded
by him—and then Green kissed the nape of my neck, and just knowing
what he was doing, where he was going to be, made the pressure of
power build in my womb, in my lungs, in my stomach, and he hadn't
even... I was being stretched... and he was almost going to breach my
other entrance, going to....

Oh Goddess, there he was... and he was inside of me. They were
inside of me, and they were moving, and the world was fracturing and
the power was building, and stronger and stronger and *oh Goddess* my

lungs were crushed, my body was crushed, my sex was crushed... *Christ, let me... oh... please...* by the weight of their bodies, they were... *oh... ah gods...* inside of my body, the coming together of lovers, beloveds, *ou'e'hm* and *due'alle*, the unity of us....

And Nicky, *ou'e'alle*, lover who owed me his allegiance, touched my hair from the side, and I almost wept because I knew the logistics, the plain necessity of the coming together of the four of us, and I couldn't do it—it was too much—and my control began to splinter, and my body began to shake, and a helpless scream of unraveling was loosening in my chest, and the power threatened to burst me, to explode from my skin like deadly rain, and if I had to, *if I taste... I can't... oh, don't make me... I need... I need....* The glow of my panic was pressing against me, tinting Bracken's skin with blue—*no, no no no.... Please Nicky, give me some....*

...And then Nicky did an amazing thing.

He turned my head to the side, and he kissed me.

Such a simple thing, a kiss—his tongue, tasting of me, tasting of Green, slipping into my mouth—and I was suddenly not just a vessel for power, not just an explosion of pleasure, I was me again, I was me with the men I loved, and we were rising, rising, building, crashing, crescendoing, exploding into climax—and the scream I loosed into his mouth wasn't unraveling, it was becoming....

Safe... whole... united... I thought, and the pressure built in my chest like a cosmic tidal wave unleashed on a solar system, and my body shook with the force of orgasm. The four of us, bound up in my body, released power that rolled in electromagnetic pulse waves throughout the hill... and rolled and rolled and pushed through the bodies of the men into the bodies under the hill, binding everybody we loved, all those under our protection, through their skin, into their blood, inoculating them against the infection of anger, of wanting, of endless soul-wrecking need that was our enemy, and binding them within their own selves, individual, impervious to being breached or violated. We were safe, those under this hill, we were safe and I was still in the freefall of orgasm, still riding the shaking, trembling, crashing wave of the holy dark. I became aware that Green was whispering to me, his chest smooth and warm against my back; that Bracken was whispering to me, and my hands were clenched in his shoulders, his skin soft against the hard muscles and collarbones; and that Nicky had broken off the kiss and had splashed over my body, against my side, when I had invaded the hill with sex. I had done it, we had done it, we had come together as one, and they were catching me, they were holding me, and I was still myself.

I collapsed forward against Bracken, drained of everything, including the will to move. My eyes closed, and I was dimly, only dimly, aware of the wetness running down my thighs, in the cleft of my bottom, and against my side, and of busy fingers tracking it over my skin. I caught a glimpse of Bracken, grim mouth pursed as he concentrated, and then my eyes closed because I was too spent to move, but I knew that they were naming me with words upon my skin. They named me in their hearts, with all the ways they could name me, could scrawl me on my own body with their seed, and I lost track of moments in the little tickly pleasure of being touched this way, until Green was inside of me again and I washed us both in a final trembling come.

At one time I was held against a hard chest in a shower as hands moved over me and made me clean, but I mostly remember my surprise when later, after I was bathed and dressed in Green's T-shirt and asleep between Bracken and Green, when all was done, and the ritual completed, I was still me.

I woke up sometime near dawn. Green and Bracken had left to walk the land, and Nicky and I were in each other's arms.

I moaned a little, contented and happy, and burrowed deeper into Nicky. His hand came up hesitantly, pushing my hair from my face, and I leaned into his caress, accepting it. He grew bolder, leaning his head down, his lips hovering just inches from mine, and I opened my eyes enough to see him—serious, yearning, trying so hard not to take too much for granted.

I loved Nicky too.

I kissed him and he kissed me back, and I pulled away although he tried to follow me. I kissed my way down his naked mortal body, reveling in the reality of freckles and small moles and cinnamon-colored nipples, a pale stomach that contrasted with the backs of his hands and the lighter tan of his arms. Dark, rust-colored hair covered his arms and was starting to sprinkle his chest, and that trail eventually led down to his phallus and tickled my nose as I tasted him—he tasted of soap and sleep. He groaned tightly, but I was still in the mood for teasing, so I moved my way toward lighter hair that covered his calves and his thighs, and I kissed those too.

Finally he grunted and rolled me to my back and spent a heaven's moment licking my sex, burying his head between my thighs, and then kissing up under my T-shirt to my mouth. I remembered our last time together and that thing I had forgotten, and I tried to say something to him now. What came out was "Nicky... baby...," but he knew, bless him, he knew. "They'll will it to wait...," he reassured. "I asked." And I was grateful, so grateful, because I could have waited for birth control, but I didn't have to, so I wrapped my legs around his slender hips, happy at how well he fit. He sheathed himself inside of me, and I groaned and wiggled and closed my eyes and stroked his chest, and he pounded, intense for a moment, his golden bird's eyes popping as he poured himself into me, and I groaned at the pleasant tingle that took over my body as he finished.

He pulled away from me and I rolled into his arms, making happy little "mmm" sounds. "That kiss last night," I said, because I wanted him to know, "that was brilliant. It was exactly what I needed when I needed it. Thank you."

"My pleasure," he said sincerely, and I rubbed his chest, enjoying the unfamiliar feel of the hair beneath my palms even as I fell inexorably asleep.

"Nicky?" I said, wanting to remember this before I went.

"Mmm...."

"Date night is officially dead."

"Praise the Lord," he breathed happily, and I smiled as we fell back asleep, breathing in tandem.

Not long afterward, Bracken and Green came back to bed, Bracken crawling in behind me and Green spooning behind Nicky.

"What have you been doing?" Bracken asked suggestively into my ear. He reached over to my hand and played with my fingers, twining them and circling them, and I clenched his hand in mine and smiled in my sleep.

"Making love," I mumbled. "All good?"

"All great."

And then we closed our eyes and slept until almost noon.

I WOKE as Arturo reached around a still sleeping Green and Nicky to tap me on the shoulder. I squinted at him, trying to make sense of my surroundings, and put a finger on the urgency that had Arturo—dignified, handsome-as-sin Arturo—practically doing the pee-pee dance in agitation.

"Wha's wrong?" I slurred, tugging at the comforter to make sure it was up around my chest, because my T-shirt had rucked up during that lovely moment with Nicky.

"Your mother's here," he whispered harshly, and I forgot my bare boobs and sat bolt upright in bed.

"My mother's *what*?" My parents had been to the hill before, but part of Green's protection of the hill was to put a geas on it—a spell of hazy memory—so that no outsider would remember it if they ever found it.

"Chloe brought her," Arturo hissed angrily, and I swore. Of course—we'd rescinded the geas for Chloe, because we knew we could wipe her memory if it didn't work. "They're out in the living room right now, cooking up enough bitch to choke a moose. We need you out there."

"Holy shit." I scrambled out of bed, too rattled to even see if I'd woken anybody else. "We're in Green's room. How did we get in Green's room? We started out in my room—did we migrate? Were we naked? Did we just materialize here?"

"Does it matter?" Arturo asked, putting a hand on my shoulder to keep me from looking around in a complete attack of frantic.

"It does if I don't keep any clothes in here, Arturo!" I exploded, wondering if I should feel like a guilty kid after that wonderful moment of powerful woman I had just pulled off. "We're right across the hall, and my mom will see me run over to my room to get dressed, and I'm about to confront my very human mother in a T-shirt after leaving a bed with three naked men...." He put his other hand on my other shoulder and breathed deeply, nodding so I would do the same, because I was losing it big time. There was something different about Arturo this morning... something gold and rust-colored, a glowing from him.... I closed my eyes and focused, figuring I'd get to that other thing later. "Short answer, yes. It matters. But that's okay. I'll deal. I'll just run across the hall when she's not—"

"Cory, are you in here?" She sounded irritated as she shoved the door open—its seal had been broken by Arturo, who was always welcome. Of course she sounded irritated. Chloe, the bitch, had been intercepting her phone calls for almost a month, and now she was hunting me down in my own home.

"—looking," I finished weakly. "You're so fired as a doorman," I hissed at Arturo. He smiled gently and dropped a kiss on my forehead before I turned to my mother with a sickly smile.

"Hey, Mom," I said lamely, and behind me I heard all three naked men sit up and mumble things like "oh, shit" and "fuck-it-all" under their breaths. "We were just getting dressed and coming out to meet you." And at least that was the truth.

Mom took in the scene with narrowed eyes and a rapidly reddening face. "Corinne Carol-Anne Kirkpatrick...."

"Op Crocken Green," I finished for her, deciding that since I was busted, I was going to be busted for the whole enchilada, and mom could make of my life what she wished.

"What?"

"My name," I said bravely—I hoped. "My full name here is Corinne Carol-Anne Kirkpatrick op Crocken Green. Bracken's full name is Bracken Brine Granite op Crocken Green," I turned and indicated my beloved, who had caught a towel thrown by Arturo and was standing up looking as decent as he could. The tattooed wreath of oak, lime, and rose that wrapped his wrist and forearm stood out sharply against the white of the towel. I turned to Green, who had managed a pair of jeans from beside the bed. He gave me the gentlest, proudest, most compassionate smile, and I managed to return it in kind. "And you already know Green."

"And this young man?" She leveled a finger at Nicky, who had stood too, and next to Green he truly did look young—or at least short, at a bare five foot six or seven next to Green's near full seven feet. His tattoo was on his arm, and all that ink made Nicky and Bracken look dangerous. I squinted at the sidhe and realized that none of them, even Arturo, were wearing glamour. So this really was full disclosure day, I thought, and felt a little relieved.

"Dominic Kestrel Kirkpatrick Green," Nicky said, raising his eyebrows at me. I smiled a little, hoping I could give him my true gratitude later.

Mom nodded, clearly not understanding. "Nice," she snapped. "And what in the hell are they all doing with you in bed?"

"It's Green's bed," I said automatically, stalling for time.

"I don't care if it's the president's bed, what in the hell are you doing there with three naked men?" Her voice rose to a shriek at the end.

Oh, Goddess... this was going downhill fast, and I was starting to think I would have to throw my body in front of it to make it stop. "I think Bracken's wearing shorts," I said inanely and then shoved my fist in my mouth and bit down to try and keep anything else that stupid from coming out.

"Cory, if you don't give me a decent answer right now, I'm calling your father and he's going to drag you home by the hair and commit you to a goddamned nuthouse—now what in the hell are all these men doing in your bed!"

I was fucked blind if anyone, even my father, was going to take me out of my bed with my men. I took a deep breath and let it out on a sigh. "We're married, Mom—where would you expect to find us all?"

"You keep saying that, but I don't see a...." She trailed off, and I looked guiltily to where a ring should be, only to discover that there was one on my finger. It was beautiful. The tattoo on my back consisted of three interwoven diamonds of oak, lime, and rose, framing the emblems of Bracken, Nicky, and Adrian. The ring was the same thing—except the diamonds were horizontal, not vertical, and the center diamond had Green's lime tree with emerald inlays for the limes, in the tiniest detail. Adrian's rose was only there in the wreaths. Lime leaves, oak leaves, and roses with tiny blood rubies in the center created the lattice weaving that made up the diamonds. There was a hawk, with a tiny topaz as its eye, for Nicky. Bracken's symbol was a sword thrust into a rock, and the sword had an onyx handle and a diamond blade, with garnet blood dripping from the (migosh!) honest granite of the tiny boulder. It was small, for all the minute detail, and the gold was colored red and gold and white as it wreathed, and the beauty of it caught my breath. I must have been truly asleep when Bracken or Green or Nicky had placed it on my finger.

A little awestruck, I showed my mother, who actually stopped midrant and gasped.

"It's beautiful," she breathed, and I turned to Bracken with a radiant smile.

"It's perfect," I told him, and he bowed slightly, waving his left hand. He had one too, and I would bet that if I looked closely, his would have my oak leaves woven in with the other symbols. I looked to Green and then to Nicky and realized that probably when the men had come to bed, they had placed rings on all our fingers. I didn't think the elves did jewelry—especially Green, who couldn't afford to owe his allegiance to anybody. But he'd chosen to wear this symbol, for me. For all of us. My eyes grew wide and bright. "They're perfect, aren't they?" I asked, and Green nodded. "Absolutely," he agreed, and I wished I had time, so I could get a better look at everybody's rings, and praise Bracken for his creativity, and....

And my mom was still looking at me like I was about to be disowned.

"See," I said brightly, "we have rings!"

"You *all* have rings?" she asked acidly, and I gave it up and decided to own my love life.

"Yup." I nodded my head and did that weird thing with my lips that dared her to make a big deal out of it. "We all have rings. We're all bound together, Mom. I could explain and totally lose you, but what matters is that we're happy. All four of us are happy, and this is more of a lifetime commitment than you can possibly imagine. It's more permanent and lasting than any marriage ceremony, and we must make it work. So we are—and we're happy, and there will be children...." I smiled, and I realized that my face had gone soft, and a sweet smile had moved through me. "Not right now—not until I'm done with school— but they'll be pretty, Mom, the prettiest children you've ever seen. And we'll love them. They'll be so loved... and we'll be happy."

I was crying. Holy shit, first I got all soft over the thought of children, and now I was crying! What in the hell was wrong with me? I wiped my face with a shaking hand and realized there were black spots in front of my eyes, and my knees were suddenly a little weak. Green was there to catch me before I could even sit down on the bed.

"You're hungry," he said, nuzzling my cheek, and I nodded, surprised.

"I don't remember this from last summer," I said fuzzily, and Bracken moved up to Green's side and laughed.

"I do," he said shortly. "It felt like I spent half the summer forcing cheeseburgers down your gullet...." He sobered. "And the other half just begging you to eat at all."

Mom made a restive sound, and we looked at her, me from my familiar perch in a beloved's arms. "See, Mom?" I said with another Jell-O smile. "They're taking good care of me. I guess I am that special after all."

She opened and closed her mouth, and I gnawed on my lip and tried to do my job. "Mom, I'm sure there's something in the kitchen to eat—do you want to have lunch?"

"I came with Chloe…," she said uncertainly, and I cut her off.

"Chloe's leaving tonight, with the kids, and she's not coming back." Mom looked at me in surprise. "I bet you called like fifty times, right?"

Mom nodded. "I was hurt—I didn't think you were planning the wedding at all," she said honestly. "I still don't know how you're going to plan a wedding for four," she said with a snort, and I guessed she hadn't figured out what she wanted to say about that.

"You'll have to talk to Bracken about the wedding plans," I said, and my beloved looked up happily, like this was a topic he didn't get to discuss enough. "He's been doing most of it on his own while I sleep. But Chloe kept your calls from me out of spite—and she's not welcome back here. So if you'll let us get dressed, we'll be out in a second for lunch."

Mom nodded, still thin lipped and bewildered—but maybe some of the authority that I'd developed in the last year was showing, because she did what I said, Arturo following to escort her out. After the door closed behind her, the four of us were left to look at each other shakily, and Green laughed with so much joy I couldn't even be sorry.

"Well, luv, I'd say we're effectively out of the closet," he said bluntly, sitting down with me in his lap.

"Goddess," I sighed and laid my head on his chest. Bracken motioned to Nicky, and they left to go get dressed. "I didn't think I'd ever tell her, Green," I said, dazed. "I thought I'd be someone different for my parents for the rest of my life."

"You can't box parts of your life from the people you love," Green offered wisely. I laughed, because I had come to that same conclusion all by myself, but it was wonderful to hear it seconded.

"I love you more than the sound of my heartbeat," I told him gravely. "Now dress me and feed me before I pass out and make things weirder."

"My wish is but to serve you, my lady," he said softly, and I nuzzled his bare chest.

"You're wearing my ring," I said, and he looked away from me, a sorrow on his face that neither of us could do anything about.

"It's *truly* the least I could do," he said, and I could taste the bitterness falling from his lips, so I kissed them and made them sweet. He came up for air, laughing a little, and nuzzled my neck until I gasped. "We did it, you know," he said. "Our people are safe—from Hollow Man, at least, and maybe from like dangers."

"Don't we have to test that or something?" I was kind of skeptical, even though I'd felt my power rippling through the hill like an EM pulse.

Suddenly Green was cold sober and all business. "Don't worry, luv. I'm sure he'll take care of the testing all by himself."

He set me carefully on the bed and finished dressing. I probably could have gone to get my clothes like a big girl then, but I got to spend so few intimate, small moments with Green that I took advantage of this one and sat and watched him dress. The sprites had been at his hair this morning—it shook out long and straight and lemon yellow, and he brushed it and braided it deftly.

"I could do that, you know," I said mildly, and he looked over his shoulder at me and grinned.

"You're not my valet, luv," he said through half-closed eyes, and I flushed. The point was made moot in a moment, when Bracken came in fully dressed himself and with an armload of clothes for me.

"Where the hell are my jeans?" I picked up the three-quarters skirt and the fitted blouse and cardigan with my fingertips.

"No jeans this morning," he said briefly. I tried to stand up to have this argument, but my knees went out from under me and I sat down hard, looking in bemusement at the black spots in front of my eyes.

"I'll get you for this," I sighed as he picked up the clothes and dressed me like a two-year-old. We both paused for a moment to watch the contrast of his tattoo against the freckled whiteness of my thigh. "Why am I dressing in librarian chic today?"

"Think of it like Easter morning," Bracken said seriously, doing a button on the back of the shirt that I ordinarily would have just let flap in the breeze. "There's a formality to a morning like this—and your mother needs to see you look serious to the hill. After the way you introduced this whole thing, we need to give her some legitimacy." With that he looked at Green and frowned. "Is that what you're wearing?"

Green was wearing jeans and a fisherman's sweater. I thought he looked pretty spiffy, but Bracken was wearing slacks and the sweater I'd knit him, and he looked a little more formal. "Green gave Mitch's eulogy completely naked, holding me," I reminded him. "He's fine as he is."

Bracken whuffed a little in laughter, and then, as I stood up and started walking out to the hallway, he swung me up in his arms against my protest.

"If Green could eulogize Mitch holding you, I can greet our mothers holding you," he said with dignity while carrying me into the front room, stepping over what looked like a zoo full of animals on the way to breakfast. Pumas and giant housecats and a couple of wolves, some really large rabbits, and about thirty different breeds of dog all snoozed or nuzzled in twos. A familiar tawny cat stood up on her hind legs and put her two paws on my chest so she could lick my face.

"Good night, puss?" I asked, stroking Renny's ears gently, and a purr that probably rumbled the floorboards started from her chest. A large, dark brown cat with slightly crossed blue eyes stood up on his hind legs and whuffed shyly at me, so I scratched the sweet spot between his eyes. Max purred too, and the two of them hopped down and crossed the room, curling up into a satisfied pile of happy cat and licking each other's necks and backs and ears with broad pink tongues. Fleetingly, I wondered what the living room had looked like while I'd been having my own nuclear meltdown. Then I shuddered and decided I didn't even want to know.

"They couldn't make it to the were-rooms?" I asked Bracken, flushing because my mom was standing in a corner of the kitchen by the refrigerator, looking really freaked out about the animals. Apparently she'd been too whacked out by whatever Chloe had told her to notice them on the way in, and now all of her freaking out was happening in front of these rather predatory beings. It was a good thing most of them were in a sex coma, because I saw a few of them sniffing the air in a lazy, "I can wait for this mouse to run across my muzzle before I eat it" kind of way.

"Mom, calm down." I was trying for reassuring but ended up with exasperated. "Nobody's going to eat you—especially with the spread on the table." Wow—I was really impressed. There were croissants and cheesecakes and pastries of a thousand types, as well as crackers and hummus and cheeses and every fruit known to man, from canned grapefruit to mango to kiwi—everything but peaches. In fact, there was pretty much every sort of breakfast food I could possibly imagine, except meat. I smiled brilliantly at Bracken's mother, who was fluttering about me looking anxious. "It's awesome," I said sincerely. "I have no idea where you found the time. Thank you so much for preparing this."

Blissa hummed and glowed incandescently with pride, and Bracken nuzzled my ear, letting me know he was pleased. I made to move out of his arms, but he clenched me even tighter. I sighed and looked out at the living room. The were-animals were looking hopefully at the pastries, and some of the elves had woken up and were wandering in, and I looked at Green for help because this was a social thing—which meant I was lost.

"Come eat, everybody," he said in a carrying voice. Then he looked at Blissa to confirm something. "And I understand there's another breakfast in the were… uhm…." He looked at my mom and for the first time seemed a little disconcerted, then sighed bravely and carried on. "The weres' common room has a breakfast with," he shuddered, "more protein."

There was a happy sound of animals whuffling and rising to their feet, and suddenly the zoo began to migrate downstairs. Nicky had emerged from the hall just as Green made his announcement—and I don't know what he saw in my face, but he made a "one minute" sort of gesture and trotted back down the hall. Bracken's mother handed me a plate full of what looked like cream puffs made of wheat bran before Brack set me on one of the stools near the counter that semidivided the kitchen from the living room. I waved my mom to come sit across from me, and Green and Bracken made themselves comfortable around me, leaving a stool for Nicky and a couple of places at the table. I looked around for Arturo, but he wasn't in the room, and I wondered where he was.

"Come eat, Mom," I said through a full mouth. "It's good stuff."

"It wasn't here when I got here," Mom said dazedly. "I wasn't in the room more than three minutes. Where did the food come from?"

I shrugged and smiled and offered one of those bran pastries to her. "Bracken's mom made these," I said, hoping it was true. "Try one, they're awesome."

"What about Chloe?" she asked, and I looked up to see Grace's daughter, back to the door, eyeing me and the men around me with stark, unfriendly eyes.

"Chloe isn't welcome at our table," Green said evenly and looked up from the sidhe he had been greeting to pin the woman against the door with one of the coldest looks I'd ever seen him give. "Are you, Chloe?"

"Like I'd eat with you people," she spat, and I looked at Green, pained.

"The boys will be out in a moment," I said, because I didn't want them to see us having this discussion. "I think that's where Arturo went."

Green looked far away for a moment and then returned with a snap. "They went to the were-table," he said, his mouth quirking up. "They wanted to see the weres turning."

I remembered that day with Eric and Renny and was faintly alarmed. "I hope they have—"

"Robes." He nodded, and I felt reassured. The sidhe children, I was sure, were used to all states of dress and undress, but not these human children—I didn't want to scar them for life with something they wouldn't understand. "Arturo said he set up for it this morning after we walked."

"Okay, well, then in that case...." I glared at Chloe.

"In that case," Green said, his voice hard, "Chloe, you're not only not welcome at my table, you're not welcome in my home. You can go outside and stay there until your mother wakes up, and then you can say good-bye." Chloe's mouth opened, but Green cut her off. "We hoped you could be a part of us, of our family—but that's three times now you've done something spiteful and petty to members of my family, and twice your malice has put my beloved in danger. You don't get a third chance."

"Bringing me here was dangerous?" my mom asked, and I turned to her sharply.

"Don't interrupt Green," I hissed and turned back to him.

"You need to go outside," he continued, "and for the next few hours you need to know this: you won't remember your time here, but your children will. Your children will be invited back, and you will be powerless to say no. Your children will know their grandmother and her people, and you will believe that she is dead, as you have always believed—but this time, you won't dream of her."

Chloe gasped, and for the first time since she'd fainted in Grace's store, she looked truly frightened. "You can't do that to me!" she protested, but Green was relentless, and I was behind him.

"We have to, Chloe," he said. It was the only gentleness he'd shown her this morning, and it wasn't much. "If your mother visits you in your dreams, you may start to remember—and we need you to forget. You brought someone here who didn't remember the way. The last stranger we let remember the way was Officer Max, and he's one of us now. Cory knew her way since her first night here—but she's truly special, and we couldn't make her forget if we tried. We are powerful, but we can't fight against the might of God's world, Chloe. Our best weapon is the fact that nobody believes we exist, and you've taken it upon yourself to strip us of that by simply being petty and foolish. You are too old to be petty and foolish. You need to grow up, but you are too dangerous to be allowed to grow up here. So go outside, so that we may eat, and sit and think upon what you've lost. And don't think of leaving, or doing anything else malicious, because your car won't start and you've seen for yourself that it's a hell of a walk to anywhere but here. When your mother wakes up, you may say your good-byes. I'd think about making them count, because they're the last things you'll get to say to her. Twenty years ago, your mother was dying of cancer, and she took the only way open to her to watch you grow up. Today, think of it as though you are dying of ignorance, and you had the only cure and threw it away. When your mother says good-bye to you tonight, it will be like you're the one who died and left her to continue on with her life—with your children."

Chloe was in tears now. I almost felt sorry for her—but I looked at my mom, who was dazed and upset and would probably need her mind rolled to cope with half of what she'd seen today, and I thought of Grace and of the heartbreak this was going to cause her, and my pity melted like frost on coffee. She'd had her chances, and I of all people knew that you only get so many. One night I'd stopped just looking up and had taken what the Goddess gave me, and it had almost been too late. Chloe had never even looked up.

Wordlessly, moving stiffly—I think Green was compelling her against her will—Chloe tucked her hand behind her, opened the door, and stepped outside. We resumed eating, and my mom stepped forward on shaky legs and sat down silently at the table.

Various members of the household came up one at a time to whisper in Green's ear and smile shyly at me. I'd grin back because I was pretty sure they were telling him that they had felt it—that the combination of sex and power and protection had rolled through the hill and through their skins, and we had made our people safe. The people coming up to us were almost all higher elves or sidhe, with the occasional werecreature dressed hastily in jeans or robes or, in the case of Renny, in one of Max's shirts and a pair of white cotton panties. Max had returned and managed a pair of jeans, unbuttoned, and a white T-shirt, torn. I raised my eyebrows at the ripped neck as he came by and kissed my cheek, and he flushed so hotly I could see sweat prints form on his china plate. I looked around and noticed that most of the lower fey—the ones who looked the least human—had tactfully stayed away, and I doubly cursed Chloe. This was our time, the hill's time, to honor us, to say thank you—and they couldn't, because they were afraid of the humans in our midst. We were having a wedding for my parents—we should have at least been allowed to have this breakfast for the hill.

I sighed and tried to shake it off, but it was hard with my mother sitting right next to me, eating stolidly through some of the best pastries a human had ever tasted. I cleared my plate and was looking fretfully at the spread on the table when Nicky showed back up, his arms loaded with plates of ham, sausage, and scrambled eggs with cheese.

"Have I mentioned I love you?" I said with no qualifications whatsoever. Nicky grinned and started dumping protein on my plate like I hadn't eaten for a week. In spite of the stacks of pastries I'd just eaten, my stomach was starting to agree with him. Max and Renny came up with hopeful eyes, and Nicky and I made a plate for them. I stuck my tongue out at Renny as she snitched a piece of bacon off my plate after I'd already given her a stack, and Max mumbled thank you, and then they found a corner of their own to sit and eat. I realized that the only reason they had stayed up here with the fey was for me. They were my special friends, and I was touched. For one thing, I bet the were breakfast was a lot more lively than the dignified sidhe.

Another sidhe came to talk to Green, and I took one look at that so-purple-it's-black skin and said, "Twilight?" Twilight turned and smiled at me, silver tears tracking their way down his face.

"It was good, Twilight?" I asked gently, and in response he took both my hands in his and kissed my forehead.

"It was lovely, little Goddess," he choked out, and I beamed back at him. He was so gorgeous now, so lovely and whole and unscarred. Green and I had done that, and I was so proud of his health and wholeness that I could cry. "I've never had such a ritual, such pleasure and love. I couldn't have made that on my own little hill in a thousand years."

I flushed. "It was all of us, Twilight." Goddess, I hoped Mom didn't figure out what any of this meant. "It took all of us. Not just me."

Twilight kissed my forehead again and walked away with his plate, and I smiled at Green using all my teeth, then started to dig into breakfast—phase two.

"Corinne Carol-Anne!" my mother admonished. "If you keep eating like that they won't be able to fit you through the door." I'm not sure if it was the only thing she felt she could control, or the only way she could express her disapproval in the face of all this glowing approval aimed at me from other people, but it did the trick.

I looked woefully at the half of a sausage between my fingers and swallowed what was in my mouth with a thump.

"Green...," Bracken growled at my side, and I looked at him in surprise.

Green nodded, as though this was something they'd discussed before, and turned to my mother. "Ellen," he said gently, "I would hate to separate another mother and daughter this morning for the sake of the people on my hill."

My mother looked at him in surprise, but she'd seen him order Chloe out of the room. She might not have understood all that had gone on between them, but she certainly understood the implied threat. She looked at me helplessly, and I looked back with even eyes. No one contradicted Green in his own hill, least of all me.

Mom looked down and wiped her mouth with a napkin, then looked up at me with a lost expression before nodding. "I'm sorry, sweetheart," she said, looking embarrassed. "You're looking really good right now— I'm not sure if I told you that."

It was a start. "Thanks, Mom," I said and went back to my well-earned breakfast.

We finished quietly, making small comments to each other mostly to watch the other person smile. There was understated touching. Nicky and I were perpetually bumping hands, Green took every opportunity to nuzzle my hair, and Bracken's hand never left my knee. All in all, I knew my mother felt left out, but I couldn't help that. Finally I found a way to involve her, and asked Bracken what I was going to be wearing for our wedding. Then he was off and rolling, and my mother was hauling ass behind him, picking up the slack. I was relieved. She might not have understood who I was marrying, or what she'd interrupted this morning, but she knew I was wearing an off-white dress with a crown of wildflowers and a bouquet of red thornless roses, and that she could send invitations to Aunt Jeanie (Dad's sister) so Uncle Dan could send their regrets, because he never left the house. "They'll probably send you salt-and-pepper shakers," Mom sniffed. "It's what your father and I got, and they were so hideous we gave them to you to break when you were a toddler."

Excellent, I thought to myself. *We'll put them in the room for the sprites and brownies and the other tiny ones of the lower fey, and they can collect magic dust and house copulating sprites.* It was all good.

Finally I mopped up the last crumb on my plate and was almost full, and the room started to clear out. Renny and Max came up to me, and Renny was sending impatient looks my mom's way because it was obvious that she wanted to gossip. I looked at Green. "Green, can we find someone to take Mom home?" I asked hopefully, and Green nodded. "You and Bracken can go. You can check on the stores and the gas stations for me too, if you like."

He was up to something. "But Green... that whole thing with Chloe.... It's almost three in the afternoon—we won't be back until way after dark."

He nodded evenly. "Yes, luv, I'm aware of that."

I frowned. "You shouldn't have to do that alone," I said tentatively. "I mean...." I looked at Mom, still not sure how much she'd seen, in spite of the fact that nobody had worn glamour today. After watching Chloe's willful blindness, I was becoming convinced that people believed whatever they wanted to, in spite of the weight of evidence to the contrary. "I mean, Grace's people... and I... we sort of have... a rapport." Did that sound as lame to Green as it did to me? But how much worse would *I'm queen of the vampires* sound to my mom? I looked at Green and the sly glimmer in his eyes, and I realized he knew exactly why it would be impossible for me to win this argument.

"You can't shelter me forever," I said obstinately, and he conceded that with a nod.

"But you shouldn't have to be a part of this." He took my hand. "Please, beloved—I'm not trying to make you look weak, but...."

I shook my head. "I was the one who told Grace," I said after a moment. "I should see this through."

He sighed and touched my cheek fondly. "You are too grown-up for your own good," he said at last, and I grinned because against all odds I'd won.

"Canyagimmehallelujah," I returned suggestively, and that made him laugh fully—open mouth, open heart, happy eyes.

"In that case," he said after a moment of goodness, "we'll have someone else take your mum home, yes?" His voice shifted in that moment, his British accent growing deeper, and I wondered what he was thinking about to make that happen. He sounded very transplanted during everyday things, but depending on what or when he was thinking about, the accent became more pronounced—and often shifted regions. He looked at my mom politely. "Is that all right with you, Mrs. Kirkpatrick?"

Mom nodded, looking distracted by a deep conversation with Bracken about Renny as a bridesmaid and Grace as a matron of honor (I hadn't been aware I'd have such things—wasn't that a little bit of overkill?) and the fact that the wedding would have to be just after sunset if we wanted that to happen, especially because Marcus wanted to stand up as well. I didn't know he'd even expressed an interest—or that Bracken got up to so much after I'd fallen asleep.

"I'll take her, Green," Brack said cheerfully, and I looked at him in surprise. He winked at me, and I wondered if he was going to pull a whammy on her so she'd forget everything she'd seen today. A part of me thought that was a great idea, and a part of me was sort of depressed, because I'd been very proud of my stand for adulthood this morning. Bracken excused himself from his conversation with Mom for a second and said, "I'll sound her out, beloved. Green and the vamps aren't the only ones who can do a mind-wipe, and she's feeling comfortable with me right now. I think she can handle it—but I think she'd like to talk to one of us alone too."

My face must have been blank with surprise, because I thought he really didn't like Mom at all, but he reinstated some of my faith in my ability to read a situation by saying, "And this way, she can't hurt you anymore."

I smiled, suddenly feeling a little watery, and kissed him fully on the mouth, welcoming his surprised response. And that quickly, I was wet and ready all over again and nearly devouring his face there at the luncheon table. He pulled away with difficulty, and I realized we were both flushed and panting and that Green had his arm around my middle and had placed a trembling kiss into my hair. I swallowed and dredged up a smile for my mom over his shoulder, so muddled from the kiss I couldn't even summon an apology.

After that, it was a matter of good-byes and that gentle disconnecting guests do at the end of the party, except it was my mom saying good-bye, and the party hadn't been planned. She was so bewildered by, well, everything that she couldn't think of a thing to say to me—not "I didn't raise you to be a nympho sex-glutted ho-bag," not "Are you sure this is how you want to live your life?" and not even "What am I going to tell your father?" She was just subdued, ruminative, thinking quietly about everything—either that, or catatonic. I kissed Bracken good-bye, hoping their conversation would go well. Nicky volunteered to go with him, and I warned them both to stay out of trouble.

Bracken turned to me and grinned as he walked out the door. "After last night, beloved, maybe trouble should stay out of our business today, you think?"

I smiled tightly and shook my head. "Can somebody else go with them?" I asked plaintively. He had no idea how raw the image of him bleeding out while floating a good six feet over Lake Camp Far West still was in my mind. To my surprise, Mario and LaMark walked in the door at just that moment, and hearing my request, did a 180 out the door following Bracken. Honor guard indeed, I thought with some bemusement, and taking their job seriously. I called a grateful thank-you after them and turned to Green, who was finishing up his milk as he sat.

"That was really odd and hectic," I said with a smile, and his answering grin was lazy and incredibly self-satisfied.

"And now we're alone," he responded, ignoring the room full of weres and sidhe who were still filling in the corners from that awesome breakfast. One look into his lowering eyes, and suddenly I couldn't see them either.

I raised my eyebrows. "Whatever will we do?"

Oh, yeah. We found something to occupy the time.

BRACKEN
Unexpected Snags

MRS. KIRKPATRICK didn't look nearly as comfortable sitting next to me in the car as she had sitting across the counter at breakfast, but I suppose the presence of the Avians in the back had something to do with that.

She cast them nervous glances while they immersed themselves in quiet conversation—I gathered from what they were saying that they had felt our safety spell even from their separate hill, although the distance had dulled the sexual intensity that had made our hill so happy. As I swung Cory's new red SUV (Green had bought it sight unseen) around the broad curves of Foresthill Road and passed Scary Tree, LaMark piped up from the backseat.

"Hey—is it me, or has Scary Tree gotten darker and grown since this winter?" I didn't even need to look at it to tell him yes, it had. I wasn't sure what kind of tree Scary Tree had been when it was alive, although my mother could have told me, but now that it was dead, it stood like a hulking, silver-black skeleton against the green and blonde of the grasses, with the mind-boggling immensity of the canyon beyond it. When I was young and Green had told me that Scary Tree was a measuring stick of evil, I'd asked him why it wasn't on our hill. He'd looked at me with a half smile on his face, as though pleased that I thought everything of importance should be on the hill. Then he'd answered, "Because this tree is older than the hill by many years. In fact, I chose the location of the hill to be counter to the tree—so I know the state of the immediate vicinity as it relates to my home."

I looked at the tree in the rearview mirror as it got smaller but no less stark in relief. "Yeah," I said thoughtfully. "Either the hill has just become heaven on earth, or there is something exceptionally black and rotten at large in this area."

There was a glum silence then, and the SUV continued its soar through the cloven shelves of rock and short meadow that hugged the mountain while the canyon yawned beyond. By the time we came to the vast, green-railed two-lane bridge that spanned the canyon before Auburn, I had pulled up the most articulate version of myself and strove to make peace.

"She's not fat," I said loudly into the silence, and Cory's mother jumped with a little squeak.

"I beg your pardon?"

"You keep telling her not to eat. She's not fat." Cory would be in hysterics by now, I thought grimly. My tact had the character of a runaway garbage scow.

Mrs. Kirkpatrick blinked a little, an expression that let me see, perhaps for the first time, the similarity between mother and daughter. Her father gave Cory the coloring—the reddish hair and shadowed greenish eyes—but Ellen gave her the bone structure and, somewhere under the weariness and judgment and worry, the same sense of soft wonder that Cory once shielded with black lipstick. It was probably that quality that had sustained her quiet acceptance back at Green's, but as the SUV started the climb through carved naked granite walls to Auburn, her back had become stiffer and angrier with disapproval.

"Well, she's not a supermodel," she said sharply, and the three men in back gasped.

"Bracken... man... you can't let her...." LaMark was the most upset—perhaps because he was the youngest and couldn't see the frightened parent in the aggressive critic.

"We think she's lovely," I said, trying hard to keep my voice even. "And she's ours now."

"Well, yes, she is, isn't she? She's everybody's. For all I know, every man in your apartment complex is screwing my daughter—and you think that telling me she's pretty is going to make that all right." As an appalled silence blanketed the car, I had a queasy moment to reflect that here was another thing mother and daughter had in common— except Cory usually managed to jump to the right conclusions before she confronted a problem head on.

"I'm a gay virgin, ma'am," LaMark snapped from the back seat, "so I'm not screwing your daughter, but that doesn't mean that you're not pissing me off."

Mario snarked so hard it sounded like he was swallowing his tongue. "I was widowed this winter," he said softly, when he could breathe again.

"So I'm not in that club either. You need to see your daughter the way we see her to understand how she's loved right now."

"What's to see?" Her voice rose in exasperation. "I know what we are, son. Our family is one step above white trash—don't think I don't know that." Her voice trembled for a moment. "Cory never played wedding when she was a kid. No, my daughter used to sit in her room and play queen. She'd have all her stuffed animals and her dolls all set up, and she'd wait on them and order their lives about and tell them how to fix their problems. She'd use her headboard as a throne and put a cut-up butter tub on her head and use her grandma's quilt as a robe—it was real cute, you all would have laughed your asses off. And I had to go in one day and tell her she wasn't ever going to be queen of anything, and she had better get used to the fact that if she was lucky, she'd get to cut hair or be a dental assistant or something that paid okay and didn't make her old before her time. She cried for a week, but dammit, when she was done sniveling she was ready for the real world. She was doing good, too—I was starting to believe she just might make it through school— before you people came around and started screwing with her. It just makes me sick—she needed a boyfriend so bad she couldn't even see it, and you all played right into that. She's only a kid—how dare you fool with her head like that?"

My stomach clenched, and Nicky and I met stark eyes in the rearview mirror. The car began the final climb through the canyon while we groped for a way to change the vision of the woman who had damn near crippled our beloved queen out of love.

"We will never leave her," I said nakedly, after struggling for breath and groping for words like a drowning man flailing for a log. "We will always love her—our lives depend on it. And you may not understand who she is, or who we are, but that's because you're not looking with the right eyes, and you need to find them or you will never know her at all. She is our everything. Not just to those of us who love her like me and Green and Nicky. LaMark and Mario follow her to school every day just to keep her safe. Max may have given up his humanity for Renny, but he gave up his career and his family to be a part of Cory's life. She wasn't lying or being bitter this morning, Mrs. Kirkpatrick. She *is* that special. I just wish I was her right now, because I don't have the words to show you how."

The silence that fell was total, so all-consuming that it lasted through Auburn and down the hill, through when I got off at the Penryn exit and turned left, then left again and right, until I found the large, raw, undeveloped piece of land on Val Verde that Cory had grown up on. We rumbled up the gravel drive, the area already dry enough to start throwing off dust, and pulled to a quiet stop. I made a decision and turned to Cory's mother.

"Your daughter is painfully honest," I said, catching her gray-eyed gaze and making sure she was tracking my eyes. "I expect you to be as well. You can either forget this morning and come to this wedding blind, seeing what you want to see and being completely in the dark—" I nodded once to make sure she understood. "—or you can remember this morning and try to come to grips with the idea that your daughter's future not only involves graduating from college and working for Green, but also includes a wedding ceremony between the four of us. It's up to you, but you need to decide now—because if we ever have a conversation like this again, I won't ask, I'll simply take it all away." The one thing holding me back was the desire to honor Green. "The only memories you'll have of your only daughter from here on out will be the ones we want you to have, and that includes your husband as well. So which do you want it to be? The lie that's pleasant for you, or the truth that's glorious for Cory?"

She swallowed painfully. I could see for the first time an absolute belief in her that I could do this, that I could play with her memories like a teenager edits a comic book, and she was suddenly grasping the enormity of what she would lose if she let go of what she knew for what she wanted to believe.

She breathed in slowly and let it out, then sighed, a tiny smile quirking at her lips. One more thing, I thought with a wrench in my heart, to add to the list of qualities she had given her daughter. "She looked awfully happy today at brunch, didn't she?" Agnes said wistfully, and I nodded.

"She looked beautiful," I agreed.

"She really looked like a queen." She was begging me for confirmation. I gave it to her.

"We'd give our lives for her," I told her truthfully, and she gave a shaky nod.

"I'll keep my brains in my head, thank you very much," she said decisively and opened the car door. "Let me know what she wants for a wedding present—I was going to make a quilt, but if you wanted something else...."

"She'd love that," Nicky said from behind me, and I nodded. "She would."

And then, with a birdlike little nod of her head that she *hadn't* given to Cory but kept all to herself, she shut the door with a *chunk* and walked across the yard, giving her husband a kiss as he paused from pushing the lawnmower over the lush grass of the season. He said something to her as I went to back out and then looked at us, raising his hand in a puzzled farewell as we finished backing and threw the car into drive.

It was so quiet as I retraced our steps toward home that I could almost hear the churning in everybody's stomach.

"Let's make a deal," Nicky said tightly, about midway up the hill to Auburn.

"We unload that conversation onto Green and then try to forget it ever happened?" Mario asked and answered, and the rest of us nodded.

"I'm in," LaMark said on a puffed breath, and everybody looked at me. I kept trying to say something, anything, but I had this thing in my throat that would hardly let me breathe. I could see Cory, tiny and plump, being regal and gracious and happy, telling a story: *Listen here, my people. Once upon a time, there was a princess who believed in herself, and she could do anything, and then a well-meaning queen convinced her that her entire fate was a dark accident. Now she can still do anything, but she will never believe in herself the way she did when she was tiny and plump and wore a quilt as a chaperon and a butter tub as a crown.*

"I'll never forget that," I said at last, aware that they were still looking at me, waiting to see what Cory's *due'alle* would do with an understanding he had never wanted. "I'm all for telling Green... and for never mentioning it to her at all." I swallowed. "But I'll never forget it." *Never.*

And, silly us, we thought that was the worst thing that would happen to us that day.

LaMark and Mario hadn't been fed like Nicky and me, so we stopped for lunch in Old Town Auburn, and by the time we got to the top of the hill and off the freeway it was nearly seven o'clock. After the freeway overpass and right before the canyon to Foresthill Road is a McDonald's with a vast parking lot for busses headed to Reno, and that was where the police cars were gathered, cherry-top lights flashing urgently. In the center of the circled cop cars was Chloe's oversized champagne-colored truck. Chloe was talking to an officer, her white face chafed with tears, her shoulders trembling and her head shaking in violent denial. The boys were nowhere to be seen.

CORY
Unraveling

GREEN AND I couldn't make love *all* afternoon, and we'd slept in plenty. About an hour after Brack took Mom home, we left Green's room with hair all wet from the shower. He went left to the front room to talk to his people, and I went right to Renny's room to see if Max was still there or if Renny and I could talk.

Renny answered with a soft "come in" when I knocked, and I was surprised to see that Max was still in her room. He was face down on her dainty queen-sized bed, fast asleep on the pale yellow comforter. I looked around the room, noting that the bare wooden walls had been stained a faded sage green with stunning bursts of beige and tawny brown.

"When did that happen?" I asked curiously. She had two chairs like I did, but hers were the kind with plump middles and wooden scrolled legs and edgings, and they were done in an antique white—which was good, because it contrasted nicely with the long tawny cat hairs that covered the fabric. Renny was sitting in one of them, knitting.

"Last night," she answered calmly. Then she looked at me and smiled, the kind of soft smile I knew I must get sometimes when I thought of my beloveds. "Thanks."

"My pleasure," I replied, raising my eyebrows suggestively, and she looked at me sideways.

"My God, I certainly hope so." And we both laughed a little.

"So…," and I was only kidding, "do I get to be a bridesmaid?"

"No," she responded seriously. I blinked back at her, surprised and not a little hurt. "We're going to have a justice-of-the-peace thing for his parents, and a little thing here that Green will officiate."

"And I don't get to stand up with you?" Maybe I should have said "congratulations" first, but I was now *really* shocked, because this was a lot more planned out than I had anticipated, and I didn't get to be a bridesmaid.

Renny rolled her eyes and switched her needles. "Jeez, Cory, you totally rank me. It wouldn't fit your station at all."

And now I gaped at her, grasping for words in the worst way. "Renny... we went to high school together. We read the same books, for sweet Goddess's sake."

"Yes, we did." And now her eyes left her knitting and concentrated totally on me. "And it would be like Queen Elizabeth waiting on Anne Boleyn—"

"Anne Boleyn was her mother and died when Liz was a kid—"

"Yeah, but she was a lady in waiting first, and it would be a total reversal of rank, okay? Queen Elizabeth doesn't wait on anybody. You don't either."

"But, Renny...." I blinked tears now, stung and totally derailed at the track this conversation had taken. "Renny, you're the best girlfriend I've had since middle school...."

Renny smiled sweetly at me and put her knitting down, put her hands on mine, and squeezed. "And you're the best friend I've ever had too. But... but even when you were friends with Davy, it was more like you were a secret agent trying to be regular people. You didn't ask to be Queen of the Vampires, you certainly didn't ask to be High Faerie Queen of Northern California... but as silly as those titles are, that's exactly what you've become. And I'd die before I dishonored you, even if you don't see it that way. You'll be there next to Green as he officiates, and I'll steal something from your closet for the justice-of-the-peace thing, and you can be a witness, and don't worry—no one else is standing up with me since you can't, not even Max's bitchy sister who thinks it's her God-given right. But Lady Cory of my hill doesn't wait on anybody, not even her best friend, and I'll make sure you remember that, because we've put our lives and our safety and even our honor in your hands."

I'd roomed with Renny—she'd gone an entire week without ever saying that much, and now what she did have to say hurt me like nothing I'd expected.

"What do you want for a wedding present?" I asked thickly, when I was pretty sure I could speak.

She smiled her best cat smile and picked up her knitting again. "I'll think of something," she threatened, and I shook my head.

"So, do you think Max likes being a cat?" He'd seemed like a natural this morning.

"I hope so," she said calmly, "because I plan to boink him silly as a cat, and I want him to enjoy it."

My eyes got wide, and I had an inappropriate girlfriend question to ask. "So… is cat sex better than people sex?" But at that moment, Green opened the door and bobbed his head toward the front room, so I never found out.

"The vampires are up," he said quietly. "It's time."

I stood up and grimaced at Renny. She nodded her head, like a bow, as I turned to leave.

"What is it, luv?" Green asked as I seized his hand and started off down the corridor.

"Who wants to be a bridesmaid anyway?" I sniffed, and he stopped right there in the hall, knowing half the hill was outside in the front yard waiting for us.

"You did," he said softly. "But your friends won't let you wait on them."

"It's a dumb rule," I pouted childishly, and then I ran into my room to get something because I didn't want to hear his answer to that. He waited for me, and together we moved outside toward the waiting court.

The front door opened out onto a landing that overlooked the gardens, with a flight of stairs to the front lawn. We opened the door and looked out on the entire kiss of vampires and all of the sidhe. The weres had apparently decided to sit this one out, but that didn't stop Gavin and Graeme from being thrilled to be getting vampire rides from Ellis, Marcus, a subdued Kyle, and any other vampire willing to heft them ten feet into the air for a moment or two and then set them down. Ellis and Graeme were eye level with the landing about a second after we opened the door, and Graeme gave us a cheery wave.

"Are you coming to say good-bye, Cory?" he asked breathlessly. "Grandma says we can come back in the summertimes and stay for a whole month! We're going to call it Camp Green, and we'll get a written invitation and a car and driver and everything. Ooop!" Because Ellis took that moment to roll his eyes and drop quickly down, just to hear the delighted squeal that came with the maneuver.

"Yes," I called down to him as I pattered down the stairs with Green at my heels. "Yes, I came to say good-bye to you guys, and yes, we're all glad you get to come in the summer." That last sound brought a strangled sniff from Chloe, and I looked at her coldly as I drew near.

"Don't worry, Chloe. You'll think it's a free summer camp and be thrilled to send them off."

"How can you do this?" she growled, watching miserably as her children played as naturally in our world as they probably did at the local park at home.

"Since you may have forced us to do the same thing to my own mother, Chloe, I'd think you'd have figured it out. Green and I... we'd give about anything to keep our people safe. Your mother understands this—I think she loves us for it. Your memory is such a small price to pay, in the long run."

"What about my sister—"

"What about her? Have you told Regina what you've found here?"

Chloe's muttered "No" didn't surprise me—Grace had told me that, from what she'd gathered when visiting the women in their dreams, Regina and Chloe hadn't maintained much contact. "Regina's a sweet girl," she'd said proudly, "and still very idealistic—she teaches children and hopes to change the world. Chloe raises her children, and hopes the world will change for her."

"So if you haven't told her, then there's no reason for your mom not to check in on her now and then," I said reasonably. "And she'll say hi to the boys, of course."

"How can you take them away from me!" Chloe almost wailed, and I looked at her in surprise.

"I can't," I told her, blinking. "I can only give them the opportunity to know your mother. You've already rejected the chance. There's no reason they have to, right?"

With that, Grace tapped me on the shoulder, her broad freckled features looking strained in the fading twilight, and I gave her a twisted look of my own. "I'm sorry, Grace," I said, and she nodded.

"Do you trust me to do it, Lady Cory?" she asked, and Chloe's gasp ripped us both a little. I cringed.

"Of course I trust you!" I did. Implicitly. "But you've been hurt enough already. I told you that Green will do it. It was our decision, we'll take care of it."

Grace nodded once, and a crimson tear sneaked out, matting her long cinnamon-colored lashes and smearing across the side of her face when she dashed it away.

"Signal Green when you're ready," I said roughly, moving aside and squeezing her shoulder.

Grace nodded and turned a bleak face to her daughter, looking more vampiric than I'd ever seen her look—even more vampiric than the night we'd claimed Kyle for our own.

Thinking of Kyle, I left the two of them to their good-byes, whatever they might entail, and went to where the boys were still getting vampire rides. Kyle was standing, waiting his turn, looking like he was barely holding himself together. The men and I hadn't seen him since the night of Davy's funeral, but then, we'd had other things on our minds.

"You look like hell," I said quietly, smiling and waving at Gavin, who was looking fierce and determined not to be afraid of the ten-foot gap between his feet and the earth. Kyle's pale face was corpse white and gaunt—it was almost his feeding face, standing there on the lawn and playing with children—and his shoulders wobbled dejectedly toward the ground.

"That's funny, 'cause I feel like shit," he said laconically, and I smiled just a little, as he'd meant me to.

"You know... Green doesn't have to sleep with you to help heal you," I said after a moment. "And there are women here who will take some of the pain away until you can bear it. And your kiss mates will do anything they can...."

"They have been," Kyle said simply. "It's not the sex—although I'll probably come see Green later—but...." He looked at me, and suddenly he seemed wise, when once upon a time I would have said he was denser than dark matter. "It took you months, Lady Cory. I know, because I asked. In fact, the general consensus is that you and Bracken and Green will never be the same."

I swallowed and looked at him calmly. "We shouldn't ever be the same," I said roughly. "But we can go on and be happy. In fact, that's what we've been doing."

I didn't give him time to reply, because I ran to intercept Graeme before he went up again.

"Aww, Lady Cory—one more ride?" he begged, and I laughed.

"You can each do one more ride, but I have to talk to you first, okay?" They both gathered near me, and I dropped down to their level, although I was so small anyway it felt a little redundant.

"First, I've got a present for you." A little shyly, I pulled the two hats out of my pocket. I'd striped one of them blue with yellow and the other one blue with red, and then, because I wasn't that good with color yet, I'd gone and bought patches—Superman and Spiderman—and sewn them on. Graeme greedily snatched at the Spiderman hat, and Gavin took the Superman hat with quiet gratitude. They thanked me and put the hats on their heads to show me they fit. I was pleased, because I really did love these kids, and this way I was sure they would be able to remember us. Then I had to settle down to business.

"Okay, guys. Someone told you that you get to come back, right?" They nodded eagerly, and I took a deep breath. "Has anyone told you that your mom won't remember us?" There was a stunned silence. "You're flying with vampires, higher than high, so you know I'm telling the truth, right?"

They nodded solemnly, and Gavin looked almost frightened.

"Now, you guys haven't done anything wrong, but your mom...." I sighed. "You guys already know that this place is *special*, right?" More solemn nods. "Well, you have to love a place to keep it special. Your mom doesn't love this place... and we just can't let her come back to it, okay?"

"I'm sorry," Graeme said earnestly. "I'm sorry my mom was mean to you...." He was crying, and I felt lower than fleas on roadkill.

"No no no no no...." I gathered them in for a hug that was sweet, so sweet. Their little arms clung to me and they burrowed their faces into my shoulder, and I just wanted to die because this hurt them and I was a part of it. "This is not your fault, guys, and it's not altogether your mom's fault. Sometimes, grown-ups... they're just not ready for a place this special, that's all. But we want you to come back, and you're going to start recognizing people—elves and fey and weres and things— just because you believe, okay? So I'm going to give you a password." They'd stopped crying and were looking at me now with avid eyes. "If you see someone you think would fit in with this hill—they might even have a tattoo...."

"Like Arturo's? And Grandma's? Like Bracken's?" They chimed in, and I nodded, relieved.

"We all have one—all of us but Green. So if you see someone with a tattoo like that, and you're afraid—either of them or of someone else—you just have to say 'We're Green's people.' Can you remember that? Just tell them that you're one of Green's people, and they'll keep you safe, because that's what Green's people do."

They nodded solemnly, and we had another hug, and then I shooed them back so they could have their last vampire ride. I turned toward Grace and Chloe just in time to see Chloe crumple to the ground and Grace help her down, scarlet tears tracking her pale face.

"Oh, Grace...." Because Green and Arturo were rushing to them, and anyone could guess what had happened. Grace hadn't waited for Green after all.

Arturo gathered her to him. I saw it then, that faint bronze light that had caught my attention this morning before my mother had walked in. Oh... oh, Goddess. I touched my own neck, feeling Adrian's three marks—the ones that bound me to this hill, to the vampires, and, in domino fashion, had bound me to the three men who had shared my bed, and even to breaking the hearts of the two little boys shrieking with excitement on the lawn. The pain, the exquisite, joyous pain of that binding was a thing I couldn't ever forget, not for a day or a minute or a heartbeat. It was the scent of my beloved on my skin, and he had....

I was breathing too fast as I watched Arturo shoulder his way through the crowd, hugging Grace to him. She was touching his face and murmuring an explanation even as I watched. I wouldn't trade my life for anything, I thought painfully, loving them both. I didn't expect Arturo would either.

Swallowing hard, I moved to where Green was setting Chloe behind the wheel of her truck and whispering softly into her ear. Chloe's eyes opened and her posture straightened. She looked straight ahead, just like an expectant little doll, and waited for further instructions. We signaled the vampires then. They flew the boys to the car and we got them all buckled and secured, and their overnight bags settled as well. Green was checking Chloe's cell phone and giving the numbers to Cocklebur, a slightly built, small-statured sidhe who was writing them down—preparing, I guess, to make sure the Redding vampires had a way to ensure we left no loose ends.

Finally, the truck grumbled out of the drive in a spatter of gravel, and the people on the front lawn began to disperse. I walked straight into Green's arms, aware that although I had been dreading the experience like a dental checkup, the reality was so much worse than the anticipation that I might never be able to go to the dentist again.

"Will Grace be okay?" I asked urgently, and Green's mouth twisted.

"No," he said after a moment, "and yes. Either way, it's over. Let's go upstairs and wait for our boys, shall we?"

Forty-five minutes later, I was starting to get worried—Bracken had left a message with one of the weres that they were going to stop for dinner for LaMark and Mario, but they should have been home by now. Green and I had been reading my lit assignment together—he had the best reading voice in the world—and I had just allowed my restlessness to launch me off his lap so I could go grab my flip-flops and my car keys, when the phone rang.

It was Bracken, and the nightmare began.

I wasn't sure how many cars went, or who all was in them. All I knew was that Green, Grace, Max, Renny, and I all stuffed ourselves into the Caddy as Arturo drove. I had just enough brainpower to check the rearview mirror and make sure the hearse was following us, since I knew there were a lot of vampires in the air and no guarantee we would be returning to the hill before dawn. I hadn't even been able to look at Grace as we'd loaded in.

"We should have sent an escort," I said as we spanned the bridge. It was the first thing any of us had said since we'd loaded into the car, and I was pretty sure I was just voicing everybody else's thoughts.

"We didn't have a choice," Arturo said harshly, and I could have kicked myself. He loved those kids—we all loved those kids—and here I was grinding salt into his flesh about my own shortsightedness.

I must have made a sound, because Green squeezed my knee reassuringly. "He's right, luv. If we'd sent an escort, she would have known she was being followed, and that would have tipped her off. The mind-wipe was too recent for her to see one of us in her rearview mirror. We had no way of knowing they'd stop to use the loo before they got on the freeway."

"It was probably Graeme," I said tightly. "That kid's got a bladder the size of a pea."

Arturo made a horrible sound, between a laugh and a sob and a howl, and that was the end of conversation for the next ten minutes.

We didn't pull up to the McDonald's parking lot but went instead to the Denny's across the street, where Bracken and the others were waiting tensely outside of the SUV and pacing in panicked bursts. As we unloaded, Bracken took me into a hug that had more than panic in it, and I was too tightly sprung to wonder what. Then he looked at Max, and both men nodded. Max had changed into a shirt that wasn't torn and had a leather jacket on that made me think achingly of Adrian, and he strode off into the night with Renny trotting at his side to ask his fellow cops what had happened.

I did the pee-pee dance while he was gone, unable to hug Bracken or Green or to hold Nicky's hand. I had a picture in my head, an idea, a tug, a feel, and I wanted to pin it down before I told everybody to follow it. I wanted confirmation of what I already knew before I made an ass of myself by thinking I had a power I might not.

Max came back looking grim, and Renny was subdued and upset at his elbow.

"She stopped here so the boys could use the bathroom. They parked in the upper parking lot, went inside, bought a couple of Happy Meals, and walked back to the car. Chloe's story is that someone knocked her down and grabbed the boys—but she didn't see a car or a van or even who knocked her down. She's a little out of it, but there's no bruise on her head, so I think they're taking her in for a tox screen. Other than that, they've got nada."

We nodded tensely. Then I turned to Green, thinking hard. "Green— they're ours, right? I mean, they're mine. I was the power focus, I sent it rippling through everyone's skin, they were there last night. I've marked them in a way, right?"

Green nodded. "Yes. And you should be able to sense where they are—it's the reason I didn't lock you in your room when Bracken called."

I snorted. "As if!"

"Yes, as if!" he shot back. "Because here's the thing, Cory, and you need to remember it. Everyone else here—" He gestured to everyone in the now crowded parking lot, from the people in the Caddy to the Avians to the vampires unloading from the hearse and the SUV full of werecreatures and sidhe. "—all of us are protected from the abomination that is the Hollow Man's blood. It can't hurt us, it can't poison us or enthrall us—we're safe. That includes the boys. If he had hurt them any other way, you would know it by now." He nodded urgently. "So everyone is safe from his worst weapon, yes?"

I nodded back yes, wanting him to hurry up.

"That is, my beloved, everyone is safe except you. Your only safety is if all of us—" His nod took in Bracken and Nicky. "—are with you.

So no haring off into the wild dark yonder. No springing a trap so you can get inside of it." He gave Bracken a meaningful look, and I flinched, because not too long ago I'd done just that to save Bracken's life. "We're going searching, and yes, beloved, we're following you—but you need to promise us that you'll put your safety above all else."

"Green...." I fought to stay calm, to keep my face from squinching and my voice from breaking. I fought to keep the tension of hysteria from my body, because haring off into the wild dark yonder was exactly what I wanted to do. "Green, those boys are *ours*. Davy wasn't ours, and I can live with that, but those boys are *ours,* and I can't live with keeping safe if—"

"The hell you can't," Grace growled behind me, and I turned to meet Grace the Vampire in all her glory. Her wide, freckled face was gaunt with the changes of her species. Her eyes had gone from limpid brown to whirling so redly that the blaze of them lit up the blood under her skin, and she glowed—she glowed like a demon and her mouth was all fangs, and they were extended and ready to rip me apart.

I gasped and kept myself from closing my eyes and backing up from her in shame and fear, because Green and I had done this. Green and I had put her grandchildren in danger, and now they weren't letting me go get them back.

"I cut Chloe loose for you, my Lady," Grace ground out, her voice a hollow growl. "I let those boys go, knowing that there was a danger beyond our hill, and I did it for you, and for Green. And I'd do it again. So don't fuck up my trust by getting killed—do you understand, my queen?"

I blinked twice and breathed in hard. "I understand," I said into the thundering silence that was filled with only our harsh breaths and heartbeats. "I understand that I'll get them back, that's what I understand," I barked. Then I whirled around and opened the door to the Caddy. "They're across the overpass, down Bowman, and then take Luther Road." Until I'd said it, I had no idea that was where the buzzing in my stomach was leading me, but I knew it was truth. After thinking of nothing *but* the boys and my fear for them for the last half hour, this thing in my gut was more than a feeling, it was more than a pull—it was just knowledge, dropped into my brain like a slide into a projector, and I could see what they saw, recognize what they knew, and my urgency was spurred on by their fear.

"NOW, people!" I snapped, and bodies were diving for cars and we were off and running. Somehow, without jostling or shuffling, Bracken and Nicky ended up in the Caddy along with Grace, Green, and me.

"I meant it, Cory," Grace said from the backseat, but her voice was closer to normal and that moment of crisis was over.

"Down Luther," I said again as Arturo got near it and he gave me a droll look, as panicked as I knew he was.

Luther Road was often used as a shortcut between Highway 80 and Highway 49, and it had a few home-run businesses on it, but the streets that shot off from it were purely residential. There were houses with half-acre lots and trees in their backyards, long driveways, and a variety of floor plans. It was sort of what subdivisions had been like before they became tiny houses and tinier yards. There were no streetlamps, no sidewalks, and no sculpted lawns. Here, in the dark, I could only follow a feeling and the blurry impressions I got from the boys as we traveled the same space. Those impressions came from about two hundred feet up, but I didn't share this with anybody. I only hoped they were as brave with our enemy as they had been with friends on Green's front lawn.

The impressions began to waver, though, when we hit the second round of turnoffs into the residential areas, and the first hit of evil filtered through the car's ventilation system. Grace and I both made gagging noises in tandem, and I gestured frantically for Arturo to turn right down Matson and then pull off to the side.

"We're close," Arturo said needlessly. I nodded, then slammed the door open and exited the still moving vehicle to fall to my knees on the graveled road shoulder in front of a long stretch of watered crabgrass and try to get my stomach under control.

The hearse was hard on our heels, and the other SUV as well. I noted that Kyle, Marcus, Phillip, Bryn, and Ellis were in the hearse; the SUV was full of werecreatures, including Leah, Steph, Joe, and a couple of wolves I didn't recognize, as well as Cocklebur and Twilight. I grimaced as all of these definitely odd people piled out of three cars in one of the more crowded subdivisions, but the vampires were looking decidedly gray around the gills, so I figured maybe we could claim food poisoning if someone asked.

"Thank the Goddess," Marcus said softly, coming up to touch my shoulder in sympathy. "The smell is bad, but it's so much better than it was that night...."

He was right, I thought, nodding my head. The literal stench of abomination had faded, and after a moment I could say, "I'll be okay." Bracken hauled me to my feet. I was still breathing hard to keep my stomach under control, but much more functional than I expected to be.

I looked at him sourly. "You will never know how lucky you are," I accused, and he kissed me softly on the forehead.

"You're okay, bird dog. Now track."

I was in the process of obeying orders (autocratic bastard) when he suddenly laughed, the sound odd and jarring in the middle of all this tension.

"You brought your *knitting?*" He gestured to the quilted tapestry bag over my shoulder, the amazed smirk on his face making me want to kick him.

"I brought my *gun,* genius," I snapped back, taking satisfaction in the "oooohhh" dawning on his handsome face. "It's in my purse inside the bag." I smirked at him and then looked at the vampires, nodding northish (or so I thought) up Matson. I could see, even from where we'd pulled up short to stop, that there was a big stretch of green with a horse enclosure smack in the middle. There were some trees scattered around houses back from the horse area, and that area was haunted with trees and shadows and smaller intimate buildings among big houses, private driveways, and excellent hiding places for the bad guy.

"Fan out," Green said, his voice carrying but still soft enough to stay under the radar. "Stay in clumps—no one person goes anywhere alone, always in twos or threes. Give a shout-out to whomever you look to if you find anything."

And with that we set off down the sweet little suburb, Green and Bracken flanking me, and Nicky crossing the street to follow Grace and Arturo. We all moved as quietly as we could, but I told Marcus to have the vampires stay on the ground. I'd seen an aerial battle, and I'd been on the ground during one, and it seemed to me that a group on the ground had a defensive advantage over a group in the air. Some Air Force pilots out there might have disagreed with me, but working with jets was a lot different from the perspective of an anti-aircraft gun. And besides, Hollow Man had been flying when he first snatched the boys. If he had them now, there was nothing in the spell I had cast the night before to keep them safe if he dropped them from two hundred feet in the air.

Summer was nearing and the night was pleasant, but the neighborhood was extremely quiet. I didn't know what to make of this—shouldn't there be joggers? Teenagers killing time? Neighbors visiting? Maybe they thought about it, took one look outside, and decided "mmnnnoooo... not tonight." Maybe they'd been doing that for a while. Maybe the whistle from the nearby train was a lonely sound tonight, or the trees whispering overhead seemed too sinister, or the dark seemed all-encompassing. We had encountered an enemy before who had existed among humans in this way, and I still didn't understand how an entire block of people could just tuck their heads into their houses and tell themselves that it was all in their imaginations.

We kept walking, even though the stink made it hard on the vampires. The were-animals kept shifting nervously in their shoes, and I was sure they were hearing the same thing we were smelling, but everybody looked determined. Suddenly the smell got worse, and without warning there was a flurry and rustle and animal noises as every werecreature in our party just shifted without preamble, and seemingly without conscious thought. Nicky and the other Avians launched into the air away from their respective groups, heading toward us. They started flying about five feet above us, and in a little more time (they had to get free of their clothes) there was a pack of wolves, pumas, dogs, and a giant misplaced housecat heading toward us as well. They circled me, the elves, and the vampires, facing outward and growling into the night.

"Think he's close?" I asked gamely, and Bracken and Green grabbed my hands without any humor whatsoever. I heard a frustrated yowl and looked across the street to where Max was rolling on his back, trying to get his oversized paw free of his cool black leather jacket. He was hissing and spitting up a storm, and I felt bad for him. "Oh, c'mon— Grace, Arturo, can someone help him out?" Poor Max—he was way too new to the whole cat thing to come out and play cop.

But nobody was paying attention to me. The vampires were trying to stay upright, the werecreatures were surrounding me and letting out a variety of loud, scary animal sounds, and the elves, including Arturo, were squinting into the night in frustration. Everyone knew he was out there, everyone knew he was close, but no one could pin him down.

And then a pale shape came fluttering out of the dark, knocking the Avians aside even as they shrieked and attacked it back.

"Nicky!" I screamed as I saw him hurtled to the ground, and Green and Bracken clutched me closer and swore because they could see the birds getting thrown about but they couldn't see the assailant. Grace and the other vampires launched themselves with moaning growls of fury, and they moved in hyperspeed, but they were still too slow. They flew at the pale shape only to be knocked aside two and three at a time. Marcus got thrown to the ground much faster than he'd flown into the air, landing at our feet with a horrible splat, and I had a moment to be glad there were werecreatures here who could feed him so that he could heal quickly. Then I was hauling at Green's and Bracken's hands, trying to get my gun out of my yarn bag so I could shoot this asshole out of the fucking sky.

Because the vampires and Avians were losing. Grace got thrown aside, sailing into a huge old oak tree about fifty feet away and getting tangled in the branches, and then Phillip, and then Kyle. They all came back, they all hurtled into their enemy using the Goddess's speed and their own force and momentum, and I heard grunts from the Hollow Man and shrieks of pain from our own people, but still they got thrown back. The Avians took over while the vampires were recovering, including Nicky, who had pulled back from his first fall and hadn't even hit the ground. The Hollow Man moved too fast—with an elf's grace and a sorcerer's cunning and a vampire's speed and force—and for all that he had done his fighting with other people's bodies so far, his own body was more than enough to defeat us when we weren't bound into one cohesive whole.

"I need my hands!" I shouted, because the elves weren't letting go of me, and in desperation I made two fists and willed my power into them to make Green and Bracken give me some room. They let go with frustrated oaths, and I ignored their dirty looks and took a step back to throw some fireballs at this fuckhead—but I couldn't, because the vampires were swarming around him. They were right overhead, and Kyle took a blow to the jaw that must have shredded his lips on his teeth, because blood splattered on those of us below, hitting my cheek and painting Green and Bracken with crimson speckles. I swore and ordered Green to clear the sky. "Make them move!" I shouted, and he did that thing, that carrying, "I'm the leader" thing with his voice, and hollered, "My people, clear the sky!"

And as a whole, every creature in the sky that was ours dropped to the ground. I threw two powerballs at the Hollow Man's chest and hit him dead on.

The first ball of fire made him stutter in the air, obviously hurt, and the second one made him shout—a sound that caused the were-animals at our feet to crouch and whine and snap—but neither burst of supernatural energy destroyed him. I had grabbed Bracken's hand and was charging again when he dove out of the sky above us and came straight toward me.

The elves couldn't see him. I screeched and tried to grab a blurry, fast-motion arm with my own nuclear-fusion hand, but Green and Bracken could only feel the passage of the body, watch me struggle with the flesh, and finally shout in frustration and anger when those arms, those clammy cold arms with flesh like giant maggots, wrapped around me and ripped me off the ground. Bracken held on until my shoulder gave a wrench and I howled. Then he let go, the look of despair on his face as he fell that ten feet to the ground almost breaking my heart through the bubble wrap of fear around it.

Oh yeah, I fought like hell. I caught that chilly flesh with my nails, pumped power into my hands, and grabbed at earthworm-cold muscles and skin until Hollow Man screamed in surprise and pain and actually dropped me.

The wind blasted at my ears and the dark whirred in an airbrush of gray, and I desperately remembered that I could fly on occasion and pulled enough power to form a shield between me and the earth. Just when I was slowing into a controlled fall and bounce, I felt that repulsive flesh around my waist and I was jerked upward again, this time dangling upside down over an indignant, corpse-cold back. My yarn bag slid off my dangling arm to be caught by one strap just before it fell. I watched in dejection as my leather purse—with the damned gun—jounced out of the gaping opening and spiraled to the ground with a thump I could only imagine. With a pissed-off groan, I wriggled some more—until it dawned on me that he seemed to have a goal. If he had a goal, that was probably where he stashed the boys, and hitching a ride on his nasty self was my one way of saving them.

I stopped struggling abruptly and settled for a power-aided punch on the back that made him grunt.

"You *fuckhead!*" I bitched, punching him some more and looking down to where, separated by a big slice of dark sky, Bracken and Green were flying after me, but at a severe disadvantage. They were unable to see my captor and losing my own form into the darkness as we blurred away from them with blinding speed. "I will never hear the fucking end of this, do you realize that? They're gonna lock me in a fucking box and not let me out until I'm ninety." I pounded his back again with my own small strength and a giant cathartic "aaaaaarrrrrrrgggggghhhhhhhh!" and then settled down for the ride.

The sewer stench of Hollow Man never really got better, but eventually, after I'd resigned myself to being in his company for a while, it got to the point where I could ignore it and wonder where we were going.

As it turned out, we weren't going all that far. As Matson continued, there were enormous amounts of green, moonlit lawn—I wasn't sure if they were rich people's lawns or golf courses, but the big-ass house by the pond at the end of the side road beneath us was definitely a one-family residence. The mother-in-law cottage about two hundred feet behind it was close enough to the train tracks to shake when the damn engine went by, and it was here that Hollow Man landed.

The cottage itself was sort of standard—made for one or two people and some guests, stucco walls that would probably be tan in the sunlight but that just looked dim and pale now. The weirdest detail of the whole night was listening to the Hollow Man (maybe I'd find out his real name now) search the pockets of his wool slacks for the keys to the entryway while I hung suspended over his shoulder—which was bony, by the way, and digging painfully into my ribs and abdomen.

Once he let himself in, he didn't linger, and I had a vague impression of a living space with a really big leather couch and three or four bedrooms—any one of which could have held the boys—before I was hauled down stairs into what looked like a basement. A basement? A mother-in-law cottage with a basement? It had a pool table, a futon, a gorgeous throw rug in azure and fuchsia, a refrigerator that was probably meant to hold beer, and steel walls that were probably thicker than my waist.

"A bomb shelter?" I asked out of sheer stinking curiosity. "You managed to find a mother-in-law cottage with a bomb shelter? Who in the hell are these people?"

"Rich and paranoid," he snapped, dumping me on the sky blue futon. "And visiting Spain for the winter." He stepped back from me and frowned, looking past my shoulder to the undecorated wall behind me, and I got a good look at our adversary at last.

He wasn't much to look at. Short, that was my first impression. He was shorter than Nicky and taller than me, which probably made him around five foot four, but I'd seen people (my old English teacher for one) who could carry that height and make it look big. This guy was not one of those people.

In life, he'd had acne—not the horrible kind that made me feel so bad for some of the guys in high school, just the irritating kind—the kind that got picked and scarred and picked some more, and then left absurdly shaped scars around his cheeks. I would place a bet that about the time his acne had cleared, his hair had begun to thin, because at death he'd had what looked suspiciously like a bland blond comb-over on what had probably been a twenty-five-year-old oily scalp. Now he was a twenty-five-year-old walking corpse with a baby-shit green complexion. No wonder he'd borrowed Jon Case's body, I thought with a stab of pity—I'd bet all of the bodies he'd snatched for his own use were good-looking. I'd gotten so used to being around the Goddess's get that sometimes I forgot what it was like to be human and homely and to feel, deep in your gut, that everything from your hair to your pores repelled the rest of your species as a whole.

But still, at one time there must have been something innately attractive about this guy, right? Twilight had loved him. A member of the sidhe had chosen him, had lavished the kind of care and attention on him that I got on a daily basis, and had planned to care for him that way until he died, presumably in worse physical condition than when it had all gone horribly wrong. I wondered if I'd have time to figure out what it was about him that had made him desirable, or if I was just going to have to kill him and get it over with.

"I wouldn't do it," he said in what was an admittedly handsome baritone voice. He looked at me glumly, assessing my tense, poised body and the way I was charging power like mad.

"You got a good reason why I shouldn't?" I stood up and smiled toothily, waiting for the buzzing in my chest to get big enough to force it into my hands and throttle him with it.

"Whatever you'd do big enough to kill me would probably destroy the house, right?" he asked, leaning back on the pool table with an irritating nonchalance. I nodded, knowing where this was going but wanting to hear him say it. "You'd kill the kids—and that was the thing that got you out here, right?"

"If you've hurt them," I said pleasantly, letting my force ease up a little but keeping it in reserve in the back of my throat like tears, "there's not a power on the planet that will save you. You know that, right?"

"Your people won't do anything to hurt you...."

"They know I'd die for those kids," I broke in. I'd made that pretty clear. "What do you want them for?"

He blinked and shrugged a little. "I'm hungry," he said plaintively. "I'm hungry, all the time—"

"You're a vampire! The soul-stealing kind!" Oh, please—he couldn't be this stupid, could he? "What did you expect when you went begging the Houston vampires to turn you?"

"Well, for one thing, I expected a little fucking respect!" he burst out, sounding surprised. "All those other vampires... people are nice to them."

"Well I'm the queen of the fucking Northern California vampires, shithead. If you wanted some respect, maybe you could have tried talking to me instead of going after my people!" I thought of poor Chris Williams. "Or any people," I finished sadly. "Did you really go to all the trouble of snatching those little kids for a meal? There are plenty of humans who'd roll over on their backs, spread their legs, and beg you to take them, bleed them, and do it again—why'd you snatch *my* people?"

"They glowed like you," he said distractedly. "The boys, I mean. I thought maybe they'd be supernatural. I like supernatural blood. Humans don't... don't satisfy me...," he said, sounding surprised and sad. His pasty, greenish face assumed a stiff expression of pique. "I can drain them and drain them.... I drained your little friend, once I realized she wasn't you, and I was still hungry. But supernaturals, they last awhile. They make me feel... alive...." His voice trailed off in a dreamy way, and I wondered sickly how many of his own people he'd killed just because he hadn't figured out the nature of his own existence.

"How long have you been murdering your own people?" I asked, not wanting to know but feeling I had to.

"I don't know...," he said, looking a little disconsolate. "The year I turned.... Let's see, that movie had just come out...." He smiled a little, and for the first time I could see just a little bit of humanity in him, a little bit of boyishness, but it still wasn't enough for me to know what Twilight had seen. "*Ferris Bueller's Day Off*," he remembered with joy. "I loved that movie."

"Thirty years," I said blankly. "You've been killing your own people for longer than I've been alive." For some reason, that totally blew my mind. "Why! For the love of the Goddess… you had a sweet setup in Houston—a good home, emerging powers, Twilight as a lover—why? Do you know how we tracked you down, Hollow Man? We tracked you down by *smell*. The things you've done to yourself—the things you've done to others—you've become an abomination to your own people. Why?"

"What did you call me?" he asked, seeming to ignore everything else I'd said.

"The Hollow Man." I flopped disconsolately onto the futon, wrapping my good arm around my knees. He obviously needed me for something—and I wasn't going to fight him now, when he was right about me not wanting to hurt the boys. I might as well make myself comfortable.

"Why would you call me that?" he asked, looking unhappily at his shiny black shoes. He'd looked everywhere but at me since he'd dropped me in this little cold room.

"Because you unmake everything you touch," I said, blinking up at him. "You're never satisfied." He was such a nonentity, standing there with his attention wandering around the bare-steel room. I'd expected more. I'd expected a big gothic bad guy with a Bela Lugosi accent, and I got the kid who didn't go to prom and never got over it.

"Well, I never get enough!" he burst out, toeing the very pricey throw rug under the pool table. "I mean, I've got this sorry-assed power where I can move shit around, but really—what can you do with that?"

"Well, you could have fought crime," I suggested nastily, "but you chose to throw losers at me instead." The images of Chuck and Shane, their heads split open because this guy had thrown them at me like softballs, rose in front of my eyes like black spots.

"It didn't get that big until I turned," he groused. "Until I died, all it really did was break shit."

"That's because it's all you chose to do with it!" I thought longingly of the boys and that wonderful day in the garden when just the tiniest bit of sun had peeked through the clouds, filling their shield bubbles full of rainbows. "These power things—they're really only as big as our hearts, you know," I said, trying to get through.

"But I'm not really hollow." He was still stuck on that. "I mean, I've got flesh and blood…."

"You've apparently got everybody else's flesh and blood." The terrible waste, the horrible deaths.... He was so empty. Was it all because he was so empty?

"Yeah—that one guy had a great body. I could have walked around as him for a long time." He narrowed his eyes and looked disgruntled. "And then your boyfriend...."

"Husband."

"Ripped his heart out. And you killed my other friends."

"You threw them at me!" Again my stomach heard the thud of Chuck's head as it hit the wall, and I swallowed hard.

"It's hard to get friends," he said sadly. "People don't really like me."

"Yeah, that's a shame. Do you realize that you corrupt everything you touch with your... your need? People don't like you because once you touch them, they blow up!" An image of Ellen Beth flashed before me, her eyes rolling whitely in the mask of her lover's corrupted blood.

"That's not my fault!" he whined. "I mean, I need to eat. And they like it when I feed. It's not my fault it's not enough. And they talk to me, and they agree... but it's not enough. Nothing is ever enough—and we ask ourselves, what do we want that we don't have? What do we need? And we need, and we need... and then I'm all alone, needing without them. It's not my fault they leave me...."

His whine was beginning to grate on my nerves, partly because I was starting to feel for him. He really did seem lonely... maybe the corruption of the blood wasn't his fault.... I shook myself and stuck to the important things. "Can you tell me again why you needed the boys? You can't infect them, you know."

He nodded, still sunk in his own sense of having been wronged. "I know. You did something to them. I can't bite them—my teeth sort of bounce off."

"You can't bite any of us," I told him frankly, thrilled to know that what we'd done had worked. "You might as well go away."

"I can bite you," he said. "Your skin doesn't smell the same." And then he looked up at me pleasantly and smiled, meeting my eyes for the first time. Terror settled into my stomach like a sleeping puffer fish.

His eyes were pale, pale blue, almost translucent they were so colorless, and they were empty, puzzled, devoid of anything but his own self-pity. He smiled wistfully for a moment. "I bet you'd taste wonderful. You're pretty powerful, aren't you? Power tastes good. The sylphs taste okay, but Twilight…." He shuddered in a really repulsive ecstasy of sensuality. "Twilight was the best. He was the closest I ever came to full."

"That's because he loved you," I said sadly.

"Yeah." He smiled happily. "That was nice—it was nice that he loved me. But he was holding out on me. All I wanted was everything he had. How can you love someone and not want to give them everything?"

I thought of Bracken and Green, doing everything in their power to keep me safe, to keep me alive and whole and well—and of Adrian, who had died trying to do the same thing. "Sometimes everything is not yours to give," I said sincerely.

"No." He shook his head. "I never got any breaks. My mother left me—"

"She died, Hollow Man. That's not the same as leaving you."

"She was gone. She just didn't want to stay with me, and I wasn't cute enough to adopt. Twilight loved me. He promised me the world, but…." He shifted restively, shrugging off the tremendous, earth-shattering bounty that was a sidhe lover as though regretting not buying shoes. "He didn't really give it to me. If he'd given me all he had, I wouldn't have… I wouldn't have just wanted more. I think he just wanted to watch me wither and die, like my mom. He wanted to keep me mortal and dependent on him. Love the poor human…. I was a charity case, that was all, and his charity wasn't worth shit."

Oh… oh, Goddess. This guy was scary. I'd faced the vengeful and the power hungry, and I'd been able to get hot and angry and do my job. This guy—this guy scared me cold, clammy cold, the chill of his smooth maggot flesh. "Let the boys go," I begged from the heart.

"I can't," he said, surprised. "I can't feed off of them, but I marked them, so they can't go back. They're mine," he smiled happily, "and I'll give them what no one gave me. I'll make them immortal."

I blanched, my breath suddenly whooshing out of me like I'd been hit. "Oh, Goddess," I whispered. "Goddess… oh jeez…. Hollow Man, tell me how many times you've marked them." *The first is empathy,* I heard in my brain. It was a vampire mantra—one I hadn't heard when Adrian had marked me but that Marcus had told me since I'd come back to the hill and started blooding my people. *The second is telepathy, the third is physical sensation, the fourth is immortality.* Adrian had marked me twice while he was alive, his soul blowing through mine like a breeze blows through your hair. The third time had been as he'd died, and his soul had blown through me on its way to… to Green's hill, I guess, where he haunted us still. The third time, instead of his physical sensations, he'd given me his kiss of vampires to protect, the power of blooding his people—it was the only power that I, a living, breathing human, could absorb from him. If he'd marked me a fourth time, my life would be as tied to his as Bracken's was to mine. I would have died when he did, and as much as I might have wanted to die the morning Green and I woke up to a world without him, I had plenty of reasons to live now. And the idea of this guy's polluted soul blowing through the bodies of those sweet little boys made me sick.

"How many?" I repeated. From what I understood, it was hard for a vampire to do more than once in a week, but this guy… this guy took over new bodies on what was apparently a regular basis. He knew how to move his pale starveling soul with ease. How many times had he fouled their hearts with the texture of his yearning evil?

"Only once." He nodded. "But it was sweet…." He writhed, and I tried to keep my dinner down. "So sweet…. Imagine how sweet it will be if I'm in their bodies when I move my soul through them?" He swallowed convulsively. I noticed a thin trickle of spit tracking down his skin and thought I would barf on his shiny black shoes if he didn't shut up. Oh, Goddess. I had to undo that abomination. I had to find some way to wipe that taint off their poor, helpless little souls.

"Can't you just…." I tried to keep the tears out of my voice, not that he was noticing anybody else's unhappiness but his own. "Can't you just let them go?"

"They taste so good…." He closed those colorless eyes and breathed deeply, serene in his own impending satisfaction. "They're the best break I've ever gotten."

"I bet I'd taste pretty good," I said cheerfully, hoping to distract him.

He eyed me and nodded. "Yes," he said. "But you'd taste better if I was inside you. I'll wait until you're weak and I can be inside you. That's what I've been waiting for since I saw you at school, you know. To be inside you and taste you. You were so bright, walking through that campus. I wanted your boyfriend—"

"Husband."

"—but he could destroy me, so I had to settle. You and your friends were like army searchlights. I just wanted to be a part of you… to have you…."

I stood up, ignoring the stench and moving up to him to plead, to see if I could beg some sense into his dreamy, off-center self. "You have no right to us." Those little boys…. I couldn't blow up the house, or I'd kill them—but if I let the house stand, what would happen would be worse.

"Your boyfriend—"

"Husband."

"—would carry you through the halls and the quad, and the world would part for you. You were like the goddamned queen of every-fucking-thing. I wanted that. I wanted him too—God, he was beautiful. But mostly I wanted to be carried through the world like I was the king of every-fucking-thing… and now I'll have you to taste. And I'll have the boys, bound to me, worshipping me while you suck me and kiss me and worship me. I'll have everything."

"You had everything," I whispered sadly, looking past his pathetic, lost-kid face and thinking of Twilight and his little house and the werecreatures he'd nurtured, and the love that shining creature had blessed this pitiful *thing* with. "You had everything, Hollow Man, and you lost it. And one way or another, you are not going to survive this night."

He backhanded me then, his vampire muscles and hyperspeed motion throwing my body against the futon and my head into the steel wall behind it. Pain exploded in my skull and in my nose and cheekbone, and the world began to fade.

"My name is Steve," he said softly and then slammed the door as the world went black.

GREEN
Picking Up

GREEN WATCHED her fall and thought his heart would stall right there in his chest until he saw the shining shield she'd created to catch herself. Then she was jerked upright and pulled into the darkening night, and he wondered if he'd ever breathe again.

He was blurring, blurring toward her, air whooshing past his ears, but Hollow Man was in the air too, and Green couldn't fly fast enough, and they were fading, fading from his sight, and then they were gone.

"*Buggerfuck*!" Bracken howled behind him. He dropped from the sky to fall to his knees and beat the concrete with his fists until his skin shredded and the concrete cracked. "Buggerfuckingcowshittingcock-slurpingsonofabastardscumsluttingwhore!" Bracken continued his pound into the pavement with that truly awesome show of language, and Green just stared into the sky with disbelief. She was gone. He couldn't see her anymore. All they had done to keep her safe, and she could just be hauled off into the dark yonder without him. Bracken was still on his knees swearing brokenly, and without thinking about it Green walked back to him and put his hand on his brother's shoulder to calm him down. They'd never find her if Bracken hurt himself in despair.

He pulled on Bracken's shoulder and they lifted into the air to find the friends they'd left behind. The vampires were pulling themselves up from where they'd been smacked and stunned, and the werecreatures trotted over, whining softly and offering throats so their friends could heal. As he and Bracken landed, three Avians touched down by them and turned, checking out torn skin, bloodied limbs, and bone-deep bruises as they stood.

"Goddess!" Nicky swore softly, putting his own bloody hand on Bracken's shoulder and squeezing gently. "Well, at least we know he wants her alive."

"Yes." Green nodded automatically and forced himself to think. Think (*she was just taken from me*) think (*she's vulnerable*) think (*oh*

Goddess, I can't) think (*can't do this again*) think (*oh Goddess please please please don't do this to me, not again, not so soon after... not when we've nursed her back to health and she's starting to live that promise, that fabulous promise of what she's always been meant to be*) think... breathe... think.... The Hollow Man's presence seemed to block all telepathy, but that was not how her bond worked with everybody. "Nicky, Bracken—you're bound to her magically. Can you feel her pulling at you?"

Nicky said yes, and Bracken stared at his bloodied hands dangling at his thighs and nodded. Green took another deep breath and sent a surge of healing through Bracken's shoulder, and they both watched for a relieving moment as the rips in Bracken's skin and the cracks in his bones reknit. "You know she gets upset when you hurt yourself," he said gently, and Bracken visibly pulled himself together and took Green's offered hand to stand.

"We know she's alive... and we know the boys are," Green said. Everybody nodded, seeming to take some strength from the knowledge. Renny and Max limped over to Green and thrust disconsolate heads under his hands. He stroked them, gaining some strength himself. "The vampires can track us to his general area by scent. The weres can protect them when the smell gets too bad. Nicky and Bracken can keep us going after that. We stay together—completely together. If he caught the boys to feed, he's been sorely disappointed, and none of us are safe."

"What are we going to do when we find him?" Grace asked, her voice edging on hysteria, and Arturo put his palm in the small of her back. "No, I'm serious. We just got our asses kicked by one guy—"

"Because Cory wasn't using her power," Green said firmly. They couldn't afford to fall apart now. "Because we were all so busy protecting her we didn't give her a chance to do her job. She's known all along how to defeat Hollow Man...."

"No," Grace said.

"And we didn't listen."

"*Mijo*, no," Arturo seconded.

"But we know now, don't we—and the three of us have a way to keep her safe as she does it, and that's what we're going to do."

Bracken made a broken sound, a terrified whimper, and Nicky looked at him with wide, hurt eyes. "We know she's alive," Green snarled in the face of their doubt. "Now it's time we believe in her the way she's always believed in us. But first we've got to find her...." He swallowed, the myriad things that could happen between the snatching and the retrieving swarming him before he had a chance to ward them off. He swallowed again and made a defensive gesture with his hands for the purely mental pestilences of fear that were besieging him. "And we've got to find her soon. I don't know our enemy. Everything he's done so far has been beyond our comprehension. I... I don't think we *can* know him. I don't think anything in us can understand this... this moral vacancy—but we know it's got her and the boys, and we need to get them now."

And with that he looked to the vampires, who nodded him north again, and as a whole they turned and headed that way. They had to stop several times to tend to the wounded. The hurt ones hadn't wanted to slow the group down, but eventually the limping and the whimpers and the occasional stagger brought concerned attention their way, and Green healed them.

Cocklebur had sustained a wrenched shoulder, trying to grab at Hollow Man as he'd come for Cory. "You came closer than anybody but Bracken," Green praised softly as he healed. The slight little sidhe blushed and bowed slightly—he hadn't been Cory's biggest fan when she came to the hill, but now he loved her as much as everybody else. Twilight put his arm around Cocklebur's shoulders, and the two of them stayed staunchly by Green's side when they resumed.

Steph and Joe were okay, but they whined at Grace's feet until she fed from them just a little and they knew *she* would be okay. Marcus had regenerated from much of his internal injuries, but he needed to feed to supplement the healing, and Leah offered him a willing throat while Phillip helped to support his weight. Max would have done it—but as he padded up to offer, his back leg folded, and Renny trotted to him, nuzzling his neck and whining. Bracken took a look and laid a gentle hand on the new werecat's neck.

"You got hamstrung in the fight," he said gently. "He was moving so fast I didn't even see. C'mon, let's have Green get a look." And with that he hefted the big animal in his arms and trotted up to the front of the group, where Green was tending to an already mending rip on Mario's arm.

"Man, I really liked those jeans," Mario was complaining, trying to keep things light. He was standing in the middle of someone's lawn, buck naked. "I can't believe I lost *everything* in trans."

Arturo gave an amused grunt and blurred away in hyperspeed, returning with an armload of clothes. "I don't think the weres are going to need them," he said, and as Green turned his attention to Max, Mario started putting on Max's clothes—including the leather jacket, which he stroked appreciatively.

Max turned baleful eyes on him from Bracken's hold and growled, and Green fondled the dark brown ears. "He'll take good care of it, Max—it's the envy of every non-sidhe on the hill." And then he ever so gently ran his hands down the back of the injured leg and sent a breath of healing through the sundered tissues and ripped tendons. Max gave a whimper and a mrreowwlll, and Renny almost knocked Bracken over in her attempts to reach him. After a moment he started struggling out of Bracken's arms, and Bracken put him down, as good as new. Max licked his hands in appreciation, then moved to Green and did the same.

Arturo watched all of this with raised eyebrows. "And to think—I would have killed him last summer without a second thought."

"Lucky us, you didn't," Green said, and they moved on.

The going was slow. The Hollow Man had occupied this neighborhood for a long time—his stink was all over the place, from the roots of the grass to the leaves on the trees to the ether above—and the vampires had to think very carefully before they chose another direction.

The werecreatures were so incensed by the sound of the wrongness that often they would whine and growl at the wind through the trees. A train went by once, off in the distance, and the sound so unsettled the two werewolves that they became naked, beautiful young men in one heartbeat, furry, magnificent wolves in the next, and so on until they finally collapsed in a heap of exhausted human limbs and panting, sobbing breaths. LaMark—who had lost his shoes and jacket in trans— limped back to them. He knew them from his time in the weres' common room, and he looked up to Green. "I'll take them back, leader," he said quietly. "They can't do this anymore, and I'm about done in. I'm sorry."

Green grimaced in sympathy. "Go ahead, brothers. Thanks for what you've given us."

LaMark helped the two young men up, and they looked back at Green abashedly. They appeared disconsolate and ashamed, and Green nodded his head and gave them a wave as a salute. Everyone else kept inching toward the epicenter of the agony.

A minute went by, then another, and Green became breathlessly aware that midnight had passed and dawn was nearing. It was all he could do to not wrap his arms around his middle and howl to the night sky to bring her back. He was looking desperately up to the barely waning moon at the northwest horizon when he saw something tiny and bright flicker across it and toward them in a glitter of azure and sunrise orange. He knew those colors. His breath caught, and so did Bracken's.

"Holy shit. Is that who I think it is?" Nicky asked, hope throbbing in his voice. Green and Bracken nodded yes, their pulses thready with the exhilaration of finally, at last, a lead.

Then Bracken saw what was trailing behind the tiny creature and said, "Aww, fuck. Is that *what* I think it is?"

Green saw what he was talking about and groaned himself. "Goddess," he swore. "She must really be desperate."

That thought shook everybody from their trance of hoping at the moon, and the whole group of them took off running in the direction of Cory's sprite.

CORY
The Queen of Every-fucking-thing

I DON'T know how long I lay flopped awkwardly on the futon, stunned and unconscious, but when I surfaced it was to a buzzing that *wasn't* in my head. I looked up and there was, of all things, a sprite flitting anxiously about my face. I held up a steadying hand to make it stop moving quite so quickly, because I was getting dizzy and queasy all over again.

The poor thing screeched to a halt and hovered over my face, and I smiled in reassurance—then the dizzy and queasy reasserted themselves with the force of an anvil falling on my head. Groaning, gasping, gurgling on my own blood—which was running down my throat again from my goddamned broken nose—I rolled off the futon onto all fours and did what I always do when I get hurt. I felt much better when I was done, and I looked around blearily for something to wash off with. There, in the corner next to the refrigerator, was a sink I hadn't noticed earlier, and I made it my top priority, sort of. I was going to stand up—really, I was— but when I put a hand on the futon, it wobbled, and then I wobbled. I decided that maybe standing up was for pussies, so I crawled to the sink on all fours, hoping the world would stop spinning when I got there. No such luck. But after I'd hauled myself up by grabbing the blessedly stable counter and pulling with all my might, and washed the blood off my face and rinsed and spat, I thought maybe I could learn to walk in a place where the furniture got bigger and smaller and did a little nautical dance around any point of reference I might choose.

I barely made it back to the futon without doing the Nestea Plunge on that beautiful carpet. When I did get back, I fell on it hard enough to make the wood creak and looked anxiously at my tiny companion.

"Heya," I whispered gruffly, and she got close enough for me to make out features instead of just the insane glimmer of lights that usually came with sprites. Sprites tended to look like something animal; this one looked like a pet mouse I'd had in the third grade before Griselda, my mother's cat, had gotten it, except she was blinking rapidly in sky blue and sunset orange—my colors, or so Green had assured me last summer. "Are you *my* guardian sprite?" I asked loopily, and she nodded, her little Tinker Bell wings blurring with happiness.

It would figure that they'd sicced a sprite on me, I thought ruefully. Of course, I'd done the same thing to Davy—and it wasn't like they loved me *less* than I'd cared for my friend. "How long ya been with me?" I asked. I gave up trying to focus my eyes for a moment and just let them drift closed.

Her insistent buzzing made me shake my head (*ou—uuch!*) and open my eyes, and I tried again. "Did they assign you tonight?"

The tiny, furless, mouse-featured head bobbed once, and I smiled gently (I hoped) to let her know that it was well and dandy that she'd been hanging out with me, probably staying invisible (if they could do that) while we tried to hunt down our enemy like a bear in a cave. "So... can you go get Green and tell him where I am?" *Pretty pretty please with a cherry on top of the Goddess sundae thank you very much?*

No dice. The little sunset wings drooped in a staggering display of depression for a being four inches tall, and I shrugged and tried not to let my own disappointment show. Two tiny hands came up and shielded the even tinier eyes, and I realized that her problem would be the same problem the elves had when we'd been fighting. She could probably find Green—but she wouldn't be able to see the Hollow Man's lair. The Goddess's creatures tended to work on such a metaphorical level, this little house had probably dropped out of sight for the elves as soon as the stench became overpowering for the vampires. I nodded sympathetically and then had to close my eyes to keep the whole world from bobbing in time.

I opened my eyes again and reached slowly to the floor where my yarn bag had fallen, because I was terrified and hurt and hell, it was there. I mean, I had a couple of pointy sticks, a little pair of scissors—he could be cut, right? He'd been nursing healing wounds even as we'd spoken. Maybe I could use the itty-bitty scissors to dig into his wrist and snip a big artery or something—there *had* to be a reason the darn things were forbidden on airlines, didn't there?

If I could have done so without pain, I would have shaken my head. It was Green's sweater, that's all. Nothing lethal, just sticks and string and a tiny bit of human magic soaking into the fiber from my heart and the oils on my hands. And suddenly I had an idea—as Dr. Seuss would say, A Wonderful, Awful Idea.

"You wouldn't be able to *bring* something to Green?" I asked hopefully. The little wings perked right up and the horrible, clashing colors (my horrible clashing colors) started beating like a disco ball.

The first thing I had to do was go over his sweater and tie the little ends I'd left into knots where I hadn't already. That wasn't so hard—I'd done most of those. The unnatural part was when I had to worry my finished loops off on the back, the front, and the first sleeve so I could attach the yarn and have it rip out all in one smooth rope—my little companion could probably drag the front of the yarn quite some distance, but if it caught on a snag some thousand yards out, I couldn't say for certain it wouldn't break. Although, as I eyed the perfect cables, the hours of work and heartbreak and hope and prayer for Green's safe return that I was about to destroy in one flight of the Goddess's smallest emissary, I thought it wasn't the yarn we had to worry about breaking—it was my heart, dammit. It was supposed to end up a sweater, not a lifeline out of the Minotaur's maze.

I narrowed my eyes and tried to focus on some other solution to getting the hell out of this damned basement so I could go shove my foot up the Hollow Man's ass, and realized that I'd been seeing double the whole time I'd been tying knots. No wonder they were so nervous about me, I thought with disgust. Bracken practically got eviscerated, and he was back to breaking things within the hour. I got one lousy backhand to the face and I was about totaled. Ruefully I looked back at the sweater, now bound together from piece to piece by strategically placed knots, and decided I should probably attach the spare balls of yarn to it as well.

Finally I was done and ready to sacrifice Green's beloved sweater to the greater good. "You really *can* find Green, right?" I asked apprehensively. It would really suck if I did all this and it didn't work, but the sprite's tiny little bottom gave a flounce of impatience. I said a small prayer over my soon-to-be-demolished work before I pulled the needle out, gave her the snipped end of the working yarn, and told her to go find Green. She buzzed cheerfully, a whole art deco Christmas tree of lights in a four-inch space, and zoomed to the door. She stopped there and made herself germ tiny (I assumed, since I could still see the yarn), then disappeared through the keyhole, the sleeve zipping toward nothing in her wake.

I collapsed on the futon and tried to keep myself from passing out by doing math. We'd been about two miles away from Hollow Man's house when I'd been abducted—which was how many yards? But it didn't matter, because they *must* have gotten closer since I'd been here, so if there were two thousand yards of yarn in the sweater and they were a mile away…. Aw, fuck it. I'd just sit here and feel the blood trickle down my scalp and watch my work self-destruct and pray for rescue until the Hollow Man saw the magic yarn zooming from his house.

I didn't have long to wait. "What in the hell is this!" he roared as he came crashing through the steel door, swinging it open both quickly and ponderously at the same time. I looked at him through my swollen face (my eye had closed up while I'd been tying knots, and I couldn't breathe out of my nose anymore) and said, "What is what?" I could be flippant, I thought carefully, because the sweater had stopped unzipping about five minutes earlier—all that was left was the beginning ribbing on the bottom of the back. Not the whole enchilada, right, but by golly, that was a start.

"What is this string?" he asked, looking at me propped up in the corner of the couch and cradling the last of the yarn on my lap like a dead pet. He bent to pick it up but dropped it with a howl that surprised me enough to sit up. "What did you do to it? It *hurts*…."

Great, I thought fuzzily. If I'd known that, I could have just thrown it on him whole and saved myself a whole bunch of work. "Did you think I was just going to sit here?" I asked him around the cuts on the inside of my mouth. Carefully, I sat up a little more. I'd been charging as much power as I could since the sprite had disappeared, and since I'd just been loved by the three men I loved and was terrified for the boys and more pissed off than words that I'd been captured, pain or no pain, that was no small amount of magical fusion at my disposal. I just had to be very, very careful about how I used it.

"You *hit* me, leave me alone here and promise to torture someone who's mine, and you think I'm just going to cry about it?" I stood up and pretended the world wasn't spinning. "Assmunch, I've got so much more to live for than that, and you've got a lot to learn about love." And with that, I let my power loose—not as a ball or anything that would blow him up, but as a shield around him.

He shrieked and, please-Goddess-let-it-be-so, I could swear I heard the howls of dogs and hisses of giant cats somewhere in the distance.

Then he charged at my shield, and I planted my feet and froze my will and grunted in triumph when he slammed into the glowing bubble of magic and bounced back, leaving a smear of burnt orange spitting on the side of the field.

He hit the shield again, and again and again, and each time I gritted my teeth and pitted my power and will against his power and will, and eventually he squatted in the middle of the circle and glared at me from his feeding face, and I snarled back, even though his feeding face was truly horrific.

When their feeding faces take over, most vampires simply look like highly sexual predators—hollowed cheeks, popping tendons, glowing eyes, extended jaws and teeth. They are almost beautiful, in an alien, terrifying way. The Hollow Man was different—his feeding face revealed him for what he truly was. His flesh seemed to be running down his face like melted wax to reveal porous, brown, moldy bones beneath. His musculature, his skeleton, even his skin seemed to be rotting, wasting away, leaving only the teeth—pointed, porous, and jagged—to support that decaying flesh. No wonder he stank—he was decomposing even as he walked around in undeath. The vampires don't decompose, because they are kept alive with the Goddess's will. This guy, he'd corrupted the Goddess's will. He'd had Goddess-born power and abused it, and all that was holding him together were the rules of the magic, not the love. He truly was hollow. From his heart to his mind to his flesh, there was nothing of substance, not even his blood.

"You can't keep me in here forever," he hissed. Like all vampires, his vocal cords had changed—but his were raspy, undeveloped, and his hiss was truly that, like a pissed-off kitten with laryngitis. "I'll get out, and then I'll kill you, and I'll take over your children, and your lovers will die from the pain… and then I'll drain them too."

I stared him down, from the hideous flesh to the eyeballs that didn't glow but only rolled around greenly in their rotted orbs. "I don't have to keep you in here forever." I grinned ferociously, the pain of moving my cheek and jaw muscles agonizing but worth it. "I only have to keep you in here until they come to get me. And in the meantime, you're not hurting the boys and you can't set a trap for my lovers and you're just fucked. So sit back and enjoy, because we've got something truly nasty planned for you when this is over."

At that moment I heard Green and Bracken blow through the front of the house, shouting my name.

"And buddy, this is so fucking over," I growled, then shouted, "Down here, guys!" through my broken lips. "Have Grace get the boys and get out of here—they're somewhere upstairs."

There was a racket, and an "I've got them.... Oh, Goddess..." before I heard Arturo urging Grace out of the house, hopefully soothing her and telling her that there was some way, please Goddess, some miracle that would take that dark mark off their souls.

And then there was a distinctly un-sidhe-like clatter and the door to the basement room completely disintegrated, and I was sandwiched between Green and Bracken as they tried to crush the life out of me with their relief and their beautiful love.

"I liked the sprite," I said after a moment, as the shield brightened to a blinding sheen because their touch was pumping me full of what I used to keep my power strong. Then I coughed and sputtered, because even though Bracken was hugging me from the back, Green hadn't healed me yet, and Bracken's touch was making my nose bleed again. Green rubbed his thumb gently over my shattered cheekbone and my swollen jaw and eye, his wide-spaced eyes narrowing in a distinctly uncharacteristic charge of anger.

"Is everybody okay?" I asked, still sputtering, but Green's fingers were gently probing my bruises and wiping away the still spilling bright red blood.

"Everybody's fine," Bracken said breathing into my hair—which felt wet—and looking at Green over my shoulder. Green was showing me what his true rage looked like. I realized that he might have scared me a few times, but I'd never seen him as angry as he was now.

"Is that him?" he snarled, squinting into the power bubble at what, to him, must have been a dark blur.

I nodded my head, massaging his chest with my hands to try to calm him down.

"I'll kill him," he growled, his voice sounding very Victorian cockney. "I'll pull 'is fookin' guts ou' wi' me teeth." He took a huge, shuddering breath and turned toward Hollow Man to do just that, and I reached up and caught his beloved face in my hands. I touched the corners of his eyes, his elven ears, his long jaw, and felt the muscles there bunched up in a snarl of pure hatred. How could I have ever put this man—this sidhe—into a box of "gentle lover," I asked myself, amazed at my own stupidity. Bracken was stroking my hair, just my hair, not touching my scalp with his fingers, and I took Green's hands in my own and kissed them.

"Heal me, beloved," I asked, looking with grateful tears into both sets of Green's eyes dancing around in my fractured vision, "because I've got something worse in mind."

Green shuddered again and nodded, and bent to kiss my brow. I felt that queasy slide of flesh that meant my body was using magic to regenerate—it never felt quite human to do that. I also felt that Green was tired. How much had it cost them, I wondered as I turned and hugged Bracken, then touched the blood that had soaked into the sleeves of his sweater from wounds that I couldn't see now but had been there. How much had it taken to wade through the Hollow Man's evil and come to my rescue? I stood on my tiptoes, supported by the broadness of Bracken's hand on the small of my back, and kissed his jaw, watching his shadowed eyes close in gratitude that I was still alive, and then looked at both of them and at Nicky, who had just come down the stairs. I reached out my hand to him, and he stopped standing hesitantly and rushed in for the hug and a grateful kiss, his dusty animal smell clinging to me reassuringly. Then I stepped away from all of them and said it.

"You know what I need to do, right?" Goddess, I hoped they did, because I was feeling strong now, but the Hollow Man was pacing his magic prison of light like a bull and I couldn't hold him there forever.

Green stepped forward, took my hands, and nodded. "And you know what we need to do, right?" he asked seriously, and I nodded back.

"You need to remind me who I am," I said quietly, and Nicky broke the moment.

"You'd better forgive us," he said seriously, and I managed a grin from my now healthy, healed face. Nicky used both hands to rip off a piece of his sweatshirt and gave it to me to clean the blood off, and I was grateful.

"If you call me a bitch, it had better be written across my fat white ass," I told him. I smiled grimly at all of them, meeting their eyes firmly and with all the confidence I didn't feel. "I love you all," I said, and then I moved to the couch and grabbed the itty-bitty scissors from my yarn bag and turned toward my shield.

I'd never stepped through my own power before—it was exhilarating and commonplace at once. It was my power, so it was an extension of me, but it was the part of me that everybody else saw and I only generated. I felt pretty damned good, I thought as I stepped through, and then I sobered, there in the shining bubble of my magic alone with Hollow Man again.

He lunged, of course, but I was ready for him—and so was Green, because visibility or no visibility, it was his power that pinned Hollow Man to the floor.

"You wanted to taste me?" I asked tauntingly. His eyes rolled, and he *whined*—a grown man whining because he didn't get his way was almost as repulsive as that horribly sullied flesh. "You did want to taste me, didn't you? You wanted to be inside me while you tasted me." Bracken made a wild animal sound outside the shield, but I ignored him. He'd trust me—I knew he'd trust me. "That's what you said, right?"

"I blow people up," he said, his dreamy, wandering voice still focused on that thing, that elusive thing he wanted, but couldn't name; needed, but couldn't have; imagined, but couldn't know. "I'm part sidhe. You can't kill me—not with sunlight, not with decapitation—I know. The sylphs tried. I don't burn, I don't dissolve… I just am…."

I bent over him and used the pointy ends of the scissors to prick a blunt hole in my thumb. Then I grabbed his hand, pressed flat against the lovely fuchsia-colored rug, and did the same thing for him. "You blow up people who don't know who they are," I told him, enjoying the little human whimper that came when I made that wound just a little bit bigger, digging in past the mottled brown and green flesh of his hands until a blackish, orangish ooze began to seep out. "You've been lucky that way. Sylphs are waiting for love to cement their identities. Werecreatures wouldn't have become werecreatures if they weren't searching, waiting, trying to find that thing they needed but couldn't name. Chuck and Shane and Chris—they were all lost creatures, poor creatures, without an identity of their own." I moved my thumb, dripping a little blood up the center of his chest, and watched him eye the blood hungrily. "Jon Case, he'd just started his first love affair with another man—he was still surprised to find out who he was."

"Not me," I said, savoring this knowledge, knowing that if I was wrong it could be the last good thing I felt, but also knowing in my gut that I was right simply because I felt it—and my identity was not just a good thing, it was a *great* thing. "I know exactly who I am. And if I ever forget, I've got people I love more than life to remind me. So… who are you, Hollow Man?" I asked, watching a fat red drop of my blood plop on his chin. "Do you really want to know?"

Then I held my thumb over his mouth, and at the same time as another fat drop fell past those rotted teeth into the black-mold cave that his mouth had become, I steeled myself for the awfulness and licked the blackish ooze from his wrist.

You can't brace yourself for something that horrible, never in a million trillion years.

It was nothing, nothing at all—no love, no hate, no pain, just a knowledge that you were empty. It was such a familiar feeling. I remembered it, deep in my stomach—nights behind a cash register, pounding drivel into my computer, hating my professors for looking through me and my customers for looking past me, hating my parents for not seeing who I really was and myself for not being worth the seeing. That hate, that need… you could deny it, you could feed it with sex and drugs and food and with other people's pain, but that need… that need to be seen, to be known, to be recognized…. Who had ever recognized me? Who had ever seen me for what I could be? Who had ever believed I was capable of more than just some lousy fucking job under corpse-fluorescent lights, pissing off the dumb-fuck locals because I fucking could….

"Beloved," Green said, and I jerked to myself. I was me, I was violently angry, I was capable of hurting people because I just fucking could….

"Beloved," Bracken said. I loved Bracken… I loved to piss him off. God, he was so overbearing sometimes. Wouldn't it be great if he just beat his own head into a bloody….

"Cory," Nicky said. What in the hell was he whining about now? Couldn't he see I was goddamned busy? I was trying to run the fucking world, and who gave a shit about his poor hurt little ego anyway, and *Jesus* his fucking drivel was fucking killing me…. And I was so goddamned angry, so consumed with impatience and fury, and couldn't they just give me, just once, just goddamned once, a little fucking respect? No one knew… no one gave a shit… they just wanted and took and wanted— and I could just scream, scream and blow the world up with my magic, because I was powerful and burning and they were jack-diddly-squat….

"Corinne Carol-Anne…" Oh, Goddess, I wasn't saying these things out loud, was I? I stood straighter at the sound of their voices saying my complete name in sync and thought my mouth tasted like dried puke and thought it was glued shut with that lactic acid thing, and couldn't one of those assholes get me a glass of—"Kirkpatrick op Crocken Green."

—water? Oh, Goddess… what had I done? They hadn't heard me, had they? I had been spewing filth…. I was so stupid, such an idiot to not recognize them, how could they love me, how could anyone love me? I was so goddamned dumber-than-a-box-of-snot stupid, coming in here like this. Who did I think I was? I was nobody. How could I kill this guy, how could I make it all better when I was nobody? My head heart and my chest hurt, and it was just what I deserved—I'd killed a hundred vampires, it was my fault, mine alone that Adrian was dead, he'd flown in to defend me, if I'd just been able to keep my mouth shut….

"Beloved of Adrian," Green said firmly. "Beloved of my heart," he continued. "*Ou'e'eir,* stubborn woman, lovely lass, beautiful lover…," he continued on, saying things in Elvish, and I teared up just hearing his lovely, lovely voice telling me who I'd earned the right to be in his eyes. Then I heard Bracken speaking. "Stubborn bitch, *due'ane,* beloved of my heart, beloved to my brother, beloved to my leader, terrible tease, lost little girl, warm woman in my bed, Cory op Crocken…." And then Nicky. "Bossy heifer, *ou'e'ane,* sweet kid, wise student, friend and lover, confidante, terrifying leader, beloved of Green…." And I listened and listened and heard them resonating in my heart, resonating in my soul, in the core of the person I had come to be, and then I knew myself.

I was a good person. I was kind. I was fierce. I was powerful. I was beloved. And I wasn't angry—I hadn't been angry for a very long time. I took a breath and felt clean and free, when I'd felt tight and bound with that chronic pain of want, and then I knew, really knew, how close I had come to being lost—not just tonight, when I would have died a stranger to myself—but a year ago, when I had been that stranger, with only the little seeds of who I was now growing in my heart.

I could have been Hollow Man. I could have let my bitterness, my alienation, my anger become my whole world, my whole heart, spending my life staring at my shoes and needing love without giving it until I just needed and needed and needed and swallowed up the world with my bottomless, endless want—but I hadn't.

I *had* looked up, I *had* reached for what the world had to offer, and now I was the person who loved three men with all that I was, and I was loved in return, and there wasn't anything better in the world than that.

With an effort, I swallowed and stood from where I'd been crouched over the Hollow Man's writhing body. He whined and thrashed and swore at me… and then, piteously, called Twilight's name. I looked up at Green and he shook his head. Apparently, "Steve" had been dead to Twilight for too long—the only reason he'd come tonight had been for us.

"He's not coming," I croaked through a throat that felt like it had been arc-welded together with recycled tequila. I looked down on the dissolution of a human being who had used senseless power to feed too much nagging need. He was still repulsive, but now even his anger was gone. He was consumed with the struggle of forces inside of him, and I knew the feeling and the terrible, terrible cost it exacted on your body and soul.

I was soaked in sweat, and my sweatshirt was already bloody from my nose, so I was pretty sure I stank as well. My hands were shaking so badly I almost stabbed myself in the eye with my thumb when I went to pull them through my ravaged hair, and my breath was shuddering out of my chest like I'd just run five miles at warp speed. But I was alive. I'd started to come apart, to unravel, to lose everything that was me, but I hadn't—my lovers had kept me whole simply by loving me because I was me.

"You died to him thirty years ago," I said now, proud of how solid I sounded even though I felt almost translucently weak, "and I'm glad he's not here to see you now. This ends now, Hollow Man." He grunted and started a mrewlling whine that I knew was going to get worse before it ended. I turned on wobbly knees and left him to suffer through the horror that was coming next.

My shield was weak, but it still infused me with my own power, and I barreled through it and into Green's waiting arms. Bracken leaned over my shoulders from behind and Nicky wriggled into Green's embrace somehow. I trembled inside their circle of faith until I thought the chattering of my teeth would sever my tongue, but we stayed there and served as witnesses to the final abomination.

Hollow Man struggled, straining against Green's restraints until his flesh actually started to strip away. His raw, rotting skin rubbed against that warm, living light of power, and the whine escalated, became a howl through clenched, decaying teeth, and then a wail of raspy anguish. Then, with all that was inside of him, all of the hate and the anger and the emptiness, he opened his mouth and screamed. Goddess, I'd never heard such a scream. It felt like the train outside was passing the house, then it felt like the train was crashing through the building, and I watched in fascination as a crack opened up in the concrete floor under the shield even as we crouched and held our ears (well, mine were muffled by lovely big male bodies) and screamed in the pain of the sound of his shriek.

"It hurts!" he cried. "It hurts! It's bright and it hurts! What did I do? Oh, Twilight, pleeeeeeeezzzzzz...." And then, oh Goddess, the agony of that wail, the excoriating pain of a soul-freezing void that would never, ever, ever be filled. But still we stayed to listen, to watch, to *smell* (the stench made black spots dance in front of my eyes), because we had to. He had hurt us and stalked us for so long, and Davy and Kyle and Chris and Shane and Chuck and Ellen Beth and Jon Case and Hallow all deserved justice, all deserved vengeance, all deserved balance—and balance was what was struggling inside Hollow Man even as he screamed, a balance against the sunshine that was my blood and the blackness that was his body, heart, and soul. It went on forever, until our own throats were sore with shrieking in time to it, but the sound of our screams was muffled and inconsequential next to the wail coming from him, and his thrashing, flopping, dying body seemed to stretch at the seams, to bubble like a faulty balloon.

Abruptly the scream died away, to be replaced by an animal whimper of simple, excruciating physical agony and a moan that finally, finally stirred my pity because it was the first human sound he'd made since he'd dumped me in this steel room. Abruptly the whimper died away to a gurgle, and his body splatted against the walls of my shield like a poodle in a microwave.

Balance had been achieved.

I MADE them let me walk out of the house on my own, just as soon as I'd guzzled water from the faucet and rinsed the streaming sweat and leftover blood off my face. Green, who hadn't stopped touching me and who had wrapped his arms around me from behind even as I cleaned up, started to swing me up into his arms, but his muscles trembled and I stopped him.

"Were there many injured?" I asked Bracken quietly, both arms around Green's waist and looking back over my shoulder. "During the fight?"

"Almost everybody," Bracken said, eyeing his leader with compassion. I took that narrow, beautiful, pointed face in my hands and kissed Green's sensual mouth until he moaned softly. Then I pulled away and touched foreheads.

"I'll be okay, *ou'e'hm*," I whispered. "If everyone's out there, let them see us walk out together, okay?" He nodded, his jaw trembling, and I leaned my head against his chest.

"That was so close," he said, and he was the only one who had the courage to tell me. "We could see you growing transparent... your skin threatening to fly off your flesh. Oh, beloved... we almost weren't enough."

"But you were," I choked, not wanting to think about how close I had come to losing my center. "In the end, that's all that matters."

I didn't look at the rest of the house as we walked up the stairs and out the door—I didn't care what it looked like. I was left with a vague impression of white walls and pricey, dark wood trim after the gleaming steel walls of the bomb-shelter basement. I didn't care who had lived there, and I could only hope that, as weird as it had sounded, they really were in Spain or Brazil or Bumfuck South-of-Hell, and not greasy spots in the main house or piles of dust in the garden. My capacity to give beyond the people on our hill had been blasted out of me by my own struggle for self. I was Green's hill; Green's hill was all I could save.

We walked out the door into the teeth-chattering predawn chill, and I looked gratefully to my people as they surrounded me. Renny and Max almost knocked me over, and I wrapped my arms around them and hugged, wincing in sympathy as the blood matting their fur from their poor ears soaked into my jacket. Nicky's ears had bled too, the blood sticking his hair to his head like feathers. Mario was right behind them, dressed in Max's jacket, and he too had splashes of crimson gleaming wetly in the dark. I could only hug them and be hugged by them and commiserate and weep to get out of there, to go home.

Twilight had his arms wrapped around Marcus and Phillip as they sagged against him. Cocklebur was doing the same for Kyle, and they looked at us like people waking out of a coma. I caught Twilight's eyes to see how he was doing.

"I don't even remember his name," he said simply. "Did you ever find out?"

I tried to live as the Goddess made the elves—but I ate meat because I had to supplement my diet, and I was happy to limit the number of lovers in my bed because I just wasn't wired that way, and I had just blooded an enemy to kill him. I was not an elf.

"No," I lied softly. "He was just the Hollow Man." We nodded together, and then, as one many-legged entity, we started to walk back across that terrible expanse of starlit (the moon was down now) green lawn toward the cars. It was getting perilously close to dawn, and even though the smell and the fatigue it caused were dissipating even more as we moved from the little cottage, we were all still weak, and I didn't think anybody was in any shape to go hyperspeed. I looked around.

"Where are Arturo and Grace and the boys?" I asked, and a sudden foreboding flashed through me. I wasn't done this night, not by even a little.

"They went for the cars," Mario said quietly. "There was something wrong. Grace wouldn't say what, but she was really freaked out. I don't know how she could move that fast—she was as wiped out as the rest of us."

I nodded and tilted my head back to the cleansing stars, made a concerted gathering of thoughts and energy, and directed it at Grace. *"They're marked,"* I told her. Then I stumbled, because I was tired and not paying attention, and Bracken swung me into his arms. I let him, I *clung* to him, trying to swim to some shore of understanding through our exhaustion.

"Goddess… they smell like him…." Grace's voice in my head was hysterical, and I was so new at this brain-chatter thing that I couldn't get a handle on her.

"Green, tell Arturo to calm her down," I begged. "Tell her I've got an idea, but they need to come get me and the vampires." I groaned, because the only other place we could put the vampires was in the trunk of the Caddy, and that's probably where they were right now. Oh, Goddess… I was so confused. I couldn't do people and cars right now… I could only think of the boys….

Marcus and Phillip were suddenly there at my elbow, even as Bracken strode through the night. "We'll get ourselves to safety, Lady Cory," Marcus murmured, with a sweet kiss on my head that sent a shock of awareness through me that rebounded off Bracken. I saw Brack's eyes widen. He gave Marcus a tired grin that we both ignored—but the buzz was there, and it gave me enough strength to focus my thought. I looked over at Green for help, and he nodded.

"Grace and Arturo are in the Caddy with the boys," he said. "Nicky, you need to go with the weres in the SUV." Before, I think Nicky would have protested—now he simply nodded reluctantly and accepted. Green continued speaking, almost to himself, setting up the logistics in his own head. "No one can fly right now, and we're a fucking breath away from dawn, and I think whatever Cory's got in mind has to happen before then. Right, luv?" he asked, and I nodded, so grateful for him that I almost wept against Bracken's neck.

"Yeah…," I breathed. "I think at sunrise that mark is there to stay." And then I was in Grace's head, and I was explaining, in part, what I had in mind.

We were walking down a large expanse of grass, cutting across it toward Matson, when we heard a beep behind us and turned. I grunted, half in humor, half in frustration, because we had to backtrack across a huge expanse of lawn.

In a burst of power, Nicky and Mario morphed and elves and vampires blurred, picking up the were-animals on the way. In moments we were stuffed in cars and heading toward home.

Green and Bracken were in the front of the Caddy with Arturo, and I was in the back with Grace and the boys. They were barely breathing and completely unconscious. In spite of the stench of the Hollow Man that permeated them, I hefted Graeme from her and held him in my lap, squeezing him to me and trying to stave off despair.

"Tell me how it works," I said to Grace. *Plan. Plan and think and plan some more, and maybe we won't have to face the possibility that they're lost forever.* "Marking. Vampires die their day death and their souls pass through their loved ones, and it leaves a mark. What does it feel like—how do you know it's done?"

"Cory… I…." Even in the darkened car, I could see her embarrassed, anxious glance at Arturo as he drove. "That damned stubborn man just stayed with me, that's all," she fretted, smelling the top of Gavin's head instinctively and closing her eyes in pain when she scented evil instead of puppy-dog little boy. "And then I was inside him and through him, and I felt… all of him. We were like one person. His heartbeat was mine, his blood was mine, his past—" She rolled her eyes. "—all bajillion freakin' years of it, was mine. I knew it. And then it was gone, but… it was like the smell of incense in your clothes, the smell of your beloved on your soul." She looked at me in the empty dark. "How can they live with that stench on their souls? How can they love and laugh and play and grow if they stink of all that need!"

"We'll fix it," I said fervently—hoping, hoping against hope that I knew how to make it true.

We had gotten to Foresthill Road and crossed the bridge when Bracken said something to Green and Green gave an order to Arturo. Suddenly the car was swerving off the road onto a turnabout, then jumping the turnabout and heading toward Scary Tree, the canyon yawning beyond it.

"I hate Scary Tree," I said blankly, loud enough for the men to hear me.

"Scary Tree sucks up bad power in the area," Green said tersely. "You want someplace for that shite to go, right?"

Right. "Oh." Oh, Goddess, I was really going to do this.

The car fishtailed to a halt on the still drying grasses about a hundred feet from Scary Tree, and we all got out. I was struggling to pull Graeme out of the car when Bracken stepped in and took him from me, while Arturo did the same thing for Grace. We scrambled out after them and started trotting across the field under a sky that had gone from purple velvet to charcoal gray. "Green, I need you across from me." Behind us I heard the SUV and the hearse go off road, and we stopped—not close enough for the tree's shadow to touch us, but close enough to see the green-speckled red canyon beyond.

"Nicky, hurry," I called over my shoulder and fell to my knees in the thick grasses that had grown lush during the rains and were barely starting to die now, a crackly, cat's-tongue carpet. I worried about snakes and then thought we might be a little high up for rattlers. I wasn't sure, but I was with elves who probably had snake repellent pumping through their veins so I stopped borrowing trouble and reached out for the boys. I wrapped an arm around each child when Bracken and Arturo gave them to me.

"It's like that night at the lake, right?" I asked no one in particular, looking up at Green and Bracken with eyes that were probably as terrified as I was.

Grace nodded and put her hand on my shoulder. "Sweetheart… if you don't think you can do this…."

"I can't live with myself if I don't try…," I whispered, then looked at Green again, trying to hold on to my courage. "But I'm not as strong as I thought I was…." He'd said he could see me fading, growing translucent, getting ready to fly apart.

Green fell to his knees across from me and put his hands on my shoulders. "But all together, we are as strong as you know we are," he said, and the shaking of his hands in my hair as I'd recovered from Hollow Man haunted me.

"You really can't lie, can you?" Please, beloved. Please lie to me and tell me this is going to be just hunky-fucking-dory…. Please.

"Not at all," he said so calmly I had to believe him. Then, evenly, "Nicky, Bracken, come here with us. She's going to push herself through them, and she needs to have us to know when to go back."

"Holy fucking Goddess," Bracken breathed, falling to his knees next to me in shock. "If I'd known that, I would have picked her up and dragged her home."

Nicky sank down to my other side, his mouth open in surprise. "You have got to be shitting me." They each set a hand on my knee, Green's hands on top of theirs, our arms a lattice of protection over the boys who now lay prone on the ground in our center. The warmth of my lovers' fingers started to radiate up my legs, easing the predawn chill. They loved me. I could do this.

"Marcus, Phillip," I ordered tersely, "get in the hearse. Take them with you." I nodded toward Kyle, Grace, and Ellis, and was a little miffed when none of them moved.

"No offense, Lady Cory," Marcus said, taking a nod from Phillip and the others, "but fuck off. We're here until we know our queen's okay."

I took a breath that stammered in my throat and took a look at the ever-lightening sky and thought, *I have to do this.* And then I thought about Green, and how badly I wanted to be with him alone right now. So badly that even sitting across from him was too far away, so badly that his touch on my knees was not enough. And an ache began to build in my chest. It was like my power, but it was a yearning, a pain, an agonizing need to be with my beloved, and it was forcing me toward him. I kept my muscles locked and let it force me.

My body stopped breathing, but I wasn't in it, so it didn't bother me. I was inside Graeme—smart, seeing everything, even flaws, secrets, and lies. Feeling his mother's hands on his forehead when he was tired or worried, hearing her sharp voice on the phone with his father, the texture of his favorite blanket, the exact pattern of shadows on his bedroom wall at night, the even, comforting sound of his brother's breathing in the bed next to him, the fierce desire to protect Gavin from harm, from censure—which Gavin often got—from his father. And over it all, starting to seep into his skin, the knowledge that the world was evil, rotten to the core, frightening, terrible, and that no one, no one at all, could save him from it....

I will, baby. And then I pushed through the space between us, through the boys' prone bodies, aiming toward Green, my self oozing through Graeme's pores, squishing the evil out like the stink of sweat, feeling it evaporate as it hit the air. I was exhausted, my vision of the world wavering between the two boys. I wanted to breathe, I wanted to be myself, I wanted to return....

Green. I had to make it to Green.

Gavin.... Sweet, sweet boy.... His wonder at the little bald creature who would be his little brother, his acceptance of everything from Santa Claus to his father's criticism as true, his unwillingness to ask for better from his parents in case they should take away from him the burning, bright, and proud little man who loved him unreservedly, who kept him safe. The soft fur of the kittens he fed under the house until his mother took them to the pound, the models his brother asked to have for his birthday so he could give them to Gavin, who was magic with his hands, and his patience and his fervent wish to not attract any more attention than necessary. The indefinable, unnameable difference that would make his life difficult, make his life sweet, define who he loved, and alienate his parents.... And bad things were already going to happen—he knew it, he'd heard his dad use bad words for people like him—and this haze, this terrible smell, this horrible slimy gunk slithering down his skin was a small price to pay for not saying anything, for just holding it in and stamping down on his heart so no one would know he was different, no one would yell at him no one would hurt him anymore....

I won't hurt you. I'll make it go away.

Green. And again that other push, one more mighty heave, and my body was bursting with the need to breathe and the evil was evaporating, misting from my soul into the air—but my whole psyche was writhing, swollen with the need to breathe, with the need to feel the inside of my own skin, with the need to....

Touch Green. Oh, Goddess, there he was. I could smell the faint wildflower of his skin, the mint of his breath, feel the silk of his flesh, the wine of his blood, and then I was inside....

No. Oh, beloved, you can't stay....

He pushed me out gently, like a toddler being put back in his bed. Bracken and Nicky were calling to me—I could hear their voices screaming my many names, feel their hands on my thighs, on my shoulders, and they needed me, they needed me they needed me.... The silver light of dawn blurred by my vision and the wind passed through my soul, and in a whirl of the people around me I was suddenly....

Gasp! Sweet, sweet oxygen, sweet, sweet air in my lungs. A breath, and another and another, and awareness of bodies in my arms, of bigger bodies embracing me, of Gavin and Graeme, clean and as pure as they had been two nights ago, smelling like sweaty little boys, fast asleep in my arms. Of Bracken and Nicky, shuddering, sobbing in reaction and relief that I was all right, of Green, reaching across the space of our bodies to touch his thumb to my lip and his fingers to my cheek, the golden light of the horizon just peaking up beyond his....

Holy shit.

With strength I wouldn't have guessed I had, I sat up, freeing my face from that press of love and relief.

"Vampires, get the fuck undercover!" I said distinctly, and there was a breeze behind me as my people went hurtling toward vehicles. I heard Grace's surprised squawk as Arturo shoved her in the Cadillac and threw a tarp on top of her, then slammed the lid, all movement in hyperspeed, and the faint hum of machinery as everyone else shmushed themselves into the back of the hearse and pushed the buttons that dropped the back platform down and pulled the rolltop lid over them.

Then I pressed my cheek to Bracken's coarse, tangled hair and felt helpless, exhausted tears sliding down my face. The sky didn't look as bright as it had a moment before, and I had a chance to wonder at the gray filming between myself and the world before I felt the rough tongue of a werecat on the back of my neck. I mumbled something incoherent, and then the gray turned to black and I was fast asleep.

BRACKEN
Binding Off

I KNEW that she was alive because I was alive—that is the nature of our binding. But you cannot tell panic that the thing it fears most has not happened because the thing it doesn't fear at all has not happened either.

When her shoulders stopped moving with breath and her face lost color and she slumped forward like a newly minted corpse, Nicky and I shouted at her until our throats shredded and our breath ran short.

It was worse than her struggle with the Hollow Man, because then every name we called had seemed to bring her back to herself. This was like shouting at a coffin for the dead man to wake up, and that's what we did while our hearts pounded against our chests with the force to shatter our ribs.

Adrian hadn't left a body when he died again—vampires don't—and he had been my only loss. To see her with her life force absent, cold, still, was as alien to me as a crimson sky, and as horrible as the nearly transparent forms of the two little boys sliding down her tiny lap into the deep grasses.

In a heartbeat, Graeme's body was as solid and real as the screams rending my throat. The small group of our people standing behind us, watching in horrified fascination, gave a collective gasp, and I wondered what had happened to Scary Tree. Cory's lips were paling as I watched, and then bluing, and she hadn't moved, twitched, gasped, or shuddered—and now my heart had stopped its pounding and sat, simply stalled, while I continued to scream at her, beg her, plead with every face she had ever shown me to please… oh Goddess, please… please….

And then Gavin became real, and we waited breathlessly for her breaths to begin. In that awful, waiting silence, Green gave a cry—an anguished, agonized cry, as though he'd just lifted a weight that had ripped his intestines open with its dark-matter mass—and as the cry began to echo off the canyon beyond, Cory's chest heaved, gulped, and expanded in a giant shudder, and Nicky and I collapsed weeping on top of her.

She looked up at Green from the tangle of arms around her, and he was touching her face with pale shaking hands. Then her eyes widened, and she screamed at the vampires.

I hadn't even thought of the vampires as gold touched the sky.

Cory's head bobbed drunkenly, and her eyes started to wander. Behind her, Renny licked the back of her neck and her hair, leaving it in an amazing tangle.

"Renny, you bitch, I'll be damned if I don't get to be a bridesmaid," she said succinctly and then collapsed within our arms, while Green toppled to his side and got quietly sick in the grass.

Nicky reluctantly let her go while Arturo and Mario picked up the boys, and I hauled her limp body into my lap and looked at Green with an outrage I couldn't quite get a handle on.

"You lied?" I asked quietly, looking at the man I had known and trusted my entire life. Then, a little louder, "You *lied*?"

He spat and grimaced and shook his head. "Not about that," he rasped. His beautiful sunshine hair was coming out of its braid, and he passed his hand around his face and pulled tendrils out of his eyes. LaMark was suddenly there with a bottle of water he'd gotten from the car, and Green took it gratefully.

"You didn't lie about believing in her?" Just to make sure. Just to reaffirm that the man I loved more than life hadn't let me down.

"I knew she could do it." He sat back and put his head between his knees, his arms at rest by his sides, and tried to get a hold of the sickness that takes us over when we lie. "But…." His breath actually rattled in his chest. "She… her spirit… she… was trying to get to me. That's how she pushed through the boys—she used me as a goal. She got there," he gave me a thin memory of a smile, "and there her body was, cold and blue, and I thought what we all thought, although I knew it wasn't true…." His voice got rough like fine-grain sandpaper. "And then I could feel her, right? Feel… her?"

I nodded. His accent was back with the faintest of cockney overtones, the one that recurred when he was the most frightened or angry or sad. Nicky moved next to him and laid his cheek against Green's shoulder, and Green wrapped an arm around his bound lover and took comfort where it was offered.

"Her soul touched mine…," he continued, "and…." A tear of true silver leaked down his cheek. "And it *smelled* like her… and I thought, sure, I could keep her safe if she was just here, inside my skin."

"Oh, no…." Now I knew what the lie had been. "And you told her you wanted her to go…."

"And here she is." He reached out, and I moved her so he could stroke her face again. He closed his eyes—relief? love? the pain of both?—and tried for another smile. This one came out better, but it was still such a lie he should have gotten sick again. "And here she is," he repeated softly, "and aren't we all glad I lied."

SHE SLEPT for a solid twelve hours after that.

We decided to keep the boys until she woke up to talk to them. It was probably a horrible, insensitive thing to do to their mother, and damn us all if we gave a tinker's shit. She had earned the right to see them safe and whole before they left.

We bathed with her before laying her down—she'd been covered in blood and vomit and the sweat stink of fear, and so had we all. Nicky had needed to leave the shower when he realized how heavily her hair was crusted with blood. He hadn't seen her, really seen the extent of her injuries when we'd blurred into the room and found her standing next to that glowing bubble of triumph and spelling out Hollow Man's doom with a broken nose, broken cheekbone, and probably a cracked skull as well. I knew it was a sight that would haunt me in every restless sleep for the rest of my short and mortal life.

Green slept next to her for the first four hours. He had been exhausted to the point that his legs shook when he swung her up out of my arms from the car, but I wouldn't have taken her curled, contented, sleeping body from him for anything in the world. I gave him the privacy and the honor of being alone… of lying in the darkened room, listening to the wonder of her breathing and scenting her skin.

Green awoke and stumbled out of bed a little past noon, reaching for a can of trail mix and his computer. He needed to make inquiries about the house that Hollow Man had died in, to see if we had to worry about exposure or police investigations or any of the things that could haunt a group of people that shouldn't exist. After an hour of poring over the computer, he padded down to Renny's room to wake Max for a little help and ordered me to go lie down with my *due'ane*. I had been sitting in the living room, trying to figure out how to knit so I could help her fix Green's beloved sweater.

"You need more sleep," I said, trying to focus my eyes on my needles. My mother, who had been the one doing the teaching, reached out gently and took the work from my ungainly hands and kissed my cheek.

"I'll have the sprites wash out the thistles and stains from the rest of the yarn," she promised. The sprite we'd sent with Cory had apparently appeared back at the hill and asked for help after we'd followed her trail back to the cottage, and an entire fleet of sprites had gone back to the golf course on Matson and gathered Cory's treasured yarn up into neat little balls and brought them back.

"But will it...." I floundered for words. "Will her touch magic still be in it?" I asked fuzzily, worried. "If you wash it... will her touch go away?"

Mom laughed. She was a pixie—her laugh tinkled. "Silly boy. I've washed the sweater she's made you ten times—you wear it most of the week. I bet it's still as strong as the day you first wore it." She sobered and patted my face like she had when I'd been fourteen and showed up shamed with a truckload of peaches. "After the sacrifices she's made to keep her family, darling, do you really think those can be washed away with a little water and some re-spinning?"

My brush with mortality still haunted both my parents—I could see it sometimes, when danger was near. I shook my head, watching, fascinated, as the world spun behind my bleary eyes.

"You do what your leader tells you, Bracken," Mom said gently. "Go to bed." And I caught her in a hug, careful of her wings. I used to sit at my mother's feet while she read to me and be mesmerized by the rainbow shimmer, but now all I could think of was that she and my father had been proud of me, so proud, and that nothing they'd said to me in my whole life had hurt me as much as Cory's mother had hurt her when she was a child.

"Go," she ordered, her four-foot pixie body wriggling because I was so much bigger than she was. I shambled off to bed, slamming my shoulder into the doorframe from sheer weariness on the way out.

I slept soundly. When I woke up, it was near dark, and Cory awoke enough to snuggle into my arms. Nicky had joined her, and followed her across the bed into the snuggle. I didn't mind—we'd shared very well this last week. She'd said I was free-falling off a cliff and he was the first night of spring—I could live very easily, knowing my place in her life was assured.

She woke up in the dark only a few moments after I'd awakened to listen to her breathe. The sun was dying from the sky, and only the littlest bit of light snuck under the door. She was sandwiched between Nicky and me, and her eyes met mine in such honest relief, such terrible love, that I could hardly blink. Those shadowed, brightening green/brown eyes would never look at anyone else the way they looked at me.

She put her hand on Nicky's hand around her middle, and I could sense the careful—almost panicked—suppression of her disappointment that Green wasn't there. She took Nicky's hand to her lips and kissed it, still looking into my eyes, and he dropped kisses in her hair and clenched into her, shuddering. I sheltered them both with my big shoulders and my own embrace.

"Green was here for the first few hours," I said, understanding.

"How long have I been out?" Her voice was gravel and honey.

"I think the vampires just woke up."

She grunted, then said, "Ouch! I think I sprained my brain-chatter op center."

It was all I could do not to smack her upside the head, but Grace spared me the trouble by bursting in with a tray full of food and a mouth full of acerbic scolding.

"What in the fuck do you think you're doing, trying to talk like that after what you did?"

"Were you just *waiting* there with all that food?" Cory asked, blinking hard and trying to sit up. Her arm went out from under her, and she landed awkwardly on the mattress next me like a fish on its side. I sat up fluidly—my sleep had been adequate—and pulled her up next to me, sitting her on my lap. She didn't object, and she and Grace kept talking throughout the procedure.

"Yes," Grace snapped back. "How do you feel?"

"Like someone's scooping out my eye with a melon baller," Cory returned sourly, reaching up to rub it. Grace took her hand away and looked. She'd turned on the lamp next to the bed, and I could see now that Cory's right eye was bloodshot. I wondered what else Green had healed during his too brief sleep next to her.

"Yeah." Grace's voice became, if anything, sharper. "Green said you'd damn near blown out a blood vessel—you stupid, thoughtless, willful,"—and now her voice broke—"blessed, blessed child. Goddammit!

My queen, you can't ever do that again… not even for me. Do you understand?"

Cory grunted like she was being squeezed too tight. Then she thumped my forearm with her fist, and I realized that I had been the one doing the squeezing.

"Bracken…," she complained—and then Nicky, who had sat up behind her, smacked her upside the head. "*Nicky!*" She glared at all of us, her eyes narrowing. "No. No to all of you. I have no intention of dying and letting you all down, but I'm not giving up risking myself to help our people. If I didn't risk anything, *you'd* be dead, you big goober." She smacked me on the chest. "And Nicky, you'd be dead or worse, and"— she glared at Grace—"the boys would be in hell or worse. I *am* going to give what I have to give, and I *am* going to be a goddamned bridesmaid! Ouch!" She put her hand to her eye and whimpered, and I cradled her head against my chest.

"But maybe some food and rest first, you think, my queen?" I asked, feeling smug.

"Asshole," she said, stroking my chest. "Nicky, feed me pie."

"The prime rib first," Nicky said, sliding off the bed in his boxer shorts and moving to the chair by the bed. "Does this mean the weres are eating well tonight?" We could practically hear him salivating.

Grace was still recovering herself, but she nodded. "There's plenty there for both of you," she said, her voice still broken.

"You haven't seen her eat," Nicky said. Cory's open eye bulged with indignation, but her mouth was full of cow so she couldn't say anything.

"They're all right, aren't they?" I asked. Steph, Joe, and Arturo had snatched the boys up as soon as we'd gotten home, whisking them away to a guest room like a pack of mama bears. I was guessing Arturo had spelled them to sleep until we figured out what to tell them and how to get them back to their mother now that there was a statewide Amber Alert for them.

"They're fine," Grace said, a dry laugh forcing its way out. "That man has them playing some insane electronic thing. I'm surprised you haven't heard Graeme shouting from here."

Cory swallowed a giant bite with an audible gulp. "Grace…." She gnawed on her lower lip and sighed, leaning her head against my chest and stroking it for comfort. She didn't even look at Grace as she spoke.

"Grace, Gavin... Gavin's...." She grimaced, not liking the word choice given her. "He's wired... he's wired to love men, the same way Arturo's wired to love women. I know that sounds dumb for a little kid, but... he's just wired that way. He's known forever, and his father isn't... he's not a nice man about that sort of thing. You've noticed that Graeme's protective of him, right? Well, there's a good reason, and...." Finally, she looked at Grace, heartbreak in her face. "Grace, we're going to need to get that kid and bring him here when he hits puberty, okay? We're going to need Graeme to have a way to get in touch with us, because Gavin won't—because his whole life he's been taught that if he reaches for anything that makes him happy, it's probably wrong. Gavin... when he's sad, he—he's like you!" she blurted. "He holds it all inside his chest. But he's been holding this too long... and if we don't save him, he'll end up as lost as everyone else this hill has saved, and...." She was getting upset, her first sign of true, panicky emotion since she woke up. "We can't let that happen," she finished, soft, sobless tears falling on my bare skin. "But we have to give him back... all we can do is watch him and hope...."

Grace was on her knees, holding her hands and stroking fevered hair from Cory's hot face. "Oh darling...," she breathed. "I'm the grandma... don't you know by now that's all I *can* do?"

Cory nodded mutely, and my eyes went to the intricately worked Irish Chain quilt on our bed. It was one of the few things she had taken from home. I had a sudden thought about her grandmother, whom she had never talked about, ever, and a question I thought I might never ask.

"I'll bring them in, then," Grace said matter-of-factly. "Max is going to take them into the station and say he found them by Scary Tree—it's close enough to the truth. All they remember is that you saved them. They don't know how, but it's the one thing we got from them." She laughed a little. "'Cory's a superhero! She saved us, Grandma!' I told them that superheroes needed their secret identities. I don't think they're going to have any trouble keeping a secret without our help."

"So what's my superhero identity?" Cory asked musingly, and her voice was blurring. She was getting tired—overwhelmingly tired—and she had barely eaten. I nodded at Nicky, and he shoved a bite of potatoes and prime rib in her mouth. She gave a goofy little laugh around her full mouth, then swallowed. "The only superhero names I can think of sound like a porn star's stage name...." Nicky fed her again, and she kept talking through her full mouth. "Orgasmo-chick." She giggled. "Sexual

Frenzy...." (*giggle swallow giggle*) "Buffy the Boffer...." (*giggle giggle giggle*) "The Big Bang!!!" And she collapsed into gales of laughter on my chest while the rest of us looked at her in shocked amusement. We didn't even have to spell her to sleep—her laughter died abruptly, she gave a little hiccup. And fell asleep.

Green came back in after Grace went out and told him that she'd fallen asleep again. He took her off my lap and nudged me out of my spot with his hip, then sat cradling her, looking exhausted.

"You need more sleep, leader," I said quietly, and he gave me a wry smile.

"I agree. But Hallow's here. He wants to thank her, and—"

"She needs more healing," I told him frankly, knowing it would be the one thing that would keep him here in this quiet haven of soft yellow light and comfortable things while he rested.

He grunted and his head tipped back against the headboard, his eyes half-closed already. "Tell Hallow I'll be out in a few...," he mumbled.

Nicky and I waited until his eyes were closed and his breathing had softened, and then I moved her to his side and we both eased him back. He stirred for moment, said "Just another minute...," then clutched her to his chest and fell asleep.

"Gods," Nicky sighed as we walked out of the hall. "Sometimes there's a benefit to being second banana...." Then he toddled off to his room, hopefully to finish his sleep uninterrupted.

I wandered into the front room to talk to Hallow. He was sitting at the table playing backgammon with Max, who was responding to gently probing questions about accommodating his change to a preternatural being with extremely human grunts.

"I understand that the Goddess night was extremely intense," Hallow was saying. "What did you think?"

"I think I just won," Max said without triumph. "Renny, do we have any pie?"

Renny, who was sitting in the chair next to him, stood up to get some out of the refrigerator—but Max, running on sheer human panic, beat her to it, practically knocking over his chair in an effort to get the hell away from that table.

"Would you like some pie?" he asked with that bright, false hospitality of a child uncomfortable with an older relative—or a new husband dealing with an in-law.

"That would be lovely," Hallow said with a straight face and dancing eyes. "Bracken, would you like to join us?"

Not really. "Pie sounds great." I missed cramps and the sweats by inches.

Hallow laughed and pinched the bridge of his nose—a gesture very like Green's. "I'm off duty, people," he complained. "I didn't just drop out of the sky at dark thirty to psychoanalyze the whole hill."

Oh, well, in that case.... "I'd love to join you," I said with some genuine relief. "If you don't mind me asking...."

"Why am I here?" We nodded, Max and Renny with full mouths. "To thank you all, of course," he said seriously. "Most especially Green and your child-Goddess."

"Little Goddess," Max corrected with a swallow.

Hallow shook his head. "You are all so loyal—it's a truly good thing. Just...." He grimaced. "Just don't forget that even after all of this, she's only two human decades...."

Max made a pained sound and rolled his eyes at his beloved, who had only just turned twenty. Renny patted his thigh and went back to the half of a chocolate-caramel-cream masterpiece on her plate. Grace had been busy this night, cooking her relief and her gratitude into dessert.

"It's not like you're that old either, Max," Hallow added kindly. "Besides, I honestly just came to say thank you. Half the time when we were talking, Lady Cory was trying to console me. I wouldn't let her—I thought she needed to worry more about herself. But...." His fine, handsome face suddenly became grief stricken, and I remembered with a faint sense of shame the thing that Cory had never forgotten—Hallow had suffered a loss much like ours. We had been so involved in our great adjustment that I wasn't sure if anyone but Green and Cory had given a thought to his well-being. "But...," he repeated and shrugged, "she exacted justice, she kept her people safe. I'm one of her people, and some of that justice was for me. I just wanted to say thank you, that's all."

"She'll be asleep for a long time," I said, cocking my head to invite him to wait.

"I don't mind waiting," he said, and Max turned miserable eyes to me. He obviously didn't want to play with the grown-ups anymore.

"Would you like to play chess?" I asked hopefully.

"I'd love to—but I refuse to let you win," he said with some amusement.

"Damn Adrian," I muttered, running back to his old room to get a chess set, but I said it without heat. He had intended to live forever—I might never have known how badly I sucked at the game I had loved learning at his feet. But then, if he hadn't died, I might never have improved, either. I was so busy musing on this that I almost tripped over my own feet when I threw open the door to Adrian's room. The light was on and Kyle was sitting on the bed, listening to music on a set of tiny headphones. I froze in the doorway, not sure who was more stunned, Kyle or me.

"I'm sorry," I said after a moment, swallowing past the pain of seeing another person in this bright yellow room that I had loved. "I didn't realize...."

"Marcus set me up here...," he said apologetically, scrambling up and swinging his legs over the bed. "He said that no one was using this room right now...."

I shook my head and swallowed again. "No," I acknowledged. "No one's using it. It's...." Goddess, I had known this was coming. "It's fine," I said at last, meaning it. "Only this is where we keep the chess sets...."

Kyle's face—that stoic, still human mask that hid a pain I was too acquainted with—suddenly lit up. "That is an *awesome* collection," he said enthusiastically. "I'd love to play with some of those—that Civil War one is soooooo cooooool...." Then his face fell, as though he suddenly remembered that he was grieving and a stranger here. "But I'm not that good anyway," he mumbled, looking away.

"Well, go ahead and get it out," I invited, thinking that's what Cory would do. "Uhm... Hallow and I were going to start a game. You can play loser."

"Don't you mean winner?"

I shook my head glumly, thinking that Hallow probably learned how to play from Green—I got the feeling they were of an age, with a history. "No, no... the only way we'll all get to play is if one of us plays the loser."

Kyle laughed a tiny bit, just enough to make me think that, like the rest of us, he'd survive. "If you're sure?"

"Yeah. No problem whatsoever."

He got the set and went ahead of me, and I glanced behind me before I shut off the light.

Adrian, when will you love me?

Forever and ever.

A LITTLE before Cory woke up, Green strode purposefully into the living room and set himself up at his computer. Hallow and I looked at each other with questions in our eyes.

"Shouldn't she be up soon?" I asked—I'd been expecting her up for a couple of hours. We'd been playing marathon chess, so the time went by fast, but it was nearing two in the morning.

"I would imagine so." He kept his voice expressionless, and he was staring at his computer in the same way Cory had been staring at her knitting the morning after Davy died.

I know my eyebrows shot up to my hairline, and Hallow's did the same. "She will be aching to have you there," I said baldly.

"She's not even awake yet," he protested, and I was immediately earlobe-deep in the final realization of why Cory needed more than one lover.

"You're avoiding her," I accused, and he gave me an "oh please" look that should have made him sick—but because he hadn't spoken, I think the curse grazed by him by a hair's breadth.

Hallow tapped my shoulder and looked up at the doorway where our beloved stood, barefoot, wearing a white T-shirt that could have been either of ours—in fact, she'd been wearing our clothes so often, I think we'd been sharing each other's shirts as often as she'd been wearing them. She looked tired, her eye was still a little red, and her hair was a wild, tangled disaster floating around her pale face, but she had a mutinous cant to her jaw and that knit little pucker between her eyes. She took a long look at Green, oblivious in front of his laptop, and nodded, then changed her tack just a little.

I don't know how she made that pad to the couch sexy, but she did. She reached from behind the high-back (Hallow and I could see that when she bent at the waist, her feet came off the floor) and wrapped her arms around her beloved's shoulders, then bit him sharply on the ear.

"Beloved....," he complained, but she reached out (her little feet kicking furiously) and snapped the laptop shut over Green's loud protest.

"You lied," she said clearly. Green's shoulders slumped and his chin lowered to his chest, and for an awful, dreadful moment, he looked as defeated as I'd ever seen him.

"I'm so terribly sorry," he said rawly, and she moved her head around and nipped his other ear.

"It's a good thing you did," she replied matter-of-factly, "because with what I want to do to you, do you know what would happen if I tried it while I was floating around in your body as some sort of disembodied soul?" She bent over to his ear again and whispered something obscene, absurd, and so funny that Hallow and I choked on our own tongues, and Green burst into the startled laughter of the naughty little boy. Then he turned and looked her in the eyes for the first time since Scary Tree.

"You think so?" he asked, his chest still shaking with laughter. His eyes, though, were sober and yearning, and so terribly in love.

"I don't know." She smiled wickedly. "Do you want to try it with me on the outside of your body and see?"

He became a blur as he vaulted over the couch and swept her down the hallway.

"Oh damn," I sighed, watching them disappear into our room and feeling the last couple of days catching up with me. "Where am I going to sleep?"

Hallow looked in the direction they had disappeared, the last traces of trouble fading from his clear brow and lake-blue eyes. "I would imagine," he said thoughtfully, "that give it another game of chess—two games at the most—and you can sleep with them in your own bed."

Kyle raised his eyes to me and shrugged. Worth a try.

It took two games.

THE STILLNESS of the pre-gray dawn had settled over the house. Only the vampires were still awake, and their day was winding down too. Hallow had opted to stay over—I'd offered him a guest room, and I'm sure he was asleep almost as soon as the door closed behind me. I could hear the pad of my sidhe-quiet feet on the carpet as I opened the door to our room.

Green's back was to me, and his face was buried in her chest. Her arms were wrapped protectively around him. She was still stroking his hair, although I could see from the doorway that he was fast asleep. Her T-shirt glinted silver in the light that came in from the hall—elven tears, saturating the fabric.

Her chin lifted as I opened the door, and she nodded to me, her eyes limpid in the darkness when I closed out the hall light behind me. I realized that the room was still too permeated with the four of us together for me to tell if they had been making love. I hoped they had—Goddess, how I hoped they had. Green needed to be loved.

I undressed and wiggled in between the wall and her tiny body, sliding under the sheets behind her, and she wriggled back against me, gently pulling Green with her. Her T-shirt had rucked up a little under the covers, and her bottom was bare and smooth and her thighs were damp. That was a wonder and a comfort to me.

I wrapped my arm around her and she grasped my hand in hers, twining our fingers and putting our hands on the back of Green's head. Together we stroked his hair some more, until his breathing was so completely even we knew nothing could wake him.

"Are you hungry?" I asked into the quiet. "Do you need anything?"

"Mmmm...," she replied, probably meaning she was too sleepy to eat. Then she surprised me. "Yeah," she said. "Tell me about our wedding."

"Hm?"

"Our wedding—you've been planning it when I've been asleep— you have this whole wedding planned for me, and I don't know what it will be like."

"You want to hear it now?" I leaned in and rubbed the back of her ear with my lips.

"I want...." Her breath blew out, and I could only guess at the heaviness weighing on her. What must it be like, I wondered wretchedly, to hold Green's life in your hands?

"I want hope," she said at last. "I want the hope of peace, of a life with all of us. We're so close, Bracken. We're so close, and I just want to see it...." Her voice wobbled a little, and I kissed the back of her neck and began to speak.

"It will start just before sunset, because I want to see the sun in your hair," I said, thinking about how a late June sunset would make her hair like a halo of quiet flame.

"What day?" she asked, dropping a kiss in Green's hair.

"Two days after Litha." Our hands stilled. When she didn't say anything more, I continued, "So the vampires will be strong. I've talked to Grace and Marcus—when the sun sets, they'll all zoom up and just 'appear' in the middle of the guests, invisible in the twilight...."

"That'll be awesome...." Quiet laughter in her voice.

"Yes... they're planning to wear dark, washed-out greens and purples and blues—it will be like the night coming alive."

"What'll we wear?" The curiosity in her voice was painful.

"You'll wear what I set out for you," I told her primly, laughing in soft falls over her protesting "Bracken...."

"It will be the color of sunlight," I said when she'd kissed my fingers and asked me nicely. "Not white, not gold or yellow or off-white. It will make your face glow and your eyes look extraordinary," I told her reverently. "But other than that—it's a surprise. And Green will wear the same color...."

"And you?"

"No, I'll wear sort of a chocolate brown/green—it goes, I've checked already."

"Like your eyes...." She sounded amused.

"You like my eyes."

"Yes, but I've never suspected you of vanity." Her voice was getting blurry again.

"Hush and let me finish." I disentangled our fingers and stroked her hair back from her face instead. She leaned into my touch like a drowsy kitten. "Nicky will wear a dark rust color, like his hair. Arturo will officiate—and he can be stark naked if he cares to be, so don't ask."

She giggled a little but let me continue.

"We'll simply gather together at the crown of the Goddess grove, by the spring, and it will be... perfect. Your parents will be there, and any other family you have, and you'll be wearing the best wedding dress ever, with that purple stuff over your eyes, and they'll think you look..." *like a queen* "like an angel. They'll think you're radiant and lovely and that they've never seen a happier bride, and they won't care how many men are up there with you, they'll just..." *for once* "do what you do, beloved. They'll accept, and they'll love."

"Will the boys be there?"

"Absolutely...." Although I hadn't planned on them at all. "We'll have them escort your family to the crown of the hill."

"What will we say?" Her blurry voice was breaking, just a little.

"Whatever we want, whatever is in our hearts. You'll do most of the talking, of course."

"In front of all those people?" Yes, this would be hard for her.

"You can't speak a little poetry for your beloveds?" I teased.

"I could sing…," she murmured, so close to sleep I almost couldn't hear her. Then her voice wandered off, still sweet, still in key, but sleepy, syncopated, a dreamy version of "Lifetimes," her voice wobbling on the word "anyway."

"That would be perfect…." I hugged her even tighter.

"Tell me more…," she whispered.

And so I did.

CORY
Weaving in Ends

IT WENT almost exactly as Bracken had said it would. Elves aren't supposed to be precognitive, or anything like that—maybe it was just because he loved me so much that he planned everything that would make me happy, and his vision was just that clear.

Bracken, Green, and I spent Litha night itself in mourning, sitting on the crest of the Goddess grove, watching the sun die through the trees and speaking of Adrian. Because Litha was a day of weakness for vampires, we knew his ghost wouldn't be there, and that was good—because the hard thing about having the ghost of your lover hanging out to talk to you when you want him is that you sometimes forget that he's gone, until you want his touch so badly that not having it is like having him die all over again. So we mourned the first anniversary of Adrian's death, and the next day we prepared to celebrate the beginnings of our lives. Kind of poetic, really.

The wedding was perfect, although not quite as perfect as Bracken's vision—nothing ever really goes the way you plan it, right? Nicky's parents hadn't come. No amount of pleading on the parts of any of us would change their minds, and so we had all—Eric included—spent a little part of ourselves serving as a sop to his unspoken sadness. My stupid aunt showed up and was on the verge of getting fried by all the angry glances in reaction to her impertinent questions when Arturo saved us all by brain-wiping her into being quiet and forgetting everything but the fact that it was a beautiful day.

It was beautiful. The trees had grown enough from the night of their birth that you could barely see that they were really erotic sculptures of Green, Adrian, and me in the throes of our first joint encounter. Somehow that made the grove more sensual, in the same way that the curve of Green's neck or the point of Bracken's ears could, in a gilded moment, turn me on more than their bare and sculpted flesh. The sun was leveling across the top of the hill as we all gathered, and an unexpected breeze sprang up. The men looked breathtaking, in such a heart-full way that I cannot describe it. I can tell you what they were wearing, and that Green's eyes looked more green than emeralds and his hair brighter than gold, but I cannot tell you the way my heart or the pit of my stomach vibrated when he looked at me where I stood, all nerves, in the center of the place I loved most, surrounded by our people.

Bracken was so full of quiet pride that I almost wept looking at him. Nicky was so shy, so radiating with joy at being included in our little group on top of the hill, that I did weep. Green caught the tear on his finger and whispered "*Anyaen*" in my ear. It meant "mine," and he'd only used the word twice before. It was so absurdly perfect for this moment that I shed another tear, and another, until my throat almost clogged when it was time for me to sing.

But it didn't. And when I was done, there were tears in everybody's eyes.

When the sun set and the vampires joined us in the twilight, the incense of blood magic joined us, and the hill became a place of mystery and joy.

We celebrated until dawn, and the four of us made love until the next dawn, and our hill spent the week sated and saturated with pleasure and wonder. It was truly the most wonderful thing of all—the freedom of balance.

Eventually it ended, but it was a time of perfection. It gave us strength for whatever the big bad world would hold in store for us in the future—like the 120-degree day that Bracken and I chose to go to the college to collect everybody's report cards, for example.

July had been hot—hideously hot—all over the country. Toronto reported temperatures in the 110s with a devastating humidity, and places like Arizona and New Mexico had atmospheres just south of hell. Sacramento and its piddly little unhumid 120 seemed almost silly to complain about—but the elves all huddled in the temperateness of the hill, and even the vampires barely stirred out of Green's protection, unless it was for a midnight skinny dip in Lake Clementine.

I was all for going to the college alone—or with Renny and Nicky, who did fine in the heat—but Bracken insisted on coming, and Nicky was busy with the Avians, and Renny and Max were… doing whatever they did when Max wasn't working. (Yes, I have a pretty good idea of what that was—no, I do not need a clear mental picture.)

The sun was already coming off the concrete in murky waves of brilliant ozone when we pulled into the parking lot by the levee—Bracken had said he wanted to look at the river on our way out, since I'd told him I'd be running on the bike path there this year. As a wedding present, Green had given me a smooth and even running route around his hill. Now, when the elves walked their land, I could run on my little trail, and we could sort of do our things together. It was so cool... and then I'd felt bad because I hadn't given any of them a wedding present, and Green had laughed.

"What about my sweater, luv?" He wore it every morning—another thing to thank the climate on his magic hill for, because otherwise it wouldn't see the light of day until November.

I flushed. "I didn't really... I mean, after it got unraveled, Bracken's mother and Grace knitted most of it back up! It's not really my work," I burst out, trying not to be too upset by this but failing. It had been such a wonderful gesture—they had knit back up every stitch that I'd had, right to the three (count 'em!) miscrossed cables in the front—but it felt like when Bracken had done my physics homework (which I hadn't let him do after March), because I personally hadn't finished all of it.

Green's indulgent smile had vanished then, and he'd framed my face in his graceful hands. "This bloody sweater led me to you, beloved. You gave up all of that sweat so that I could have you back. If you can't feel the pain of that sacrifice—and how hard you tried to mask it—in every stitch, you're mad. You made it. You had help fixing it, but you had by Goddess better claim your work."

Yeah, well, the argument about wedding presents had ended then.

So today we made the trek from the far parking lot (where the SUV could at least be in the shade) through the campus to the administration building just to print out everybody's grades at the kiosk, because we were all too impatient to wait for our report cards.

It was already ninety-five degrees outside, and Bracken was visibly wilting, all near-seven feet of him, as we were trekking back. This was probably why I only overreacted a little when I saw my physics grade.

"How in the blue fuck did I get a B in physics?" I demanded.

"Apparently you did well on the tests," he said mildly. I looked at him with narrowed eyes, the last fragment from that sleepy conversation filtering behind my eyes.

"So, mighty Kreskin... if you can see our wedding this clearly, can you tell me if I'm going to pass physics?" I was so tired... so almost... nod... darkness... so close to....

"By the skin of my balls...," he muttered, and I startled a little and woke up.

"Wha?"

"Go to sleep, beloved," he ordered.

"You'd better not do any more of my...."

Apparently he'd willed me to sleep after that, because I didn't remember any more of that conversation—and I knew there were homework assignments I'd missed between March and May.

"You *asshole*," I said with feeling. "I told you I wanted an honest grade from that class."

"You got an honest grade," he replied mildly, turning behind himself to give me a hand up the levee. There were stairs not far away, but it didn't occur to either of us to use them. "Anyone who could think of physics while trying to figure out how to crash a car into a power bubble deserves at least a B."

I blushed. "Who told you that?" I knew I'd been bouncing around in everyone's heads that night, but I wasn't aware that my panic-physics had been so widely broadcast.

"Marcus and Green. Green didn't know what that part was all about when it was happening. Marcus thought it was funny." He gave me a final heave, and we stood up on the crest of the levy. There was the bike path below us, winding like the rattlesnakes that loved it too—and the low water beyond, clothed in green blackberry bushes and cattails at its marshy skin, gliding insouciantly under the bike bridge.

"Nothing about that night was funny," I said grimly, shivering in horror at my nightmare vision of Bracken bleeding, *dying* under Grace's hands.

"Marcus thought *that* was," he said soothingly, trying to distract me. I wondered if he'd ever understand that the vision of his blood dripping through my power was as awful to me as... well, I guess there were so many times I'd come close to death, he could take his pick. But the distraction worked, because suddenly I was remembering Marcus on the night of the wedding. His humble, handsome face had been bashful in the ambient violet light of the grove as he had lowered his lips to mine in a traditional kiss for the untraditional bride.

"Uhm…." I blushed. Marcus would never say anything to either of us, I knew, but… "Uhm… Marcus, Bracken?"

"Marcus is like Andres," Bracken replied with a small smile, his pond-shadow eyes looking out at the rocks on the far side of the levee. The rocks on our side were, per tradition, painted white and spelling out the name of some fraternity against the plain tan-brown of the river dust. The soil at Green's hill was red, I thought irrelevantly, and then Bracken attended to what I'd said. "If they are to be—if we're to be, and a vampire is to be part of us, it will happen or not happen in its time." It was too hot to wrap me up in his arms, so he settled for a quick kiss at my temple instead. "You should know that by now."

"Mmmm." He was right—Bracken was often right, but I wasn't going to tell him that. "It's pretty, isn't it?" I asked instead, sort of surprised. The river was broad in this spot—sliding, gliding, swollen from late snows in early May, moving down from the mountains by Green's hill past this busy, grimy center of concentrated humanity. My land breathed in and out, lived and died, at the fall of the rains and the drink of the sun, but I frequently forgot that the river that bound these drives together lay right at my feet.

"It would be prettier clean," he said sadly, "but yes, running water is always magic. This is too."

A wind came off the water then—a hot wind, but it dried the sweat off our skin so it was still pleasant. It shook the broad, translucent leaves in the trees above us with the white bark and the cobwebs of plant fur, and we stood for another moment, looking at the tranquil magic of our river.

But it was getting hotter by the second, and I had to get my elf to the safety of his hill, so I was the one who turned to scramble back down the bark and eucalyptus-leaf covered levee, knowing he would follow.

"This is a good place," my friend, my beloved, my husband, said as we were trotting slowly back to the car. "It will be good to come back in September."

I smiled at him, grateful. "Yeah—it really will." And we navigated out of that icon of human learning back to the sanity of Green's hill.

Stay tuned for an exclusive excerpt from

Rampant, Vol. 1

Little Goddess:
Book Four, Vol. 1

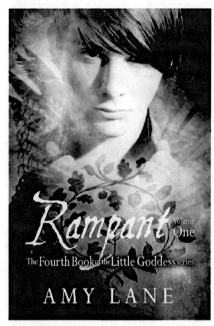

Lady Cory has carved out a life for herself not just as a wife to three husbands but also as one of the rulers of the supernatural communities of Northern California—and a college student in search of that elusive degree. When a supernatural threat comes crashing into the hard-forged peace of Green's Hill, she and Green determine that they're the ones in charge of stopping the abomination that created it. To protect the people they love, Cory, Bracken, and Nicky travel to Redding to confront a tight-knit family of vampires guarding a terrible secret. It also leads them to a conflict of loyalties, as Nicky's parents threaten to tear Nicky away from the family he's come to love more than his own life.

Cory has to work hard to hold on to her temper and her life as she tries to prove that she and Green are not only leaders who will bind people to their hearts, but also protectors who will keep danger from running rampant.

Coming Soon to
www.dsppublications.com

CORY
Buzzkilling

GETTING BAD news when you're suspended fifty feet above the ground is the definition of buzzkill.

Green and Bracken were below me, ready to catch—don't get me wrong, I'm not stupid. But there I was, holy shit and canny a gimme hallelujah, I was *flying! Suspended* off the ground, hovering in the crystal-shard February blue, watching the fat-sheep clouds scudding much farther above me and shivering convulsively. Below me I could see big clumps of crocuses and pinks defiantly brightening Green's gardens. In the foothills they were rare—but in Green's hill, the rare was commonplace, and that crunchy sweet smell was teasing us with the promise of spring as I practiced my flying.

Last year, I'd been put in a position where being able to fly would have been *extremely* handy, but my lack of control had completely biffed *that* opportunity, so my husbands and I (no shit—we all had rings, Nicky too, who was a bird in his other skin and currently flying around my head annoying me with hawk-shrikes of encouragement) were out here practicing my stuff. You never know when you might plummet hundreds of feet from a bad guy's nasty, slippery, dead-fleshed grasp, and a little initiative might make hitting bottom a lot more comfortable, right?

So there I was, arms spread like a psychotic bird (because Nicky wasn't psychotic enough for both of us, he was so worried), and Green and Bracken just *freaking out* whenever my flight plan deviated and it looked as though they couldn't even hyperspeed it fast enough to catch me, and I was trying not to have too much fun.

I mean, it was sort of fun, even if it was cold enough to freeze the balls off a female Yeti (is that a Yetina? I have no idea), but I was terrified, and I'm not that great at driving fast so what in the *fuck* made me think flying would be such a swell idea? Besides, my life was so intimately tied with the three men helping me that getting hurt or killed with what was, essentially, a training exercise, was absolutely unriskable. So I was having fun, but I was working *very* hard at being in control of myself—hovering, swooping, diving, and unintentionally scaring Bracken enough to make his sidhe-pale skin blanche almost green. Green, on the other hand, was handling the panic well. The occasional frustrated "Beloved..." would waft up on a warning breeze, but mostly he had faith that I wouldn't put myself in more danger than necessary.

But I guess you can't help but buzz a little when you're, well, *buzzing*, so it was a definite distraction when Hallow, my professor-cum-shrink, pulled up in a rather spiffy white Lexus, looking as though someone had died.

Dammit, you don't look like someone died in my world unless the news is pretty fucking dire, right? I mean... people *do* die around us, all the time.

I came dropping out of the sky like lead shit from a helium duck.

Green and Bracken both screamed, "Fuck!" and then scrambled to find a place below me, but I beat them to it, putting a big fat slice of power below me and sort of skimming off it like one of those big bounce-house slides. I whooped up for about ten feet at the end and then set another cushion of will beneath me, coming to a rest about two feet off the ground on all fours before sinking slowly until I hit grass, like a Labrador on a punctured air bed.

Bracken collapsed next to me, his haggard face buried in his hands, his onyx-black hair in disarray around his perfect, inhumanly beautiful triangular features.

When his eyes met mine, they were murky and dark with hints of green like a pond in shadow, but when he opened his mouth, all of that murkiness disappeared.

"I cannot fucking do this. It scares the piss out of me every fucking time."

I sat back on my haunches and scooted into him, leaning my head on his shoulder. "At no time was the subject in real danger," I murmured, mimicking the dry voice of a TV documentary narrator. He grunted and jerked away, and I looked up to Green for help.

Green smiled and blew out an exasperated breath, shaking his hip-length butter-colored hair down his back. "Really, mate—after everything else we've done, you can't take a spin in the garden? Your mother let you do this when you were four."

No one could resist Green when he was determinedly good-natured, and Bracken was no exception. He looked up, the corners of his sour grimace quirking upwards, and shook his head. "It's a good thing I'm mortal, mate—I don't think I could take scares like that for a millennium."

And now *I* wanted to smack *him*. The big hoser had given his immortality up for me, because I was mortal, and he'd just rubbed salt in that wound. Typical, for Bracken.

I smacked the back of his head for real, and felt much better.

"Oww...." And then, also typical Bracken, he realized how badly he'd screwed up before he could get mad. By the time Hallow walked up, he was repeatedly smacking his forehead with the heel of his hand, and Nicky had landed in the open patch of green I'd fallen on and was rolling barefoot on the frost-melted grass.

I was about two breaths away from ripping into Nicky like a kid into a Christmas present for losing his *handmade* woolen socks when I remembered why I'd fallen out of the sky in the first place.

Hallow had the same preternaturally beautiful features as Green—triangular bone structure, overlarge eyes (but his were blue), clean lines. Unlike my beloved, though, Hallow's beauty had never moved me. I liked the guy, but that didn't keep me from spitting venom at him now.

"Who died?" I demanded, and for all his professorial dignity, Hallow managed to look sheepish.

"I'm so sorry about that—I do have bad news, but it's not that dire." He wore his hair long, like Green's, but his was plaited and pulled back from his aesthetic features. He was playing with the end of the braid.

So no one died. But someone was about to. "Cough it up, dammit!" I growled. I had been doing so well this time around—some of my other flying attempts had rewritten disaster movie scripts—and if he was going to drop in and make me just drop, well, he'd better have a damned good explanation.

Have you ever heard bad news that made your eyes glaze over and your brain black out? I understand it doesn't happen for *really* bad things, like death or dismemberment or even cancer, but I knew a girl in high school who swore that it happened whenever her current boyfriend broke up with her. Apparently it made the next ten minutes after each breakup horribly awkward, because she would deny all knowledge of the preceding conversation.

When I came to, I was staring at Hallow with eyes that were dried by the wind and with a little bit of drool tracking the corner of my lips. The men were all staring at me as though I were a rabid bear, and I had to ask Hallow to repeat what he'd just said.

I swear to the Goddess I was listening the second time, and it still didn't make any sense.

"What do you mean, I'm not going to graduate?" This much had seeped in, but it was like getting cold maple syrup through the baked hardpan of a planetary desert.

Hallow grimaced uncomfortably. My sudden-onset senility was worrisome to him, but since I'd been working my *ass* off for nearly the last four years to try to get my BA ASAP, I had to admit that the 180 degree mind-fuck was leaving my cortex a little sore.

"You *will* graduate, Lady Cory—"

"Would you stop calling me that like it's going to calm me down?" I snapped, and he gritted his teeth and continued.

"It's just that you have too many units right now to graduate with a bachelor's degree."

I blinked slowly. "How in the fuck is that even possible?"

Hallow took another deep breath and waded in again. "You took so many units last year that you have more than enough to graduate. But you don't have them in the right places. If you take the classes you need in the right places, you will have so many units that you will have enough for two bachelor's degrees. If you take the nine units of thesis work, you'll have enough for two bachelors and a master's degree. Which I suggest you do. But it means that—"

"I don't graduate this year." Okay. I was finally starting to understand.

Hallow sighed and let out a whole lot of tension from his shoulders. "That's right, my lady, you'll have to wait until next year."

Now, two years ago I would have pitched a fit of cosmic proportions— six zillion light-years from here, some species that registered emotional sound through its skin would have shuddered, turned brown, and said, "What in the fuck was that?"

But I was older now. I was more mature than that. I was the leader of my fucking people, and I did not pitch fits over bizarre twists of bureaucratic insanity, I simply... I just.... Oh Jesus... I was going to be the first person in my family to ever graduate from college. I'd about worn my impending letters like some sort of badge of triumph over the ignominy of white-trashdom that I'd been trying to shake my entire life.

"Uhm, Cory?" Bracken said gently, throwing himself under the bus of my potential meltdown. He was used to it. Our relationship had the passion of a sailor addicted to the sea—the storms were exhilarating and the smooth sailing was a thing of beauty, and he could weather the rolling thunder of my bitchiness like no other lover.

"Beloved?" Green asked, even more gently. Of the three of them, his sweetness, and the kind and even keel of his beautiful soul, could be the only things that would calm me down.

Nicky, my shape-shifting accidental lover, had no such finesse. "Well hell, Cory, what are you going to do?"

I turned to him and blinked rapidly, trying to slam this bit of unwelcome news into perspective. I mean, shit, hadn't I just thought someone had died? I'd been prepared to deal with *death*, for crap's sake, couldn't I take a change in my goddamned plans?

I growled, grunted, and tried again from grinding teeth, finally finding my outlet.

"I am going to go knit."

And with that, I turned on my heel and stalked through Green's glorious gardens, blind to their loveliness, and pounded up the stairs to the landing and into the living room, leaving my three husbands wincing in sympathy behind me.

Renny, my best friend and part-time giant tabby cat, had a built-in radar as to whether or not I needed a girl friend or a kitty when I was upset.

She was curled up in a big purring tortoiseshell blob on the olive-turquoise-violet colored quilt at my feet as I sat cross-legged on the gi-freaking-normous bed I shared with Bracken, knitting Nicky another goddamned pair of socks.

Nicky actually stuck his head in first, but I glared at him, and he cringed when he saw the burgundy, brown, and lime-green yarn I was working with (always trendy for Nick!) and ducked right on back out. One of the things that made our polyamorous marriage work was that Nicky had learned to recognize when I needed my man friend with the nice body and comforting smell and when I needed one of my beloveds who could steady the world when it rocked beneath my feet.

I should have been ashamed that this was one of those times, but what the fuck. Sometimes even Lady Cory, beloved to Lord Green and queen of the goddamned vampires, could get stuck in a petty, shit-kicking funk about dumb fucking bullshit that complicated her life, right?

Well, not for long.

Bracken stalked in after about half an hour, so lost as to what to do for me that he was actually squinting in puzzlement.

"What are you making?" he demanded—and he was probably unaware of how arrogant he sounded. He was trying, honestly, to make conversation.

"Socks for Nicky," I replied mildly, and his frown deepened.

"Little fucker lost the last pair in trans," he said, and I nodded glumly. It happened sometimes. Nicky was an Avian, a bird shape-shifter, and they were the only species that actually didn't have to strip naked to shift. They carried their clothes and stuff on the oil in their feathers—except when a bird is stressed or tired, that oil gets a little thin, and something has to go. I freaked Nicky out by almost plummeting to my death, and he lost his socks.

"You like Nicky," I reminded him. It had not always been so, but Bracken had finally accepted Nicky's accidental and unintentional place in my bed and my life. Still, it didn't hurt to remind Brack that Nicky had his place. Besides, there were things we could do with three people in a bed that we couldn't do with two, and Bracken was just bi enough—and had been raised with enough sexual diversity and privilege—to enjoy those things.

We were bound. If either of us took our pleasure outside our marriage or any of my pre-existing bindings (like, say, Green or Nicky), the other one would die horribly. There is always a flip side to the passion of the Goddess's magic, and this was one of them. Marriage? Fabulous—but you'd better make good and damned sure that you were in it for the long haul. If I had been a sidhe instead of a human sorceress, Bracken and I would be locked inside this binding for a lot more than a mortal lifespan—not that either one of us would have minded then either, not even a little teeny bit, but like I said, he'd been raised with some freedoms.

In the context of those freedoms, Nicky had gone from being a nuisance to a perk—even if he was only my perk. Bracken was bound to me and Nicky was bound to me, and the two of them had learned to tolerate each other, except in bed.

In bed, Bracken had taken to being my primary lover like sex was a competitive event. It was like a sweet lovers' game, except the stakes seemed to be the increasingly colorful state of Green's once pristinely finished wood-paneled walls. My losses of control—even small ones— in bed tended to change the state of the world around me. Sometimes it was cute—olive, turquoise, and lavender paneling in the living room, for example.

Sometimes it was huge. Green and I, with our beloved vampire, Adrian, had completely reformed the crown of Green's hill, complete with trees doing erotic things with their trunks, if you can believe that bullshit. Bracken and I had created a hotel.

Sometimes it was terrifying. The things I had done upon Adrian's death were an object lesson of why power shouldn't be allowed to run rampant.

So Bracken strategized and Nicky accepted—and I treated their efforts with affection and passion and as practice sessions to control my body, my mind, and my magic.

No—I loved my husbands, all three of them, but no combination of us would ever be what Green and Adrian and I had been, and I knew better than to try.

Right now, Bracken was wishing that he didn't like Nicky quite so much, because it was much easier to use my lesser lover as a scapegoat than to figure out a way to comfort me. Not knowing how to comfort me was item number 2657 on the list of things that made Bracken cranky— and per usual when he was cranky, he found some way to purge that emotion from his extremely passionate system.

"You never make me socks!" he accused, perfectly serious, and I fought the urge to laugh.

"You hate stuff on your feet!" I responded. It was true. All elves did. Even outside just now, in the chilly February, Bracken and Green had been barefoot. "Besides, I just finished your sweater for this year!" I fingered the gray wool on his arm. The yoke of the thing was a dark, masculine green and purple over a cream background. (My first venture into Fair Isle patternworking—I was very proud.)

"Well, I wouldn't hate it if you made it!" he protested, a little panic in his voice—really bad shit happens to elves if they lie, and he was obviously hoping he really felt this way and wasn't just saying this to make me feel better. He brightened when the nausea and cramping didn't start, and he continued on, a little more confident. "But I wouldn't want them in...." Bracken wrinkled his nose, and I held out my hands. Those colors. Enough said. "And they'd need to be strong. But not plain." He stroked the smooth fingering-weight wool between my fingers. "And it needs texture... this is ordinary. If I'm going to wear something on my feet it needs to press your fingertips into my flesh."

I nodded, completely bemused, and unbidden, a pattern for Bracken's socks began to emerge in my head. "Man's colors, lots of texture, not plain...."

"And not feminine either," he emphasized, and I stifled the urge to chortle. From his square shoulders to his frequent glower, there was not an effete inch to Bracken's bisexual skin. I could make these things in pony-puke pink, and on Brack, it would be the next navy blue.

"Not a problem," I murmured dryly. "Bracken... love... you really don't have to...."

Bracken stood up and paced a little. If this were a death, a true tragedy, he'd know how to deal—he dealt very well with me when I was upset or unhappy, or feeling inadequate. But something like this—something that was frustrating and (I admit it) self-inflicted—well, he was at a loss.

"Of course I want you to make me socks," he said softly, coming to a halt in front of me. An elegant hand with blunt, square fingers appeared under my chin and tilted my face so I would look at him. "You know I love the things you make for me."

"I meant," I murmured, feeling a helpless, foolish little smile steal across my face, "that you don't have to come with me for one more year."

He looked honestly surprised, and then he looked honestly pissed. "You think you're going there without me?" He backed up, eyes flashing, and I grimaced. Any little hint that I might *possibly* feel unworthy, and he acted like I had stomped on his damned-near-prehensile big toe.

I laughed, shaking my head and wondering if now was the time in our relationship to stand up and soothe over that powerful, vast body with my own little hands. "I'm just saying that you don't have to live with my own personal fuckup, okay?" I tried to smile winningly, and he was almost buying it, almost in my arms, when it suddenly occurred to him that now I was the one calming *him* down.

He shook his head and kissed me hard, literally leaning over Renny-the-cat's body to take my mouth with his, until I whimpered just a little in surprise and arousal.

Renny reached out with precisely extended claws and flexed those large crescents into Bracken's leg.

He jumped back and yelped, and she gave a cat chuckle and settled down into her paws again. "What was that for?" he demanded. Renny, being the supreme bitch-kitty that she was, made a show of cleaning the pads of her front foot with a rough pink tongue.

"You almost squashed her, Brack!" I protested, much of my funk almost completely gone.

"I was just trying"—he glared at Renny, who continued cleaning undisturbed—"to tell you that I…." He shook his head sheepishly. "I like school. It's fun. Some of my favorite Cory moments come when we're working together like that."

My mouth quirked up, and I wondered why my chest didn't explode. "And that you wanted socks," I added, wondering if he was going to back down on that.

"Absolutely," he said, and once again he looked surprised when he didn't double over and barf.

I leaned into him over Renny, and I was about half a heartbeat from kicking her out of my room when a tiny sparkly pink creature popped into thin air about two inches from Bracken's face and started speaking in Bumblebee or whatever. Sprites: the fey equivalent of the cell phone.

"Now?" Bracken asked reluctantly, and even I could interpret the emphatic little foot stomping that went with the little guy's (girl's?) sparkling tinkle. Bracken scrubbed his face with both hands and nodded, and the sprite disappeared.

"It's Da," Bracken sighed. "Apparently they're having trouble stringing lights for the ceremony tonight, and they want…." He flushed.

"*Oi'anga*," I supplied with a smile, and he nodded. I was having one hell of a time learning the language of the fey, but this word I had down cold. It meant "the tall one." Bracken's mother and father were lower fey—they were not only less humanoid looking than their gigantic offspring, they were also much smaller. Bracken frequently got called into service as a walking ladder. As my husband, he had also become a reluctant and baffled liaison between the lower fey and Green, the leader of the sidhe—the high elves. Bracken had spent much of his seventy-seven years of life avoiding any responsibility that didn't get him laid. He'd been horrified to realize that being my lover made him a corner in our little triad of power, but he hadn't been able to leave his new status any more than he'd be able to leave me.

"As long as they remember you're my *due'alle* first," I muttered direly, and he grinned.

"I'll make it a priority to remind them, *due'ane*," he replied, and I stopped him before he made an accompanying gesture.

"If you bow to me, you'll be best friends with your fist for a week," I warned, and he grinned unrepentantly and did a full-fledged, head-at-his-knees bow with a flourish, and I was suddenly in my complete, leather-stewing funk again even as he dodged lightly out the door. (Sidhe always moved lightly—it didn't matter that he was over six and a half feet tall. I couldn't move lightly when I was fifty feet in the air. Bastard.)

I sighed and scrambled over Renny's cat-chuckling body onto the other side of the bed, where I got on my knees and yanked out a big clear-white Lexan. I scanned through the plastic lid, decided what I wanted wasn't in that one, and then yanked the other one out from under the bed.

Renny was suddenly a naked young woman kneeling next to me. She'd opened the first box and was sorting through the elbow-deep pile of lovely hand-dyed fiber within.

"Jeez, Cory, it's a good thing you work at a yarn store, because you might run out of this shit and that would be a shame."

I looked at her sideways. Her flyaway brown hair was sticking out all over her head like a lion's mane, and her eyes were their usual dreamy, unfocused brown. "It would help," I said mildly, "if skeins wouldn't just walk out of the boxes sometimes when I thought they'd be where I left them."

Renny didn't have the grace to flush. "You have the best taste," she murmured, taking a blue-gray wool/tencel/cotton blend out and stroking it. Her bare shoulders did a sinuous little dance, and she reached into the box for the other five skeins. It didn't take a genius in color theory to know she was planning a sweater for her husband, Max. Max had blue eyes and dark hair and would probably look awesome in that yarn—I'd thought so when I'd recommended it to Renny while we were working, and she'd refused.

Bitch, I thought affectionately. It was like it was more fun to hunt and kill the little yarn cake herself as long as it was under my bed.

"What are you making?" she asked, her yarn carefully hoarded against her bare breasts. It was funny how, in a place like Green's where everything was so very sexually charged, Renny (and hell, almost anybody—even Green and Bracken when they felt like it) could run around naked and inspire nothing but curiosity as to whether or not she was cold.

I pulled out a black, brown, and red-speckled yarn and eyed it with satisfaction. "Apparently I'm making a pair of socks that says 'I'm a big strong bundle of hypersensitive testosterone who can eat small animals raw for breakfast but who wouldn't mind touching another man's bare ass.'"

Renny smirked and was opening her mouth to make a retort when the door opened again. There was only one other person who would open our door without knocking, and that was the one person Renny would leave the room for as a sign of respect. In a morphing flash of bare white skin and fluffy brown tortoiseshell fur, she streaked out of the room, leaving me to clean up. Bitch.

Unhurriedly I put the lids on the yarn boxes, leaving what she'd picked out for Max on top even as I pushed the two boxes back under the bed. Then I tossed Bracken's ball of sock yarn on top of the bed and launched myself at my beloved Green with enough force to surprise him.

"I'm fine," I murmured, rubbing my face against his white linen shirt. "I'm fine, I'll live… don't worry about me."

Heaven was in Green's arms. They folded around me like I was a shattered bird, and his job was to put me back together again without disturbing a single hollow bone.

"I know you're fine, luv," he murmured into my hair. "You're stronger than letting something like this shake you. I just wanted to comfort you, that's all." He backed up, and I smiled besottedly into his clean-lined, masculine, and lovely face. His sidhe-pale skin was flushed and warm from an armload of little ol' me, and his green eyes were glowing for me alone. It had taken a long time for me to accept that he could love me with all of his heart, and I took this moment to bask in that affection for a moment like a kitten in the sun.

Playfully he backed up and unbalanced us so we sprawled upon the bed, and I grinned up at him sunnily. He held his fingertips to my plain mortal face, and I leaned into his touch like lightning in a ball. I didn't know what everyone else felt when he touched them—I imagined it was the difference between what a high school teacher feels for her students and what she feels for her teenaged children. She might enjoy the company of all those others, but she would lie down in traffic and die for her own.

That was how my Green loved me.

My small mortal body often felt as though it would peel back and split from the gigantic swelling of my soul when he touched me like this, tenderly and with passion. How could something as stupid as another year of school overwhelm me when I was loved like this, by this man-god? It was impossible. Small things could be overcome.

"You may comfort me any time you want," I said softly, rubbing the curve of his pointed ear. He smiled and leaned into that touch—I think it was a sidhe weakness, because Bracken liked it too.

When he lowered his head to kiss me, the tears I'd been ruthlessly squashing back trickled forward, and he stopped in the middle of my best kiss and wiped them away with his thumbs.

"See, luv, you are upset!" he chided. I shook my head. I wouldn't be upset, not when I had him, and Bracken, and Nicky.

"I'm happy," I told him gruffly. "I'm happy—I'm so happy that our disasters can be measured in headaches and not heartaches." And then all that mattered was his lips on mine, the taste of his tongue, his hands, warm and sweet, touching my stomach under my sweatshirt.

I sighed, sinking into him with the eagerness of an addict sinking into euphoria, and he rushed through my skin with my fix. My hands went to wriggle under his sweatshirt and jeans, but he sighed and pulled away. I'd seen that expression in his eyes before, and this time I didn't need to rack my brains to know why we had to stop.

"The ceremony...." I didn't need to finish the thought, and he nodded apologetically. Our recently appointed (shanghaied!) alpha werewolf and his chosen mates were being formally bound on the top of the hill tonight, in the Goddess grove. Besides the fact that the entire hill would be there and it would be rude to be late, Green and I were sort of officiating.

"If it was our own shindig, luv...." He trailed off meaningfully, and I managed a grin. If it was our own shindig, we'd have our own quickie and make the world wait for us. But it was someone else's shindig, and not just any someone else—it was someone we'd come to care for, and someone who so often expected to be overlooked or abused. If it had been our celebration, we might have been late and unapologetic. If it was a good friend's party, we might be late anyway, and they would understand.

But it wasn't ours and it wasn't anybody else's, it was Teague's. And while Jack and Katy would forgive us, we wouldn't do that to Teague for all the world.

"Goddess!" I groaned, throwing my head back against the mattress. "Are you sure he's back already?"

Green blinked at me. "Back from where? Where would he be going right before his wedding?"

I blinked back at him. I thought Teague would have told him—sometimes I forgot that people treated me like I was exactly equal to Green. I never knew what to do with that. Green was 1800 years old; I would be twenty-two in July.

"He went to see Lloyd and Spider," I told him now, hoping I hadn't done anything wrong. Teague had left early this morning—before the vampires went to sleep, actually. I didn't realize that he had slunk from his lovers' bed like a con man from his virgin mark until Jack had come looking for him right before I went out to practice flying.

"Really?" Green asked, a quirk of private amusement on his lips. "I wonder what his tattoo will look like."

I shook my head. I had no idea, but I did know that it would be very private to the three of them. Since my little visit to Lloyd and Spider, Green had marked all of his people with an insignia—mostly through one big blast of magic that we had performed together with a whole lot of help. Anyone joining us, either as a were or a vampire or just a friendly human, came through their transition with the mark on their skin.

The werewolves were no exceptions—Teague's was on his right wrist, Katy's was on her ankle, and I had no idea where Jack's mark was. Whatever Teague was doing right now, it was something different, just for his lovers, and that was his business.

Green looked distant for a moment, and then he came back to me. "He's just hitting the driveway now. It really is time."

I covered my eyes with my hands. "Aw, crap—Bracken was going to help me get ready!"

Bracken was good at that sort of thing. He had good taste, and I privately had to admit that he knew how to make me look like the Lady of Green's House when often I would have just blown off the occasion in jeans and a T-shirt. Yes, Bracken was good at picking out the clothes and the makeup and choosing the hairstyle, but looking at Green's grin now I remembered who bought the clothes and told the sprites to buy the makeup and suggested the hairstyles to the sprites who did them in the first place.

"You planned this!" I accused, not upset in the least. Green and I got so little uninterrupted time together that even having him help me get ready would be a treat.

"I didn't, I swear!" he denied, holding up his hands and laughing. His playful grin faded, though, and he gazed at me fondly. "But that doesn't mean I won't appreciate every second of it, if that's good with you."

Of course it wasn't a question. Green was in my arms and he loved me. It was all good with me.

Little Goddess: Book One

Working graveyards in a gas station seems a small price for Cory to pay to get her degree and get the hell out of her tiny town. She's terrified of disappearing into the aimless masses of the lost and the young who haunt her neck of the woods. Until the night she actually stops looking at her books and looks up. What awaits her is a world she has only read about—one filled with fantastical creatures that she's sure she could never be.

And then Adrian walks in, bearing a wealth of pain, an agonizing secret, and a hundred and fifty years with a lover he's afraid she won't understand. In one breathless kiss, her entire understanding of her own worth and destiny is turned completely upside down. When her newfound world explodes into violence and Adrian's lover—and prince—walks into the picture, she's forced to explore feelings and abilities she's never dreamed of. The first thing she discovers is that love doesn't fit into nice neat little boxes. The second thing is that risking your life is nothing compared to facing who you really are—and who you'll kill to protect.

www.dsppublications.com

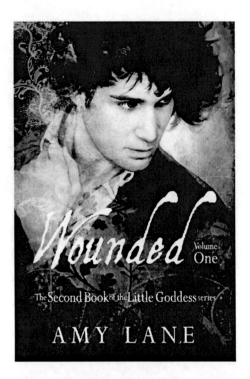

Little Goddess: Book Two, Vol. 1

Cory fled the foothills to deal with the pain of losing Adrian, and Green watched her go. Separately, they could easily grieve themselves to death, but when an old enemy of Green's brings them back together, they can no longer hide from their grief—or their love for each other.

But Cory's grieving has cut her off from the emotional stability that's the source of her power, and Green's worry for her has left them both weak. Cory's strength comes from love, and she finds that when she's in the presence of Adrian's best friend, Bracken, she feels stronger still.

But defeating their enemy is by no means a sure thing. As the attacks against Cory and her lovers keep coming, it becomes clear that their love might not be enough if they can't heal each other—and themselves—from the wounds that almost killed them all.

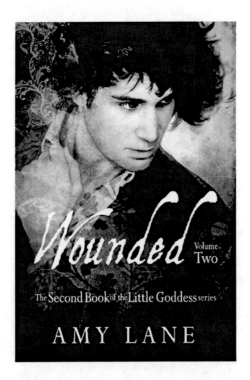

Little Goddess: Book Two, Vol. 2

Green and Bracken's beloved survived their enemy's worst—with unexpected vampiric help.

But survival is a long way from recovery, and even further from safety. Green's people want badly to return to the Sierra Foothills, but they're not going with their tails between their legs. Before they go home, they have to make sure they're free from attack—and that they administer a healthy dose of revenge as well.

As Cory negotiates a fragile peace between her new and unexpected lovers, Green negotiates the unexpected power that comes from being a beloved leader of the paranormal population. Together, they might heal their own wounds and lead their people to an unprecedented place at the top of the supernatural food chain—a place that will allow them to return home a better, stronger whole.

www.dsppublications.com

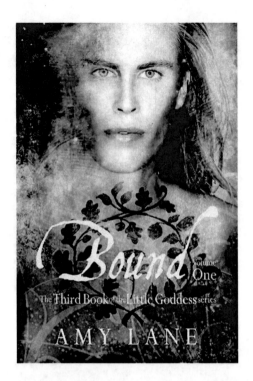

Little Goddess: Book Three, Vol. 1

Humans have the option of separation, divorce, and heartbreak. For Corinne Carol-Anne Kirkpatrick, sorceress and queen of the vampires, the choices are limited to love or death. Now that she is back at Green's Hill and assuming her duties as leader, her life is, at best, complicated. Bracken and Nicky are competing for her affections, Green is away taking care of his people, and a new supernatural enemy is threatening the sanctity of all she has come to love. Throw in a family reunion gone bad, a supernatural psychiatrist, and a killer physics class, and Cory's life isn't just complex, it's psychotic.

Cory needs to get her act and her identity together, and soon, because the enemy she and her lovers are facing is a nightmare that doesn't just kill people, it unmakes them. If she doesn't figure out who she is and what her place is on Green's Hill, it's not just her life on the line. She knows from hard experience that the only thing worse than facing death is facing the death of someone she loves.

Loving people is easy—living with them is what takes the real work, and it's even harder if you're bound.

www.dsppublications.com

AMY LANE is a mother of two college students, two grade-schoolers, and two small dogs. She is also a compulsive knitter who writes because she can't silence the voices in her head. She adores fur-babies, knitting socks, and hawt menz, and she dislikes moths, cat boxes, and knuckle-headed macspazzmatrons. She is rarely found cooking, cleaning, or doing domestic chores, but she has been known to knit up an emergency hat/blanket/pair of socks for any occasion whatsoever, or sometimes for no reason at all. Her award-winning writing has three flavors: twisty-purple alternative universe, angsty-orange contemporary, and sunshine-yellow happy. By necessity, she has learned to type like the wind. She's been married for twenty-plus years to her beloved Mate and still believes in Twu Wuv, with a capital Twu and a capital Wuv, and she doesn't see any reason at all for that to change.

Website: www.greenshill.com
Blog: www.writerslane.blogspot.com
E-mail: amylane@greenshill.com
Facebook: www.facebook.com/amy.lane.167
Twitter: @amymaclane

CPSIA information can be obtained at www.ICGtesting.com
Printed in the USA
LVOW07s1938150116

470668LV00030B/796/P